RUIN

By

Rebecca Guy

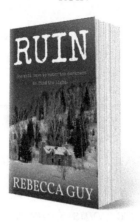

Want exclusive behind the scenes content and extra's?

Want to be the first to hear about promotions, discounts, forthcoming titles and competitions?

Get all this and more each month by signing up to my mailing list - It's free and I never spam!

Details at the end of the book.

Follow on Instagram, facebook,and pinterest.

Www.rebeccaguy.co.uk

To my children, Millie, Alex and Max.

For keeping my eye on the ball.

*Forge your dreams. Make it happen, and
remember, anything is possible.
Reach for the stars, little guys.*

Prologue

Kent news 05/12/16, 5.58pm

'That's the news for the area this evening, the time is 5.58pm, here's Dan with the travel update.'

'Thanks Lena, well if you're heading out of the city this evening avoiding the A20 is a must. A major accident involving a number of vehicles has closed both sides of the carriageway resulting in stationary traffic for around six miles. The air ambulance is in attendance but with casualties still trapped in their cars, there are no signs that congestion will ease anytime soon.

Police say the accident, which occurred around 5pm this evening, is particularly complex. If you're caught up in the commotion it's looking like a long wait, so please bear with the emergency services as they determine the best course of action for reopening the road to get you moving.

Elsewhere in the area, there's slow traffic through the roadworks on the westbound side of the M20 between junctions 6 and 7, and eastbound, heavy traffic through junction 4.

Wherever you're trying to get to please take it easy and allow extra time for your journey as people try to find alternative routes around that major accident. For the good people stranded in their cars tonight, I'm sure Lena has some great feel-good tracks to keep you company while the emergency services do their work. Stick with us, we'll keep you updated as we know more. Back to you Lena.'

Chapter 1

Emmie Landers stamped on the brake and the Honda's tyres screeched on the cool tarmac. The seatbelt locked, throwing her back into her seat as the car came to a sliding stop.

She blinked, heart pumping.

Pulling her mouth back in an embarrassed grimace, she glanced into the rear-view mirror. The road behind her was empty.

She let out a breath, rolling her eyes.

Jeez Em, that's one way to get out of starting a new life, kill yourself first, cleans up all the mess in one go.

She cackled and pressed the button to lower the driver's window. Cold air poured into the car, lifting her dark fringe from deep blue eyes. Breath clouding before her, she leaned out of the window to look back at the small wooden sign, covered with stray branches stripped bare by winter. It hung lopsided, making this side only marginally clearer than the one she had just passed. She squinted at the weather faded writing in the growing dusk.

BRUADAIR.

That was the place.

Pushing the button to retract the window she jammed the car into reverse and backed up, stopping adjacent to the the sign. She peered into the gloom at a single track lane in bad repair. Large trees and overgrown hedges lined each side, and potholes were prevalent in the ageing tarmac. Grass poked its way through the cracked surface marking the central line of the lane with a patchy mohican.

Emmie checked the car's digital display – 3.34pm - which made her officially late to meet the estate agent..

She pursed her lips. Better late than never.

The car's headlights flicked on against the impending dusk as she turned onto the lane and steered her way up the narrow track, swerving to avoid the worst of the potholes and stray branches which reached from the hedges like arthritic hands. Emmie wrinkled her nose. She had an idea she may need an open mind for this viewing.

Rounding a bend, an old farmhouse came into view and her spirits rose at the signs of life within the lit windows. She slowed, peering into a dimly lit kitchen, trying to catch a glimpse of the occupants, curious as to the type of people who lived up a lane like this. She was still craning her head when the steering wheel wrenched from her grip, scraping through her hands as the car dipped sharply left. Fighting to control the vehicle before it railed into the hedge, she yelled as it bounced back out of the large hole with a thud.

'Christ, couldn't someone fix the damn road?'

Heart thudding, she passed the gated driveway and outbuildings and drove on with more caution, back into the murkiness of the darkening landscape.

Just as she was beginning to wonder how far up the lane this blessed house was, the road stopped abruptly. In front of her sat a small picket fence and gate in dire need of repair and a fresh coat of paint. To the right was a grass clearing where a small Ford sat parked neatly. Emmie raised her eyebrows. Driveway? Well, it was different. One point to the house.

Grinning, she pulled the Honda onto the grass beside the Ford and climbed out of the car, taking a moment to stretch her stiff joints after the long drive. The relief of stretching her legs fell away as she turned to look at the house she had come to view. Heaving a sigh, she felt the last of her optimism fade away under sagging shoulders.

Beyond the picket fence the path to the house was barely visible; hell, a machete might even be in order to get through the tangled mess of grass, brambles, gorse, and bracken.

What she could see of the house didn't fare much better. Light from inside illuminated parts of the wall revealing holes in the mortar, like missing teeth, between the grey stone. The stone porch looked precarious on its column legs and most of the guttering was broken, it hung limply down the house like tinsel on a neglected Christmas tree. Tiles were missing from the roof, one of the two chimney stacks had fallen, and there was a broken window thrown in to boot.

Pulling her wool coat around her against the cold air, Emmie blew out a long breath as she thought of Bryson Estate Agent's particulars.

Tired and rundown, they had stated. In need of restoration.

This house isn't tired, it's half dead, and what it needs is a demolition crew. Are desolate wrecks really all I can afford?

Emmie bit her lip fighting the urge to get back into the car, but she had driven eight hours to view this house, and despite whether it was worth it, she couldn't bear the thought of driving up here just to drive straight home again. Besides, her sister was right, it was time to move on. Three adults and five children squashed into Natalie's four-bed detached down in Surrey was never going to be a forever deal.

She looked back at the house.

Maybe I should just buy a tent.

'Ms Landers?'

A deep voice cut into her thoughts, and Emmie looked to see an elderly gentleman in a grey suit and heavy wool coat coming up the path. He stopped to un-pluck a bramble that had stuck itself to one trouser leg before continuing toward her.

'Ms Emelia Landers?' He enquired again.

Emmie froze, wondering erratically if she should say she was just passing by.

In limbo, and aware of how ridiculous her reaction was, especially given the that there was nowhere to 'pass by' to, she fought the urge to giggle.

'Hello?' The old man bellowed. The sound stretched and echoed. Emmie thought of the officer on the lifeboat after the Titanic sank in the film, *Hello! Is there anyone alive out there?!*

He was only missing a torch in the fading light.

This image enhanced the already suppressed laughter which erupted from her nose as a loud snort. Eyes watering, she quickly looked down into the collar of her coat, shoulders shaking as she searched for a tissue.

Christ, Em. What is wrong with you? Get a grip.

Blowing her nose, she struggled to choke back the next wave of laughter as she looked up at the man who had now stopped by the gate and was watching her bemused.

'Sorry, allergies.' She offered, getting herself back under control and making her way toward him.

In winter? Crap... well, it's said now.

His bushy eyebrows rose as he regarded her. She shrugged nonchalantly and smiled.

'Ms Landers?' He asked for the third time.

'Yes.' She said, accepting that she was going to have to look around this ramshackle and make the right noises even if she never intended to come here again.

'Mr Roberts, from Bryson Estate Agency. I'd just about given up, thought you'd seen the place and gone back the way you'd come.' He chuckled and offered his hand.

She shook it with a smile, his mild manner and slow Scottish dialect setting her at ease. For a moment she was transported back to her childhood when many family holidays had brought them to Scotland - touring in an old split screen camper van, pitching in the wilderness; sitting around campfires in the dark, telling stories, or singing along to her father's guitar.

It reinforced the fact that this was the right decision. Scotland seemed the most natural place in the world to choose to start over. It gave her a warm, excited feeling in the pit of her stomach, and it made her feel comfortingly close to her father, whose passion had been everything Scottish before he had died four years ago.

Looking at Mr Roberts' genuine smile, she felt foolish at her earlier behaviour.

'Come this way,' he said, holding back the offending trail of bramble that hung over the pathway. She skirted around it and followed him down the overgrown path.

The garden was huge, just over six acres wrapped itself around all four sides of the house which comprised its own stream, small woodland, orchard, and masses of grassland for the children to play. As they walked, Mr Roberts pointed out the boundary lines barely visible in the murky distance.

Bordering the property were miles of fields belonging to two farms, one of which was the farm she had passed down the road. To the right of the house rose the southern edge of a hill range that stretched out for many miles north. Bracken Cruach, the nearest craggy peak to the house, looked more like a mountain than a hill to Emmie, but research had told her it was indeed a hill and far from the highest peak in the range.

Emmie felt warmth swirl in her stomach.

Apples from the orchard, our own stream, picnics on the hill. The kids would love it here -

She broke off mid-thought as Mr Roberts turned their attention to the house and her heart plummeted.

She stalled, running her eyes over the dejected facade.

'Aye, There's much to be done, it's true,' said Mr Roberts, catching her hesitation, 'But it will be a superb little property with some time, love, and attention. The majority of the wounds are superficial according to the surveys.'

'It's always what you uncover when you scratch the surface though isn't it?'

Emmie's heart gave a jolt as she inadvertently recaptured one of Scott's favourite sayings from their house hunting days as newly-weds. She momentarily wished she could go back to those days and tell herself, then ten years younger, to scratch under the surface of the marriage too. *'Scratch harder Em, see what he's doing to you?'*

Mr Robert's voice filtered into her thoughts, and she took a deep breath of cold air to steady herself as she turned to re-focus on him.

'... won't be without its problems, as all houses are,' he was saying, 'this one wears its heart on its sleeve; it's what it says on the tin - it's cheap, and it needs a lot of work. Other houses may look perfect but scrape under the surface, and they could end up costing as much to put right.'

Fully back in the present Emmie smiled. She could almost see the house beaming with pride.

Unfortunately, it didn't make it look any better.

'Let's go inside,' she said shivering as disappointment and a cool breeze wrapped itself around her.

Chapter 2

Mr Roberts opened the wooden front door to a large hallway with stairs to the first floor against the right-hand wall. Emmie noticed a door to both her left and right and another directly ahead past the oak-panelled stairs. Mr Roberts led her left, into a large square kitchen area.

It was empty - whitewashed walls dirty, the only light was a bare bulb in the centre of the room. The floor was coated with a film of earth, what flooring was underneath was anyone's guess.

Emmie tried not to look horrified as Mr Roberts pointed out that it would fit a decent amount of cupboard space and a table large enough to eat at. He had an imagination; she had to afford him that.

Numb, she followed him across the kitchen to a small utility. She dutifully poked her head inside and noted that this was the room with the broken window. She wrinkled her nose, and felt immediately guilty as dad's ingrained motto of 'find the positive in every situation', flit into her head.

Well, it's only a small pane, I suppose.

Chewing at her lip, she followed Mr Roberts through a door opposite the large kitchen window. An equally well-proportioned room sat at the back of the house. Emmie found herself nodding involuntarily, her gaze drawn to the sunset which dipped over the hill above the orchard, perfectly framed by the filthy patio doors ahead of them. Find the positive.

What a beautiful view. A playroom, maybe? Charlie could have his x-box in here.

The area was exclusively painted with white-washed grime and fashioned with a bare bulb. On closer inspection, and in keeping with the rest of the décor, the sliding patio door appeared to be off its runner. Emmie rolled her eyes as the positive faded.

Nope, there won't be an x-box in here, Em, because this house is too much work.

Emmie smiled and nodded as Mr Roberts informed her that the back of the house faced west making this a lovely spot to sit out on summer evenings facing the hills and the orchard. She followed him across the room.

'And if it's a little cold to sit out,' he was saying, 'you can always soak up the sun in here.'

He opened the door, and they stepped into a large sunroom. Emmie gasped, mouth dropping open as her wide eyes scanned the area.

'Wow.'

'Impressive, isn't it?'

Emmie nodded. Full-length windows running floor to ceiling and a glass roof afforded fantastic views of the darkening landscape over Bracken Cruach and the woodland. Dirt and debris littered the floor, and one of the handles was missing from the french doors, but she barely noticed. She was busy imagining a summer evening, sitting in here with a glass of wine and this view. Bliss.

Emmie grinned as her heart swelled, this was exactly the kind of scene she'd had in mind when she thought of living up here, she hadn't expected to find a room to match it. She was still taking in the darkening scenery when she realised Mr Roberts was on the move. Past a door on their right that apparently led back into the hallway by the stairs, and to a set of double doors further along the same wall which led into an airy living room with dual aspect windows and a central fireplace to their left. One window looked over the front garden to the picket fence and their parked cars, the other looked to the side down an incline to the forest and stream and then up the side of Bracken Cruach itself.

Oblivious to the dirt and grime, Emmie mentally placed some furniture and a rug in front of the fire. She grinned.

Cosy. I could have roaring open fires and roast marshmallows. Scott would hate that. It's absolutely perfect -

She stopped short, quickly shaking her head to dispel the images. She had to stop her imagination from running ahead, positivity or not, the reality was she couldn't afford this house. In the condition it stood? No problem, but there would be no money left to make the place liveable, and with Charlie and Grace being just eight and three? It was stupidity.

A lump thickened in her throat, the emotion taking her by surprise. She heaved a shaky breath.

Mr Roberts put out a hand indicating that she go to the other end of the room where a door on the right led back into the hall past the bottom of the stairs. They were back by the front door before Mr Roberts turned to her with a warm smile, making his face crinkle into a road map of lines.

'You haven't said much. I know a little of your position, and I know it seems a lot of work. Do you want to carry on viewing?' He said.

Emmie felt her pulse quicken. She didn't want to leave, not yet. Just a while longer to dream.

'I'm sorry, it's just a lot to take in. I didn't expect it to be in such a state. It's an impressive amount of space and a fantastic position but, well, now I know why it's so cheap.'

'Aye, it's a lot of house for the money, and it will be a superb place given time. It just needs a little love. It's been empty for far too long. So should we go upstairs?'

Emmie smiled and shrugged.

'I'm here now, why not?'

The double-width stairs were wide, but not imposing. A square landing halfway up allowed them to curve to the left before continuing to the first floor. At the top, a corridor ran ahead of them, while a small galleried landing swung to the left allowing a view down into the hall and to the front door.

At the end of the gallery was a large bedroom facing the front of the house. It swung back around the stairs in an L shape the bulk of the room sitting over the living room below. It had a good feel, and built in wardrobes to boot. The floorboards in one corner looked like they had been chewed by something large, but at least she could hang her clothes.

'You have big mice up here,' Emmie said lightly, pointing to the corner.

Mr Roberts chuckled, but in Estate Agent mode told her the boards wouldn't be too hard or costly to fix. Emmie smiled as they came back out of the room. A 'family bathroom' sat through a door to their left. Her heart sank as she looked inside.

There could be a toilet issue here ... and a washing issue. Let's face it there's a slight 'living' issue with this house.

She mentally calculated the cost of a kitchen and bathroom before shaking her head with a sigh. It couldn't work, and it tugged at her heart. The house felt comfortable even in its dilapidated condition. She knew it was just her imagination, the more time she spent inside, the more she felt she belonged here. It felt... right.

The corridor opposite the stairs led to two further large bedrooms, one to the back of the house, above the playroom, and one to the front. This one sat alongside a fourth much smaller room. Emmie peeked inside.

This could work as a studio, small, but...

Stop! Em, Jesus Christ. It can't happen.

She blinked back unexpected tears.

And why the hell am I so emotional?

Luckily Mr Roberts was striding ahead as he informed her of a vast loft space and pointed out the large square in the ceiling just ahead of the stairs and then, far too soon, they arrived back at the front door.

'Well that's all there is to see, It's getting late. I don't want to keep you, I know you have a long drive back. Just briefly, what do you think?'

Mr Roberts smiled looking resigned, he already knew the answer. She almost felt guilty for saying it aloud, and weirdly, it seemed worse to say it with the house listening; like she was just another viewer to let it down.

'Well, the er, space is, er, great. The house is larger than anything I could have expected to own. I'm sure the garden could be fantastic, and the kids would love the woods and stream. It's almost at the top of my budget. There's no way I could afford to fix the broken roof tiles never mind install a kitchen and bathroom.'

Mr Roberts was nodding and smiling. She was right, he had heard it all before, but how could he expect a single mother to take on something like this? She wasn't made of money, and there were the children to think about. Weren't there?

How bad could it be? What if I just...?

Her head raged with the stupidity of taking this on, but even as her head screamed, her heart pulled, and she heard her voice forming the words.

'I'd like to make an offer.' She said.

Chapter 3

'You did *what?*"

Natalie stopped laying the table and looked at her sister wide-eyed, and then she swung her head left.

'Nathan, put that knife down, this instant.'

The three-year-old ran around the table brandishing a butter knife challenging the dog to a sword fight. The boxer, Minnie, was cowering under the table eyeing him warily.

'I put in an offer.' Emmie cupped her coffee with her hands and sighed as the enormity of what she'd done hit her.

'Are you insane?' Natalie looked back to her eyebrows raised, 'How are you going to manage a project like that? You'll be all alone up there Em. You are not some twenty-year-old on an adventure, this is real life, and you have responsibilities!'

'Thanks, I know.'

'What on earth were you thinking?... Nathan! Minnie does not want to play. I said put the knife down. Boys, it's seven thirty, get dressed or you'll be late for school, and where the heck is Lucy? Is she even up yet?'

Charlie and James grumbled and shot each other a look. It was nice to see a glint of humour from Charlie who had changed from a chatty and confident young man into a quiet and sullen little boy over the last two years. Emmie knew he had good reason, but she still worried, and she still wished she could erase all of his hurt.

The boys threw down the x-box controllers and headed for the stairs as six-year-old Lucy appeared in the doorway with a dramatic swoop.

'Ta-da!'

A cape made from a fleece blanket flew out behind her, and covered Grace's head gently as it fell. Grace giggled delighted.

A hush fell over the room. Both of their faces were painted so exuberantly they could have acquired jobs with the travelling circus. Blue eyeshadow covered Lucy's eyes up to and over her eyebrows, Grace's went further, covering her nose and forehead. Rosy cheeks befell each girl from eye socket to chin and mascara had been drawn like sun rays around their eyes. To complete the look red lipstick covered Lucy's mouth nearly from nose to chin. Grace's went further with streaks down her neck and a long smear wobbling up her left cheek.

Emmie glanced at her sister, trying to conceal a grin. Natalie stared in disbelief and horror, mouth open, spoons still in her right hand waiting to take their place at the table.

'Lucy?' she said carefully, 'have you been playing with mommy's make-up?'

'No, mommy.' Lucy shook her head innocently, she removed the cape revealing her school uniform and sat down at the table ready for breakfast, 'I got ready for school, see?'

'I'm Cinderella,' Grace added sitting next to her and smoothing her blue Cinderella dress over her knees before looking up at Lucy adoringly. Lucy grinned as she picked up the box of cornflakes to pour into her empty dish.

Emmie smiled, the happiness on Grace's face filled her with warmth. Grace had cried far too much after Scott had thrown them out, and it was good to see she was getting back to her old self, even if Charlie was taking a while longer.

She wiped Grace's face and helped her with breakfast as she watched her sister rant and fuss over getting Lucy's face clean before school.

Breakfast was accomplished in record time; dishes in the kitchen, table wiped, shoes and coats on, and children out of the door and into the care of the school walking bus. Only Cinderella remained, and with no nursery today she lounged on the settee watching 'Peppa Pig' as any young princess would.

'So let's talk,' Natalie said as Emmie shut the front door.

Emmie sighed and wandered into the kitchen to make more coffee, aware that Natalie was following her.

'There's nothing to talk about, Nat. I'm buying it, The bid is in, and

I very much doubt there are any other mad contenders, it will be mine, warts and all.'

She turned to face her sister with a smile that fell away as she realised Natalie was scanning through the paperwork from Bryson's Estate Agency.

Shit, leaving that around really won't help your case Em, great start.

The now familiar house details and pictures of the orchard, wood, and stream were being scrutinised under Natalie's uncompromising frown. Natalie offered only one word.

'Why?'

Emmie tried to gauge her sister's mood.

'You really had to be there,' she said lightly shrugging her shoulders.

Natalie glared at her.

Oops, wrong mood.

'Look, Nat, I don't have a lot of options right now. Yes, the place is a mess, but it offers a great sized house with loads of space for the kids to play. The estate agent said most of the wounds were superficial. I know it will be hard, but once we're through the first year, we should be well on the way to a great life in an idyllic setting.'

'How will you heal these little wounds? You will have. No. Money. Left.' Natalie spat as though Emmie had no concept of this alien thing called money. Emmie tried to keep her cool.

'I'm aware of that,' she said keeping her voice light, 'but I do have money saved, commissions to fulfil, and a couple of payments outstanding. We should be good for a while.'

'Oh, well that's great Em, and just when do you think you'll get time even to run the business, never mind complete a painting?'

'I'll find time Nat. I have no choice.'

'You also have no help, no friends, no family. You'll be completely cut off.'

Natalie slammed the papers down on the table and folded her arms looking furious.

Emmie watched her chewing on her lip.

'You asked me to get out, Nat, I'm getting out. You should be happy. What the hell was I supposed to do? Tell me, because I have no idea what part of your brain thought I would be able to buy a palace with my measly divorce settlement.'

'I did not tell you to 'get out',' Natalie said quietly, 'I certainly didn't want to see you in a place like this, so far away.' She flung a hand toward the papers.

Emmie flushed, feeling her temper rise.

'A place like what?' She said, 'The house is fine, it needs work, so what? Where was I supposed to live?'

'It's Scotland!'

'I love Scotland, and it's not a million miles away.'

Natalie huffed and ran a hand through her dark, shoulder length hair, clearly frustrated.

'Em, you cannot possibly be basing this love on the view of a child on holiday! Really? God damn it you're not even moving to an area we stayed at.'

Emmie rolled her eyes and turned away. She poured water into the two cups and idly stirred the teaspoon. She didn't hear her sister cross the room until she felt Natalie's hand on her shoulder. Emmie carried on stirring hearing Natalie sigh heavily.

'You were supposed to live nearby,' she said, 'where we could see each other without planes, trains and automobiles getting involved. I don't like the idea of you driving all up there and having to deal with this yourself after everything you've been through. The accident *and* the divorce weren't all that long -'

'I've already driven up there. I'm absolutely fine, Nat. What was I supposed to live in down here? A shoebox? be realistic.'

Natalie pouted and stared out of the window. As the silence stretched the irony of the situation was not lost on Emmie. Here she was lecturing her super-sensible, super-realist older sister on being realistic. What the hell was going on?

Emmie stirred her coffee slowly not knowing what to say. Natalie glanced at her watch, and the awkward silence was broken with her sigh.

'Look, I need to get ready for work, and I need time to get my head around this. I'm not happy. At all. But I don't want to argue with you,

Em.' Natalie avoided her gaze as she picked up her coffee and took a long sip.

'Fine, I need to do some work myself, the money will be useful to do up some old house.' Emmie mumbled into her cup. Natalie closed her eyes briefly, cup still in her hand.

'Please don't be mad, I'm just worried about you.'

'I'm not mad, and you don't need to worry.'

Natalie stared at her and Emmie gave her a small smile.

'I'm not mad Nat.'

Natalie rolled her eyes. She mouthed sorry before taking her cup and heading for the stairs.

Emmie let out a breath and grinned at her sisters retreating back.

Chapter 4

Natalie Hampton rapped on the bathroom door.

'Are you done in there?'

A muffled voice came back, raised over the noise of the shower.

'Um, not really?'

Natalie sighed agitated, 'Wrong answer Michael, I need to talk.'

'Am I in trouble?'

'What? No! I need to talk about Emmie.'

There was a clatter as a bottle dropped into the bath, closely followed by a curse.

'Could I finish my shower first?'

Natalie thought he sounded annoyed but this was important, maybe she'd better cut to the chase.

'She's leaving.'

How was that for a bombshell?

'Oh, ... that's great.' Floated back to her through the wooden door

Great? Is this guy for real?

'She's buying a place in Scotland, no kitchen, no bathroom, no roof, could do with being razed to the ground, no talking her out of it.'

'Hmm?'

Natalie frowned.

'No family around her, no friends, a whole wreck of a house, and six acres of messy garden.'

My God, is he whistling?

'Mike?'

'Yeah, hun, six acres sounds great, plenty of room to hold her infamous barbecue parties!'

'Mike,' Natalie snapped, 'we cannot go to a barbecue eight hours away every sunny Sunday. Get out of the shower. Can you even hear me?'

'I believe you said Emmie is leaving for Scotland.' The muffled voice replied, shower water still running.

'Yes, leaving for Scotland!' Natalie growled through gritted teeth.

The shower finally stopped and seconds later the bathroom door opened revealing an incredulous looking Michael. A hand towel barely met over one hip just about covering all he had as he dripped puddles onto the floor.

'You asked her to leave,' He pointed out annoyingly.

'I know,' Natalie said.

'So, she's leaving. That's good, right?'

'It's not good, she didn't need to find anywhere quite so soon, we could have managed a while longer.'

'How long did you need? Another nine months? Maybe we could extend, or move into a bigger place. We could all grow old together.'

Natalie felt hope well up inside her. Could they? Could she save her sister from this disastrous move?

Michael's face gave her all the answer she needed. She cast her eyes downward and blinked as tears threatened to emerge.

'Why so far?' She whispered, 'I thought she could rent a place down the road until she could afford to buy. Or at least in the area, why bloody Scotland? I need my sister here Mike, and she needs me whether she knows it or not. I almost lost her in that damn accident and I don't want to lose her now. I don't want her to go, she's not ready.'

Natalie's lip trembled and the tears finally let go.

Michael pulled her close with his free hand, wetting her pyjamas as he kissed the top of her head.

'This is what we wanted. No, we *needed* it, Nat. We are all going insane.' He said gently. 'Don't you think Em may need it too? It can't be fun living in a home that's not your own. She needs this as much as we do and she needs to make the decision where, when, how and why on her own.'

'I'm her big sister, Mike, I'm supposed to protect her and keep her safe, how can I do that from here when she's all the way up there? She's buying a wreck, in the middle of nowhere, in another country. She's so blasé, but she doesn't understand, and I'm worried sick.'

'Really, Nat! You make it seem like she's moving to Outer Mongolia. She's a few hours away, not even across water. She has to do this for herself, work it out for herself, all you can do is tell her we're here if she needs us. She's thirty-four, that's not so little anymore, Nat.'

Natalie's breath hitched. She wiped her tears with the back of her hand and nodded.

'I know,' She said, 'It's just this time last month I would have killed to get her out from under my feet, but now it's a reality. She's actually going and I don't want her to, especially not so far away. I'm tired of the lies, and I'm scared for her.'

'Emmie will be fine, honey, she's stronger than you give her credit for, she's had a tough couple of years and she's still standing. She will make this work, she has no choice, she knows that. Let's help her get where she needs to be and we can deal with the rest later. One step at a time.'

Michael cupped Natalie's chin and lifted her eyes to his.

'She will be fine.' He repeated, 'You know that don't you?'

Natalie nodded. She had always been the strong, sensible, level-headed one and she needed to draw on all her reserves now. Emmie needed support, not a laden weight around her neck.

Natalie looked at Michael, her knight. He had put up with so much lately, their home had not been their own for almost a year and he hadn't uttered a word against the situation. She had instigated Emmie moving in, and now her moving out, and Michael had supported her at every turn. She was incredibly lucky.

He was pretty handsome too, she thought, looking into his familiar face and big brown eyes. He smiled down at her.

'Okay?'

She nodded.

'Good,' He said, 'because it's the middle of winter and I'm standing here in little more than a facecloth. I'm getting back in the shower, I'm bloody freezing!'

Chapter 5

A month later Emmie was sitting at the dining table, laptop open, staring at the documents from the solicitors. She had taken a chance putting in a low offer straight after the viewing, and to her surprise the vendors had accepted before the closing date and taken the house off the market. A solicitor was sought and Missives put into place almost immediately. The whole process had run with precision, and now anxiety bubbled at the speed the vendors had wished the house gone.

Were they laughing now, toasting her stupidity with champagne?

She sighed. Any other house sale dragged its feet, this one felt like it had moved too quickly and yet, here it was, clear as day, 'Missives have been concluded', ready to go. The date of entry was just two weeks away.

January 3rd.

New year, new house, new life.

Shit!

Emmie snapped the laptop lid shut as her heart thumped. Suppressing the urge to throw open a window and scream for help, she took Grace to the park and pretended she hadn't seen the email at all.

After two glorious, if cold, hours in the park Emmie had returned home and put a shattered Grace down for a nap. She opened the laptop with trepidation and signed into her email account.

Damn. It was still there. A big dose of reality in glorious twenty-two-inch black and white.

Her heart thud against her ribs.

Am I really going to do this?

'Bad news?'

Emmie jumped and spun around in the chair. Michael stood in the doorway of the dining room, tugging the tie from around his neck and opening the top button of his shirt. Friday was a short day for Michael, the one afternoon he left his advertising firm at a decent time of the day to be home with his family. Except, Emmie thought, that his 'family' didn't arrive back until late afternoon giving him approximately three hours of man time, which involved sitting on his backside.

She smiled in faux delight at his question.

'Not at all, it should be fabulous news. I'll be moving out in approximately two weeks,' she paused and heaved a sigh, the smile leaving her lips, 'so why do I feel like shit?'

Michael put the folded tie down on the table. 'Hitting home what you've taken on?'

'I'm not entirely sure what I was thinking, maybe Nat was right. I should have stayed here and put up with a shoe box for a while, at least I'd have family and friends around me. I'm going to have to do this alone Mike. All alone. And with two kids. All I thought at the time was how they would love the garden,' She huffed out a breath, 'They won't have a house, but they'll have a bloody garden so that's all right then, isn't it? We can camp in the orchard and eat apples, do you think there's any fish in the stream? Got to keep up the kid's omega 3.'

Emmie put a hand over her mouth and tittered nervously.

Michael played along, 'It's a possibility, but I think the stream may have a habit of freezing over in winter. Do you have a double-storey tent or do you intend being snowed in for a few weeks of the year?'

'I don't have a tent. There's plenty of loose floorboards in the house though we could build a tree-house in the wood.'

'Hope you won't need to pee in the middle of the night. Could spell a few broken legs.'

'We could hang out the window it's not like there are any neighbours to see.'

'Hmm, you know what they say about shitting on your own doorstep.'

He was deadpan as he unfolded the paper from under his arm and shook it straight ready to take himself into the living room. Emmie wrinkled her nose.

'Out the *window* Mike, I'll make sure it's at the back.'

He looked at her raising his eyebrows.

'And the cold...?'

'Underfloor heating, it's wondrous what's out there these days. You spend far too much time at the office, Mike, it'll be a veritable palace!'

'Unlike the actual house.'

'Pah, houses are so over-rated, who needs one anyway?'

Mike let out a laugh and Emmie giggled feeling better.

Where the hell did her sister find this man? She needed to shop at the same store, except her man wouldn't have the beer gut and spend his days at the office. Her man would be a bohemian art and nature lover, calm and chilled, and he would have zero issues with control and keeping his temper - unlike Scott. Oh, and a few building skills may come in handy, she mentally added that to her man list. Now she just had to find him. And pigs may fly.

Michael popped her bubble.

'I'm sure you'll find a way Em, and I'm sure you had a reason when you bought the place. Maybe it'll resurface when you get back, the novelty is just wearing off that's all.'

'Why does the word 'novelty' scare me?'

'you know what I mean. You could have brought a dozen other places in the same condition, some for less money, something must have made you buy this one above the countless others.'

'Madness?'

Michael laughed, 'Time will tell. Hey, I bet a year from now this will feel like a small blip. Call Kevin McCloud, when it has a spot on 'Grand Designs' you'll be laughing thinking back over this whole conversation.'

Emmie snorted, 'Grand Designs? It's got more chance of being on 'Help! my house is falling down!'

'It could be a real bona fide 'country house rescue' maybe?'

'No, Mike, it's a real bona fide 'Beeny's restoration nightmare' except it's not Sarah Beeny's, it's bloody mine.'

'Okay, I can see why you feel like shit.'

'Thanks.'

'Always a pleasure.'

Emmie threw a chair cushion his way laughing.

Not for the first time in her life though, she felt like she was in a hole, and who knew how long it would take to climb out of this one. Would there even be any hand holes?

Chapter 6

The Saturday between Christmas and New Year Natalie and Michael organised a small farewell party at the house.

Emmie had agreed to close friends and family but apparently, they had invited the whole of Surrey. The house was crammed with people and she had smiled and thanked so many well-wishers that her jaw ached. She needed to find a corner to be alone with her wine, but she wasn't sure it was going to be possible.

Pushing her way through to the conservatory a familiar face caught her attention. She stopped short and narrowed her eyes.

Well, Christ, isn't that Martin Stomes? Where the hell has he been dragged up from? And when was the last time I saw him anyway? At the University of Kent when I was 21 years old? I think maybe it was.

Martin looked up and caught her eye. He grinned and raised his bottle of bud to her. Emmie pasted a smile and raised a hand in return.

Oooo-kay, weird.

Emmie quickly turned to go before he decided to come over and start reminiscing about their 'way cool' uni days. In the far corner, she spotted Amy and made her way over. Amy broke away from the group she was with, still laughing, as she saw Emmie and held her arms out.

Emmie walked into that welcome hug and squeezed hard. Of all the people around her, Amy was the one she would miss the most. They had been best friend's since primary school. Amy had been there through all the significant moments in Emmie's life; her first boyfriend, first kiss, first fumble, marriage, pregnancy, childbirth, babies, children, divorce, losing her home. They had laughed through 'Bridget Jones' Diary', cried through 'Titanic', peeped from behind cushions at 'Halloween' and now what?

Amy couldn't move to Scotland with her, in fact, Amy didn't own a car and Emmie was confident the number 233 bus didn't go to Perth and Kinross.

Emmie sighed heavily and Amy pulled away and held on to her hands.

'Feel like I lost a toe,' she said.

Emmie grinned, 'Is that really all I'm worth?'

'Absolutely, I think I'm being generous!'

Emmie nodded, tears brimmed and she swallowed back a lump.

Not now Em, get a grip.

She made a face at Amy, crossed her eyes and took a large shuddering breath only to look up and see 'Uni Boy' Martin giving her strange look before quickly turning away. Great. He wouldn't forget that parting look in a hurry.

'Do you want to escape for a bit?' Amy said.

'Nah, it's my party I can't disappear. I'm going to hold it together like a big brave girl and see it through to the end. Isn't that what I tell the kids?'

'All the time', Amy agreed, 'They never listen, why should you?'

Emmie giggled. Then she sighed and took a sip of wine.

'What the hell am I going to do with my Friday nights now? I'm going to be eight hours away. Our movie, wine, and chocolate sessions have officially become obsolete. Next Friday I'll be gone.'

Amy pouted. 'I know, it will be so weird, I just know I'm going to hate Friday's forever. We've had some great times haven't we?' Then she suddenly chuckled, 'Hey remember that time you were doing the 'bend and snap' trying to pull the barman in Frankie and Benny's after we saw Legally Blonde?'

Emmie narrowed her eyes.

'Not funny Amy.'

Amy's Chuckles turned to laughter.

'You bent alright, but the only thing you managed to snap was the heel off your shoe, remember? You fell off the bar and rolled into that girl, who threw her pint all over her boyfriend, remember, huh?'

'I do, it was bloody agony.'

Amy gasped for breath, 'I know, but falling, *and* the shoe, *and* the girl who looked like she was going to punch your lights out, oh my god, I couldn't breathe!'

Emmie pretended to frown, 'Go on, laugh. Just to add insult to injury they were my one and only ever pair of Christian Louboutins.'

'You were so pissed, and didn't a certain good looking barman...' Amy trailed off.

'Help me up and give me a roasting about being on the bar? Yes Amy,' Emmie said deadpan. Amy wiped at tears and straightening up took a breath about to speak. Emmie cut her off.

'No, I didn't ever see him again,' Emmie glanced at Amy and grinned, 'He was probably gay anyway, no straight man is that good looking.'

Amy snorted and laughed loudly causing a few well-wishers to glance at them with smiles.

'I, at least, would have gone back to check.'

'You wouldn't have checked until you were in his bed.'

Amy shrugged. 'Of course, too little, too late by then.'

Emmie grinned and rolled her eyes as Amy's laughter subsided and she looked at Emmie with a sad smile.

'You know, there's going to be a huge Emmie shaped hole in my life after next week.'

Out of nowhere, a tear slipped down Amy's cheek, Emmie brushed it away quickly.

'Stop, please, you'll start me off too, and if anyone knows what my crying face looks like it's you, so you understand the predicament.'

Amy sniffed and straightened, wiping at her eyes, nodding.

'You're right, I'm not going to ruin your night by making you show that face to all these people.'

Emmie chuckled and hugged her friend. She was busy savouring the feeling when over Amy's shoulder she saw Michael catch her eye and beckon her over.

'Crap, here comes Mike. Seriously, can I not spend ten seconds alone with my best friend before I leave for the other end of the British Isles! You know, I'm pretty sure he's been following me all evening to make sure I don't disappear.'

Amy laughed, it was a good sound, Emmie was missing it already. She broke away from the hug and looked at their now empty wine glasses.

'Shall I get us more wine, after I've spoken to his highness?' She raised her glass and wiggled her eyebrows.

Amy pursed her lips, 'I think that's an excellent idea!'

The wine wasn't just a good idea, it was essential. As the night was drawing to a close it appeared Michael had taken it upon himself to make a speech and was busy summoning everyone to the large lounge as he pulled Emmie along.

'This isn't necessary, Mike, really. Let me go quietly in a wine-induced stupor, please.'

'I'm not going to let my favourite sister in law go all that way without saying a few words.'

She glanced down at the notes in his hand.

A few words? It looks like a short story to me.

They reached the fireplace, Emmie's heart thudding behind her ribs. She stared at the coal hoping she would get away with facing the fire.

Michael Hampton cleared his throat and asked for quiet raising his hands like a preacher hosting a sermon. A hush fell over the room, people that had previously spread over all three downstairs rooms now crammed together into the lounge area and spilt out into the hallway. Michael pulled Emmie to him and turned her to face the crowd placing an arm around her shoulders.

'As you know in just a few short days my favourite, and very brave, sister in law will be leaving us to begin a new chapter in her life.'

Emmie felt her face get hot as the attention turned to her and Michael continued his speech. As she blinked into the bright flashes of camera lights she resisted the urge to ask for no photo's of the prize beetroot to end up on Facebook.

'It has been a difficult couple of years for all of us, but not least for Emmie who has taken some of the hardest blows life can throw at us and still managed to come through it with dignity and humour. There's a way to go yet, but she truly has emerged stronger, and somehow more rounded.'

'That'll be the chocolate!' Someone shouted from the back.

Laughter rolled around the room and Emmie grimaced, hands unconsciously drifting to cover her tummy.

Michael chuckled as he let the laughter subside.

'The very fact that we're having this party proves she is ready to step back into the world again, I'm hoping the fact that she's going so far away has no bearing on us,' he grinned and glanced Emmie's way, 'It's a huge project that she is taking on, but bravery and gusto has never really been an issue where Emmie is concerned, and I'm sure she can pull this off. I hope you will join me in raising your glass, as I think I speak for all of us, when I say she is truly an inspiration, and deserves all the happiness I'm sure will come her way.' Michael smiled and lightly squeezed her shoulder through the cheers and clapping that ensued.

'Is Scotland aware of what's coming *its* way?' someone heckled, and clapping gave way to laughter that rippled around the room. Emmie squinted into the crowd to see if she could spot the culprit that announced that clanger before Michael started again.

'Okay, okay,' he hushed expertly right hand in the air, 'I know Emmie is dying to get out of the spotlight and mingle so I'll get onto the main reason I got roped into this.'

Michael turned to Emmie and took a breath.

Emmie looked back at him not daring to breathe, eyes wide.

What the hell? Oh, this is going to be bad, right? Keep it together Em, don't cry.

'Okay,' Michael started, 'We had no idea what we could possibly get you that would be of the most benefit with the money we raised from a little collection we did.'

They did a collection? Shit. I will not cry ...

'So we decided to buy 'time' from friends and family that can offer a week, possibly two, to help you get set up and moved into a habitable home. We managed to gather a veritable troupe happy to patch, clean, paint and shop. Cameron and a small group of his builders have promised to stay until the place is fit to live in. We even found a week of Glen's time so you have a plumber to get a kitchen and bathroom installed at the very least.'

Emmie's hand drifted to her open mouth as she glanced over at Glen who smiled at her and raised his glass.

'So, 'Michael continued, 'it appears you won't be getting away from us all as soon as you'd hoped Em. Sorry.'

'Er,' Emmie stuttered struggling to get words over the lump in her throat.

She swallowed hard, biting her tongue and blinking back the tears that threatened.

'Er ... I don't know what to say. I'm overwhelmed. Thank you so much. All of you. I'm not at all sure what I ...'

Emmie paused as murmurs and the sound of scuffling arose from the hallway. Were people on the move already?

She took a breath and carried on.

'Er, anyway I'd like to thank Mike and Nat from the bottom of my heart for helping me through some of the toughest years of my life so far. I have a feeling the next year-'

The mumbles became talking and people fidgeted, heads swivelling.

What the hell is going on?

Emmie shrugged and turned to put her wine glass on the mantelpiece, if they didn't want to listen, then she sure as hell wasn't bothering to talk. Stuff them. She was glad she was leaving anyway. Tears stung her eyes. Did they really not care?

The crowd swam before her and through her blurred vision she saw an apparition, dressed all in black.

It was almost right in front of her when the familiar smell of aftershave and hair gel hit her nostrils and the hairs on her arms stood on end as her heart started to thump.

Scott.

But different. His complexion seemed pasty and a lock of perfectly groomed dark hair hung onto his forehead. Knowing how much he hated any bit of his appearance being out of place she fought the uncontrollable urge to smooth it back for him.

'Hi sweet pea, looking good,' he said mouth curling into a sneer, 'So. I hear you're going on an adventure to start a new life, good for you darling, but really, you didn't assume I was going to just let you waltz away with a couple of small things that belong to me did you?'

Chapter 7

Emmie was sure her heart could be heard pounding three streets away. She opened her mouth - shut it - opened it again but nothing would come out. His condescending tone transported her straight back to married life, and the subsequent divorce, when Scott had played so dirty she hadn't known who he was.

She felt herself bristle.

He has no control over you any more Em, remember that.

She focused on the stray lock of hair. Something was out of sorts with him, he certainly wasn't at his best, but she found that encouraging.

She opened her mouth again.

Scott raised his eyebrows at her, 'well? A simple answer would suffice, the whole acting like a fish thing is getting us nowhere.'

Emmie flushed, temper rising, 'Where in the hell did you come from?'

'Oh, Emelia, I'm a little disappointed that you forgot our marital home so quickly, let me refresh your memory. Small detached on court street, around a five-minute walk -'

'Shut up,' Emmie snapped cutting him off,' I'd like to remind you that although you live in Court street, a five minute walk by your own authority, the last time you saw, or even breathed a word to your kids was nearly six months ago. Six. So what gives you the right to stand in my sisters home and demand to know what's happening in mine and the children's lives?'

Scott smiled and rolled his eyes at the couple next to him then he sighed and shook his head, face smoothing into fake sympathy. Keeping the smile firmly in place he took a step closer.

'Emelia. Darling. I couldn't give a flying fuck what's happening in your life, honey, but I absolutely do have a right to know what you're planning to do with my property, and if I've heard right and you're off to bonny Scotland then I'm afraid, sweet pea, that I shall have to interject.'

Emmie seethed, heart pounding in her ears. Her whole body shook with control, she wanted to punch the smug smile right off his face; instead, she laughed, a harsh loud splutter.

'Are you serious? Property? Is that how you describe your own flesh and blood? My God, do you have any idea what you've put us through? I sat on Grace's bed night after night with her sobbing for you, Charlie has never stopped asking if he can see you. He's changed so much you wouldn't recognise him, my heart breaks for them every day that you don't contact.'

'Emelia, I'm not here to mend your poor shattered heart, I tried and failed at that long ago, not sure I could even find a heart in there …'

He knocked the man next to him playfully and winked, which was so out of character she struggled to comprehend the action. Scott wasn't someone who 'touched' people. Especially without a spray of hand gel at the ready.

A bitter, stale whiff reached her nose as he stepped closer and she had it.

He'd been drinking, which wasn't something he usually partook in. Emmie was starting to feel that she had come off the better half of a divorce she hadn't wanted, and it was giving her courage.

She straightened and spluttered a laugh.

'Grow up Scott, this isn't about us, they are eight and three-years-old, good job they didn't inherit your brains, what kind of chance would they have had then?'

A few people in the crowd snickered, Scott reddened and Emmie could see that vein pulsing in his temple. She stared at it musing that you could know someone so well that such a tiny notion was a dead giveaway of just how much you were hitting a nerve. She had also forgotten just how quickly his temper could flare up. A flutter of fear rippled through her chest and she quickly squashed it. There was nothing he could do here in this crowd.

She took a breath, the notion spurring her on, she hadn't often had the nerve to stand up to him, preferring to assuage his anger rather than ignite it, now she didn't have to deal with the fallout, she found it empowering.

She swept her hand around the room motioning to all the guests.

'Just for the record would you like to tell everyone exactly what you would give up in your precious little life if your children did indeed want to return home with you? Let's see, you're at the office 6am until 7pm Monday through Friday, except for the cheeky round of golf on Friday afternoons.'

Scott's face reddened further, his mouth tightening, and Emmie covered her own mouth with her hands.

'Oops, sorry. I wasn't supposed to know about that one, right? Oh well. So, anyway that leaves the weekend.' She stopped and held up her hand, 'Oh no, my mistake, it's back to the office Saturday to catch up on paperwork. So what's left? Ah, that's right. Sunday. Sunday is 'family day' right Scott? Maybe you could be a father to them on Sunday; they can manage the rest of the week on their own surely? Are you confirming that you wouldn't run a mile if Charlie said 'ok dad, I choose to live with you, I'll pack my bags now?'

The room had gone deathly quiet and Scott swallowed, adams apple bobbing. He was furious. His right thumbnail scraping and digging into his first finger rhythmically. It was another sign that didn't escape Emmie's attention. When he got really angry he could draw blood. Once, with his accountant, it had actually dripped onto the new Persian rug, only one drop. He hadn't noticed but Emmie had, she had watched while it darkened and finally dried as he ranted on. At the time she had been terrified of the thumb digging, it meant he had gone past the point of no return, his anger would only escalate, and that was when anything not tied down in their home would start flying as he raged.

Here, he didn't have that option, and Emmie could almost feel the self-control radiating off him.

'My life isn't comparable to the life that I had with you, darling.'

He sounded calm but Emmie wasn't fooled, she saw his jaw working under the outward control.

'I'm a changed man, I feel only pity for you, and do you know what else? I couldn't give a rats ass if you take the children to Scotland.' he spat the word at her like it was venomous, 'I've done my grieving for them, they're already gone darling. No, the two things I'm interested in are the diamond necklace of my mothers that I see you're putting to good use tonight, obviously of great sentimental value to me, and the wedding ring, of great monitory value. I would like them returned before you leave or you will be hearing from my lawyer. I'm sure you could do without that expense while you do up your little shack.'

There were gasps from around the room. Everyone seemed to be entirely still, faces frozen in shock like someone had pressed pause on the movie. The atmosphere was suddenly dense, and Emmie knew everyone was waiting for her next move. She swallowed hard as tears welled in her eyes. Michael, whose mouth had been open since Scott had entered the room, regained his composure and put a firm arm around her shoulders simultaneously comforting her and warning her to think about how she answered. Emmie barely felt it.

She gaped at Scott as images flashed through her mind, her movie on fast forward. Grace's tear-stained face as she asked for her daddy, and bedtime as she asked for one extra cuddle to make sure that mommy didn't want to go away in the night too. And Charlie, how quiet he had been since they split, the haunted look that he continued to wear since his dad stopped contacting.

When did he stop loving them? How could he stop loving them?

'You selfish bastard,' she whispered. 'You think I give a fuck about your mothers necklace and a sodding ring?'

Her hands shook as she fumbled with the clasp of the necklace. It finally gave and fell to the ground with a thud. The wedding ring she slipped off easily. Picking up the chain she hurled them both in Scott's direction before turning away as the tears slipped down her cheeks.

Thanks, sweet pea,' he said lightly retrieving them from the people who had managed to catch them, 'have a nice life.'

Emmie turned away, catching a glimpse of Martin Stomes, who was grinning as he disappeared out of the room on Scott's tail.

Yeah, and you can fuck off too, Uni boy.

Chapter 8

January 3rd arrived cold, blustery, and grey. The bleak outlook perfectly matched Emmie's mood, the gusting wind mimicking the swirling nerves in her stomach; one minute still, the next spinning like a rotary line in a force ten gale.

Despite her anxiety, the small moving truck was loaded and on its way early as planned, followed by a small trail of cars piled with tools and helpers. Driving behind the truck, Emmie felt as if she were in the middle of a funeral procession. She teetered between desperate tears, unease, anxiety, and frantic nerves. She felt thoroughly sick, while trying to remain enthusiastic for Grace and Charlie who were chatty with excitement. That day, she would remember as one of the hardest of her life, and the drive; one of the longest she had ever taken.

By the time they arrived that evening, Emmie was drained and on edge, and the sight of the house, dilapidated and desolate under a moonlit sky, only made her feel worse. Any enthusiasm she had retained for the children's benefit drained away, and she was glad of the joviality her helpers had brought with them as they climbed out of their cars. Jokes pertaining to the state of the house, and jibes about 'what her idea of a bargain was' brought on raucous laughter and elbow nudging. It was a gentle tease at her expense, but Emmie wasn't bothered, to be honest it was the only thing keeping her afloat.

After the initial mass excitement of hauling in items and boxes from the truck, the group poked around, fresh mugs of tea in hand, tapping at plaster, opening doors, stomping on floorboards, flicking away of cobwebs, until it was gone 11pm, and well past freezing.

The investigation had discovered a long forgotten pile of firewood stacked at the side of the house. Mike grabbed a few logs to build a fire in the living room, while Cameron, the builder, patched up the window and made the back doors safe for the evening.

That first night everyone huddled together on the floor of the living room, in front of the fire, like a huge sleepover. Grace and Charlie loved every minute, but Emmie didn't sleep a wink in a house that felt neither safe nor secure. She lay watching the flickering light of the waning fire as she listened to the ageing building creak and moan under a brisk wind.

As the fire grew dim she wondered what in the hell she had done. Scott was a bastard, sure, but had she really needed to go so far?

The following week Emmie threw herself into working on the house with the rest of the crew. The building, thankfully, turned out to be structurally sound and the fallen chimney superficial. Cameron and his team cleared the significant work effortlessly, even boarding out the loft for future use. Within days the house was both warm and watertight, with a new boiler, basic kitchen, and simple bathroom installed.

Meanwhile, everyone else scrubbed and cleaned, sanded, filled, painted and shopped. They joked there had been more blisters, broken nails and hammered thumbs in those few square feet than there had been in the neighbouring village of Bracken Hill in the last ten years.

And, okay, so the whole house was trade-paint magnolia, and the floors were only furnished with rugs, but it looked fresh and clean. The up-cycled furniture was starting to feel like it belonged and even the large, donated, grandfather clock in the living room appeared at home. Emmie had initially baulked at the hefty gift, but just a week later she was already attached to its steady ticking and occasional chimes. The sunroom had the only new furniture in the form of a three-piece wicker suite and a small table.

It was basic, but it was enough.

As the house came together people finally tailed off, saying their farewell's in small groups. When only Natalie and Mike remained the peace that descended over the house was glorious; but when they finally left too, it had taken all of Emmie's willpower not to beg them to take her back home.

Now Emmie sat alone opposite the fire, in the living room. She absently twisted the stem of the wine glass back and forth between her fingers.

Natalie and Mike had left after lunch, and after a few tears, Emmie had been fine. She busied herself with tidying, making dinner and playing with Grace and Charlie, pleased how easily this living alone lark was coming to her. But as an impenetrable darkness had descended outside, Emmie began to pace the house unsettled. And now, with the children in bed, the quiet felt plain eerie.

Perched on the edge of the settee, she watched the low light of the fire make shadows on the walls. It popped and crackled, as the grandfather clock ticked it's presence quietly from the corner of the room.

With new central heating installed she didn't need the fire, and hadn't intended to use it with the children around, but she found it necessary tonight. Its openness reminding her of a campfire, which made her think of her dad - a small comfort on her first night alone.

She took a sip from the glass, swallowing harder than necessary.

Dad.

He would have been so thrilled with her purchase she would have had to kick him back home. Emmie smiled.

I did it, dad. Here I am in my very own house in the highlands.

All alone.

Crap.

Her breath quickened as she glanced around. The room suddenly seemed huge, the house unmanageable. Unsettled, she rose from the settee with a sigh, and wandered into the hall. There wasn't a sound from upstairs, the children had fallen to sleep within seconds as they had every night so far.

For the tenth time tonight Emmie pulled the handle of the wooden front door.

Still locked tight. Chain still in situ.

As if anyone is lurking around anyway, who the hell walks three miles up a track to burgle the house at the end that has nothing in it?

She chewed her lip.

In the kitchen, the gentle hum of the boiler firing the central heating was a small comfort in the silence. She entered and looked out of the large window over the front garden, which was lit by a new carriage light attached to the stone porch.

Shadows, shapes, fence, car. Nothing moved.

She gulped the last mouthful of wine and rinsed the glass at the sink. Only hours ago the same sink had been full of cups, glasses and plates, the side littered with remnants of lunch, pop bottles and tea bags. Now it was all clean, only the solitary wine glass remained.

Turning from the window, Emmie grabbed the magazine from the dining table, shivering slightly in the draft that emerged from the open playroom door. She smiled as she remembered the viewing with Mr Roberts, and how she had tried to stop herself from imagining the playroom, now it was a reality in the house she thought she couldn't afford. Funny how things worked out.

As she crossed the hall back to the living room there was a small, but distinct noise. She paused with a frown, head turning back toward the kitchen.

Thump.

Low and muffled. From behind. From the playroom.

Grace wouldn't be that stealthy. It must be Charlie, and Emmie had an idea why.

His hand held consoles and tablet were kept in the cupboard down here, he probably couldn't sleep and had crept down to get one of them.

Throwing the magazine onto the settee in the toasty living room she crossed back the kitchen.

The door to the playroom was shut.

She tugged it open it to tell Charlie to get back to bed, but the room was empty. The cupboard shut. A controller wire hanging out as he had left it earlier.

Emmie frowned.

It was cold in here. So cold she could see her breath. She crossed her arms over her chest rubbing her shoulders as she looked at the patio doors dismayed.

Bloody hell, those doors let out a lot of heat.

She put a hand to the radiator, noting it's pumping heat, which was doing nothing to warm the room.

Thump.

The sunroom.

Eager to get out of the cold, she crossed the room and opened the door.

It was empty. And as cold as the playroom. The only difference here was that the air felt 'stirred' as though someone had been there only moments before.

Opening the door into the hall, Emmie paused. Then, a new noise, now from upstairs.

Ssshhh.

It sounded like material dragging on the wooden floor. Charlie must have come down in his bedclothes to keep warm. Shutting the door quietly behind her to keep the cool out of the warmer side of the house. She listened at the base of the stairs. There was no further noise. Emmie felt her muscles relax as warmth encompassed her again.

Charlie must have known he had been rumbled and gone back to bed.

Grinning at his sneakiness, and impressed with how quiet he had been, especially climbing the stairs, she went back to the warm living room. She concluded that the cold in both back rooms must be due to the vast amounts of glass. Nothing she could do about that yet.

Satisfied, she picked up her magazine and began to read until she was tired enough to collapse into bed, where she would hopefully sleep soundly.

Chapter 9

The sound of laughter woke Emmie from a fretful sleep full of dreams crawling with dark shadows, strange noises, and a very scary looking Grace asking her to fix something. She turned to face the window and saw sunlight glinting off the trees like frosty jewels. It was warm and comfortable in bed, and with a satisfied moan she snuggled further down.

Just ten more minutes...

She closed her eyes to the brightness just as a shout bellowed up the stairs.

'Mom! where are the cornflakes?'

Her eyes snapped open. She sighed blowing out her lips. What the hell was she thinking? There was never 'just ten more minutes' when kids were involved. She threw back the covers and stepped out into the cold morning air.

'Mom!' Charlie's voice shouted again.

'Coming,' she grumbled as she grabbed her slippers from under the bed and stuffed her feet into them. She passed through the bedroom doorway pulling her fleece nightgown off the door hook and folding herself into it as she descended the stairs. At the bottom, she met an amused looking Charlie.

'What the heck happened to you?' He said, eyebrows shooting up.

'What do you mean, honey?'

She yawned and ruffled his hair as she passed him.

'You look a bit of a mess. Mom, I didn't know hair could look that bad just from sleeping!'

Emmie stopped turning back to him shocked. He looked good, brown hair flopping into his deep hazel eyes, a smirk lighting up his face. This place was doing him good, the change in him in the few days they had been here was already immeasurable, and now here he was recovering his old dry sense of humour. Emmie played along, feigning mock annoyance.

'A mess, huh? I'll have you know, Mr Fancy-pants, that while you and Grace were asleep we were attacked by stealth ninjas. I was up all night making use of my black belt moves to defend our territory and keep you safe.'

She threw her right arm around his neck pulling his head down into a gentle headlock, scrubbing his hair with her left hand. He yelled and Emmie released him laughing before heading to the kitchen. Charlie followed her, grinning as hc smoothed down his hair.

In the doorway she stopped short.

A scene of devastation unfolded around her. Kitchen cupboards were open, cereal boxes strewn, four different kinds of cereal merging artistically on the floor.

A rogue trail of coco pops lead under the kitchen table where a milk carton was lying on its side, milk still trickling onto the tiled floor.

Emmie surveyed the scene with a sinking sensation in her gut.

What the hell? I think those ninjas did a number on us.

Then she spied the source. There on a dining chair, legs tucked under her, brown curls hanging in her face was Grace, proudly eating the breakfast she had made for herself.

Sensing movement, she looked up from her bowl and grinned.

'I'm a big girl mommy, I made coco pops, see?'

'Uh huh, I see Gracie.'

'They're yummy.' Grace said as she shovelled another spoonful into her mouth.

'Yeah, coco pops are your favourite aren't they? Unfortunately, most of them are now on the floor, why didn't you let Charlie help?'

Grace shrugged as she spooned more out of her bowl. Emmie turned to Charlie struggling to keep her temper.

'Really? Finding the cornflakes while they were still inside the box was so hard?'

'It wasn't me! I had no idea. It wasn't in this mess before, I swear!'

Charlie looked genuinely as shocked as Emmie felt.

'It was the funny man', Grace said giggling, 'He makes me laugh mommy!'

Emmie turned back to Grace with a sigh.

'Grace, we have been through this before with your little 'friend' making a mess. We've had this talk, haven't we? You tell him no.'

Grace looked suitably sorry, eyes cast downward, pouting mouth.

Emmie looked at her. Grace was a good-natured child, always eager to please, but after the culmination of the accident, the divorce, and the absence of a father who had always been there, Grace had started to do naughty little things in secret. On being found out she would blame the funny man, who would have committed the crime, or at least told her to do it.

After a few months, calm talks, and some very controlled anger from Emmie's side (especially when Grace had hidden her keys and phone down the toilet). Grace had finally come out the other side and the episodes had stopped.

The move here must have triggered her anxiety, and although the fact that this was happening again filled Emmie with foreboding, she also knew that they had beaten it before and they could do it again. She just needed to keep her cool.

Emmie picked up the milk carton and the empty boxes.

'Shame the funny man didn't stick around to tidy up after himself, eh?'

Grace slipped off her chair to help as there was a knock at the door, Emmie looked into the hallway surprised.

Did I not just move to the middle of nowhere? Who the hell is knocking my door at 9.30am?

She padded across the tiled floor into the hall and unlocked the wooden door swinging it open. Emmie's gaze travelled upward and, with an involuntary gasp, she took two steps backwards.

On the step was the biggest, burliest, bushiest man she had ever seen. He stood at around 6 foot 6 inches, had a mop of wild brown hair and a beard to match. Not much of his ruddy face could be seen other than clear green eyes.

Across the brambled garden, parked by the gate, was an old Land Rover, rusty patches on the wheel arches, and a large dent in the rear end. On the passenger seat was a Rottweiler, barking incessantly through the gap in the passenger window.

'Hallo lass, I'm from the farm down the road. I wanted to introduce myself.' Emmie turned her attention back to the man taking in his boots, jeans and checked shirt. 'I'm William Bruce. Bill to my friends. The wife's Maggie, can't be here today. Sure she'll make herself known at some point.' He smiled showing yellowing teeth.

His accent was so thick Emmie missed most of what he'd said other than his friends call him Bill. Did that mean she should call him Bill or not? Trying to process what he had said she flicked her eyes to the truck and the dog. Bill caught her eye-line and glanced back.

'Brutus, Shush!' he bellowed making Emmie jump.

Brutus was apparently not in a listening mood and offered a series of savage barks, jumping at the window.

'I said shush! I can't hear myself think,' Bill shouted again.

He turned to Emmie with a smile that didn't reach his eyes.

'Damn dog, always hated this place. Shouldn't have brought him here it only upsets him.'

The dog hates my house?

'Oh,' Emmie said, 'Erm, well, I'm Emmie. Pleased to meet you, William. Or should I call you Bill?'

Bill's eyes bored into hers, a sneer playing across his mouth.

'I said my friends call me Bill. What do *you* think you should do, lass?'

Emmie squirmed as her heart pumped. How was she supposed to respond to that? She was getting better at deciphering his accent, but he was making her uneasy.

'Erm ... I ... er,' Emmie said, trying to think of the best way to answer without antagonising this huge man.

Then, as quick as a barefoot man in hell, the sneer disappeared, his eyes lit up and crinkled at the corners as he broke into a huge grin.

'Well, of course you should call me Bill!' He said clapping Emmie on the shoulder and almost knocking her backwards. He broke into deep slow laughter that shook his whole body. At that moment the dog quit barking and took up whining, head cocked to one side. Bills laughter turned to splutters and coughing. He plucked a hankie from his breast pocket and covered his mouth until the coughing subsided before standing, hands on his thighs breathing heavily. Finally, he looked up, and the dog was off again barking out of the gap in the window. Bill looked back over his shoulder.

'Brutus, I said shut the hell up!'

The dog took no notice and Bill turned back to Emmie, a smile playing on his lips. He looked at her just long enough to make her uncomfortable, eyes moving down her dressing gown, to her slippers and back again.

'You moved here alone?' he said gruffly.

Emmie didn't want to answer but also didn't want to appear rude and bring back scary Bill.

'well, I ...erm, I'm here with my children. Grace and Charlie. I recently got divorced and needed the change of scenery, so, yeah, here I am.'

'Aye,' Bill said slowly nodding. He pulled a packet of cigarettes from his pocket and put one into his mouth, eyes on hers as he lit it. He offered her the packet and she quickly shook her head. Even if she had smoked she couldn't have taken one from him. Her uneasiness swelled with the silence.

'Project,' she squeaked, her voice cracking.

'Big project for a city girl,' Bill said blowing smoke. 'You'll be needing a hand, no doubt. I'll come up to help when I can.'

Emmie balked, the last thing she wanted was to be alone up here with this man.

'Oh no, I couldn't ask you to do that, I'm sure I'll manage fine.'

Bills face darkened and she found herself quickly backtracking, lightening instincts working subconsciously to keep him calm as she had done for too many years with Scott.

'I mean …. I'll be fine, really, but I will let you know if I need you. Thank you, you're very kind.'

'Aye,' Bill said again and took a final puff of his cigarette before throwing it on the floor and smothering it slowly with his foot. 'If you need anything; eggs, meat, cheese, butter and the like, we're a working farm we can provide them for you. For a price of course.'

'Right, I'll keep that in mind, thank you.'

'It's a long way to the village from here. Long way to anywhere.'

Emmie looked at him and swallowed hard as his eyes held hers.

'Just saying,' he said finally, 'wouldn't want you to get caught short.'

She was wondering how to respond for the second time when he suddenly shrugged his shoulders.

'Well, I'll be away. Lots to do. Supposed to be a storm coming up in the next few days. Tend to be big ones around these parts, stay indoors, wouldn't want any accidents with the bairns. You'll be wanting some candles, the power gets knocked out every time. Old lines. Too remote to bother updating. Ted tried with the council for years with no joy.'

'Ted?'

'Lived here before the place went to ruin. Got struck by lightning during the big storm of '99. Killed outright. I found him next morning when I popped up with his daily eggs, burnt to a crisp on the back patio. Awful affair. Wouldn't want to be finding any of you out there.'

Bill smiled, but his eyes offered no mirth. Emmie's pulse quickened. The thought of old Ted, fried, would be with her every time she looked at the patio now.

Thanks, Bill, old pal.

'Well, I'll make sure we're all inside. Thanks for dropping by.'

Emmie went to shut the door but Bill put his hand out, stopping it and pushing it back. He took a step nearer as Emmie took an involuntary step back, hand still clutching the doorknob. Bill's eyes bored into her own.

'Take care up here, all alone, won't you, lass?'

Emmie didn't answer, her heart was pounding. She tried to push the door against Bill's hand and he looked down as though just realising it was attached to his body. Hastily he removed it from the door.

'Aye, they say it's going to be a big one, you take care now.'

Bill grinned and bowed his head slightly as he backed down the pathway. Then he raised his hand and turned, striding toward the Land Rover where the dog was still barking manically.

Emmie slammed the door shut hard, turned the key in the lock and stood with her back against it breathing heavily.

Shit. What a weirdo.

As her heart slowed she pushed herself shakily away from the door. It was only then that she caught sight of her reflection in the gilt-framed mirror which hung on the wall opposite. She blinked.

Bloody hell! He must have thought I was Einstein reincarnated!

Pushing her hair down with her hands she returned to the kitchen to clean up, hoping Bill would be one of those neighbours who liked to keep himself to himself.

Chapter 10

The weather remained fine and dry through the rest of the week but Saturday was on the change. It was cold and gloomy; dark, dense, clouds bulged heavy in the sky giving the air an oppressive feel.

Emmie flicked the switch on the kettle and grabbed a cup from the cupboard.

As she waited she surveyed the front garden. She had attacked the mass of brambles hanging in the path yesterday, cutting off the stragglers and pruning them back with mere kitchen scissors. It had been laborious, and Emmie had kicked herself for not having the foresight to bring any tools with her, garden or otherwise, but at least it was looking better now.

Life was starting to settle down, and it reflected in Charlie's first two days at his new school where he came out full of enthusiasm and complete with two new friends. Grace was due to start nursery next week giving him time to settle before Emmie had to deal with losing both of her children to the education system. They were growing up too fast, and it thoroughly wrenched at her heart.

She also hoped that, over time, Charlie would give up trying to get his tablet at bedtime and fall into his usual pattern of sleep.

Twice more over the week she had heard his thuds and the swish of the duvet. Each time he had managed to thwart her efforts to catch him in the act, and each time she had made a mental note to get someone to check over the windows at the back of the house.

The playroom had been icy cold on more than a few occasions, and yesterday even the afternoon sun hadn't been able to warm the room.

Emmie hadn't warmed to the room herself, it had a strange atmosphere. She always felt watched, which she knew was silly, especially as Charlie spent lots of time in there and never mentioned feeling anything untoward.

The kettle clicked off and she busied herself making tea before moving into the living room, where Charlie was busy counting as Grace hid.

Emmie put her tea on top of the little cupboard which held the books and board games and started to empty it out placing them on the floor next to her.

Today's mission was to find the little white shoe box which held the few precious photographs she owned. Inside were a couple from her childhood and a few of her father, but mainly it contained pictures of the children. All of the family photographs had been stored on Scott's computer which was now inaccessible. It hurt to think of all the memories he had saved while she only had the handful that had been printed over the years.

She had taken the box the day Scott had told them to leave, and later, in anger, she had torn up and thrown away any picture showing him, even from the back. There was nothing left of him in there now, and that was how she liked it, but consequently, the remaining few pictures were immensely important and, with everything unpacked, it niggled that she still hadn't come across them.

When the cupboard came up empty, she replaced the books and games and turned to the TV cabinet as Charlie reached a hundred and started his hunt for Grace in the hall.

Emmie conducted her search methodically, ending up back in the living room an hour later, sweating and frustrated.

I know I packed that box, I remember doing it.

She chewed at her lip.

Or maybe you thought so, you were stressed and anxious back then, Em. Perhaps you left it behind.

It was a possibility, she supposed. She turned back to the hall with a sigh as Charlie crashed down the stairs.

'Mom, have you seen Grace?'

She turned to look at him surprised.

'No, honey, I don't think she's been downstairs.'

'I can't find her she's disappeared.'

'Well, isn't that the idea of the game? She's obviously found a good place to hide.'

'She doesn't do hiding mom, she stands behind doors and sits under the kitchen table, and I can always hear her giggling.'

Emmie frowned.

'Well she can't have fallen off the face of the earth Charlie, she has to be here somewhere. Have you tried all of the wardrobes and under beds.'

'Everywhere I can think of.'

'You know she moves around when you're trying to find her don't you? A running hide she calls it.'

'I know that, but I can always *hear* her.'

Charlie looked at her, eyes pleading, face etched with anxiety. She smiled at him.

'Come on, I'll help you to look. She can't have gone far.'

They scoured the house thoroughly before it started to worry Emmie that he might be right. Usually, there was a sign that Grace was nearby. A giggle, a movement, even just breathing, but today - nothing. All of the rooms were quiet and empty. Grace seemed to have vanished.

No. We've missed her somewhere. She's doing a very quiet running hide that's all.

Even so, Emmie's pulse quickened as she tried to push down the panic that wanted to run wild inside her.

They searched again. Looking everywhere. Calling Grace's name over and over, and when this search turned up nothing Emmie threw open the front door in desperation.

'Grace!' She yelled.

Outside the clouds had finally divulged their swollen contents to the ground. The rain came down hard and fast, a dip in the front garden already forming a small pool. Emmie stepped out anyway, circling the house closely, but scanning whole the area, screaming Grace's name across the open land.

Finally, desperate and soaked to the skin, she returned to Charlie who was sitting on the bottom step of the stairs, tears wetting his face. He swiped at them as she entered but one look at her face and he was crying again.

Emmie's heart thudded wildly. She shivered in the cool air. When you had looked everywhere, what the hell happened next?

Call the police?

And tell them what? She had lost her three-year-old somewhere she couldn't possibly get lost?

She can't have vanished. There is no possible way.

Sitting next to Charlie, she put a wet arm around him. She was shaking now, through both fear and cold, erratic thoughts tumbling over each other with worry. She wanted to join Charlie in his tears but she knew that would only upset him more and achieve nothing. He sniffled against her soaked jumper before pulling back.

'Where is she, mom?'

Emmie brushed the hair out of his eyes with a cold, shaky hand and pulled him back to her swallowing the lump in her throat.

'We'll find her Charlie she can't have gone far. We'll have another look and then maybe we'll have to call the police. They will find her in some stupid place we would never think to look.'

Her voice shook, but not excessively, and she sent up a silent prayer of thanks. She didn't want Charlie to know just how worried she was, Grace had only been missing forty minutes it was hardly time to file a missing person report. Still, that didn't stop the fear twisting through her and sinking deep into her stomach where it settled like lead, hard and cold.

She held Charlie until his tears subsided and went to get him a tissue before they set up search again, but back in the hall, Charlie put a finger to his lips in such a grown-up manner she momentarily had a glimpse of what he may look like in ten years time.

He pointed up.

'I think I can hear something,' He whispered, 'Upstairs.'

Relief almost buckled Emmie's legs. Willing to clutch at any straw offered right now, she held her hand out to him.

'Let's go upstairs then.'

Upstairs Emmie didn't think she had ever listened so hard, but the silence was absolute. Crippling fear quickly replaced the relief that had flooded through her downstairs. She was about to tell Charlie he must have been mistaken when she heard it.

A faint thud – two - seemed to come from the direction of her bedroom. Charlie heard it too, his eyes widening in hope as he all but dragged her to the room. There was another thud, louder in here, and Charlie pointed toward the wardrobe that ran the length of the wall. Emmie nodded agreement. She threw open the large double doors.

On the left were shelves with folded jumpers, jeans, belts and bags. Emmie ran her hand over each shelf, even the ones that were far too high, but there was no Grace. The floor was littered with shoes and boots, but it still would have been easy to see anyone hiding on the floor, and Charlie was moving the clothes that were hanging across the rail at the other side of the wardrobe, his puzzled face revealing she wasn't there either.

Emmie wondered if she was going crazy. The back of the wardrobe was the wall over the stairs. It went nowhere. If the thuds had come from in here surely Grace was in the wardrobe.

Except that she wasn't.

Emmie ran her hands quickly over her face, grasping the back of her neck.

She felt like screaming.

Breathe Em, breathe. The noise came from somewhere let's listen again maybe your direction is a little off.

'Mom? I'm sure ...'

Emmie put her hand up to stop him as another succession of light thuds emerged - from the wardrobe.

She looked at Charlie, who looked back at her with an identical look of bewilderment. Together, with an unspoken urgency, they emptied it. Emmie threw the clothes off each shelf as Charlie took out shoes and what he could reach off the rail. The rest Emmie tugged down until they were facing an empty space. White walled and completely bare. Emmie stared, panting hard, as Charlie let out a small moan.

This is horse shit! I don't have a wardrobe that goes to Narnia it's impossible. So how the hell are the knocks coming from in here?

And yet, they came again, quick thumps from inside.

Charlie got inside and started to bang on the back wall with his fists. Emmie stood shocked for a beat before spurring into action.

'Charlie, no. You'll hurt your hands.'

She stepped forward putting a hand out to grab him as a small square of the wall opened with a click. It swung outward, spitting with it a very upset Grace.

Charlie jumped back, yelping in shock as Grace fell to the floor drenched in sweat, tears rolling down her flushed little face. Emmie scooped her up, and sank to the floor, Charlie huddled close to her left side and Grace pooled in her lap. Grasping both children tightly in each arm, Emmie let her tears flow with theirs, immense relief leaving her shaking violently.

'The … the funny man showed me, mommy, he t…told me to hide in there. I was stuck.'

Emmie's blood ran cold as she kissed the top of Grace's head.

'It's okay Grace. You're safe now.'

But she didn't believe it. The implications of Grace's statement scared her to death; naughtiness was par for the course but this was a step too far.

The funny man had to go. And fast.

Chapter 11

Emmie inspected the space in the wardrobe. It was small but easily big enough to accommodate Grace - she estimated around three feet high and four feet wide at the opening and going back another three feet or so. It was empty and painted as white as the back of the wardrobe. She ran her hand over the inside.

Brick.

The walls of the house were old and thick, and a little investigation revealed that three foot was approximately wall thickness before the wardrobe jutted into the room.

The door was wooden and a good couple of inches thick which accounted for the lack of noise from outside as Grace banged on it. It had a push lock - push to open, push to close - explaining the lack of handle from the outside and, when shut, it fit almost entirely flush. In all the time she had been here, and even when she had filled the wardrobe she hadn't noticed anything strange about the back wall. Now she knew it was there it seemed glaringly obvious.

On the inside of the door a piece of leather, which had probably been a belt at some stage, was nailed to the wood. Once inside, there would be no way to get out without pushing from the front, but if you could pull the door hard enough from the inside, the mechanism would pop the door open again. Grace must have pulled the strap, clicking the door shut, but hadn't been strong enough, or more likely she hadn't understood, that pulling the strap would also let her out, rendering herself stuck.

Completely stuck.

Emmie stood back frowning. Why such a space should exist at all was odd enough, but a hiding space so deadly for the children worried her. She vowed to bring them back up here and explain how the door worked just in case anyone managed to get stuck again, although the experience had scared Grace so much Emmie didn't think she would be silly enough to go in for a second try.

The photograph appeared as she was folding jumpers ready to put back in the wardrobe. It fluttered out of the pile, landing face up on the floor, giving her the second shot of relief within the last twenty minutes.

So, the box was here after all, although Emmie had sellotaped the lid tight before the move. Now it was open, which meant that someone small wasn't telling the truth.

Stacking the pile of jumpers onto a shelf, she bent to pick up the photograph with a smile. It was an old one of her father, stood atop a mountain, stick in one hand emulating a walking aid, looking out into the distance with a smile on his face. Emmie was stood beside him, no more than seven or eight years old, her hand was around his back and his free hand dropping down to curl around her shoulders. Unlike her father she grinned at the camera, dark hair blowing, cheeks reddened by the wind.

Emmie felt a twinge in her chest staring into the eyes of the girl she once was. Not many of little Em's dreams had been fulfilled yet. In fact she didn't think her plans ever involved meeting a Scott Harvington and being beaten down over years of anger and control until she hadn't known who she was anymore.

Little Em would have said that wasn't possible and laughed until her sides ached.

The photo started to shake in her fingers. Emmie took a breath and forced Scott out of her mind.

What's the positive, Em?

Well, she had broken free from Scott, even if it had been his call, and she supposed she was already smashing the big dream by moving here. Although, if she remembered accurately, living in Scotland was closely followed by plans to marry a big Scotsman and live happily ever after up in the mountains.

The smile that had been forming on her lips now slipped to a grimace.

Well, one dream at a time, eh, little Em? And by the way, toots, if all big Scotsmen up here are like Bill you can stick that dream in your pipe and smoke it, honey.

The smile back, Emmie turned her attention to her father.

If only you could see me now, dad, out from under Scott's reign and making my own life up here.

Harry Landers had never been fond of Scott, and he saw through any lightness Emmie made of her situation. But he had never questioned her decisions over the years; moving in together, getting married, the children. Instead, he had been her go to. Her adviser. Always listening and offering sound advice, and never judging, even if his opinion was dismissed.

He was the calm, stable, constant in her life, always there when she needed him and always with a cuddle no matter how big she had grown.

The unfairness of the heart attack which had taken him four years ago had utterly blindsided Emmie. He was an active outdoor man, bagging at least two of Scotland's munros each year, including the year of his death at sixty-two. He never smoked and never drank. He had been fit, healthy, and well all of his life. The irony hadn't escaped her, and it had planted a seed back then, although she hadn't known it.

Scott had kept them near London, where the more prominent law firms were. She could paint anywhere, but Law was his career and she had never questioned it. After the divorce, and the subsequent realisation that she could cope on her own, despite Scott's opinion, she had felt that seed start to sprout. Scotland had pulled her as though it had a cord tied around her waist and was slowly shortening the length, and Bruadair had pulled her from the moment she had seen the house on Bryson Estate Agency's website.

And, okay, so we had a small hiccup today, but I can do this, it's a piece of cake, right dad?

She ran a thumb over the photo with a sigh, pocketed it carefully, and checked the small cubby hole was shut tight before going downstairs.

Chapter 12

Later that evening, pyjamas on, hot chocolate in their hands, Emmie read a couple of books to Grace and Charlie. While they were calm and relaxed she decided to have a little chat about the picture before she took them up to bed.

Putting the last book down and stretching her arms out either side of her, she pulled them in. Charlie on her right, Grace on the left, they leaned into her shoulders and she enjoyed the hug, cherishing the moment, kissing the top of their heads in turn.

'Someone's been telling porkie pies.' She said quietly. 'Who is it?'

Charlie looked up at her frowning as more vocal Grace stated her plea.

'I'm not porkie pig mommy.'

'I'm not sure about that all the food you put away today, Gracie.'

She poked a finger into Grace's side making her squirm and giggle. She let her calm before continuing.

'Seriously though, I know one of you has mommy's photo box, and you both know how important it is and how hard I tried to look for it today. I'm not mad I just need it back, so, come on, who is it?'

Charlie and Grace looked at her with equal blank stares. Emmie waited.

'Well?'

'I haven't seen the box mom. I would have told you today if I had.'

Charlie's face was innocent and wide-eyed and she was entitled to believe him, it had been the same look and tone he had used when Grace and her imaginary friend had trashed the kitchen. She turned to Grace who was also straight-faced and wide-eyed.

'What about you Grace?'

'I not seen the box mommy.'

Emmie sighed looking from one to the other.

'Ok guys, here's the deal. I found one of the photos from the box when I was putting things away in the wardrobe, so I know they're here, and I know one of you has messed with them. I won't have lies from either of you. You're not in trouble, I just want to put the box somewhere safe.'

Charlie shook his head. She looked into their eyes neither one appearing guilty. They weren't avoiding her gaze, messing with fingers, trying not to smile, fidgeting. They stared back at her as resolutely as she looked at them.

She frowned and then had an idea.

'What about your friend Grace? Has he had the box?'

Grace seemed to think a little and then shook her head.

'I don't think so, mommy.'

'So did this photo appear out of nowhere? It was in the box. Someone has had it out and put it in my wardrobe. No takers?'

Both of them shook their heads in unison. Emmie was flummoxed. How could they both be acting so convincingly innocent? She huffed out a breath and ran a hand through her hair pushing it back off her face. This was getting them nowhere, and it certainly wasn't finding the box.

'Well, there's no hot chocolate before bed tomorrow unless someone confesses before tomorrow night. You have twenty-four hours. Now let's get to bed, come on.'

Grace and Charlie moaned, pleaded, and complained over each other all the way up to bed, but neither one of them would admit guilt. If hot chocolate removal couldn't get it out of them they were probably telling the truth, it was their one sin and they adored it, not every night, but most in winter.

Maybe the photo had got caught in the jumper. The box had been stored in the wardrobe at Natalie's, it wasn't so far-fetched. She would call Natalie tomorrow, it would be good to chat, and maybe she could shed some light on the missing box.

After an uneasy day, Emmie decided to settle in the sunroom for a change. The days had been colder lately but this room had never reached the low temperature it had been that first night, and tonight it was cool but comfortable. She checked the French doors - just in case - and sat in a wicker chair, blanket folded around her, looking out into the darkness toward the orchard. All was quiet and calm.

She sighed leaning back in the chair watching the tops of the trees moving against the clear moonlit sky as her mind wandered.

Grace started school soon. They could finally settle into a routine and then hopefully, invisible man would disappear. They were in need of supplies and Emmie was in need of money. Like it or not, she had to get back to work, and she had to get out and integrate, they couldn't stay holed up here forever.

A noise from upstairs cut into her thoughts as she reached for her book from the table. She paused, listening for one of the children but all was quiet again. Grabbing the book, she relaxed back into the chair

She glanced back out to the orchard and blinked.

Something seemed wrong outside. She squinted into the darkness behind the doors. The shadows were wrong, closer somehow, impenetrable.

She leaned forward to get a closer look, book falling to the floor with a soft thud, as the noise came again from upstairs, she swivelled her head to look at the ceiling.

A low thump followed by a rustle of dragged material.

Charlie.

She got up, wrapping the blanket closer around her and opened the door to the hallway.

'Games up Charlie, I know what you've been up to. Get back into bed.'

There was another thump.

'Bed, Charlie, I mean it.'

There was no response. Assuming he had complied she shut the door and sat back into the chair, gingerly turning back to the shadows outside.

Thump…ssshhh. Thump...ssshhh.

The noise continued upstairs, slow and rhythmical. Emmie stood again, pulse quickening as she strained to make sense of the sound.

Is Charlie still out of bed? Why didn't he answer me? He would have reacted, even with just a grunt, surely.

No longer confident that it was Charlie, the nape of her neck prickled. Her heart thumped in her ears as she realised the sound was travelling, slowly and consistently, toward the top of the stairs. Goosebumps littered her arms. She swallowed hard.

Thump...ssshhh. Thump...ssshhh.

This is stupid Em. It has to be Charlie, just go to the stairs and tell him off. Simple.

But she couldn't move, a surge of terror rooted her to the spot. She felt as she often did in the playroom. Watched.

Hunted.

Thoughts jostled in her head each one dismissed as soon as it arrived. Heating? Could it be the pipes? The wind? Is Grace out of bed? Is Charlie playing a trick? Is something is blowing down the landing? None of them could be attributed to the deliberate, slow, repetitive noise. Nothing made sense.

Cool air pressed around her, and instinct surged, screaming at her to move; to get out of the room, get out of the house, to get away.

To RUN.

And then her stomach dropped through the floor, as she remembered Charlie and Grace. They were upstairs. And if it wasn't one of them, then 'It' was between her and the children.

Oh god, they're up there with it.

'It' what? What the hell is it?

WHAT THE FUCK IS IT?

Thump...ssshhh. Thump...ssshhh.

Louder now, down the stairs. Each slow step the thud of a footfall.

Sick with fear Emmie felt the room start to spin as she tried to drag in a breath. She wanted to run – hide - anything but to wait for whatever was descending the stairs, but she was frozen, rooted to the floor as deep as an ancient tree, unable to move, and unable to look away. She watched the door into the hall barely breathing.

Thump...ssshhh. Thump...ssshhh.

Right, up to the door.

Where it stopped.

The silence grew heavy with presence and anticipation. Emmie's eyes ached as they bored into the door, trying to detect any movement of the handle. Her breath puffed before her as the temperature plummeted. She tried not to shiver, not to move, not to break the spell making whatever *it* was aware of her presence.

Only the ticking grandfather clock reached her ears. The air was tense and charged, it felt like a standoff, a gunfight at dawn, who was going to shoot first?

A loud knocking exploded around the room and Emmie flinched letting out a yell as she dropped to the floor. She swung her head to the source of the knocking and tried to scream but couldn't catch her breath.

At the French doors, a mass of blackness was pressing and swirling onto the glass from the outside. It didn't matter what it looked like Emmie was sure it was a man, and it was menacing.

'Mine!'

The word boomed around the old house with such force that Emmie was sure the house shook around her. She scooted back to the wicker sofa, whimpering noises escaping from her throat as she climbed onto it. She tried to scream over and over but her throat was so dry and hoarse no sound came out.

It - he - was glaring at her from the doors, his attention on her.

She buried her head into the cushions, legs tucked under her and waited for whatever was to come, tears of fear prickling behind her eyes.

Nothing happened.

The silence stretched. Air taut with tension.

'Mommy?'

Emmie was in such a grip of fear she was having trouble processing the sweet voice.

Grace, it was Grace.

'Mommy? Can you fix this for me? It's very broken.'

The voice that emerged from Emmie was stiff and tight sounding like it belonged to someone else. She struggled to be normal for Grace's sake.

'Ok honey, mommy was sleeping, hang on.'

Emmie rose as normally as she could, though her whole body shook. She kept her eyes closed as she scrubbed the tears away pretending to yawn.

'Mommy?'

A light touch fell on Emmie's arm. She stiffened. The contact was bone cold, icy even.

It wasn't the touch of a little girl.

A moan escaping her lips she slowly opened her eyes.

Grace stood before her. Grey skin contrasting with her favourite Peppa Pig top, now smeared with dried blood. A long strip of Plastic fastened with a zip covered her from waist to feet like a skirt. A skirt made for someone much bigger, it stretched out on the floor behind her. Blood crusted her hair into rusty clumps and her left arm bent at an unearthly angle as it hung at her side. Emmie scanned the small figure in horror as Grace smiled showing missing teeth and held something out toward her.

Something red and meaty.

Something that Emmie realised with mounting disgust looked like a heart.

Grace's heart.

Torn from the hole Emmie now saw in the chest of the Peppa Pig top.

'Can you fix it, mommy?'

Emmie opened her mouth. This time the scream came loud and shrill.

Chapter 13

Natalie took a final drag of her cigarette and flicked it out of the small window of the tiny supplies cupboard. Her shift at Swallow Heath General Hospital had been manic, the busy A&E department she had transferred to just six months ago was starting to get on her nerves. She had not specialised in paediatrics to be cleaning up vomit from drunk idiots, getting sworn at on a daily basis, and wiping the elderly, and indeed the doctors, backsides. With three hours of her shift left to go she was flagging, she had to have a break.

She had long since discovered that the cupboard was the perfect place for a quiet smoke with a window which opened out onto a disused courtyard making it a great place to get rid of the evidence.

Coffee was next on the agenda. She quickly took a mini deodorant spray from her tunic pocket, sprayed herself and the room and popped a chewing gum into her mouth. As she moved to exit the little cupboard, her phone buzzed with a message.

Mike.

Em Called, not urgent, call her if you get a minute.

Natalie cursed, she had meant to call Em every day since they had left her and hadn't had a chance, a few quick texts were all she had managed between manic shifts. She quickly typed back.

Thanks Hun, just going for coffee, I'll call if I can. See you at 9.30ish. x

As she reached for the door handle the phone buzzed again.

ok.

She looked at the message and chuckled to herself. Men; Last of the big texters. Pocketing the phone she took a breath and opened the door, trying to look purposeful as she came out of the cupboard. Stepping into the clinical corridor she put her head down and quickly walked toward the vending machine.

'Ah Natalie, there you are, you're needed at reception.'

Natalie stopped, pasted a smile and turned to face Kay, Team Leader over the reception staff. She was a small blonde lady, usually quietly spoken, but this lady had fabulous organisational skills and a fabulous temper to match. She had been in post just a year and had already whipped those half soaked receptionists running the front line of A&E into shape with numerous flow charts and forms.

'Oh, I was just grabbing a coffee, that bike crash victim ran off with my break, I'm gagging.'

She smiled but Kay didn't reciprocate. It was definitely one of those shifts.

'I guess coffee will have to wait. What's happening?'

'Little boy came in with facial swelling and breathing difficulties, suspected anaphylaxis. Adrenalin was administered in the ambulance and the boy is fairly calm now but the parents have been here with him a while, they're a bit put out they've not been seen by a Doctor yet. I want you to go through a few routine checks with them, appease them a while. God knows when Dr Chopra is going to get round to them.'

'What happened to Dr Carter?' Natalie asked, moving aside as two porters wheeling a bed came past at a near run, 'They were clearing the backlog with the two of them on shift.'

'Phone call,' Clipped Kay, 'His wife I believe, been outside with a coffee for the last 40 minutes.'

Kay pursed her lips, her eyes hard.

'Right.' Natalie was getting the picture loud and clear, 'I'll go and check where there's a clear bay, then I'll be right with them.'

Kay was already walking briskly down the corridor.

'Don't bother, there isn't one.' She called back, not turning around, 'I've asked Nancy to move Mr Dawes up to the stroke ward to free up bay 2. No way he's going home tonight anyway. She's moving him now, I've got a domestic on standby. By the time you've finished talking to the parents and got to the bay, it will be all clean for you.'

'Great, I'll get right on it,' called Natalie walking back in the direction of the reception.

Anxious parents with an attitude brought on by fear, this would be a battle as she was clearly no Doctor. People weren't stupid they would know she was buying time. Bye, bye coffee. Roll on 9pm when her shift officially finished.

It was after 10pm when Natalie got home that evening. She was ratty and exhausted, and wanted nothing more than her bed, but she knew she had to call Emmie. Natalie couldn't care less if she didn't see a single person for the next three days after that shift, but Em was all alone up there in Scotland, she probably hadn't had a decent conversation since they had left.

Throwing her keys and phone onto the table, she said a quick hello to Mike, changed, and was on the settee with a beautifully cooked lasagne and a glass of wine in less than ten minutes.

Call as I eat?

Her stomach growled as the cheesy aroma filled her nostrils. When the heck had she last eaten?

Mike watched her, 'I managed the whole recipe with no catastrophes and the kids wolfed it down. They're still alive so you have nothing to worry about, it's delicious.'

Natalie looked back at him and the decision was made.

Fifteen minutes later, with a silenced stomach, she dialled Emmie and waited as the phone rang out hoping she hadn't gone to bed.

There was a click on the line.

'Hi Nat, What bloody time do you call this?'

A surge of warmth flooded through Natalie. Trying to stop the grin that was spreading across her face, she quickly frowned and feigned mock annoyance.

'Late. Some of us have jobs to go to. You should be thankful I phoned you at all, I was debating leaving it until tomorrow.'

'Oh, please. There's no way you'd have left me hanging, you worry far too much!'

Natalie laughed. 'Pah, it's your optimism that I won't leave you hanging that puts the pressure on me to call so late.'

Emmie snorted on the other end of the line.

'If you hadn't called you wouldn't have slept. You worried yourself to death over Mike's stubbed toe last week, I can't imagine what you'd have had in store for me, I'd have been in all sorts of mess up here!'

Natalie had to admit that Emmie was right and she couldn't help but laugh. Emmie joined her and it was good to hear, Natalie's grin was firmly plastered on her face.

'How are you, honey?' she asked.

'I'm doing great, Nat, I love it up here. It's going to be fabulous for work, it's so peaceful, and the location is stunning. It's starting to feel like home now too. Everything is unpacked properly and in its place and I've even attacked the brambles in the front garden so that the path is passable. I can't wait to get some flowers and shrubs in there next summer it'll make the place look beautiful.'

Emmie sounded excited her words coming thick and fast. Natalie smiled and shifted back on the settee, sipping the last of her wine as Emmie chattered on.

'I've finally got Grace into Nursery at Charlie's school. It's just mornings which means I can work and then spend afternoons with her before collecting Charlie. It's perfect. Charlie is settling in already, and Grace starts next week so we can start getting into a proper routine. They're both doing so well. It's fabulous here, Nat, I absolutely love it, my own space is exactly what I need to put everything behind me and start again fresh. Did I say that this is possibly the best thing I could ever have done?'

'No, Em, but I get the gist. Everything is fabulous. Which is great to hear because I didn't know whether it may be too far off the beaten track for you.'

There was a funny rumbling from Emmie's end but as Natalie was about to ask what the noise was an indignant Emmie cut back in.

'As it happens, Nat, my kindly neighbour Bill already popped round for a chat. He offered me eggs, butter, milk, all kinds of stuff from his farm down the road. It was wonderful to meet him.'

Natalie sensed the sarcasm in Emmie's voice and frowned.

'What happened?'

'Well, he did come over for a chat and to offer me those things, which should be a nice gesture, right? He was just a little weird, you know, creepy weird. Maybe I'm being harsh and it's just the way they are up here. His dog wants shooting either way, I couldn't hear myself think. He left it in his truck by the gate and the bloody thing barked and howled right up until he left. He said the dog had always hated my house, I'm not sure if I should be offended!'

Emmie tittered and Natalie thought she sounded on edge, the laugh a bit too forced.

'Well,' she said, trying to reassure Emmie, 'I wouldn't be too bothered what he thinks, I mean, he doesn't have to live there right?'

'Bill?'

'The dog.'

Emmie Laughed. In the background was that rumble again, but this time Emmie gasped.

'What is it, Em?' Natalie asked, concerned.

'Storm. Bill said that it would be a bad one. To be honest, it's been rumbling and raining on and off since 4pm I thought it had passed us by but, God, it's getting fierce out there now. I've never seen lightning like it!'

'Dad used to say storms were better to watch out in the country, remember?'

'He was right, I can see every fork lighting up the sky for miles.'

There was a sudden loud crack followed by a rumble. Natalie jumped and held the phone away from her ear as she heard Emmie shriek on the other end.

'Bloody hell,' they said in unison.

Natalie whistled through her teeth, 'That was really loud.'

'You should try being here, I thought the roof was coming in!'

Natalie giggled.

'What's so funny?'

'Remember what mom used to tell us? It's only God moving the furniture around in heaven, once he's happy with the arrangement it'll stop.'

Natalie heard Emmie giggle on the other end of the phone.

'Remember when we got older? We'd count the distance between the lightning and thunder to check it was moving away,' she said

'Yeah, that's right,' Natalie said smiling at memories of the two of them crouched behind the settee, their eyes peering over the top to check when the lightning flashed so they could begin to count. She wondered if Emmie was putting on a brave front, when they were little she used to be terrified of storms.

Another loud boom and the phone line crackled and fizzed in Natalie's ear.

'Em, are you still there?'

A few more bursts of static and Emmie was back.

'... said he found him on the patio, fried to a crisp. Said he wouldn't want to repeat the experience with one of us. I was a bit creeped out to be perfectly honest.'

Natalie was taken aback, heart skipping a beat.

'Woah, woah, what? The line isn't too good, what were you saying?'

'I said Bill was telling us to stay indoors during the storm. Apparently, the chap who lived here before got struck by lightning. Bill said he found him next morning fried on the patio.'

'Fried? As in dead?'

Natalie was incredulous. Who the hell was this Bill with his stories? And how on earth do you manage to bring that into conversation on the first meeting with your new neighbour?

'Dead as a dodo,' replied Emmie.

'Well, God, did he have to relay that little nugget of information on the day you first meet?'

'Hmm, it was a bit weird like I said, but I think it was because of the storm, he was looking out for us. Well, at least he doesn't want to find another body on the patio and that makes him normal right? Although if you hear of us fried tomorrow remember it's probably foul play. Look into the neighbour.'

Emmie laughed but all Natalie could force out was a high pitched, strangled noise. Christ did she have to be up there alone, on a stormy night, and with a weird neighbour? Natalie wrinkled her nose. Why hadn't she forced the issue of the shoebox in Surrey? She heard Emmie yawn and the phone line crackled again with another thunderclap. Natalie looked at the clock, 11.05pm. Emmie cut into her thoughts.

'Well, I have my first proper outing tomorrow to the village store. I'm desperately low on supplies now and since Grace tipped half the cereal and milk all over the floor in one of her fits of 'the imaginary friend told me to do it' I now have no cereal left for tomorrow. Should have gone today really but the kids were playing so we've had a lovely, lazy day. Oh while I've got you, Nat, remember the little box I had with the photos ...'

There was a loud boom and Natalie jumped out of her skin as the line went dead. She held the phone up in front of her face and shook it before putting it back to her ear.

'Em? Are you there?'

There was no reply and the dial tone reappeared in her ear. Natalie raised her eyebrows and severed the connection, she pressed redial but got an engaged tone. She rubbed a hand through her hair staring at the phone.

Emmie had sounded well enough and seemed to be enjoying herself up there for now, but Natalie's stomach twisted with worry and uneasy desperation. Emmie may think she had come through the worst, but it would all come crashing down again eventually, it had to.

How long did they leave it? What could they do with Emmie so far away?

She felt despair start to crawl over her. The therapist had said not to push Emmie until she was ready to face the truth. She wasn't ready yet, and even if she were, there wasn't a damn thing Natalie could do about it right now.

Natalie took a shuddering breath, giving herself a mental shake.

Let it go for now. Let it go and be happy for her while things are good.

Chapter 14

Emmie stared at the phone.

'Nat ... are you there?'

She waited a moment longer and then pressed the button to end the call, she wasn't sure she could keep up the cheeriness anyway. The photo box would have to wait.

Trying to override her apprehension after last night, when she had awoke gracefully on the wicker chair with a loud scream and a painful crick in her neck, Emmie had started out in the sunroom, watching the lightening over Bracken Cruach. She stuck it out for an uncomfortable forty minutes before deciding she was just too close to the damn patio, and with mild relief, retreated to the living room and the ticking comfort of the grandfather clock.

Phone in her lap, she looked out into the darkness.

This was turning into some storm - the wind roared around the house, rattling the heavy front door, and whining down the chimney. Rain battered the windows and lightning illuminated both the front and side windows of the room. Natalie calling so late had kept her occupied as the storm raged, it had felt good to be connected to someone living. Now, sitting alone again, she was on edge.

Three bright streaks lit the sky in quick succession and a loud clap of thunder seemed to rock the foundations. Emmie closed her eyes clapping her hands over her ears.

Crap! Is it possible for a house to fall down through thunder?

She was determining whether to hide behind a cushion until the storm passed over when the door connecting the hall and the front room opened and in came Charlie, closely followed by a very worried looking Grace.

Emmie's heart patted its relief, she wasn't going to have to sit through this alone after all. She opened her arms and Grace ran into them, soft warm Grace, hair smelling like strawberry shampoo. Emmie buried her head in it, then she looked up and motioned to Charlie who was still standing by the door uncertain whether he should be the brave man of the house or give in to his fear. He decided in a flash as he saw Emmie's arm held out for him and ran into her embrace.

'I don't think I've seen a storm this bad ever,' He said, tucking his legs up and cuddling up to her.

'I don't think I have either,' Emmie said, hugging him a little tighter. 'It's just because you can see the whole show from here. We're lucky, it's really beautiful, look at all the forks across the sky.'

'I'm scared,' Grace said into Emmie's shoulder.

Emmie squeezed her tightly.

'There's nothing to be frightened of we're safe in here. It will soon pass over.'

'I think the house will blow away,' Grace whispered

'This house has been here for a long, long time, sweetie. Before you two were born. Heck, before mommy was born. It's seen lots of storms, some far worse than this one, and it's stood just fine.'

Unlike Ted, who saw his last storm in '99, and quit standing before it passed over ...

Another menacing clap of thunder threatened to shake the foundations and Emmie jumped. She wondered if the storm of that year was as bad as this one.

She was still thinking of Ted in 1999 trying to start his generator, as the storm of 2018 took out the power.

The lights flickered and dimmed, brightened for a second, and then went out altogether. Grace screamed, covering her face and Charlie jumped up to flick the light switch.

'It's no good Charlie, the powers out. Luckily Mommy prepared some candles earlier, just in case.'

She waggled her eyebrows at him smiling, and then wondered why she'd bothered. It was pitch black.

She reached over to the small table where she'd placed the three candles earlier, heeding Bill's warning. A lucky sheet of lightning lit the room as she grabbed the matches to light them.

Candlelight sucked.

As if it weren't bad enough being stuck in here with the worst storm on earth, now they were stuck in a room full of flickering shadows as well. Emmie's imagination went into overdrive as she tried to comfort Grace, who was now crying.

What if Ted was still here? What if he showed up in particularly bad storms as a testament to his fate? What if the place was derelict because Ted's ghost had killed everyone off? Was he the one at the French doors in her dream last night? Why had she thought that this house was a good idea?

She shuddered.

For Christ sake Em, would you shut the hell up?

But last night ... was it Ted?

She wanted to bury her head in a cushion and scream.

Charlie stopped her thoughts before they could pull on their Nikes and run any further.

'I think it may be going away, it seems to be a little quieter when the thunder comes now.'

Emmie listened, and thought he might be right, a knot loosened in her stomach. It appeared they might live to see another day, and as her fear eased, she had an idea.

'I know, I'll go and get us some pillows and blankets, we can have more hot chocolate and sleep on the sofa tonight. It'll be like a slumber party, like when we first got here.'

Grace wiped her tears, looked up into Emmie's eyes with an uneasy grin.

'I love sleeped overs,' She said, 'And I love chocolate.'

'Sleepovers,' Charlie corrected

Grace ignored him

'Can we mommy, can we?'

Emmie smiled and looked at the clock in the candlelight. 12.25am. Past midnight. They were heading toward morning now anyway. She felt the unease slip away a little more.

Venturing upstairs in the dark wasn't the ordeal Emmie thought it would be, although, trying not to set the bedding on fire as she came back down laden with pillows, quilt, and a candle, was a skill in itself.

She was relieved when she made it back to the living room where Charlie and Grace sat cuddling on the sofa, chatting quietly. She put a pillow behind each of their heads and one in the middle for herself then she placed the quilt over the chattering children and took a candle into the kitchen to make the hot chocolate.

She lit the gas with a match, glad that she had seen fit to get the gas tank filled, and five minutes later the last of the milk was in a pan on the stove. She watched it impatiently as the cold seeped around her, The storm was less ferocious now, still loud, but slowly retreating. The house had come good and Emmie was starting to feel secure again. She mumbled a thanks for sheltering them, watching the lightning flash over the lane through the window. Maybe they could play the 'counting how far away it was' game while they drank their hot chocolate.

The milk started to steam. She dipped a finger in; just warm. She poured Grace's into her cup and mixed it with the powder, before waiting for the rest of the milk to boil.

She glanced back outside as the sky lit up, forked fingers streaked towards the ground, and her eyes fell on an unfamiliar shadow by the gate. She squinted, puzzled, as the sky went dark again.

Another flash. It was still there, broad, tall, and with an odd shape at the top.

What is that?

She kept her eyes trained on the fence until the sky lit up again.

The shadow moved.

Emmie flinched, heart banging, eyes glued to the spot as the landscape plunged back into darkness. Her breath caught as her mind raced.

An animal? Too big, surely. And it's upright.

The next few flashes came and went with Emmie none the wiser but then she caught it moving again, revealing a more familiar shape.

With a gasp she staggered back from the window hitting the large table behind her.

Shit on a stick, that was most definitely a man. SHIT, SHIT, SHIT, there's a fucking man in a hat staring at my house in a storm! What the fuck is up with that?

The next flash lit up the sky, the figure stared toward the house, still again.

I'm wide awake, I'm not dreaming now. Who the fuck is outside my house?

Heart hammering in her chest she realised the pan was finally boiling and quickly shut off the gas. Trembling hands poured the milk into the two remaining mugs, the intense feeling of being watched raising the hairs at the back of her neck. She needed to get away from the window, and fast. Scooping up the cups she crossed to the living room at a near run and, after putting them on the small table next to the sofa, she immediately drew both sets of curtains across the windows and shut both of the doors leading into the room.

Charlie stared at her, watching her movements and Emmie tried to calm herself down.

'The storm is going away now, no need to scare Grace any more than she has been we'll just cuddle up and try to sleep after our drinks.'

She gave them a shaky smile and joined them on the sofa curling her legs under her and placing the quilt over them all. Within twenty minutes the drinks had gone, the storm had all but subsided leaving only the hiss of the rain, and the children were sound asleep. The house was warm, cosy, and quiet. Even so, it was daylight before Emmie's eyes finally closed.

Chapter 15

A tired, groggy, and rather shaken Emmie bustled the children out of the door the next morning. They trudged down the path looking like Michelin men in their big winter coats, hats, scarfs, gloves and wellies. It was cold and grey, and the drizzling rain made for a sombre mood amongst the small clan.

Grace was tired and grouchy and had put up a fight with everything, from putting on her trousers to eating her toast. Her gloves had come off and been thrown across the room in tantrum five times, her hat, sixteen. Emmie had lost her patience and yelled more than once, and Charlie had stood sullenly by the door watching the drama as he waited to go.

Not getting her way with anything else Grace had insisted that she take her favourite doll to the shops, which had appeased her until she had dropped it into a large puddle of mud by the gate. Emmie rolled her eyes as Grace immediately started crying again.

Fed up with arguing she stepped past Grace and bent to pick up the doll. She was shaking off the dirty water when she noticed the half washed footprint in the mud.

Big. Man-sized.

Her heart fluttered.

Means nothing, Bill visited, it could be his.

But she couldn't convince herself. With all the storm rain it would surely have been washed away. She quickly scanned the muddied grassed area that was her driveway. No sign of the land rover's tyre marks.

And if they've gone ...

She let her thought trail off as the reality sank in. This print could only have been made when the rain had started to subside which was when Emmie had been busy making hot chocolate as the storm abated. She looked back to the kitchen window and saw she was approximately where the man had been. Her heart fluttered again.

In the half light earlier she had felt brave enough to go into the kitchen and glance out of the window. Seeing nothing, she decided she had either dreamed the shadow man or her imagination was playing on her fear of the storm. She had chuckled at the notion that someone would be out here watching the house. Why would someone come all the way up the lane to stand at the gate in a storm?

Well, it looks like that's exactly what they did Em, better check the doors and windows are locked tonight, and shut the curtains while you're at it too, wouldn't want to give him the satisfaction of being able to see in.

'Mom, Whats wrong?'

Emmie looked up to see Charlie's concerned face and realised that Grace had also stopped crying and was watching her. How long had she been sat here? She stood quickly, holding the doll at her side.

'Nothing Charlie, nothing's wrong, 'she said light-heartedly.

She ushered the children into the car and strapped Grace in without a murmur. Not for the first time in the last couple of years, Emmie wondered why parenting always had to be a game of pretence and protection.

She bit at her lip, agitated, as she settled into the driver's seat, started the car and manoeuvred back down the lane, her mind whirling. Christ, she needed to talk to someone, not pretend this wasn't happening. Why couldn't mothers be scared too? She vowed to call Amy when she got home. Amy would put a positive spin on the situation whereas Natalie would worry and pack her back off to Surrey.

The drive into the small village of Bracken Hill was picturesque. The gently undulating terrain, grey stone cottages and well-tended gardens were pretty even in the winter gloom, and Emmie found her mood lifting as she drove.

She smiled as they passed an elderly couple with shopping bags, arm in arm, laughing as they bent forward against the rain. They most likely lived here, in the village. A fact that suddenly seemed appallingly sensible; why had she not chosen to live in the village?

Her heart flipped and she realised that she missed *people.* It was strange how a large house with so much land could seem so confining, especially in the clutches of winter. There had been other houses in more populated areas, and in better repair, that she had dismissed for Bruadair. The lost and forlorn house, decaying in a mess of tangled brambles, had seemed perfectly situated away from modern life, the children having acres of wilderness to enjoy in safety.

Perfectly safe.

She huffed at the irony as her thoughts drifted to the man in the storm. Why had she thought isolation was a good idea? What was so wrong with civilisation anyway?

She turned a corner and just in front of her, sat a central triangle of grass with a couple of benches, behind them rose a small grey church and cemetery with a low stone wall. Roads pulled away either side of the church. A handful of small, neat, stone cottages peeling away to the left, and a smaller number of dwellings to the right. Amongst these sat the village amenities. A butcher, a convenience store and post office, and The Grey Lion pub.

It looked nice here in the village, quaint, quiet, safe.

Heaving a sigh, Emmie pulled the car up against the low kerb outside the shop. Steeling against the biting rain, she climbed out of the car and leaned into the back to get Grace as Charlie joined her on the path. Together they hurried into the small shop, a bell tinkling their entry.

Pushing down her hood and shaking off the rain Emmie surveyed the store. The shop was small and cluttered but also warm and homely. It appeared to sell everything from postcards to milk, and pegs to magazines. The shelves were packed tight, but everything was neat and orderly, stacked with all labels facing the front, clearly on show. To the right was a small counter with a large grey till, electronic, but still what you would call old-fashioned these days.

Behind the counter stood an elderly lady with a wizened, but kind, face framed by short grey hair. Around her neck hung a pair of folded half-moon glasses that bumped gently against her cardigan as she raised her head from something she was reading and smiled. Emmie smiled back raising her hand in greeting as she collected a basket and walked around the shop guiding her little helpers in the direction of anything she thought she would need for the coming week to keep them out of mischief.

Food and sundries gathered, and high-fives dealt out for a giggling Grace and very embarrassed Charlie, they approached the lady to pay. An elderly gentleman also shuffled up to the counter with a bottle of milk and doing the right thing Emmie waved him ahead with a smile. He tipped his head at her and grunted. Emmie crossed her eyes and wrinkled her nose at the back of his head getting another giggle from Grace and at least a grin from Charlie.

And dad used to say the Scottish were so friendly. All I've met so far are grumps and weirdos.

Emmie waited as he paid for his milk, and then immediately regretted her decision to let him in front as he and the lady discussed the weather, how Marnie was (whoever Marnie was), problems with his hip, and what they were having for tea. Emmie rolled her eyes inwardly but pretended not to be bothered. She picked up a small book entitled 'Bracken Falls' from the rack at the side of the counter and began nonchalantly flicking through it.

According to the book, somewhere in Bracken Hill, there was a walk along the river to a large waterfall. It was said to be two miles up a winding track, but the views were supposed to be picture perfect, and the falls magnificent; dropping from a dizzying height if you were adventurous enough to climb to the very top. Emmie frowned as she put the book back. She couldn't recall having seen the river after it had swung off to the right three miles before she entered the village, but it sounded fun. She decided to ask the lady where the walk started ... if she ever stopped discussing Marnie's delicious steak pie, that was.

A full seven minutes later Emmie was staring into space, gaze unfocused above the shop door, thinking about calling Amy. Grace had long since quit being patient so Emmie had given Charlie the car keys and told him to take her to the car and lock themselves in. She had hoped that she wouldn't be long, but here she was staring at the back of the same man's head, bottle of milk still on the counter. Her thoughts drifted to Grace, that coat was getting far too tight she needed to find somewhere to get her a new one, before the real cold of winter set in.

'... keep you waiting.'

huh?

Emmie snapped her head round with a jolt. The old man had gone, and the elderly lady was looking at her with an expectant smile.

'what?'

The lady chuckled and spoke with a soft, slow, voice, heavily accented.

'You were in a world of your own there, dearie, I was unsure whether you wanted to return to this one what with the rain and all. I said, hello, and very sorry to keep you waiting.'

Emmie smiled, irritation fading as she warmed to the lady immediately.

'Oh, its no problem, I have nowhere better to be in this weather anyway.'

'You English are too polite. He's a nightmare to be behind let's get that out of the way. Always wants to chat. He's lonely that's all and I don't have the heart to shoo him on. He lost his wife a few months ago. Been to hell and not come back yet, he's always around, either here or at the church. She was a good sort, cancer got her in the end, God rest her soul.'

'Oh ... ', Emmie didn't know what to say, she reddened as she thought of her impatience with him and irritation that he didn't smile.

'Anyway hen, let's see what you've got there.'

Emmie put the basket on the counter as the lady slowly rang the items through and put them into a bag.

'So, you're clearly not from around these parts, what brings you here, dear? Visiting our famous falls?'

Emmie smiled.

'I'd like to,' she replied, 'But no, I'm not visiting, I just moved here. I bought a house a few miles up the road so I'm afraid you'll be seeing a lot of me and the children, you're our local shop.'

'Oh, lovely news! Welcome, and a great part of the world you've come to. I know most of the property around this area, where is it you've bought? I'm Edith by the way. I've lived in Bracken Hill all my life, I've run this shop with my husband, Len, for thirty six years now. He usually stocks the shelves, you'll probably see him pottering around now and again. He's upstairs today watching the rugby, busy he calls it.' she smiled warmly.

Emmie laughed, 'I'm Emmie, It's nice to meet you Edith, and well then, perhaps you know a place called Bruadair? It was derelict for some time before I bought it. It's warm and watertight now, although it's still very much a work in progress.'

Edith seemed to falter, her adams apple bobbing before she spoke again.

'Bruadair, eh? The house of dreams. Aye, I know the place. It has a very colourful history.'

Emmie was intrigued, not only by Edith's reaction but by the name she had given the place.

'House of dreams?'

Edith collected herself and smiled as she started her story.

'Aye, the name. It's Gaelic for dream. The story goes that the house was built by John Watts, initially as a marital home for his wife, in 1876. It was a token of his love for her, all he owned he put into that house, but it took everything from him when his wee wife Imogen was struck with a mystery virus. She died mere days later. They had moved into the house only three months before and had grand plans for a large family and lots of social gatherings, and within those three months alone more plans had been drawn up to extend the house and plant formal gardens in front of the new orchard, but John was devastated by Imogen's death. He moved out immediately. It is documented that he went back to work shipbuilding the day after her funeral, but, unfortunately, he was found only a few days later swinging from one of the trees in the wood. The story goes he was so heartbroken that he couldn't live without her.'

Emmie swallowed.

'Oh, that's tragic, what a story.'

And that's three people I know have died at the house now, why do people keep telling me this stuff?

Edith smiled sadly and nodded. When she didn't offer any more Emmie continued. Might as well get it all out of the way while they were on the subject. It would be good to have a second version of poor Ted's demise.

'Sounds like I bought a house with a whopper of a history, I heard from the neighbour, Bill, about some poor man getting struck by lightning too.'

Edith looked up and put a hand to her chest.

'Oh, aye lass, Last night was pretty loud, but the storm of 1999 was a particularly bad one. Nasty business that was, Bill found him. It stayed with him for months. He was never really one to come down to the church until that incident. Poor Bill. Of course, that was a long time ago now, we don't see him half as much as we used to at the church, he frequents the pub far more these days.'

Emmie let out a breath and a trickle of relief ran through her. That was good to hear, if it had affected Bill that much when he'd found Ted then at least that meant that he probably wasn't going to murder them all in their beds. Maybe he was just a genuine neighbour after all.

Then a pang of fear ran through her as she remembered the muddy footprint.

Genuine or not, what sane person watched a house in the dead of night?

Maybe she was jumping to conclusions but she couldn't see who the hell else it would be, they'd have one hell of a long trek just to stand at her gate in the rain and she had seen no evidence of a vehicle last night or this morning.

'Are you okay, dear?'

Emmie snapped out of her daze and looked up at Edith trying, and failing, to smile nonchalantly.

'Yes, I'm fine, just lost in thought there for a moment.'

Edith frowned and placed her hand on Emmie's arm.

'You looked worried, what's the matter?'

Emmie looked at Edith's hand. She was a lovely lady, warm and kind, and Emmie really, really wanted to talk about what had happened and how frightened she felt. The children were safe in the car, and no one else had entered the shop since she had been there, it was a perfect time to get it all off her chest. Except ... she didn't know Edith at all, what if she thought she was a lunatic? Heck, she had no choice but to shop here so their paths would undoubtedly cross many times in the future, it wasn't like she could avoid the store.

Emmie opened her mouth and then faltered torn between her head and heart, both of which were screaming their own advice. As she grasped frantically for a decision Edith threw her completely off kilter.

'Is it the house, dear?'

'The house?' Emmie looked up shocked, 'Why would it be the house?'

Emmie hoped Edith couldn't see her heart pounding against her ribs under her coat. She was sure it was going to jump right out and land on the counter at any second. Edith put her hands up, reddening a little as she backtracked.

'Oh, no reason, just folklore I suppose. I'm so sorry, don't worry about it.'

Emmie was intrigued and horrified at the same time. *Was* something wrong with the house? Maybe Edith knew more than she was letting on and Emmie didn't have to mention her visitor from last night.

'No, please, tell me,' She said, 'I mean, no, I have no problems with the house but I would love to hear the tales, I love folklore and legends and I know this is a country full of them. I just didn't think my house would be caught up in its own story.'

Edith took off her glasses now that all of the shopping was rang up and packed neatly in three bags. Slowly she cleaned them with the bottom of her jumper before folding them up and looking back at the till avoiding Emmie's gaze.

'Oh it's just local legend dear, nothing to bother yourself about, that'll be fifty-six pounds and ninety pence please.'

Emmie paid Edith and as she waited for her receipt tried to coax the old lady again.

'Please, I would love to know. You've really intrigued me. I take legends with a pinch of salt, I promise.'

She gave Edith her biggest smile and Edith sighed, shoulders sagging downward.

'Well, if you insist. It's local legend that Bruadair is haunted. That's the reason it's been boarded up derelict for so long.'

Emmie blinked. That was it? Weren't all old boarded up houses supposed to be haunted? As Scottish legends usually went this one was pretty lame. She nodded at Edith to continue anyway.

'It is said that John Watts is still there, waiting to live out his life with Imogen. They so desperately wanted a house full of children but they didn't get time or chance, poor things. Apparently, he roams now trying to find children that he can claim as his own to complete his family. It is said that no family has been able to live in the house for more than a few months since the tragedy.'

Emmie raised her eyebrows trying to look unperturbed, but her stomach flipped as she remembered the dream and the pressing blackness outside the french doors.

'That's the legend,' Edith said shrugging and pursing her lips.

The shop doorbell tinkled loudly making them both jump as the shop door blew open, banging back against the shelves, rain splashing inside. Both Emmie and Edith stood paralysed, heads turned toward the door. A small child's windmill caught the wind and spun frantically, colours blurring as a handful of postcards from the stand blew up into the air and landed skidding and tumbling across the floor in the wet. Emmie held her breath. Then a boot appeared, followed quickly by another as a lady in a brown woollen coat bustled in through the door shaking her umbrella.

'Looks like another storms a-brewing, Edie. Wind nearly took the hat right off my head just now.'

She shut the shop door and turned to pick up the postcards.

Emmie turned to Edith and smiled shakily, blowing out a breath trying to act like she hadn't just been scared out of her wits. She noticed that Edith also looked shaken as she smiled back.

'Don't believe in legends eh?' Edith whispered

Emmie grinned and shook her head, not daring to speak. She collected her bags, receipt in hand, and said goodbye to Edith, before nodding at the lady who had finished re-arranging the postcards and was now brushing her hair down with her hands.

In the car a few minutes later Emmie folded the receipt over to place it in the pocket of her coat and noticed something written in red pen on the back. She unfolded it again and read the note.

If I can be of any help please call me. Edith.

A telephone number was written underneath. Emmie smiled, she obviously hadn't fooled Edith with her nonchalance after all. She pocketed the receipt.

Bless you, Edith, I think I'll keep hold of it … just in case.

Pulling away from the kerb she drove slowly down the road, trying to find somewhere wide enough to execute a three-point turn. Just after the pub, which she saw was also a guest house, was a gravel car park with a few scattered cars. She turned in and was confronted with a beautiful view of Bracken river, flanked by large bare trees.

Ah, so that's where you're hiding.

She drove the car right up to a low fence, facing the swollen water, and killed the engine, leaving the windscreen wipers running.

Charlie looked at her eyebrows raised.

'Just looking at the river,' She said to him, 'there's a huge waterfall a couple of miles from here, it's worth a look apparently.'

'Not in this weather it's not.' Charlie still looked incredulous.

Grace suddenly piped up from the back seat.

'It's wet and cold mommy don't make us see the water.'

Emmie chuckled. She definitely had fair weather kids.

'No I didn't mean now, sweetie, we'll come back another time. I was just looking that's all.'

She peered out of the windscreen and just off to the right noticed a sign by a small series of wooden steps leading down to the water's edge.

Bracken Falls – 2 miles

Well, now I know where to come when the weather picks up.

She turned the engine over again and backed away, turning the car a full 180 degrees.

As she shifted the car into first gear movement caught her eye and she paused as she noticed a face in one of the upstairs windows of the pub.

She thought about a cheeky wave, but then the person sank back into the shadows which seemed strange. Come to think of it something about the bearded face seemed familiar but she couldn't place where from. A wave of unease wound through her.

No! No more of this crap. Not today.

Not daring to look again, she floored the accelerator spitting gravel behind the car in her hurry to get out of the car park.

Chapter 16

The next few days passed without major incident and Emmie forgot about the face in the window. Grace's funny man decided to stick around, although he hadn't made her do anything on the scale of the cereal or the cubby hole again. Little things had moved or gone missing as Emmie had known they would, but on a positive note, he had helped her to find the door keys yesterday after they had disappeared from the lock and found their way into Grace's sock drawer.

Power was restored to the house the day after the storm and everything returned to normal, although the dreams continued for Emmie, dark dreams full of shadow men who tried to steal the children, and broken things that needed fixing. She decided to take them as a sign that she ought to get her life, and indeed, her house together.

So, the following Friday morning, with Charlie at school and Grace playing dolls in her bedroom, Emmie decided it was time to investigate the attic. The box room was proving too small to be a long-term studio, she was already tripping over canvases and losing tubes of paint and she hadn't painted a single brush stroke yet. The confined space didn't lend itself to work; everything had to be put 'just so' for the room to come anywhere near to tidy. It was getting annoying.

Grabbing the stepladders from the utility Emmie took them upstairs and set them up under the large square in the ceiling. Then she climbed until she was nose to nose with the hatch.

Here goes nothing.

She took a breath and lifted, sliding it to the right. Climbing another step she popped her head inside, a small gasp escaping her lips. The space before her was lit by the four large roof windows two to the front and two to the back. Dust motes swirled lazily in the sunshine that filtered through the back windows. There was a warmth up here despite the time of year and it drew her up through the hatch until she found herself standing on the boarded floor, gazing through the back window toward the orchard.

The bare branches of the fruit trees below weaved a tangled carpet reaching all the way to the foot of Bracken Hill which reared up proud in the sunlight, a patchwork of orange and brown flanking green where last summer's bracken met the gorse and grass. The small stream ran into the trees and could be seen glinting through the thick branches as it followed its path along the foot of the hill. It was breathtaking, and the light was fantastic.

This is perfect, just what I need.

She scanned the area noting the dust and grime. It would need a clean but it had been deemed safe and pest free after having some of the boarded floor replaced when the moving crew were up here.

Well, Grace is quiet, no time like the present, let's get this studio up and running.

Energised, she spent the morning cleaning and sorting while Grace chattered to her dolls below. Left alone, within a couple of hours she had made the new studio into a usable space complete with battery powered heater and radio. She assigned a place for her easel alongside a small storage unit and smaller desk, both of which she had impatiently dragged up through the large hole by herself, nearly losing an arm in the process.

Grace had watched the frantic activity from her bedroom doorway, eyes wide, doll clutched in her arms. When the show was finally over, she had retreated to her room unimpressed falling easily back into the world of dolls as if nothing had happened.

Emmie surveyed her work with satisfaction, hands on hips, sweat running down her face in streaks, breathing heavily.

The last commission deadlines were closing in and the trickle of orders she'd attained while moving and settling in wouldn't be enough to keep food on the table. But now, with a proper place to work she could get back into the task of making money, and providing for her family. She grinned.

She was really doing this. Living. Raising kids. Making a home. By herself.

Can't survive without you, eh Scott? Wouldn't cope. Can't handle a house, don't understand the world, can't wipe my own backside. For a while there I wobbled, I must admit, but that's what happens when someone takes over, takes your confidence in yourself away. I'm good now though. See what I've done here, all by myself? Hah. You were wrong, I don't need you, I don't need anyone! Me and the kids, we're going to be just fine.

Fresh and motivated by her new space, she forced Scott out of her mind as she sat at her desk under the sunny rear windows. She opened the laptop and began to get her business back on track.

A little after 1pm Emmie looked up from her screen disturbed by the silence. All was quiet below the hatch which was unusual as Grace was an avid talker, especially to her dolls. Emmie felt guilt creep over her.

I didn't even notice she'd gone downstairs, hows that for a great bit of parenting?

Not overly worried she shut down the laptop, swung her chair and took in the view. The sun was blazing under a blue sky contouring the majestic hill into a patchwork of light and dark pockets. She sighed wondering how she could ever have thought this house was a mistake.

Okay, so there was the very real threat of whoever was watching them, but here in the sunlight, even that didn't seem so bad. Anyway, she was sure he'd get bored if she diligently locked up and drew the curtains. No point in staring at a house if the occupants don't know or care that you're standing there.

Better see what Grace is up to Ems. Hopefully not pouring cereal and milk over the floor in an attempt to get herself lunch.

As she stretched, her arms reaching for the roof, Grace's chipper little voice came from below. Emmie smiled to herself, but relief was short lived as she focused on the stream of chatter.

This wasn't her usual 'doll talk' this was a conversation. She strained to listen, craning her neck toward the open hatch, not wanting to break the moment.

'Don't know,' Grace was saying, 'I be in trouble.' She paused as though listening to someone before continuing. 'Don't want to, let's play dollies ... no ... no ... don't want to ... I like dollies ... this is Emily, she's my best one ...'

Emmie's heart fluttered a little behind her ribs.

Is this the invisible man again or is there someone in the house?

She scooted the chair back across the floor with a high pitched screech and fled to the hatch in three strides.

'Grace!'

She was down the ladder and at Grace's door in seconds.

In the room all was normal. Grace, oblivious to the commotion, was in play mode again, clutching a doll in each hand as she animatedly spoke for them, brown curls bobbing with the movements of her voice as first one doll spoke and then the other.

Emmie leaned on the door frame letting her breathing and heart rate return to normal as she watched Grace play.

Then the chatter stopped and Grace, unaware of her presence, suddenly looked up at her bed a few feet away to the left. She seemed to consider it for a beat before speaking.

'Mommy said that's bad.'

Her head bobbed slowly up and down, nodding at the bed.

'She'd be angry.'

Suddenly Grace giggled and looked at her lap shyly before looking back at the bed smiling.

'You're funny.'

Emmie frowned her pulse quickening again. So here he was in person. Grace's mystery invisible man who liked to get her into trouble. Maybe this would be a good time to confront him.

'Gracie?'

Grace swung her head to the doorway, eyes innocently wide, 'yes mommy?

'Who are you talking to, sweetheart?'

'The man.'

Emmie feigned puzzlement and scanned the room for effect.

'I can't see a man, Grace. Is he hiding?'

Grace giggled and glanced at the bed.

'Over there,' she said pointing.

'On the bed?'

'Uh-huh.' Grace looked down at Emily in her lap, bit her lip and started to twiddle her hair.

'But I can't see him, Grace.'

Grace swung her head to the bed frowning and then she broke into a broad smile.

'He says he's not for mommies.'

'Not for mommies? that's a shame as I was hoping I'd get to meet your friend one day.'

Grace shook her head.

Emmie pretended to be sad and paused before asking the question she really wanted the answer to.

'What did the man say to you, Grace?'

Grace looked up big brown eyes already looking guilty.

'Don't know.'

'You must know, Grace, you answered him. I was watching you.'

Emmie smiled to reassure Grace, who's eyes grew wide and starting to brim with tears as she quickly glanced at the bed and back to Emmie.

'It's naughty.'

Emmie moved into the room and sat next to Grace on the floor. Grace hopped onto Emmie's knee and hugged her, little fingers digging into her shirt. She wrapped her arms around Grace and softly kissed her forehead.

'You won't get into trouble sweetie, I promise, I just need to know what the man is telling you.'

A coldness was making it's way around the room, making Emmie shudder and hold onto Grace more tightly.

Christ, how can a new boiler be so inefficient?

'Grace?' Emmie urged gently.

Grace studied her mothers face before finally deciding to give up her secret.

'He told me to get the photographs and hide them in lots of places.'

Emmie felt herself reel back. Why on earth would Grace mention the photographs? She had an uncanny feeling that a particular little girl had run off with them after all but she would need to be careful with her questioning or risk Grace clamming up.

'The Photos? Well, as mommy has left them back at Auntie Natalie's, I think you'd have had trouble finding them for the naughty man anyway. And you were right to tell him no, sweetie, we know how important they are to us, don't we?'

Emmie tucked one of Grace's curls behind an ear.

'Uh huh.'

'Grace, I need you to answer a really important question, do you think you can do that?

Grace looked at Emmie with wide eyes and nodded, eager to please.

'Do you think the photos are still at Auntie Nat's?'

Grace chewed her lip, flicked her eyes to the bed and slowly shook her head.

Emmie relaxed a little now she knew what was going on.

'Where do you think they are, do you know?'

Grace immediately got defensive.

'I not had them.' She said, 'it's naughty.'

Emmie took a breath. She would have to back up a little and try a different tactic.

'Ok sweetie, so could you ask the man where they are? Does he know?'

Again Grace's eyes flicked to the bed and she nodded. Just a couple of steps to go and the photos would be safe. Carefully, carefully.

'Could you tell me where they are?'

Grace shook her head quickly.

'He's your friend,' Emmie continued, 'he won't mind, tell me where to find them and I can put them somewhere safe. No one is in trouble.'

Grace's shoulders dropped. She looked straight into Emmie's eyes.

'They're in the roof.'

'The roof? You mean the attic? Grace, no one has been up there until today, why would they be in the attic?'

Grace shrugged and looked at her hands in her lap.

'I don't know,' she mumbled, 'that's what he said.'

Emmie nodded brushing Grace's hair back from her face. She had to go and look. The place had been scrubbed from top to bottom this morning and hadn't come across the box. She knew full well that it couldn't be up there. No one would have taken it up there when fixing up the floor and certainly no one had been up there since. Emmie picked Grace off her lap and sat her back down by the dolls house.

'I'll just be a minute,' She said.

Grace watched her leave the room.

Had she got up to the attic alone? She couldn't have. Of course, Charlie could, but the ladders had been downstairs and she wasn't sure he could have carried them up.

In any case, nothing had been disturbed in the attic until today, it had been obvious. Which surely meant that the box of photographs couldn't be up there.

Emmie was aware of her thoughts getting frantic as she climbed the ladder and emerged through the hatch with trepidation.

She quickly skirted around and, finding nothing, she stood, hands on hips, breathing hard.

'The man says it's on the left, in the eaves. Look up'

Emmie froze, she didn't know what was worse. The fact that Grace could apparently pinpoint exactly where it was, or that she had seemed to repeat a sentence from a much older person. Eaves? There was no way Grace could know what the eaves were, that they were 'up', or indeed, which direction left was in relation to Emmie. She tried to sound normal against the seven shades of shaky she now felt.

'Okay sweetie, thank you.'

She made her way left and walked as far as she could meeting the outside wall, then she turned and looked up. At first, she could see nothing, the light from the windows brightening the centre of the space, the edges cloaked in darkness. Dust motes chased and swirled in shafts of light, angry at the disturbance. As her eyes adjusted, Emmie scanned the Eaves and a dark shape caught her eye just above one of the crossbeams above her. She reached an arm up knocking a hollow sounding object with her hand. It shifted, nearly fell, but Emmie cupped her hand around it. Holding it awkwardly she slid it toward her until she could get a better grip, grasping the small box and pulling it the rest of the way from the crook of the eaves.

She already knew what it was but took her time before she

confirmed the fact and descended into the many questions it would unearth. In her hands was the little white shoe box with the familiar black marker writing on the side.

Printed Photos.

As she peeled back the sellotape, opening the lid, her hands shook. The photographs seemed to be as she had left them when she packed them up. The box looked clean, no dust had settled on top, so it hadn't been there long.

Who in the heck put it there?

'mommy?' Grace's voice floated from below the hatch.

Emmie opened one of the desk drawers and placed the box inside before going down to Grace.

'Did you find it?'

'I did, thank you. I put it somewhere safe,' Emmie said, and then frowned. The temperature on the landing had dropped so cold she could see Grace's breath as she spoke. It bothered Emmie. The day should be at its warmest but the house seemed to be getting colder as the day went on, even with the winter sun blazing.

Damn Boiler.

But it was a half-hearted thought. Anxiety fluttered in her stomach, something didn't feel right, and after the episode with the man, finding the box, and Grace's use of words she was feeling more than a little shaken. She needed to get out of the uneasy atmosphere in the house.

'How about we go get some lunch and then explore the orchard before we pick up Charlie?'

Grace whooped with joy before listing every item in the fridge that she absolutely needed for lunch, Emily fell from her hands as ran for the stairs.

'Careful Grace'. Emmie warned as she picked up the doll and took it back to the dolls house in Grace's room. The room felt like an icebox. Shivering, she took a final look around, eyes pausing on the bed.

'Guess she got one up on you today, Mr Whoever.'

Emmie smiled triumphantly at the empty bedspread and then caught herself.

Now I'm talking to the invisible man, this is crazy.

She left the icy room and followed Grace downstairs, unaware of the duvet sliding off the bed with a soft swish.

Chapter 17

In the Grey Lion Pub and Guest House Martin Stomes was getting restless. Almost a week had passed with no further sign of her. He was starting to think he had imagined the whole car park scene.

He had spent the week walking the village until he knew every nook and cranny, every alley and where it led. He had explored the church and grounds, had read every gravestone. He had walked to the waterfall six times in an effort to keep intense boredom at bay, but even that was becoming annoying now. It was just a shitty little village, and yet, she still managed to avoid him. How could she hide in a place so small?

He rubbed at his thick blonde beard with a forefinger and thumb and went to the table where he picked up his mobile phone and dialled.

Scott answered after just two rings, voiced strained and clipped.

'What news?'

Martin raised his eyebrows unimpressed.

'Well, hi buddy. Yes, I'm well thank you, enjoying my little holiday up here in sunny Scot ...'

'Cut the crap Martin, I've had to duck out of a meeting to answer your call which, incidentally, had better be to tell me you've found her.'

Martin heaved a sigh.

'Nope, there's not been a sighting of her since last week. I was calling to say I'm pretty sure she's not in the village at all.'

'You said you saw her, did you or not?'

'I did, definitely. but she hasn't been back since. I've walked the village day in, day out, it's a small place, Scott. Even the mice are starting to look at me strange.'

Scott huffed down the phone.

'Walk it some more. Find her. You said she probably went to the store so go ask in the store. Small places are large gossip centres, someone knows where she is, leading questions mind, no direct inferences. Meanwhile I've collected a list of all the schools and nurseries within a ten mile radius. Checking up on those should cure the boredom. Get a pen, and make it quick.'

Martin frowned, his eyebrows meeting over the bridge of his nose, one side of his mouth curling up in disbelief.

'Ten miles? Dude, you seriously think she drove ten miles just to go to the store? Five probably would have cut it.'

'you're not in Surrey any more Martin.' Scott hissed, his voice low, 'This is rural Scotland we're talking about, I had to pan six miles out of the village to find more than one school. You're totaling two schools, and four nurseries. Think you can manage that? Now get the god-damned pen I don't have time for messing around.'

'Right. Hang on.'

Scott sounded pissed, but Martin was pretty pissed himself. If Scott didn't like the way things were moving he should come up here and endure the boredom his-fucking-self. He held up the phone in front of his face and mouthed *asshole* before throwing it onto the bed. He quickly searched the room for the customary hotel paper and pen, located below the TV, and picked up a copy of the Holy Bible to lean on.

Sorry, Lord, needs must.

Then he went back to the bed and retrieved the phone, turning it onto speaker.

'Go on,' he grunted to Scott.

Scott gave him the school names, addresses and telephone numbers along with the head teacher's details. Followed by the nursery information and relevant managers names.

'Did you get all that? Read it back to me.'

Scott's voice was clipped and sharp, and Martin rolled his eyes. He was getting tired of the 'dumb twat' insinuations.

'You know, there's this modern thing now, I think it's called email. You could have sent it yourself with the click of a button, and hey presto! I would have had all the right information within seconds. It's a marvel, really.'

'Don't get smart Martin, it doesn't suit you. I am with clients all day the email wouldn't have got to you until later tonight. As it happens you called, you're bored, and now you have something to do. Get checking. The kids may be going by her maiden name so check under Landers and Harvington. Charlie Edward and Grace Amelia. And get down to the store and see what you can find out about where she is living.'

Martin heaved a sigh. At least today was looking to be a little more productive, something he could get his teeth into.

'Got it, dude.' he said, his irritation easing.

'Good. Oh, and Martin? Next time you call me a fucking asshole I'll rip yours right up to the back of your head. Got it, *dude*.'

Martin felt a hot flush rise up his neck as he heard a click and the receiver tone in his ear. He ran a hand through his shoulder length hair, pushing it back from his face and threw the phone on the bed.

Shit, it never did to piss Scott off. Now there would be hell until he got some results.

Idiot.

He grabbed his coat and headed to the store.

Chapter 18

Edith Walters was finishing her daily wander through the four aisles of Bracken Falls General Store tidying the shelves, just as she did every day before lunch. It was just after 12.30pm, a quiet time of the day here, even in summer when the sun was out and the tourists were around walking the falls.

She had already made an inventory of any items running low. Usually, she would give the list to Len so that he could restock, but today she went through to the storeroom herself collecting the items she needed in a trolley and wheeling it back into the shop.

She was busy reorganising one of the front shelves when the bell jingled. With mild surprise she looked up, dipping her nose a little to look over the top of her half-moon glasses, as the young man who was staying in the guest house entered the shop.

He had been in a few times before, usually only for chocolate, snacks, and cigarettes. A quiet fellow who didn't say a lot, she was surprised when he caught her eye and bid her good day. Edith smiled and said hello before finishing off the shelf and moving back to the counter to wait for her customer.

She watched as the tall, thin man walked silently through the aisles. He looked better kempt today than he had a couple of days ago, his hair was swept back off his face, and it looked like he had run a comb through his bushy beard. Edith wondered what his story was. Surely he must be on his way soon. Who has a need to stay in the guest house for more than a week in the middle of winter?

Tongues were already wagging of course and everyone had their theory. Not prone to add to the grapevine Edith only listened and aah-ed when necessary. She had her own theory, which she kept to herself. He was a man who came to be alone, from whatever was troubling him in his life. And that was none of anyone's business.

Still, she wouldn't mind finding out a little about his situation.

Mary Allen had said only yesterday that he had walked slowly past her house a total of eleven times during the last week, and been down the alley at the side more than once. She also said Brenda Hodges had seen him going into the church numerous times and her husband Alan had seen him three times in as many days up at the falls.

Thinking of Alan turned her thoughts to Len. Alan always made time for a daily walk up to the falls to keep the old bones lubricated and clear the cobwebs. Len used to go with him, but over the last few months, it had whittled to every few days, then once a week and finally he had stopped going altogether as he had had more and more trouble catching his breath. He was now out of puff just going up and down the stairs from the shop to their living quarters.

Edith, worried about the rate he had declined, had told him to make an appointment with Dr Gill, but Len had waved her off saying it was just old lungs in an old man. She knew it was because he was terrified. Not of the Doctor finding something wrong, but wrong enough that he would have to deal with it instead of holing up in his comfy chair watching sports and dramas all day in denial.

'... And twenty Benson too please,' the voice cut off her thoughts.

Edith looked up and plastered on her brightest smile as the man placed his items on the counter. Turning around she took the cigarettes from the shelf behind her and entered the price on the till before ringing the other items through one by one. She was about to start the small talk she often made with the tourists that passed through when the man surprised her, speaking first.

'Nice day out, the sun takes the edge off the bitter cold.'

Edith Smiled, looking up into his steel grey eyes, it seemed she may get a conversation out of this mysterious man yet. A tourist, she thought, his accent has a Southern twang.

'Aye, it is. Unfortunately, the worst of the winter is probably still to come, but today it certainly feels like everything is waking up and Spring is just around the corner.'

'It will be a shame to leave before spring, I imagine the falls change with each season.'

'They certainly do. You've been going up there a fair amount I hear, are you enjoying your break? Or is there another reason you're around these parts?'

The man seemed to stumble and colour a little, eyes flicking to the door. Edith feared she had gone too far but couldn't decide whether it was mention of the falls or the question of why he was here that had stumped him.

'Uh ... I'm here on a small assignment with my job as a, er, wildlife photographer.'

'Oh, how lovely,' Edith said, 'You should have said before. There's plenty of wildlife up by the falls alright, but I wouldn't be going up the main tourist track as you have. There's another lesser known path that veers off to the right before the bridge and carries on through the wooded area. A couple of miles up it opens out onto a field with a view right down to the falls from higher up. There would probably be more wildlife as it's so little used.'

'I see, thank you. Where would I find this path?'

'I've not been up myself but I've heard you go up the main path for about 200 yards until you come to a large oak tree, a-ways before the bridge, you can't miss it, it's the only oak amongst the birch and ash this low down for reasons only nature knows. Go around to the back of the tree and you'll pick up a deer track through the bracken which you keep following until you come out of the woods and into the open. If you're feeling adventurous, keep going North for three miles or so and you'll come to the foot of Bracken Hill. The world would be your oyster up there, we're the nearest village to the south West side so you'd be unlucky to see another person. Very pretty in all seasons, or so I'm told. These old legs won't be getting me up any hills now, the mind is willing but I'm afraid the body is not what it used to be.'

Edith shrugged as the man smiled, or was it a smirk? Catching his impatience she rang more of the items through the till. Edith thought that she had gotten as much out of him as she would for today when he suddenly changed the subject.

'Actually, I wonder if you could help me out. I'm only staying until the end of the week and I had hoped to locate my sister while I was here. We haven't seen each other for a few years. Unfortunately, I'm turning out to be a miserable detective, but I'm sure she said she was living in the village last time we spoke.'

Edith looked up surprised and warmed. Her own brother had ducked off to Australia thirty years before without so much as a goodbye. The only way she knew he was still alive now, at 84 years old, was that she received birthday and Christmas cards for herself and Len each year. She presumed when they stopped .... well, he'd stopped too. Here on Earth anyway.

'Well, I would love to help you out, dear. What's the lass's name?'

Edith rang through the last of the items and took off her half-moon glasses looking at the man with a smile.

'Emelia Harvington, or she could be going by her maiden name of Landers these days. She got divorced a couple of years ago.'

Edith thought hard but came up blank.

'Well I'm sorry dear, I'd bet I know everyone who lives in this village and what number is above their door, and I have a good head for names. Tourists come and go of course but, even so, I haven't heard of anyone with either name around here. Emelia Landers ... Harvington

...'

Edith shook her head slowly as she thought, lips pursed, and the man continued to look at her expectantly. Eyes boring into her. Finally, she let out a breath and met his eyes with hers.

'No, dear, I'm sorry.'

—— \\\ ——

Martin was getting frustrated with the elderly lady in the shop. A good head for names indeed. But that head had to be almost 100 years old. Still, she said she didn't know the name.

Drat.

Did that mean Emmie was using a new name? Was she aware that Scott was looking for her?

Well, he had seen her here either way, although he was getting less confident of the fact as time went on. If he had been wrong, he would be in deep do-do with Mr big shot Scotty Harvington.

He frowned at the lady who was now telling him she was sorry and Martin wanted to reach across the desk and show her just how sorry she should be, but he needed to keep his temper, losing it would get him nowhere, he needed answers.

'She *has* been here, I saw her,' Martin said taking care not to clip his words although his mouth felt tight from the clenching of his jaw. Old Ma Hubbard looked surprised.

'Oh, I see, are you certain? I'm sure I don't remember the name, maybe you could describe her? If she isn't local I probably didn't get it when she was here.'

Martin smiled, although with his jaw clenched tight at the insinuation it could have looked like a grimace.

'Well, I think I'm certain what my sister looks like,' Martin exuded sarcasm. He couldn't help it and couldn't stop it. Ma Hubbard didn't seem to notice.

'Aye, I suppose so dear. But then you did say it has been a few years did you not? It's possible she could have changed her appearance.'

'Yes, but she hasn't. It was definitely her I saw. She is ... or was ... somewhere around here, at least last Sunday.'

Martin heaved a controlled sigh, closed his eyes and rubbed at his temples a few times before dropping his hands. Hands he wanted to put around Ma Hubbard's neck.

'Ok, dear, so what does she look like?' She said, 'I have to tell you though, there aren't many people who aren't from the village that use the store unless they're tourists.'

As Martin described Emmie's appearance, he thought he saw a flicker of recognition pass through her eyes, but she shook her head.

'Doesn't ring any bells, dear.'

Martin stared. She was lying. He clenched his jaw hard. He looked right into her aged eyes and tried to draw it out of her telepathically until she dropped her gaze and told him the balance to pay.

She knows. Guilty as charged.

He stared at her while he felt in his pocket and stared as he handed over the £20 note. He stared as he took his change and picked up his bag. Then he looked away and left the store with a smile to himself. He thought he had scared her a little. Good, maybe next time she'd get some manners, maybe next time she would help someone out. He let the door slam behind him. He didn't say goodbye.

As the man stalked out of the shop Edith's heart almost pound right out of her chest. She would have bet her store and everything in it that it couldn't tick that hard any more without ticking its last beat, but here she was; still pounding, still standing.

For a moment she had been sure the man was about to leap over the counter and pummel her to the ground. Never had she felt a stare so intense, so full of hatred and harmful intent. She was glad she had held her own.

Oh, she had known who he was after of course. She remembered as soon as he had described the lady with the children who had just moved to Bruadair. She had also had the strange hunch that she shouldn't tell this man anything. Behind that Cheshire cat smile and floppy rock star hair, she had sensed something. She couldn't quite put her finger on what it was until that stare, but now she was glad he didn't know where the lady was. She was very glad indeed.

As she stared at the shop door Edith realised another thing. No one had seen him taking any pictures, or they certainly hadn't mentioned it.

This man wasn't who he said he was and he wasn't good news for poor Emelia what's her name, she could feel it in her bones.

Chapter 19

Martin flopped back on his bed in the guest house having achieved nothing other than smacking his head up that metaphorical brick wall. The lady in the store had infuriated him, she knew something for sure.

He had called all of the schools and nurseries that Scott had given him and even found a couple further out to call himself. All had the same response to his enquiry about the children. 'We can't give you that information sir.' He had told them he was their uncle, that their mom had had an accident, that he needed to get a message to them, that he was a police officer (crashed on that one when he couldn't tell them his number or the station he was calling from).

They asked him an untold number of questions each time, but everything came down to Data Protection and Safeguarding. He could have said he was Jesus-Fucking-Christ himself and he wouldn't have got any further.

He looked at his phone in frustration. It was impossible, he wasn't a Private Investigator he was a fucking computer technician, and an unemployed one at that. He had no idea how to do this spying business.

Just because Emmie had been here didn't mean she was coming back, he only knew that she was living in a small village not far from Aberfeldy, and he had only gleaned that information by conveniently being in the right place to overhear at Emmie's party. It had been a starting point of which he had proudly informed Scott - and boy, had Scott been impressed - he'd been trying to find where she was going for weeks.

He sighed, lying back, hands behind his head. It had been an ego shot. Scott had looked at him with admiration for a change and Martin had thought they could become firm pals again. He should have known better, there was only room in Scott's head for Scott.

Martin closed his eyes trying to think of his next move before calling Mr Ego with no news and enticing his wrath again. What a fucking joy that would be. How did it all go so fucking wrong?

At University, Martin and Scott had been firm friends. They only drifted apart after Scott passed the bar exam and made his way into one of the top law firms in South London. Dumb old Martin the Martian failed his law degree. It was his fault; too much partying and not enough studying, and that was okay because he had found out that Law was a shitty subject anyway, too many boring case studies and lawyers with poles up their arses.

Granted, Scott had also partied hard, but the law degree seemed to have been handed to him on a plate with distinctions and merits to boot.

When the time had arrived to go out into the big wide world, Scott had already met Emmie who was studying Art. Same university, different end of campus. He had made them a great life together, swanning around in top-of-the-range cars, and going on expensive holidays, while Emmie was allowed to stay at home and fiddle with her art. It was pathetic to watch, and in the end, there had been too many differences. Scott had changed, while Martin had stayed the same fun-loving guy he had always been.

Scott's loss.

But last August things changed. Martin was sat at the Frog and Toad on Queen Street, his regular haunt. The cheap beer tasted like camel's piss, but it was all he could afford on his dole money, and spending all day indoors gaming was driving him insane.

He had been in his favourite spot at the bar, back to the doorway, a clear signal to everyone who came in that: no, he did not want to chat. Even the barman had given up making small talk. They held a companionable silence even when Martin was the only person in the pub. Any talking was initiated only by Martin, and that was how he liked it. So, to say he was surprised when someone walked in one Wednesday evening, ordered a beer, and sat beside him, was an understatement. He was about to tell that someone to piss off, then he realised that it was Scott.

Scott didn't look like he had a few years ago, walking back from Swallow Heath Park with Emmie and a couple of kids. Then he had been the picture of health and domestic bliss. Martin had nearly lost his lunch on the pavement as he passed them on the opposite side of the road. They hadn't seen him, he was sure of that, they had been too wrapped up in each other and the brats.

On that Wednesday in August, however, he looked different. Hollow.

They drank, side by side, saying very little that first night, but as their impromptu drinking sessions became more frequent, Scotts barriers came down and Martin learned what had made him a shadow of his former self.

He had lost everything, Emmie and brats were gone, the life he'd had when Martin saw them strolling down the street like loves young dream was gone. Martin had listened with glee. Served him right.

Eventually, Scott had mentioned Emmie's proposed move to Scotland. According to Scott, she was doing it to get a rise from him, but she wouldn't have the balls to go through with it anyway. Of course, he wanted to keep tabs on her plans, just in case. Martin listened with apathetic indifference, he couldn't have given a toss. He owed Scott nothing, and he intended it to stay that way. But Scott was persuasive, and as he involved him in little bits of snooping Martin couldn't help but get interested. It was a hell of a lot better than staying at home gaming, or drinking alone. And Scott was good at subbing him money and beer for his efforts which was kind of addictive.

It was easy shit too, where she was, what she was up to, and who she was speaking to. Mainly he was to listen in and get any information he could about her plans.

By December, with the knowledge that she would be going to Scotland after all - Scott's face had been something else - but a lack of solid information about where to, Scott persuaded him to follow her. He gave no details, Martin was simply to find where she was living and let him know, all expenses paid, (including beer - Martin had negotiated that one himself).

Scott was adamant he couldn't go himself, he wanted the element of surprise. He didn't want to risk bumping into her in the street. He wanted to be able to ring her doorbell and see the shock in her eyes. Martin hadn't asked what Scott would do after the shock, he wasn't too bothered, but had he known just how impossible 'bumping into her' was to be, he would have laughed Scott out of the bar. But Scott had made it sound easy, Scotland was a small country right? He promised it would take no more than a couple of weeks and that Martin would be greatly rewarded on his return home.

It was a rough drinking session that day. Scott was pissed off that Martin still hadn't extracted any useful information. Secretly, Martin thought he was more pissed off that Emmie was actually going ahead with the move, overriding his confidence that she wouldn't. He did brighten, however, when Martin told him that he had heard Emmie and Amy discussing the farewell party that was to take place the following week.

Scott wasn't supposed to go anywhere near the party. Martin was only supposed to be a faceless guest with open ears, but Emmie had spotted him. She had waved, but quickly scooted off, not interested in making conversation.

It stung, he had to admit, hadn't they had been friends at uni too?

The feeling simmered only a moment before Scott had called, highly strung, and obviously on edge. He had been drinking, his voice was sharp and edged with malice. He warned Martin that this was his last chance, and told him how upset he would be if nothing solid was gleaned from this opportunity. Martin felt the first trickle of unease as threats poured forth, This was a side of Scott he had never seen, The ego had always been there, but he had obviously grown into a man used to getting exactly what he wanted, and Martin was just Martin, what if he couldn't do it?

To make matters worse, he had neglected to charge the phone, which had gone dead before Martin could tell him that the mission was almost accomplished.

Within seconds, Scott was there. Ranting and raving as the speeches were held. Emmie had looked thoroughly shocked, and after her earlier dismissal of him, it was a buzz to watch.

It was payback for Scott's threats too. Martin had an idea Scott didn't like Emmie starting over without him, but if this was his attempt to win her back, she would run a mile. In fact, she was running a fair few of them, for sure.

As Emmie threw his mother's prized jewellery into the crowd, he knew the show was over. He made his way out of the party on Scott's heels, exhilaration coursing through him.

Scott raged all the way to the Frog and Toad, Emmie getting his wrath for being such a 'fucked up cunting bitch' apparently. Martin wouldn't know and didn't care, but he took note outside the pub when Scott threw the jewellrey he had collected from her into a litter bin before going inside. They sat at the bar, Martin quietly nursing a beer as he revelled in Scott's perfect persona unravelling before him. Then the wrath had turned back to Martin, Scott's temper peaked, and a fist had arrived a little too close to Martin's nose for comfort. He felt the swoosh of air rush past his face, and as he toppled from the bar stool in a frantic effort to avoid the impact, he decided it was time to reveal his information. He had an approximate area for Emmie's new home.

Suddenly the tables turned. Martin was in control. He liked the feeling, a lot. Had Scott been surprised? Hell yes, and so grateful that Martin didn't even get an ear bashing about the dead phone. All's well that ends well.

Except that he was here, and this had been the third village he had stayed in within the last three weeks. Although Scott was footing the bill, it was getting tedious. Seeing Emmie had given him false hope. Even if she had been here, where had she gone? And what if she never came back? Was he supposed to sit here and wait forever?

When he had agreed to this he had envisaged a bit of excitement. It would be a fun break, he thought, a change from sitting around playing Resident Evil on the Playstation, but now the boredom, and answering to Scott's increasing anger and sarcasm, was just pissing him off. Scott was treating him like something he'd stepped in, he would do well to remember who had got him this far in the first place.

Martin heaved a frustrated sigh, this was getting him nowhere. He hurled the phone across the room, where it bounced off the window pane with a loud thud. He grabbed his coat and a battered cowboy hat, and stalked out of the room, pushing it firmly on his head. He liked the hat, it made him feel like Billy the Kid, and it gave him an excellent place to hide when he didn't want to speak to people, he just dipped his hat, dipped his head, et voila, he disappeared.

He walked towards the falls for the umpteenth time, but now, as he reached the large Oak tree, he took 'Ma Hubbard of the General Store's' route and branched off to the right where a tiny deer track was just visible through the old bracken.

The pale winter sunshine gave way to a light drizzle as he walked, grey clouds moving in silently overhead. No big deal, he wasn't a fair weather walker (he had walked to the Frog and Toad plenty of times in the rain). However, this permeated his trainers, jeans and jacket as he trekked through the brambles and bracken. The overhead branches of Rowan and Birch dripped relentlessly causing a stream of water to jet off the back of his hat. By the time he reached the clearing at the top of the falls he was wet through and thoroughly pissed off.

Still, he could go back to the Guest House and debate calling Scott with no news or carry on walking, so he carried on, until he came to the foot of the hill that the old lady had mentioned.

It was right what they said, he thought, if you walked through the shit in your head long enough you came out the other side. By the time he got to the foot of the hill he was feeling energised and clear-headed, anger of the morning dissipated as he'd stomped his way through the undergrowth and grass.

He wanted - *needed* - to climb the hill. He had no phone, no ties, no contact with anyone and it felt amazing. Scott might be trying to get hold of him right now, and good old Martin wouldn't pick up because he wasn't there. It would drive Scott insane, and that made Martin laugh out loud.

'Fuck you, Scott!'

Still grinning he decided that when he got back he would pack up his things and go home. This was proving to be the worst few weeks he'd spent anywhere. Period.

Scotland sucked.

If Emmie wanted to set up camp in this boring shitty place, then he wasn't about to care, Scott could come up here and find her himself. Martin the Martian was done. Over and out.

He stepped up onto a stile that cut the tie between the field and the bottom of the hill, and stared upward, pushing the brim of the hat up out of his eyes, and squinting against the light rain.

The hill rose steeply in places, and directly ahead, about halfway up, was a little section of scree that he would have to avoid if he didn't want to risk a fall. The section to his left bore a large crag of sheer rock toward the top so he couldn't get that way.

Right it is then.

He followed a small track along the bottom of the hill a few hundred yards before climbing through the grass. It was steeper than it looked and he slipped and slid in his old trainers, worn rubber soles not gaining traction on the wet grass. Eventually he picked up a small sheep track. After that he found the going a little easier and was up on the peak within an hour.

Hands on thighs, breathing hard, he stopped to congratulate himself on conquering the hill (one of the small achievements he'd managed since he got here. Shame finding Emmie wasn't another). But as he glanced up he noticed the sheep track went straight only for a short time before climbing again. He straightened and saw at least a couple of higher peaks through the drizzle.

Not to be beaten he carried on, this was fun, who knew hiking could be so calming. He felt better than he had since arriving in Scotland. He stumbled on through the drizzle, concentrating on the tiny track at his feet, looking ahead only to locate the peak and see that he was going in the right direction. The drizzle slowly became a wet mist the higher he climbed; carefully through a small patch of loose scree, and painfully through a rather large patch of gorse he couldn't be bothered to go around, until he finally reached the top.

He thought.

But another, higher peak, rose before him in the mist.

His jaw dropped. A stray black faced sheep stood in the path watching his deflation as it chewed at the grass.

'Fuck!' He cursed at it. 'A hill is a hill, right? It goes up and comes back down this isn't a hill, it's a fucking nightmare. Hiking is officially shit.'

The sheep regarded him, chewing quickly. Martin raged on at it voice rising into the mist.

'This is a *fucking* mountain where I come from.' He poked his jacket at the middle of his chest for emphasis. The sheep blinked and chewed. 'Hills are climbed in half an hour in my part of the world. I don't need hiking shoes and a backpack full of drink and shit to climb a hill. This is a fucked up fucking mountain I don't care what *you* lot like to call it.'

On 'you' he shot his hand out to point at the sheep, who decided enough was enough and turned tail, disappearing across the side of the mountain at a run.

Soaked, breathing hard, heart chastising him for his lack of athleticism, and legs shaking, Martin gave up.

Bastard nature. Just when the going got good it had to turn around and bite you on the ass.

Mentioning a drink had also made him aware that he was thirsty. A check on his watch told him it was 3.15pm.

Bugger, hiking also ate time. How about that?

No wonder he was thirsty, he had left a little after 1pm. The light would be fading fast and very soon. He should head back, there was a pint with his name on back at the Grey Lion, and that was more alluring than a return across fields and a steep-sided 70ft waterfall in the dark.

As his heart rate returned to normal, he turned to descend the hill, and realised just how high he had climbed.

With the right weather he may have found a stunning view, but with the drizzle, there wasn't much to see past a few miles. He made out what appeared to be the village of Bracken Hill below, and if he looked left, there was a small house nestled at the other side of a wood that wound itself around the foot of the hill. Beyond that was more hill, vast woodland and Fields.

His eyes settled on the house.

Who the fuck would live there?

There was remote, and there was *remote*. He preferred the closeness of his little terraced house in Swallow Heath where he at least had neighbours, even if he didn't like most of them. They were close in any case. Comrades if anything went tits up in the world. What would the person living here do in a Zombie Apocalypse?

There was smoke curling from the chimney which meant someone decided it was a good place to live. Probably someone who needed to hide, someone fucked up who should be locked away. Like a serial killer.

Maybe it was better the Zombie's get them anyway.

He shuddered. The zombie talk was starting to freak him out, and Martin became aware of just how alone he was on this hill with dusk rapidly approaching. He really needed that drink, and the chill from sweating, and now standing, was creeping into his bones as the temperature of the day fell.

In fading light, he made his way back down the sheep track as fast as he could, aware that it wouldn't be long until all light was gone. At least the drizzle seemed to be letting up, and the clouds were clearing again, although seeing the first couple of stars in the sky when he was a good few miles from his room was a little disarming.

He scrambled and slid a little faster through many (fucking) gorse bushes and along the grass, mostly on his ass until he came to the bottom - where he found he was lost.

A forest stood before him. It stretched in both directions for as far as he could see. There hadn't been a forest where he had climbed the stile which meant he had descended the hill at the wrong angle in his haste.

'What the fuck?'

He linked his hands on top of his wet hat, pushing it down on to his head as he thought. There were trees on both sides of the stile though, he remembered that much, so was the stile to his left or right? He couldn't tell. He'd been so busy following his feet he had no idea which way the damn sheep track had taken him, up or down the hill. He glanced at the trees ahead.

Go through?

Hell no. He felt far too wired. There may not be zombies, but there could be all manner of animals that wanted to eat him in the woods at night. Did bears live in Scotland? He decided he didn't want to find out. He glanced right and then left. Nothing seemed to stick out either direction, so he walked left.

As dusk turned to dark Martin was getting worried, he was dehydrated, pissed off, and not at all sure he was going the right way. The moon was out, offering some light, but he seemed to be stumbling more the darker it got. At last, he stopped altogether. He looked back in the direction he had just walked.

Turn back?

He had been walking for at least half an hour and although he hadn't got very far what if he went back and this was the right way? What he needed was a light, and that was on his phone back at the Guest House. Had he really been so happy to leave his phone back there in case Scott called? He could have turned it onto silent. At least now he would have had a light, or been able to call someone.

Karma was a bastard.

Staring to chill in the creeping cold, Martin reluctantly turned back to the left and carried on. He'd started this way, so he'd finish.

A few yards further, as the wood thinned and the land seemed to be opening up, a glimmer of light appeared through the trees. He stopped and cocked his lip, confused. At last, he got it. It was the little stone house he had seen from way up there on the hill.

The serial killer's place.

Exhausted, bone cold, and gasping for a drink Martin decided that tonight was going to be the night he had his first, and maybe last, drink with a serial killer. He would take his chances. After all, it would make a better story to die at the hands of a murderer than to freeze to death on the side of a mountain. And anyway he was desperate.

He took a few more paces along the side of the wood until the trees petered out entirely and then crossed a small stream and headed across open land toward the ominous lights of the little stone house.

Chapter 20

By 4pm that evening all light was lost from the sun, pitching the grounds into darkness. Emmie sat in the living room, her feet curled under her on the sofa, coffee in hand, watching as Charlie tried his best to teach Grace how to play *Guess Who?*.

Earlier she had brought some wood in from the store outside to light the fire. The supply was going down rapidly, and she made a mental note to add an axe to her list of tools, so that she could practice chopping some wood of her own.

She had never intended to light the fire with Charlie and Grace around, but the cold that was upstairs earlier in the day seemed to have descended into the rest of the house, wrapping every room with a chill that seeped into her bones. Emmie had checked both the boiler (working: pressure okay) and the thermostat (now set at 28 degrees) before ushering everyone into the living room, shutting the doors and lighting a fire.

She had also drawn the curtains.

Just for warmth purposes, of course.

With the fire crackling and warmth finally curling around her, Emmie felt content. Things were panning out just nicely which was a blessing after the last few years of hell.

Now she thought it through, it was only the last four years or so that had been hell, before that, well, before that had been okay, hadn't it? Putting aside Scott's need for control and angry outbursts they had made a pretty good family. Scott had been a fantastic father, doting on his two soldiers, often getting home from work just in time to sit and read with them both before bed. He never took his anger out on the children, which she had been thankful for. That wasn't to say they didn't witness it, of course, but she thought she had managed to shield them from the worst of it.

Scott often had to work Saturdays, and Saturdays at the office were always lovely, lazy days for Emmie and the kids, often spent at the park with Natalie and her kids. Some Saturdays, however, he worked from home. Those weren't days she looked back on with fondness.

Scott couldn't concentrate with the noise of the family around him, which meant his anger would fuel in direct correlation with how long he worked that day, unless the children were kept almost silent. Which was nigh on impossible. Emmie offered to take them out more than once, but Scott would always refuse. If they needed to go out, he said, they would go out together when he had finished. So instead, she would spend the hours tip-toeing around, shushing the children, cringing at every bang or shout they made, and keeping the tv on mute, hoping the pictures would satisfy them until Scott had finished. Those Saturdays were miserable, and usually ended with an 'episode' which would always be directed at Emmie.

She tried hard to keep his anger at bay, and after sixteen years together her instincts had been honed to every twitch and tick that said he was headed in that direction. She was pretty adept at working around him to diffuse most situations before they started by altering her behaviour to calm him. It became subconscious over the years. Tiresome, but necessary.

Sundays were always good, without exception Scott made Sunday a family day, whether they went somewhere for a picnic or had fun making dens indoors due to inclement weather. Sundays were the one day of the week that everyone relaxed and had fun. The day Scott put everyone other than Emmie and the children on hold. Sundays were always full of screams and laughter, ice cream and chocolate, and love. Scott gave them all his full attention and devotion, and it was these days that outweighed the toughness of traversing everyday life in the week.

The highs with Scott soared past the stars, and she felt like the luckiest woman alive, but the lows made her feel like something nasty on the bottom of his shoe.

Still, that's what relationships were about, weren't they? Emmie hadn't had any other serious relationships to compare him to. She had fallen for him completely, issues or not.

She sighed heavily.

What the hell went so wrong? I used to be able to deal with him, what changed?

She knew the answer to that. Scott changed. He had become a new

Scott, someone she didn't know. One who had slapped her so hard the force had propelled her over the coffee table, and for days afterward, a bruise had bloomed bright on her cheekbone. One who taken everything he could from the divorce, one who had disowned his children, one who liked to hurt her, one who liked to see her suffer. This Scott she couldn't deal with. And after those final two years of marriage, when his behaviour had really spiralled out of control, this Scott scared her to death.

Something hot landed on her leg, dragging Emmie back from the memories. She was shaking hard, coffee slopping over the side of the cup, as she gulped in short, shallow breaths. Knowing the symptoms of her anxiety well, she expertly applied one of the breathing techniques the therapist had shown her. One of the only good things to have come from the weekly sessions.

As she breathed she put the familiar soundtrack on loop in her head.

She wasn't to blame. Scott was a man under pressure. Long hours and masses of paperwork wore him thin, but law was his passion, and understanding that, she had let him get away with far too much. And that was okay, it didn't make his actions her fault, and it wasn't her problem any more. Scott was gone, he couldn't hurt her or the children again. She had broken free. She was safe. She could move forward.

As the spell passed and her breathing returned to normal, she looked at Charlie and Grace. They sat on the rug together, Grace giggling as Charlie asked if her man had a moustache.

'Does he have tosh?' she mimicked before collapsing into belly laughter.

Charlie was looking perplexed. He glanced at Emmie with a 'what's so funny?' look. Emmie grinned back at him.

Here is proof I can do one thing right. I can provide a safe, happy, family home for my kids. All alone too. Didn't think I'd manage did you, Scott? Stick that in your pipe and smoke it, you child dumping bastard.

Her grin widened. That felt better. No more nostalgia, no more regrets, no more self-degradation. She wouldn't do it anymore.

Emmie was stirred from her thoughts by a tapping on glass. Short and sharp, but distant. She narrowed her eyes as she listened. She thought she heard it again, but over the children, it was hard to tell. She got up, putting her coffee mug on the side table and stepped out into the hall, past the foot of the stairs.

Tap-tap-tap.

Quick and sharp, but not from the hallway. It seemed to be coming from the kitchen. She tried to remember if there were any trees that side of the house, a simple explanation, but really, Emmie knew that there wasn't a tree with branches near enough to tap at the windows of any part of the house. She swallowed hard.

Tap-tap-tap.

Definitely the kitchen. Emmie closed her eyes and rubbed at her temples. She didn't want to go and find out what it was. Period.

Do I need to? I could just go back into the living room, put on the television and ignore it. I'll look in daylight when everything isn't so ... dark.

Tap-tap-tap.

Emmie opened her eyes. Could someone be here? Maybe they'd tried the door and were now rapping windows to get her attention? She hadn't heard the door, but it was thick wood, and in light of 'shadow man' during the storm she had locked herself and the children down in the living room most nights. Shutting curtains against the darkness and possible watchers. She may not have heard the door at all.

The kitchen has blinds, but of course, they're not down. This had to be the one night she had forgotten the kitchen blinds. Stupid really as she had gotten into the habit of a hot chocolate before bed. Tonight she would have to miss it.

So now what did she do? Go in or ignore it?

She had to look. If someone was at the door, which was perfectly acceptable at 4.30pm, they would think she was a lunatic, scaling around the house like a scared rabbit.

She crossed quietly to the other side of the hall. It was darker here the only light illuminating from the living room door pulled too across the hall. Even so, she knew that it would be enough to expose her to the darkness outside. She took a shaky breath, pressed her back against the wall and very slowly edged up to the kitchen door. Had it been open she would have seen most of the window from where she was, but of course, it was pulled too.

Slowly she reached out her right hand which was closest to the door, her back flat against the hall wall. She very carefully pushed the door, trying to open it as slowly as it could. As the window sneaked slowly into view, the creak was unbearably loud grating as the hinges resisted. It made the hairs on the back of her neck creep up.

Christ, does this have to be quite so 'horror film'? Bloody hell Em, open the door and see who's there will you lets get this over with.

Tap-tap-tap.

Emmie stood stock still, hand still on the kitchen door and swung her head to the left listening. The tapping had changed direction. Bypassing the front door, it now seemed to be coming from the direction of the living room. She frowned.

Well, that's the tree theory out the window unless you have trees that walk in your orchard Em.

A nervous giggle escaped her lips. She steadied her breathing and glanced at the living room door. Not by the children, she didn't want them scared too. Emmie made it back across the hall and into the living room in three strides, shutting the door quickly behind her. There was something wrong in here, something out of place, it was colder too, but she couldn't tear her eyes away from the windows. Which one would it be? Every muscle in her body was taut. She was barely breathing.

'Mom?'

It was Charlie. Enquiring, not scared.

She put up her left hand in a gesture that told him to stop, right index finger going up to her lips.

'Ssshhhh,' she said.

She saw him get up out of the corner of her eye. He stood, just in front of the fireplace watching her. She knew he would be frightened if she didn't tell him what was going on but for the moment she had to know what was rapping at the goddamn windows.

Tap-tap-tap.

Charlie heard it too. He spun toward the window at the side of the house. Whoever it was had come around the side? Shock flooded through her. She felt violated, she had known that someone might be watching, but she didn't expect them to walk right up to the house. That was private territory, you didn't just go marching around the back. She felt like a caged animal, nowhere was safe now aside from being locked in the house?

Emmie went over to the window. With the curtain shut, she couldn't see outside, but she wanted to be as close to the noise, the watcher, as possible. Was it a person? Could it be anything else? She stood nose almost on the material waiting for the next knock. The atmosphere was tense and silent. Charlie was still too, he didn't utter a word and she loved him for it. Not only would it have sent her through the roof and given her a heart attack, but she wanted to listen. Was there anything else? Rustling? Scraping? Footsteps? Any sound of movement outside? Any sign of life other than the tapping? She moved a little closer, listening intently, the silence swelled. There was no sound other than Charlie and herself breathing in short, shallow breaths.

Then a piercing scream. Long, loud and shrill.

Emmie whirled, her heart lurching out of her chest and suddenly realised what was wrong with the room. Grace had gone, the doors to the sunroom were open, which explained the chill over the room.

Charlie was ahead of her running through the doors.

'Grace!' They screamed in unison.

Emmie reached the doors and stood struggling take in the scene before her.

Grace was standing with her back to them screaming, over and over at the French doors. Charlie ran over and was trying to turn her, both hands placed on the back of her shoulders but Grace was inconsolable, and then Charlie was screaming too and trying to pull Grace away.

Emmie, whose brain seemed to be moving through thick treacle, took a step toward the children and then caught sight what had upset first Grace, and then Charlie.

It was a man, THE man, at the edge of the patio facing the doors to the sunroom. He was still entirely in shadow, black as the night with only the low moonlight highlighting his contours.

It was the same man Emmie had seen in the storm she was sure he had the same shape, the same hat. He was tall and broad and as still as he had been the night of the storm. But now he was right here. Emmie had no idea what he wanted and had no wish to find out.

She moved toward Charlie in slow motion shouting at both him and Grace to get back into the living room. Charlie was yelling too pulling at Grace's arms to move her away from the doors. Grace was unmoving rooted to the spot, her mouth opened in a never-ending scream.

As Emmie moved into the room, her hands reaching for the children, her eyes never left the shadow man. He hadn't moved but Emmie was sure he had moved his attention to her, eyes boring into her. And then she knew what he wanted.

The children.

She was confident enough that she would have testified in court that she had heard him say it. The children were what he was after, she had no doubt.

He ... it ... stepped up to the doors, and then Emmie had them. Grace scooped up and Charlie by the arm. She stumbled to the living room catching one last glance of the man, as she turned and slammed shut the double doors.

There was an inhuman sound. It filled her head rebounding off the sides of her skull, screeching.

'Leave them alone they're mine!'

She just had time to realise the voice was her own before she was going down, falling until she hit the floor and the world went black.

Chapter 21

There was a stinging on her lips. A burning, a leathery taste, and then it was gone. She licked her lips eyes still closed. Her head pounded. She moved an arm that felt like lead and brought it up to a painful spot drumming above her right ear. A lump was growing, she felt around it and brought her hand slowly back round to her face. Slowly she opened her eyes and squinted against the light. A blurry outline of her hand appeared. Pink, no red, thank god. She closed her eyes for a moment and then remembered Charlie and Grace. She forced her eyes open and tried to sit up. Spots appeared before her eyes, the world spun, and her stomach went over.

'Don't move mom, you fell. I couldn't wake you.'

Charlie. She turned her head slowly to the right and looked at him. Her vision slowly returning she took him in as he knelt beside her, brown hair flopped over his face, concern in his eyes. He held a crystal tumbler in his right hand a small amount of red liquid in the bottom. She frowned.

'It's wine,' he said as if reading her mind, 'I remember granddad saying whisky woke people up when they'd fainted. We didn't have any, so I tried wine.'

Ah, the leather taste.

She sat up slowly.

Charlie reached out a hand. Emmie took it getting to her feet and checking herself over. Her head was pounding, but there didn't seem to be much else wrong. Just a sore patch on her shoulder that would likely become a bruise.

'What happened?'

Charlie shook the hair out of his face and looked at her, eyes wide, uncertain.

'You fell, You were carrying Grace, and you fell trying to shut the doors.'

'Fell carrying Grace?' Emmie said slowly. Then it hit her, The knocking and then the man at the back doors. The fear she had felt trying to get the children out of the way. Out of *his* way. Emmie whirled around scanning the room.

'Where is Grace? Is she ok?'

'Here mommy, I'm good.'

Grace's little face stared at her. Worried, big blue eyes glistening with tears. She sat with legs tucked up to her chest, arms encompassing them, chin resting on her knees next to the fire. Emmie gathered her up in her arms checking for injuries as Grace started to cry again.

'She isn't hurt I checked her over. She landed on top of you. She was just scared.'

Emmie looked at Charlie. He was also scared, she could see that, but he had taken care of them both calmly.

Admiration surged through her chest. She put Grace down, opened up her free arm and gestured to Charlie. He moved into her one-armed embrace, and they sat all together, on the floor in what Grace referred to as a cuddle puddle. Emmie lowered her head, kissing theirs, and tried to think. Charlie spoke breaking the silence.

'Mom. That man … what did he want?'

Emmie sighed and thought about how she was going to word this if she ever wanted the children to sleep at night again.

'I don't know Charlie. We didn't really stop to find out, did we? It was probably totally innocent, like someone lost on the hills, wanting a friendly face to help him out.'

'… and we screamed and slammed the door on him.'

Charlie had a hint of a smile playing on his lips and although Emmie didn't believe this theory, it was possible wasn't it? People must get stuck on the hills all the time, stranded by darkness, losing where they are. She played along to break the tension that had built up since the unearthly tapping.

'Well, he can't blame us. Normal people go round the front. What did he expect, looming up at the back doors like that in the dark?'

'He did tap on the window maybe he'd tried the front door?'

I think you're right, Charlie.' She ruffled his hair fondly and he immediately brought up a hand to smooth it. 'I heard the tapping at the front of the house which is why I went in the hall. I think that's what it was. The man got lost on the hills, saw our lights and decided to ask for help. He couldn't get a reply from the front, so he wandered around the back to try to get our attention. There see? Nothing to worry about. He just scared us, that's all.'

Emmie looked down at Grace who's big blue eyes were looking earnestly back up at her. She gave a faint smile and cuddled into Emmie's shoulder. Emmie squeezed her and kissed the top of her head.

'Nothing to worry about, Grace, he's probably long gone by now with all our screaming.'

'Maybe we'd better check? Shall I go and look, see if he's still there? He may still need help.'

'No Charlie!'

It came too quickly - too harsh - and a worried frown crossed Charlie's face as he pulled back to look at her.

Jeez, calm down Em, slowly and gently.

Emmie took a breath and smiled at him.

'No,' She said more gently, 'You don't need to do that, I'll go. You stay here with Grace. I'll go and check, and be back in a jiffy.'

She pulled them both in for a hug, not at all wanting to stray from the one room where strange eyes couldn't see them. Finally, she let them go and stood up. Grace immediately scuttled into Charlie's arms, eyes cast downwards. Charlie looked up at Emmie, his face grave. Emmie forced herself to chuckle and hoped it came across more natural than it sounded.

'There's no need to be so serious, it'll be fine. Keep warm by the fire, don't move, I won't be long.'

Emmie walked over to the doors and swallowed hard. Truth be told she didn't want to go in the sunroom any more than she wanted to walk through the gates of hell. But Charlie and Grace depended on her to tell them that it was okay and they were safe. She had no choice.

Before she lost her nerve, she turned to smile at the huddled children and then opened the door and walked into the sunroom. An icy blast of air hit her after the warmth of the living room, but it looked normal. She cast her eyes around the windows - *so many* - heart in her throat, and tried to see into the darkness outside. She could see nothing out of the ordinary from here by the living room doors.

The sky was clear, and she could see the abundance of stars and the colossal moon, nearly full, over Bracken Hill. The moonlight pooled in the garden and spread over the hills bathing them in an eerie silver light. Only the orchard and wood were dark, an impenetrable blackness settled within. As she stood, heart pounding, fists curled into balls at her sides, a thought occurred to her and she almost groaned aloud with the implications.

The french doors were shut and looked intact. They had been locked well before darkness had descended, but Emmie knew that she would have to check them, for her own sanity. If there was a chance he had come inside…

Dear God, please. I don't want him inside. I don't want to go over there. I don't want to check the doors. If I'm dreaming, I need wake up now, please?

She screwed her eyes shut, took a breath and opened them again. Nope, she wasn't cosy in bed. She was still in the blessed sunroom. Her heart sank, and the pounding in her head renewed its vigour. She knew what she had to do.

Licking her dry lips, She slowly walked over to the doors, scanning the many windows for any sign of shadow man.

Nothing stirred, but she felt watched. She felt as though a hundred eyes were out there watching, and waiting. Enjoying the show, enjoying her terror.

As she reached the doors, she scanned the patio taking in all of the windows, left and right in one large swoop. She had never been so glad of a cloudless sky and a moon that could lend its light.

Nothing; no shadows, nothing was moving. Outside was still and silent. Holding its breath as she held hers.

Heart in her throat, all the hairs on the back of her neck risen, her senses heightened. She focused on the handle, reaching out a shaking hand. As she touched the cold metal, a flock of crows screamed laughter, mocking as they rose up from the orchard trees in a flurry of black against the night sky casting dancing shadows all over the garden. Emmie jumped, a little whine escaping her lips.

She reached out again, and as the handle moved under her fingers, she fought what she knew couldn't be true.

The door was unlocked.

Chapter 22

Emmie stood frozen, fingers on the cold handle. Blood pounded in her ears matching the galloping rhythm of her heart. A million thoughts tore through her head.

Who is this man? What does he want? How the hell did he get in? Does he have a key? Why is he watching us? Where is he now, in the house? WHAT DO I DO?

She was caught in impossibly maddening indecision. As a mother, it was her role to protect her children from all the horrors of the world, for as long as she could. But what did that mean?

Stay? Say nothing to keep the kids feeling safe, put them to bed as usual but then leave them at the hands of shadow man who could be here somewhere in the house, *in her home,* and who wanted god knows what?

Or leave? Get out of the house while they still could but alerting the children that there was something wrong, the house was unsafe, and possibly ruining their feeling of security for who knew how long. And what would she tell them?

The grandfather clock ticked in the background and Emmie felt like she had stood at the doors for an age. She felt utterly torn, enormous pressure was building in her head, and she felt her vision pooling, blackness darkening the edges, legs starting to shake.

No! I will not choose this moment to faint.

Breaking the spell, she flung open the door onto the patio, and a gust of cold air blew into her face, blowing away the blackness and kicking her conscious into action. She shook her head.

What am I thinking? I have to get out. I can't let Grace and Charlie sleep here when there's possibly someone in the house.

She moved quickly. Shutting the French doors, she went back to the living room, thoughts in motion. Her phone was on the settee, coats were all hung up by the front door at the bottom of the stairs. Keys were in the front door. Had the kids got their shoes on? She couldn't remember, but she hoped so. Did she need anything else? She didn't think so. She made a mental checklist in her head. Kids, phone, coats, keys, car, as fast as possible. No questions, no dithering, She could explain more in the car on the way to … wherever the hell they ended up.

Calming herself a notch below hysteria she opened the doors to the living room, striding in and picking up her phone as she spoke low and quick to the children.

'Ok guys, there's nothing to worry about, but I think as a precaution we need to …'

She stopped. Grace was gone, door out into the hall open.

No … No … NO!

Crouched down Charlie was using the poker to stir the coals, and it vaguely crossed her mind that she had told him not to play with the fire as he whirled around at her voice.

'GRACE!' She shouted, 'Charlie, where the hell is Grace?'

Charlie Stood up, poker in hand looking shaken.

'What mom? What's up? She's just gone to the toilet, she said she was desperate,' He said panic rising in his voice.

The toilet? The toilet was upstairs. Emmie felt herself rise a notch above hysteria.

'Charlie, you let her go when I was checking for the man? You didn't know it was safe and you let her go? I've been gone two seconds, she couldn't have waited?'

Emmie saw Charlie's lip quiver and tears well in his eyes. She saw it but could do nothing, there would be time for hugs later, right now she had to find Grace and get out of this house. Why couldn't this kid stay in one room when she was told?

Running her hand through her hair, she spoke in hushed tones.

'Charlie, listen, I'm not sure if the man is in the house. We don't know who he is or what he wants, so we have to leave now. In the morning we can come back and check things out, call the police and get them to check things over.'

Charlie's face fell. The fear was palpable, his voice rising a couple of octaves.

'In the house? But Grace ...'

'It's okay, Charlie,' Emmie said. She took a shaky breath and stepped to him and placed both hands on his shoulders looking into his watery brown eyes, 'I'm going to find her. Listen, I need you to take the keys from the front door, grab the coats and run like hell to the car. Don't stop, don't dawdle. Run, as fast as you can. When you get to the car lock yourself in, do you hear? And don't open the door for anyone except Grace and me when we get there. Got it?'

Charlie nodded, swallowing hard. Emmie gathered him up in her arms quickly and kissed his head. Giving him a final squeeze she let him go.

'Go, now, quickly. I'll watch you from the window until the car lights flash so I know you've locked it.'

Charlie went. He grabbed the coats, keys from the door - still there mercifully - and took off into the night. Emmie pulled back the curtain and watched his shadow bob all the way to the fence. She saw the orange of the car lights as he pressed the fob to open the doors, and saw him wave as he got inside. The car lights flashed orange again showing the car was locked and she dropped the curtain.

One safe, one to go.

Grace, where are you? And where is the man?

Emmie moved into the hallway, silence surrounding her.

Not wanting to alert the man any further after the commotion with Charlie she plumbed for climbing the stairs as quietly as she could.

With each creak of a stair tread she stopped to listen before moving on.

Come on Grace where are you? You must have finished by now, just flush and head back to the stairs so we can go.

She reached the square where the steps turned up to the landing and stopped. Her heart was slamming in her chest. Taking a breath and steadying herself, she glanced down into the hallway. Now her eyes had adjusted to the gloom she could see clearly. Nothing moved, and no-one was following her up the stairs. She turned back toward the landing and continued up, all the time expecting the man to be waiting for her at the top.

'Come up, little lady,' he would say, beckoning her forward with an inane grin, 'It's all fun and games up here!'

Emmie thought her heart might give out before she had time to play any games. Her head swam and she felt the blackness closing in again. Leaning back against the wall, she closed her eyes breathing deeply.

Grace flushed and ran the water.

'I have to wash my hands now silly... that's it they're all clean... I can't play up here, Charlie says to play downstairs till mommy's back. I want to go down, it's cold up here, it's too cold...'

Emmie's eyes snapped open. Was Grace talking to the man? Her heart plummeted, but then she recognised Grace's rhythm of speech, and the fact that no one was answering her one-sided conversation.

This was invisible man. Funny how he didn't seem such a threat against shadow man.

At the top step Emmie paused. If shadow man didn't have Grace that was a relief, but the fact that she didn't know where he was proved worse. She could be as quiet as she liked, but Grace was chattering away without a care. If shadow man was up here staking them out, biding his time, he certainly knew where Grace was right now. Emmie had to move, and quick.

The bathroom door was pulled too, but the light was on. Poised for action, palms sweaty and heart thudding, Emmie took a breath, and lunged. She hit the door with her palm and almost fell into the room. Grace squealed.

'Mommy, you scared me!'

She was still yelling as Emmie picked her up, scanned the bathroom and was out. The landing was darker now after the brightness of the room. Emmie faltered, seeing shadows everywhere. She didn't stop to check if any were wearing a hat before fleeing in the direction of the stairs.

She hit them at a full run, half expecting a hand on her shoulder at any moment. At the bottom, she skidded at the door making Grace squeal again. Regaining her footing, she grabbed the handle and then they were out. Emmie heard the blood rushing past her ears, her feet slapping on the hard dirt and her breath coming in ragged gasps. Her chest was constricted, every breath sending fire into her lungs. Her arms, almost numb with the weight of carrying Grace, protested wildly, but she didn't stop.

At the car Charlie pressed the fob and the lights blinked. Emmie opened the back door and almost threw Grace into her seat before staggering round to the driver's side. She lunged inside, slamming the door and hitting the locks. Without a word Charlie gave her the keys and Emmie started the engine. She slammed the car into reverse and backed into the hedge behind before crunching into first. The car lurched forward, tearing up grass and stones, bringing a chunk of hedge with her.

Emmie didn't slow at the Bruce farm. She couldn't deal with Bill right now, whether he would help her she had no idea, but in any case he was just too damn close to the house. Right now she wanted nothing more than to be as far away as possible from Bruadair.

Chapter 23

It took Martin approximately twelve steps across open land to decide he didn't want to take his chances after all. He felt exposed, vulnerable, like whoever was in the house was watching him from the darkened windows at the back. He stopped, he would have to go back.

Except that he wouldn't have to go back, he saw as he scanned the land.

The wood stretched along next to him. The same wood he had just followed to get here. It seemed relatively long and thin now that he was looking at it from here, and this side of the wood was a vast expanse of field. Surely he could just go across that field, and it would land back into the sheep field he crossed toward the style at the foot of the hill. It was certainly the right direction, running parallel to the bottom of the hill, the way he had just walked.

Martin decided to go for it. The fields were lit by moonlight making them easier to cross than the little valley between the wood and the foot of the hill. Plus the ground was flat, the slight slope to the land in that valley had pissed him off and hurt his ankles. On the field, he would also have a chance to see the serial killer emerging from the house to attack him. It was a win, win situation.

'Right,' He said into the night, 'Lord, I'm not a begging man, but if you could cut me a little slack here, I would appreciate it. I just want a fucking drink, okay?'

Taking the silence as compliance he started away from the house striding as quickly as his tired legs would go, breath rasping in his dry throat.

Fucking dickhead, you know there's probably just some normal bloke in that house, could have been having a drink by now.

He pushed on anyway and found luck was on his side as he came to a fence which led to another field. This field was different though. If he listened hard enough, from the left was the sound of running water. The only water able to make that roar from all over here was the waterfall.

Giving a little whoop, he fist bumped the air, and strode to the left, following the roar of the water.

When the forest came into view at the top of the falls, he almost skipped for joy. He could smell that pint, feel it in his hand, the ice cold smoothness sliding down his throat, caressing it, easing the hoarse dryness every time he swallowed.

He picked up his pace until he reached the edge of the forest, which started his heart thudding for reasons other than exertion. While the fields had been easy to traverse, ahead, inside the wooded area, it was near black. With no torch and the light of the moon not penetrating the canopy above he knew this would be slow going.

The tourist path followed this side up from the car park only for a short while before crossing over the river and following up through the wood on the other side where the slope of the valley was more lenient and open. Having been up there many times, he knew the drop on this side was sheer. The trees growing right up to the edge and even down through the rock face in places. He knew he could fall off the edge if he wasn't careful. He was also worried about animals in the wood, compounding his fear, making him want to sprint.

Back at the mountain he'd had a choice, he could follow alongside the wood not venturing in at all, but here he had to go through, there was no other way.

Swallowing hard with the little saliva that would come in his rasping throat he started ahead, thinking of nothing but the beer.

Good cold beer.

Chapter 24

They were silent all the way to Bracken Hill. Charlie staring out of the window and Grace staring at her hands. There was only one place Emmie could think to go, the Grey Lion pub. She would happily pay for a room, somewhere she could switch off from the thoughts of intruders, watchers, and protecting the kids for a few hours.

Her thoughts travelled to shadow man and who he could be. There was only one person she could think of that may want to scare her; Scott. But he was down in Surrey, and it was a long way to come just to stare through her windows.

If it wasn't Scott, and she couldn't viably understand why it would be, who the hell was it? Why was this person making such an effort to scare them, and now to break into the house when they were at home? She didn't understand.

Tomorrow she would call the police, shadow man would probably be gone by then but she didn't want to scare the kids anymore, and she certainly didn't want to go back to the house tonight. In daylight, everything would seem more manageable.

Down the lane, the first signs of the village approached and Emmie felt some of the tension loosen in her shoulders, comforted by the yellow street lamps and cottages lining the street. She drove past the general store, noting the light upstairs. The shop was closed now, at a little after 5pm, but the thought of a friendly face nearby was a massive relief. Emmie had met Edith only once, but right now she was aching for familiarity.

Turning past the pub into the car park, she pulled up in the only space available and killed the engine. Gathering the children, they walked into the warmth and noise of the pub.

The normality and cheer inside after what she had been through only minutes ago almost reduced her to tears of relief. She blinked them back before making her way forward. The pub was full, almost crowded, which was weird on a Friday in January, but hey, maybe every day was a pub day in these small villages. Who knew?

Keeping the children close at her side she made her way to the bar, pushing through the crowds, revelling in the clinking of glass, the chatter and laughter of the guests, and catching that smell reserved only for old pubs; spirits and beer infused with ancient wood. It made her want to order a glass of wine, and god knows she needed one, but she had a room to sort first.

A big man stood behind the bustling bar, tall and broad, his sandy hair was short, and a neat layer of stubble shadowed the lower half of his face. He pulled back a hand-pump, muscles in his biceps straining against the rolled up sleeves of his white shirt as he filled a pint glass with ale. Catching her eye, he put the pint on the bar, said something to the customer, and came over with a warm and reassuring smile that started with his eyes.

'Hallo lass, what can I get you?' He said voice raised above the noise. It was glorious to listen to, heavily lilted and deep, but as friendly and soothing as his demeanor. Emmie smiled, feeling immediately comfortable in this small village pub. She leaned over the bar to make herself heard.

'Thank you,' she said, 'I'd love a drink, but right now I'm after a room for the night. Do I speak to anyone in particular, the landlord maybe?'

'You're looking at him, lass,' the man said, 'I own and run the place, with a little help from my son, Connor.'

Emmie followed his gaze to the other end of the bar where a boy who seemed no older than 17 stood chatting to one of the bar hoggers.

'He's a good lad, keeps the regulars in check.' He looked back at her and smiled, 'Come up this way, let me double check the bookings, although I reckon you'll be hard pushed to find a room tonight. This is the one time of winter we're always fully booked unless there's been a cancellation in the last half hour.'

Emmie bustled the children up to the far end of the bar where it curved back around to meet the wall as the man lifted a battered A4 notebook from its hook where it was held by a piece of string. She bit her lip as he looked, his finger running down the page. He pursed his lips, dimples appearing briefly.

A large woman stumbled past, bumping Charlie into Grace as she made her way to the end of the room and Emmie pulled the children in closer to the bar.

The landlord looked up, regret on his face.

'I'm afraid we just don't have anything, lass. Our Burns night ceilidh's are quite legendary around here. We've a band starting at 8pm, and we're already getting packed out as you can see. There is another village with a guest house down the lane eight mile or so, you could check there.'

Emmie's face fell, deflated and suddenly weary at the unfairness of it. Hadn't they been through enough tonight?

'I'm sorry lass, if you'd have come earlier in the week …'

He trailed off letting the words hang in the air and held his hands up in a shrug. To his credit, he did look genuinely sorry.

'That's okay, it's not your fault.' She mumbled looking at her hands. She looked back up at him and tried to give him a reassuring smile, but her mouth didn't seem to want to work. A small puzzled frown crossed his face.

'Would you like a drink lass? You look like you could use one, it'll be on the house, of course, as I couldn't help you out. Just don't tell the rest of them or I'll be out of business.' He said with a wink.

She found a small smile. Here was one of life's genuinely kind souls, she thought. She was about to decline, say that she had to go. But go where? Drive eight miles down the lane to find another full guest house? She had forgotten it was Burns night tonight, but she knew how special it was to the Scottish. The much-loved poet would be celebrated all across Scotland tonight with various festivities.

So there it was. There was nowhere else to go.

If they had to sleep in the car so be it but they'd stay in the sanctuary of the warm pub until closing time. Maybe the nice landlord would have some blankets she could use. She sure as hell wasn't taking the children home tonight.

'You know, that is just what I need. Thank you. But I'll pay my way, a large merlot and two J20's, please.'

Emmie watched as the landlord grabbed the J20's and popped a straw into each bottle, she handed one of the bottle's to Charlie, and one to Grace shouting into her ear not to drop it, as he filled a sparkling wine glass to the top and set it on the counter in front of her.

Emmie mustered another smile as she felt for her purse in her coat pockets.

Her heart stopped.

Oh Christ, no.

She closed her eyes putting her hand up to rub at her forehead, could this get any worse? She hadn't picked up her bag on the way out. No bag meant no money, no cards, she didn't have a penny to her name. She felt the heat rise up from her neck to her cheeks as she panicked. Now she had no choice. She had to take the children home or sleep in a freezing car. If she had no money, she had no options

Not even to stay here and have a drink.

Emmie felt tears prick at her eyes as she looked back to the landlord.

'Erm... I'm so sorry I seem to have forgotten my purse... I...'

Her voice cracked as the terror of having no option but to go home rose over her, and without prior warning the tears spilled down her cheeks, running silently.

Frowning, the landlord pulled a tissue out from under the bar - *do people always cry on him?* - and handed it to her. She dabbed her cheeks and tried to pull herself together under his gaze.

'Not to worry, lass. I told you they're on the house. What's all this about?'

'I'm sorry,' Emmie said with a sniff, 'it's fine, really. It's just been one of those days. I really didn't want to have to drive home tonight. I... I suppose I have no choice now. No room and no money. I'm an idiot, I'm not fit to call myself a mother. I'm sorry, I know this isn't your problem. We'll drink up and be out of your hair. I promise I will come down tomorrow and pay you for the drinks.'

The tears surged again. Annoyed with herself, she swept them away and took a big gulp of wine. The landlord watched her carefully as she drank, then he heaved a sigh.

'Look, I have a room that we're not using at the moment. It's right here next to the bar, which was a stupid decision with hindsight, many of the guests complained the noise carries through.'

He pointed to a door a few feet away from the curved edge of the bar. Emmie held her breath. She could undoubtedly cope with noise over going back to Bruadair tonight. She looked back at him with hope as he carried on.

'It needs soundproofing and updating if we're going to use it again. Tonight, well, you're certainly not going to get much sleep with the band, and it only has one double bed but if you're willing...'

'I have no money.' Emmie stated bluntly.

She waited for the blow, but the landlord chuckled softly lighting up his face. A gentle, kind face, she noted, not in the least affected by her strange behaviour and barrage of tears. The calm, reassuring smile was back, the warmth in his eyes enhanced by the crinkling at their corners.

'I know that, pet.' he said, 'I wouldn't expect you to pay for it either. It's in need of decoration and like I say the noise will keep you and the bairns awake. I can see something has happened and you're in need. If you want it, lass, it's yours, although I won't promise it's comfortable, eh?'

Relief flooded through her nearly taking her legs from under her for the second time today. She held the bar sure she was swaying slightly.

'That's so kind, thank you. You have no idea how much this means to me. I'll be back tomorrow to pay you I promise.'

'It's not necessary, really lass. I'll go and freshen the room up unless you want to look at it first?'

'No,' Emmie said a little too quickly. 'No, I'll take it thank you.'

Chapter 25

Martin went as slow as he dared, every now and then stopping to listen to the water, trying to make sure he wasn't edging nearer to the drop. Every snapping branch, movement in the undergrowth, or movement from the tree canopy made his heart pound. Each time, not having the option to run, he stood still with his eyes closed, resigned to being eaten, and willing it to be quick. When nothing emerged to consume him, and the sounds died away, he opened his eyes, checked the waterfall, and carefully carried on.

Surprise almost stopped him in his tracks when he suddenly broke out from under the canopy, and onto the far end of a car park which was rammed full. It took seeing his battered Fiesta to realise it was actually the pub car park, and then he was sprinting - no, lurching - toward the door. His sprints were over for today.

He was so tired and thirsty he decided to forgo making a stop at his room and grab a pint without getting dry. He was leaving tomorrow anyway who cared what the locals thought? He'd show any of the bastards that wanted to stare and whisper precisely what the shape of his middle finger looked like.

Stopping just outside the door he calmed his breathing and took off his hat to run his fingers back through his hair. Then he was inside and at the bar, taking the only remaining bar seat even as a lady tried to claim it. He wasn't bothered, he needed it more than this bunch, had they just walked five miles up a mountain in the rain and darkness?

Was that a 'no' he heard? Exactly.

He sat down and gestured to the young lad, who came over with a smile and poured his 'usual' without asking. He placed it on the bar in front of Martin, who downed it and ordered another straight away, ignoring looks from the people nearby.

What the fuck was going on here anyway? The pub hadn't been this full since he had arrived, now he had to brush shoulders with people at the bar. It didn't sit well with him. At least he got a little enjoyment from the looks on their faces as they realised he was wet.

Catching sight of a leaflet on the bar jogged his memory. Some band had been organised for some dead poets birthday, Barns was it? He couldn't remember, and it didn't matter because he intended to be well out of the way before all that shit started. He enjoyed the next pint, savouring the hoppy smell and the way it slid down his stomach with its cold hands, throat thoroughly soothed.

It turned out he was going to watch the festivities after all as the pints kept coming and he relaxed a little. He even made banter with the young barman about making his way down the hill in the dark with no torch. Banter wasn't something Martin usually did, but tonight, after a lousy day it felt good, and tomorrow he would be going home. That felt good too. Finished with his fifth pint he went on to order another.

Chapter 26

The room was sparse. There was no telephone, no TV, not even a window. Nothing but the bed and the couple of chairs that the landlord had placed in the room while changing sheets and spraying floral air freshener. He apologised profusely saying the room had been stripped bare as it wasn't used, but Emmie couldn't have cared less. She was just happy that she and the children were safe for the night.

At that point, the kitchen had still been still open, and he had insisted they have a few sandwiches and chips rustled up as they settled. Emmie eventually agreed. He had no idea just how much she felt indebted to him even without the food, but he wouldn't take no for an answer. He was affable, made her feel welcome and at ease, but underneath she sensed a calm authority and confidence. Emmie knew that it was the move, and recent events, which had thrown her confidence, but his magnetism pulled her. There was an air about him that said everything would be okay, and if it weren't, he would make it so. She could have cried again she was so utterly grateful, and she would be back to pay him whether he liked it or not.

An hour later, relaxed, and with a full stomach, Emmie sat in one of the chairs. She thought about Bruadair and hoped that shadow man was gone in the morning. She also hoped he hadn't taken her bag and purse as he left or that would be another thing to sort out.

Grace was snoring softly in the middle of the bed. She had barely said a word all evening, but she had eaten and clapped out as only small children can do. Still, she would need to have a cuddle and a chat in the morning, who knew what she was thinking in her little head.

Charlie had been more bothered about Emmie. He was lying next to Grace on the edge of the bed watching her and chewing on the side of his mouth. They chatted about what they thought had happened and Emmie tried to put his mind at rest as the theories of thieves and monsters came from him thick and fast.

The band struck up next door promptly at 8pm. The landlord had been right, it was certainly noisy, but not loud enough to wake Grace or to keep Charlie up. He eventually he fell asleep too, and Emmie was left alone.

She turned the day over in her head. Grace and invisible man, and then shadow man at the door. It was exhausting and frightening trying to keep one step ahead of them. She thought of calling Natalie but didn't want to worry her. She thought of Amy, but couldn't deal with the positivity she would tell her to have right now. She would talk to Amy in the morning though, she decided, before she went back to the house. In daylight, everything would seem better.

With a small plan sorted she felt calmer but that left her where? Sitting here twiddling her thumbs until bed? She blew out a breath.

An idea came to her, and it wasn't one she liked much, but it may just save her sanity. She found a chewed pencil and an old till receipt in the pocket of her coat and wrote a note.

Gone to the bar for company. If you wake and need me just open the door, I'll be seated at the table opposite. I'll be watching the door so I know you're safe. Sweet Dreams. Mom xxx

She left the small piece of paper on her chair and hoped it would be there if they woke. If not they would open the door screaming for her and she would be right outside. No problem. Right?

She still felt guilty, but she couldn't sit in this room all night.

Taking one last look at the children, she opened the door and stepped out into the bar.

Emmie was immediately thrown by the sudden volume of people and noise. It would appear the room did have a little sound insulation after all.

To her left, past the bar, at the end of the long room, she could hear the band playing what sounded like some sort of jig. She couldn't see it for the mass of people that were stretched between her and them, but she could make out the sound of a fiddle, accordion and drum amongst other instruments.

The lounge was packed full. Old men sat with pints, feet tapping and head bobbing to the beat, women shouting and clapping, children making their own fun as they weaved in and out of the masses. The majority of the noise was coming from the centre of the room where chairs and tables had been pushed back to create a makeshift dance floor. A mass of people, young and old, were shouting and laughing, standing in a line either side of the space. In the middle arms were linked as dancers moved into the centre of the corridor twirling around each other in a whirl of colour and motion before moving back to the sides. Emmie watched hypnotised as the dancers moved up and down the line in elegant motion. She had no idea how these people knew where they were supposed to be, or how they knew it was their turn to link arms.

Everyone seemed to be getting into the spirit of the music, it was infectious, and Emmie felt a smile creep across her face. It was shame she couldn't join in, but tonight she had a door to watch and children to feel guilty about. Although, She was certainly up for relaxing and tapping her foot along with everyone else.

A cheer erupted around the room as the band finished the song and struck up a waltz. The dancing continued without pause, picking up the new slower rhythm perfectly. As men and women paired off and began circling the dance floor around each other, Emmie wondered whether the landlord would sub her another wine if she promised to cough up the money tomorrow - as long as shadow man hadn't taken her bag that was.

She found him at the centre of the bar area looking her way with a smile as he wiped a glass with a white tea towel. Her stomach flipped unexpectedly, and for the second time tonight she felt the blush rise up from her neck to her cheeks.

Bloody hell, Em, is this all it takes now? A man with a kind soul and nice eyes to make you go mushy? Stop over-dramatising just because he helped you out. And by the way, toots, you came in looking like a someone who had seen the Loch Ness monster, with no money to pay for room, food or drink, and proceeded to cry all over his bar. What a bloody catch you are, a regular Kate Winslett eh? ... and believe me, honey, you're going down with the ship, he wouldn't look twice. Get over yourself.

Catching his smile as nonchalantly as she could Emmie took a breath and went over to the bar. He met her at the only available space, by the curve, put the now sparkling wine glass in front of her, and immediately poured her a Merlot. Emmie was taken aback, she hadn't expected it to be quite so easy.

'Oh,' she stammered, feeling guilty, 'Please, you don't have to. I just needed to get out of the room for a while. The children are both, um, asleep so I was just going to sit on the end table and watch the door…'

She trailed off embarrassed as he grinned.

'There's a perfectly good band playing, and you'd rather watch a door?'

She looked at him shocked.

'Oh! No, I only meant-'

He let out a chuckle and cut her off as she struggled to explain herself.

'I know, I get it. You would never leave the bairns alone under normal circumstances, but it hasn't been a normal night for you has it, lass? You need the break.'

Emmie gaped at him unable to process how he had seemed to read her like a book, was she that transparent? On the other hand, she was also grateful that he wasn't judging her. He laid a warm hand on hers gently, sending her stomach skipping over and making her heart thump.

'Go and join in, the band will lift your spirits, the bairns are safe in that room, no one will get in or out without my knowing. I'll have the door in the corner of my eye all evening. You want any more drinks you just nod my way I'll sort you out.'

'Thank you,' Emmie said, moving her hand from under his to pick up the wine glass before her heart came out of her chest, 'But I'll just sit at the end by the door, I wrote a note saying that's where I'll be. I've always kept my word, and they know they can trust me. It's the one thing I won't compromise.' She looked up at him and saw he was nodding, assessing her curiously.

'The band are great though,' She said looking toward the stage area to escape his gaze, 'What kind did you say they were?'

He smiled leaning an arm on the bar in front of her.

'They're known as a Ceilidh band,' He was saying, 'They play traditional Scottish instruments usually although some of the newer bands will add in guitar and bass. These are a band we've used for the last six years on burns night. They're old-style, fiddle, flute, tin whistle, accordion but that's what our guests and locals have come to love and expect, It's always a big success.'

A lady approached the bar, and he signalled Emmie to wait as he served two double whiskeys. She listened to the soothing lilt of his voice, watched his hands, his gestures, his expressions, and her heart took up a steady gallop.

Oh, fuck off Em, please.

Then he was done, attention back on her.

'So, They're a what? ... Cayley band?' Emmie said as the warmth of his presence surrounded her again. She must have looked puzzled, thank god it was only puzzled, as the landlord started to laugh.

'Well lass, that's about as close as you'll get with your accent. Ceilidh is just an old term used for any social gathering really, but these days the main element is usually the dancing.'

'How do they know the steps? No one seems to miss a beat.'

'There are set dances to certain songs that's all. They're simple and a lot of fun.'

'It looks fun,' Emmie said smiling, 'any other time I might have had a go.'

She looked toward the door with a little regret.

'Aye, aye lass, that's what they all say.'

He laughed again and Emmie felt herself smiling, catching his infectious good mood, enjoying his company. The wine was loosening her up a little already.

'Don't you listen to him, dear. There's no rule says you have to join in, don't let him wind you up.'

Emmie turned and found herself looking at Edith from the store.

'Edith!' She said, with a little too much enthusiasm for someone she had only met a week ago 'It's good to see you.'

'And you too lass, nice to see you down here joining in with the celebrations. I wasn't sure if you'd know about it.' Edith looked at the landlord, 'White wine spritzer please, Stuart.'

The landlord grinned as he pushed his weight off the bar where he had been leaning.

'You'll drink yourself into an early grave on the hard stuff Edie.' He joked setting about filling a glass with lemonade.

'And I'll go a happy lady, 'she replied winking at Emmie. 'I have to walk myself home later I want to be able to climb the back stairs, young man.'

The landlord, Stuart as she now knew he was called, was topping up the glass with white wine at the rear of the bar. He turned frowning.

'No Len?' He said

'No Len,' Edith confirmed, 'His chest is just too bad at the moment. It has it's up days and down days. Today is a down day. He said to pass on his good wishes, he's sorry to miss the entertainment.'

Stuart put the glass in front of Edith and took the money putting it straight in the till.

'Still no Doctor?'

Edith sighed.

'He won't have it, Stu, he says he's just an old man with old lungs, but I think he's terrified of what they will find. I can't talk him around, so I just have to live with the moaning.'

Edith smiled but Emmie could see the pain in her eyes. She put a comforting hand on her arm as Stuart rest his hand over Edith's just as he had with her a few minutes before. She started to feel a little foolish she had thought there was something in it, and then she checked herself.

Get a grip Em please, don't make your life any more complicated than it is already. Falling for the local landlord because he was kind to you wasn't in the move to Scotland remit.

Edith took her hand from under Stuarts and gave it a pat as she looked at Emmie.

'You wouldn't like to keep an old lady company would you dear? I don't fancy the nonsense the ladies around here talk tonight. Everyone thinks you need to hear the gossip when you own the local store. Really? I can't abide it. Not many tables left now though I'm afraid, we certainly won't have the best view, but we can listen to the music anyway.' She scanned the room as Emmie nodded.

'How about this one at the back here? It's out of the bustle.' Stuart said, quickly pointing to the one directly opposite the door to her room. 'I have a spare chair out back.'

Edith nodded her approval, and Emmie smiled gratefully as Stuart winked at her. He moved out of a doorway at the back of the bar as

Edith and Emmie moved to the back table. Edith took a seat as Stuart appeared further down the hall with a chair. He brought it up to them and offered it for Emmie to sit down.

'Thank you,' She said looking up at him hoping that he understood that she meant for everything, including seating them here without going into the reason with Edith.

He smiled before leaning his solid frame down toward her. For one glorious, horrifying moment she thought he was going to kiss her right there in the middle of the pub, but he put his mouth only next to her ear to make himself heard.

'I didn't catch your name, lass,' he said

'Emelia,' she said, heart pounding, and getting a whiff of cologne. He smelt as good as he looked. 'but no-one calls me that, please call me Emmie.'

'A lovely name,' He said, 'Well, enjoy your first ceilidh, Emmie. Nod to the bar when you want a drink ladies.'

Then he was gone. Back behind the bar serving another gentleman and Emmie was left with the third blush of the evening rising up her neck.

Chapter 27

Martin Stomes felt he had never been happier. The lord was shining all the luck on him tonight, and this was nothing short of a miracle. Just as he had decided it was time to throw in the towel, guess who should turn up in person? Only the little lady herself, sitting at the back table enjoying the barn dance that was getting on his last nerve.

There she sat without a care in the world laughing and chatting with Mrs 'I don't know who you mean, dear' as plain as day. If he hadn't been so happy to catch another glimpse of Emmie, he would have been inclined to go over and wipe the smiles off their smug faces. Both of them.

And Ma Hubbard, she really had it coming after all the shit he'd been through. Lying, straight to his face? Well, tomorrow he might teach her a little lesson about lies.

Tonight, however, he needed to think of his next step. Emmie was here, and there was no way he was letting her out of his sight again until he had information, but for that, he needed to follow her home, or risk her finding out what Scott was up to. It sucked royally. He was shattered, and he'd been about to go up to his room to get a good nights sleep before the trip home.

Now, the game had suddenly changed again. He would have to stay here and watch until she made a move. He couldn't risk taking his eyes off her.

He placed his hat on the bar and pushed a hand through his hair as he glanced back over at her.

Shit. How surreal is this?

Swallowing the last of his pint, he signaled to the lad for another. He sipped at this one, the volume of liquid inside him forcing him to slow down as he watched Emmie.

They had known each other quite well at University, hung around in the same circles for a while. To be honest, he had always liked her, she was lively, down to earth, and easygoing, but after she started dating Scott that changed. Scott was ferociously jealous and absurdly controlling about who she mixed with, he had often wondered how a free spirit like Emmie had put up with him all these years. Maybe it was the sex, definitely the money.

He took another slug of beer. He wasn't sure if it was just the beer goggles, but he was enjoying watching her and he'd certainly had worse jobs than watching an attractive woman in a bar.

It was a little after 11pm when Emmie finally made a move. Ma Hubbard had left a few minutes before. Martin fleetingly thought about following her out to wring her neck, but dragged his attention back to the primary focus. Attention was something he was having a little trouble with now. Every time he moved his head the room seemed to continue to move after he had stopped. It was making him feel like he might throw up, but he knew he had to hold on a little longer.

How many had he had? He'd lost count at nine and that had seemed a good while ago now.

Oh well, at least he wasn't having to foot the bill, although he had a feeling he would be paying with different currency if he had to spend all night with his head in the toilet.

Martin was starting to think he may not hold out at all when Emmie finally got up, said something to the Landlord and went through the door at the side of the bar. A little investigation with the young barman told him that this was a guest room, so it would seem she was staying the night. At least that gave him a little lea way, he'd make sure he was down before she was out in the morning.

He said goodnight and slid off the stool, holding onto the bar as he swayed. Steadying himself, he let go and staggered through the emptying bar, past Emmie's room, and down the hallway using the wall for support. He stopped at the stairs at the back of the pub and took a moment to figure out how they worked before climbing them to his room. He stabbed at the door with the key several times before unlocking it, and kicked it shut behind him as he entered. On the floor by the window was his phone where it still lay after he had thrown it. He stumbled, landing on his knees next to it and swiped at the screen.

11 missed calls

All of them Scott.

Well, who else called him these days? He thought about pressing redial, but then his stomach lurched. He crawled toward the bathroom on his hands and knees. It seemed his session conversing with the toilet would be starting early tonight.

Chapter 28

Emmie would have called it a night after the band finished playing a little after 9.30pm, but Edith turned out to be good company. She felt normal for the first time since the move and a weight lifted off her shoulders as she sipped her wine, chatted and laughed.

They hadn't asked, but even in the busyness of the evening, Stuart had brought a further two drinks over to them, each time checking they were okay and asking if they needed anything else. When Emmie had mentioned to Edith that he didn't seem to be waiting tables for anyone else, Edith had merely nodded.

'Aye. He does seem to want to look after us doesn't he, dear?' She chuckled looking fondly over at Stuart, who was laughing with a blonde woman at the bar. 'He's a good man, salt of the earth. He'd give you the coat right off his back in a monsoon if he thought you needed it. Handsome too, What I couldn't do with him if I were thirty years younger.'

That had set Emmie off into surprised laughter, and she could have kissed Edith for it. She hadn't laughed properly for weeks. After that, the laughs had kept coming and the night had flown by. She felt content, and for the first time since she had moved to Scotland, she felt as though she had made the right move and was finally meeting some genuinely nice people.

Here in the guest house, she felt safe, she wasn't on edge. She was the one under a watchful eye for a change, and she hadn't realised how much she needed it, how much the house took out of her up there on its own with no one to call for help. Coming here had been a good move, she had managed to put the house to the back of her mind, and the children had settled just fine.

Back inside the room, Charlie and Grace didn't seem to have moved. Emmie picked up a couple of extra blankets from on one of the chairs. She placed one over Charlie, now at the bottom of the bed, and put the other over her knees as she settled in the chair. Not comfortable, but safe, and that was enough for tonight. She curled her legs up under her and fell into a deep dreamless sleep for the first time since she had arrived in Scotland.

The next morning Emmie took Charlie and Grace for a walk up the falls with the sole purpose of calling Amy in privacy. Full of the beautiful breakfast that Stuart had kindly left outside the door with a knock at around 10am, the children were high in spirits, Emmie on the other hand, hadn't eaten a thing, her stomach churning at the thought of going back home.

Grace seemed to have forgotten any ill feelings from yesterday and was back to her usual chattering as they climbed. Charlie had a smile on his face too, although she knew he kept looking back to check she was okay. Each time she made sure to smile, to reassure him, and wave him on ahead.

The morning was dense with mist. The higher they climbed, the thicker it became, their coats and trousers wet within minutes, but the children seemed oblivious. The track was steep and slippery in places, and the drops were high, but it was well fenced and Charlie devoted all of his attention to keeping Grace safe as they climbed. It should have been doing them all good, but Emmie couldn't shake the uneasy feeling that followed her.

At the top, the fenced route came to a stop right over the gushing water which spurted from a large cave in the cliff below. There was a wooden bench here where she supposed many people had sat taking in the glorious view as the water fell underneath them from a dizzying height. Today they couldn't see the bottom. Even from halfway up trees seemed to appear stealthily, rising up out of the grey like ghosts, tops but no bottoms.

The children went up further into the woodland where they busied themselves with a makeshift tree swing attached to an oak. Emmie sat on the bench and watched them as she took out her phone with frozen hands. She held it in front of her checking the signal. Only one bar, she crossed her fingers that it would connect as she pressed Amy's contact. The phone rang, crackling, once, twice, three times.

Come on Amy where are you? Your phone is always glued to your hand. Pick up. Please.

The answering machine cut in and Emmie was about to leave a message when she realised she didn't know what to say. She hit 'End' and tried again. It rang long enough that she was convinced the answering machine would cut in again when Amy answered.

'Hello?' She croaked.

'Amy? It's me.' Emmie was unbelievably happy to hear Amy's voice, but Amy sounded a little confused.

'Me who?' She said yawning

'Amy, it's Emmie, surely you haven't forgotten me already!'

Amy coughed and suddenly sounded brighter although Emmie wasn't too sure it was genuine.

'Em! Gosh, wow. It's good to hear from you, how are you getting on up there in bonnie Scotland?'

Gosh? Wow?

Emmie couldn't remember if those two words had ever been in Amy's vocabulary. Something was going on.

'Yeah, ok,' She said, 'Whats up with you? You sound a little weird.'

'Weird how?'

'I don't know Ames, distracted? Whats up?'

Amy let out a long sigh.

'Christ Em, you know me too bloody well. Okay, I admit I was distracted when you first called, but you have my full attention now, I promise. How have you been?'

Emmie wasn't prepared to let her off that easily. Amy was up to something, probably in somebody's bed. She grinned.

'Who is it?'

'Who's who?'

'Who's bed are you in? Don't tell me, you finally conquered Alex Hanson?'

'Nope, you lose Ems, I'm in no-ones bed, alas, I'm sleeping alone.'

'I don't believe you. You're barely talking above a whisper, and you live alone. So where for art thou and with whom?'

Amy blew out a breath and laughed lightly.

'Oh for fuck sake, you win. Yes, I conquered Alex. Was he worth waiting for? Absolutely. He is freaking hot in bed Ems shame you dated him before you could find out what a kinky shit he was. Okay?

Satisfied?'

She heard the glee in Amy's voice and knew the little smile that would be on her face right now. Emmie laughed.

'Satisfied, thank you. You can't get one over on me even at 800 miles away. I am sorry I interrupted your hot session though, really.'

Amy was laughing too and finally sounding like herself.

'We were asleep Ems, truly, I was trying not to wake him, but he's gone to the bathroom now anyway. How are you doing? It's so good to hear your voice, how long has it been?

'Couple of weeks.'

Really? It seems like years, we need to speak more often, honey. There's so much I have to tell you! Where shall I start?' Amy took a breath and without waiting for an answer ploughed on at a hundred miles an hour, 'Ok, well, Laura Shutford at the magazine was officially fired last Tuesday, can you believe it? Miss goody two shoes, fired for stealing feature parts from the magazine for her own blog, whole *chunks* of it were out in cyberspace before the magazine left the editing desk. I'd say I was sad but... I'm now officially a Graphic Designer, how about that for kooky? They needed someone to fill in straight away and decided I was the person to step up until interviews can take place. They've almost as good as told me the jobs mine anyway interviews are a formality...'

We really do need to speak more often, Emmie thought, as Amy gushed on. She watched Grace try to push Charlie on the thin stick seat, and life suddenly seemed a lot slower up here, the fast pace of Amy's chatter was fogging her head. She tried to keep up but couldn't concentrate. It wasn't Amy's fault, Emmie just had a lot more on her plate right now than some girl getting fired. She was pleased that Amy got her promotion though, she had been working toward it for the last three years.

'Are you okay, Em? You seem quiet.'

Amy stopped talking, and the silence drew Emmie back from her thoughts.

'Sorry, what?'

'You're not okay, are you? I knew this was a step too far for you. There's no-one up there you can talk to, and it must be super lonely in that house. I couldn't deal with the lack of people either. You're a socialite, like me, you should be home Ems, you need people, come back.'

The fact that Amy thought she couldn't cope stung a little and instantly made her defensive. Tears welled in her eyes again and not for the first time she wondered what had made her move so far from her friends and family.

All I've managed to do since I got here is look over my shoulder, jump at my own shadow, scare myself and the kids, and cry. I feel like I should have moved into an asylum.

'I can't Amy,' She said, 'I'm in a mess I need to get out of before I can think of what my next step is.'

'Mess? What are you talking about? It's not a mess it's simple, sweetie, put the house on the market and come home. A and B, there's not even a C to complicate the equation.'

Emmie sighed. If she didn't come out and say it, she feared she wouldn't be able to get it out at all. She took a deep breath, now or never.

'I can't Amy, it's not about the place. I love it up here I really do. I'm doing okay, and I've met a couple of really great people. My problem is the house, or rather who is watching us in it.'

Amy sighed sounding frustrated until she fully registered what Emmie had just said.

'What did you say? Someone is watching you?... Who would be watching you at the house?'

'If I knew that I wouldn't be in this situation would I? I had to stay in a guest house in the village last night because whoever this man is broke into the house when we were there yesterday evening.'

'Holy shit Ems! are you serious? I thought the house was in the middle of nowhere how could someone break in? And why would they bother? You have nothing anyway!'

The second dig. Emmie sighed but decided to ignore it. Why was she so touchy anyway? Amy had never been tactful it was the thing that got her into the most trouble. She had been like it forever, why was it bothering her so much now?

'I don't think he's breaking in as an opportunist Amy, he's been watching us. I've seen him outside a couple of times, but I decided just to draw the curtains, lock the doors and ignore him. Thing is he was around the back of the house yesterday. Grace and Charlie saw him too. I got them into the living room out of sight, but when I got back to the sunroom, he had gone, and the French doors were open.'

'Open?'

'Well, not open. Unlocked, I mean.'

'So not open. So you don't actually know if he came into the house? Did you check everywhere?'

'No, I didn't check anywhere. My first thought was to get out of there in case we got hurt, I managed to have a quick glance around, but then we left and went to the village.'

'Did you see or hear anything? Anyone sneaking around I mean, a creaky floorboard, that sort of stuff?'

'No, I guess I didn't.'

'Right, so maybe you got it wrong and he left after scaring the kids? Let's face it if he wanted to attack you what was he waiting for? You'd already seen him by the doors, so why would he sneak around hiding? I mean how many intruders are silent anyway?'

Dead ones?

Emmie rubbed her forehead with her free hand and thought. A ghostly intruder was a ridiculous idea, and ghosts aside, Amy was right the door was still closed. He could have gotten in when she was knocked out, but the children would have heard. Charlie did say Grace was crying though so maybe not. That left her with approximately... nothing solid.

Oh, Christ, this is driving me nuts. Did I even lock the door? Is all this happening because I left the door open and scared myself and everyone else long after he had run off? Amy's right, I heard nothing and saw no evidence other than an unlocked door. I need to get a grip. He probably never entered the house.

'Emmie? You still there?'

'Yeah, I was just thinking. Maybe you're right, you know,' She blew out a breath. A headache was starting to brew. This was getting her nowhere, she needed to go home. Get this whole thing over with. 'I don't really have any evidence that anyone entered the house other than a shut door. Which, out loud, sounds ridiculous. I should just get home and check it out I'm not sure why it got so out of hand last night.'

'Well, someone is watching the house remember, so I'd say your first port of call is the police. I'm not sure why you haven't called them already, Em.'

'What and sound like a lunatic? What can the police do? It's not like they can send a patrol up the lane every 10 minutes and I'm sure they have better things to do than sit at the front of my house for days until he decides to come back. Which he won't if there's police sitting there.' She sighed frustrated, anger climbing up from her gut. 'It's just stupid Amy, I need to find out who the hell it is and why he's scaring us.'

'I know it seems hopeless. Please don't go confronting anyone by yourself in the dark though.'

'Nah, it's too damn scary at night. If I see him in the day though … then I'll kick his bloody arse.'

Amy chuckled on the other end of the line.

'Give him one from me too. Where are you now? Still at the guest house?

'The guest house, yeah.'

'Good, so is there anyone you can take with you to check the house? I'd feel better if you had someone with you, Em.'

Emmie thought about Stuart. It would be good to have a man around when she checked, especially one of his size and build, but there was no way in the world she was asking him for anything else after yesterday.

'Not really.' She replied.

'No-one? Come on Em, what about those people you've met?'

'Well, Edith has to be in her sixties so I don't think she'd be much help, she runs a shop but I reckon she would come if I asked.'

'A sixty-year-old? Jesus, Em, no parties for you up there, eh?'

Emmie thought about last night and the Ceilidh. She supposed it was a far cry from dancing on bars in clubs as she and Amy used to do but she'd still had fun. Maybe that was only compounded by the fact that she had been so unsteady. It was funny that Amy had been on the phone for less than ten minutes and was already managing to make her question her life up here and whether she was actually capable of living it.

'Well, there's the landlord of the guest house, but he'll be busy I should think.'

'He. That's a good start. You could do with a male presence, please tell me he's not 70 and walks on sticks?'

Emmie smiled in spite of herself.

'No, he's early forties I would say. Has some muscle too. But like I say I really don't want to ask him, he'll be busy, and he's done so much for us already.'

And let's face it that would be one step too far on the embarrassment meter. The man already has good reason to think I'm nutty as a fruitcake.

'Done so much like what, Em? Let you a room? That's what a guest house is.'

'Yes, but it was Burns night, and he didn't have a room left -'

Amy cut her off.

'Burn night? Whats that? Like our bonfire night?'

Emmie sighed rolling her eyes. How was it possible that Amy could get on her nerves even after not speaking for so long? Sometimes she felt she was decades older than her friend who seemed to be eternally fifteen even at thirty-four. At home, it had been endearing, but now it was starting to get on her nerves.

'No Amy, it's a Scottish celebration with music and dancing and stuff.'

'So where did you stay then if there wasn't a room?'

'He sorted an old room out for us as I was in a state, and then I had no money, so he let us have it for free. Then he fed us, plied me with wine all night, and came out with a lovely breakfast this morning. All for free. So no Amy, I am not asking him to do any more for me today.'

'All that for free? Christ Em, did you bat those baby blues at him or what? Snap him up, he may be the only man for miles around. He probably has women throwing themselves over the bar at him if he's the only one under 60 and you don't want to be a spinster for the rest of your life!'

Emmie stood to shake off the cold that was starting to seep into her bones. She walked to the edge of the railings, glanced back to make sure the kids were still in view and looked down at the waterfall watching the water cascade and tumble down the rock into a never-ending grey.

RUIN

He quite probably did have women throwing themselves over the bar at him, she thought, and that was why she was going home, coming back to pay up and not coming here again. She wouldn't put herself through it. She didn't need a man in her life at the moment, and she certainly wasn't up to flirting with one. On the other hand, she wasn't up to watching anyone else flirt with him either so she would stay away, it was simple. He's probably married anyway, she thought, although she hadn't seen a ring and he had said something about running the place with his son.

Emmie realised that Amy was still chattering and tried to bring her attention back to the conversation.

'… left anyway. So what are you going to do?' Amy was saying.

'Go back to the house, check it's secure, live my life. What else can I do Amy?'

'Find someone -'

'There *isn't* anyone, and I'm not calling the police. Look it's cold Ames, I'm going to go and get back, it's no use sitting around here putting it off. I need to go get the kids warm. We're still in last nights clothes, and Charlie has only brought a thin jacket. He'll catch his death if I stay much longer.'

Amy paused and took a breath before blowing it out.

'Ems, please, if you think there may be a chance that someone did get in please don't go there alone. I don't need to hear they've found your body on the news.'

Just another to add to the Bruadair book of the dead, eh?

'Amy I'll be fine. I think you were right. It's probably nothing.'

Amy giggled and made shushing noises down the phone.

'Get off, I'm on the phone,' She laughed again and then paused, 'Ok, When you come back, honey,' She said in her best sultry voice.

Emmie waited, slightly jealous of the affection, and the normality of Amy's life right now. She could put the phone down and carry on enjoying herself. Emmie knew she probably wouldn't even cross Amy's mind. After a lot of shuffling, a gasp and a giggle, Amy was back.

'Call me. Right after you've checked it out. Please. I need to know you're safe.'

'I will, 'Emmie replied, 'I promise.'

'OK sweetie, I'm worried, be careful.'

The careful pitched up as Amy convulsed into giggles again and suddenly Emmie didn't want to hear any more.

'Bye,' She whispered. She pressed the End button without waiting for an answer, vision blurring. No, she thought, rubbing away a stray tear. She wouldn't cry again, not today. She sniffed, tilting her chin up in defiance at her own emotions before turning to call Grace and Charlie back from the swing. It was as good as sorted anyway, she had to go back home, there was no other option.

Chapter 29

Martin woke with a banging head and a throat full of fuzz. He coughed trying to clear his throat and found all he could taste was vomit. His stomach hitched and roiled. He needed water before he lost any more of his stomach to the toilet.

Swinging his legs out of the side of the bed he lay waiting for the rest of him to comply before getting up. Every inch of his body complained and cried out for him to lie back down and go to sleep, but Martin had a mission.

Somewhere, buried deep in his mind, he knew this was a fact - although what his mission was he couldn't quite remember.

He rubbed his aching head and stumbled to the bathroom where his old friends water and paracetamol resided. He needed to clear his head. He needed to think. And he needed to get rid of the shitty taste of sour vomit.

Grabbing the glass and a couple of the tablets, he threw his head back to throw them down the hatch and threw himself off balance. He staggered backwards, fingers only just grasping the basin for support.

Fuck! Well, turns out it ain't the beer that'll kill you it's taking over the counter fucking medication. Who knew?

He laughed at his wit before placing the pills on his tongue and drinking the water greedily only stopping when his stomach cramped and rumbled threatening to re-release its contents.

Putting the cup back down, he looked at himself in the cabinet mirror.

Dude, you look like shit man.

He put both hands on the basin and leaned in closer wrinkling his nose and moving his jaw around. Why did parts of his face feel numb? He poked at his cheeks with his fingers and checked out what appeared to be mud under his chin.

What the fuck? How many did I have? Must have been a cracker of a night Marti-boy, hope you enjoyed it cause I can't remember it for shit.

He filled the basin and splashed cold water over his face and hair washing off the mud and reviving his senses. Towelling off he shuffled delicately back into the bedroom. Every bone in his body seemed to ache and scream as he pulled out his last fresh t-shirt and jeans, and when he came to his trainers, his best fucking trainers, they were filthy and soaked through. He stared at them.

What is going on here? Where did I go? What did I do?

Martin groaned. He didn't need the answer. He was going to lie down on the bed and take a little nap. His head throbbed, he needed to get these tablets in his system.

Settling back on the bed, he closed his eyes.

Something niggled. There was something he had to do. He tried to focus.

Memories came back slowly, flashes of trekking up a mountain in the rain. Of a house.

That little house made his heart thump although he couldn't think why. Then the dark forest. The whisper of leaves in the canopy, feet crunching on bracken, and the rush of water, the intense fear that he would be eaten alive or fall off the edge of the cliff to his death.

Martin's eyes flew open. He sat up quickly making his head spin, his breathing ragged, heart beating double time.

Was it a dream?

His trainers and the ache in his body implied otherwise and a sense of foreboding crept up his spine. He climbed off the bed and checked his coat, crumpled on the floor, wet and muddy, as were his jeans underneath it. He stared at them as though they were alien.

What had hell had he been doing?

He sat back on the bed putting his head in his hands. He hadn't done anything terrible - had he? He did remember getting overly frustrated with the lady in the shop yesterday, and he'd always had a temper, but shit, he wouldn't have bumped her off in the night would he?

Would he?

With enough beer in him *could* he?

He wasn't sure now that he had lost all memory. How many times had he lost all memory before? Many. It hadn't seemed to matter, but maybe it did matter, perhaps he had bumped off loads of people who had pissed him off.

Blood chorusing in his ears he tried to backtrack. How had he got back to the guest house, and his room? He couldn't piece it together. He needed a cigarette and he suddenly had the urge to visit the little shop next door. Just to see if she was still there.

The phone rang. Buzzing on the floor just under the window. Martin glanced at it frustrated, willing it to shut the hell up, and then it came back to him fast and furious.

The phone. The god-damn phone.

That was it. He had thrown the phone in temper and then gone for a walk. He had got lost on the mountain in the dark. The house had seemed sinister and the woods even more so, but that was all in his mind. He had been for a walk, got lost and had a drink when he got back. The memory of that agonising thirst and that first drink of beer flooding through him.

The phone cut off and lay silent. Martin barely noticed.

That's right, there was some shitty band on and people being far too loud and close. And oh, here it was, the bit that almost made him woozy with relief, the little lady from next door had been there. He hadn't bumped her off ladies and gents, oh no, she had been alive and well, drinking in the bar. He'd seen her at the end table with Emmie.

His mind staggered to a halt. He reeled, stunned, mouth dropping open.

That was it. Emmie had been here, like a fucking apparition, not only drinking but *staying* here. He was supposed to get up early before he lost her again.

Shit. Shit. Shit. What fucking time is it?

He threw himself off the bed ignoring his protesting body and launched for his phone swiping at the screen. 12.34pm flashed back at him. He blinked, then roared in frustration throwing the phone back down.

He pulled on his spare trainers and one of his thickest jumpers, his coat would be out of the question today, but hopefully, he wouldn't need it. His hand was reaching for the door handle when the phone started to ring again. He thumped his fist into the door frame with a grunt and went to pick up the phone.

Scott.

Martin knew he would be majorly pissed off by now, but he didn't need to miss Emmie leaving either. His head was waging war inside his skull, it felt like knives above his eyes, he needed to smoke. He hobbled over to the TV stand and found his packet of cigarettes and his lighter. He pulled one out and lit it inhaling deeply. The phone rang off and immediately started to ring again. Walking to the window and opening the little section at the top, (he didn't need to be thrown out of the non-smoking guest house right now), he aimed the smoke toward the little opening and looked down.

Emmie's car was still in the car park.

He felt a surge of triumph but knew he had to make this call quick. Clenching his teeth, he swiped to answer and held the phone to his ear saying nothing. Eventually, Scott spoke.

'Martin? Are you there?'

'Yep.'

And that was all it took for Scott to let rip.

'What the fuck are you playing at? Do you know how many times I've tried to call you? I hear nothing for two days, and then you play deaf with me? I don't think you realise I'm stuck down here going out of my *fucking* mind.'

Martin held the phone slightly away from his ear staring at the Honda. Scott was more than pissed off, he was livid, but Martin would bide his time while he had the car in view. The game would turn when he told Scott the news, for now, he'd let him rant, maybe he'd blow an artery in the process and do Martin a favour, then he could get out of this dump.

'Where the fuck have you been? Why weren't you answering my calls? I gave you a new phone so that we could be in contact at all times. AT ALL TIMES, that includes 2am, 3am and 5am if I need you. If I'd have known you were going to be such a useless piece of shit I'd have found another society dropout to do the job for me. I thought you could handle this. You said you could find her. Now what the FUCK is going on? You'll tell me now or I shall be up there in a matter of hours looking to gut you like a fish. This isn't a free holiday, Stomes, this is serious shit. I need you to find her.'

'I'm looking at her car as we speak.'

Martin heard him take a breath; his trail of anger abruptly cut short. Martin smiled utterly calm. Cigarette finished, he flicked it out of the window reached down into the packet and drew out the last one lighting it during the silence.

Oh yeah, see? Didn't expect that did you Scotty boy. Fucking asshole, who the fuck do you think you are? Prick.

'You found her?'

'Oh, I found her alright. Sorry I missed your calls and all that. I Forgot what a hoot she could be, what a fucking party girl, drank together until late. Spent the night together. Woah I got to tell ya …'

Martin trailed off blowing out a low whistle and thought he could almost hear the punch land all the way down in Surrey. It hit Scott right where it hurt, and it hit good. His voice came back low and menacing.

'You slimy piece of fucking scumbag shit, if you've so much as touched a hair on her head you'd better be watching your back. I will find you, and I will kill you, do you hear me? All you had to do was find her, tell me where she was and come back. That, Stomes, was your FUCKING mission. Not to get into the pants of my fucking wife!'

'Ex-wife, Scott. Ex.'

It tumbled from his lips before he had thought it through and Martin immediately regretted pushing too far. A guttural sound came back down the phone, almost inhuman. He'd heard Scott's temper many times, but this was on another level. Martin took another drag of his cigarette with a shaking hand and thanked the good lord that Scott was all the way down in Surrey.

'I don't give a fuck if she's my ex, Martin. You weren't to get close to her, not to touch her, not to think about her. She belongs to me. *Only* me. I want to know where the fuck she is. I'm coming up there, Martin and you'd better be long fucking gone, or I'll be using your balls for paperweights.'

Martin swallowed hard, time to relay information and calm Scott down. It had been an error of judgement, but he'd had a heavy night, he blamed the beer. Turning to rest his backside on the low window sill he looked at his room and prepared to eat his own words.

'Okay, okay, Scott calm down. I was winding you up. I've had a breakthrough; I was on a high, just getting carried away that's all. I'm sorry. Of course I know what my job is, and I'm doing it well. I've almost got her now. When I said we slept and drank together I only meant under the same roof. She was here at the guest house last night, she's still here, and I know of someone who has information too. I can follow her, or I can pursue this lady, either way, I can do this. I will get you the information by tonight, and she will be none the wiser, I promise.'

Scott was silent. Martin didn't know if that was worse than the barrage of anger, or maybe he had popped an artery after all. But then he was back, angry but controlled.

'I should tell you that my humour level is nil where Emelia is concerned. When this is over Martin, you will take great care to make sure you avoid me, and her, at all costs. I want to know where she is, an address, by tonight when you will call me for the last time before you fuck off out of my life for good. You always wanted to play around with my shit Martin, just because you couldn't get off your drunk arse and do something for yourself. I know where you live; if I so much as hear a whisper of your name when this is over I will find you, and I will kill you. You can take that as a direct threat man to man.'

The call ended abruptly, and tremors gripped Martin. A bead of sweat had formed on his top lip. He swiped at it and swallowed hard. He was wrong about Scott, dead wrong. He didn't only have a control problem he had a whole heap of anger issues too.

He almost felt sorry for Emmie, but given his life being at possible risk, and he fully believed Scott was capable, Martin would do just as he said. Get the information and leave. He wanted out of Scott's world for good.

He fumbled for his cigarettes and found the packet empty. Thumping it flat against the window sill he turned back to the window where his heart instantly ratcheted up another gear.

No! No, No, NO, NO!

This couldn't be happening. Deja vu flooding through him, he thumped on the window with a howl and sprinted for the door as Emmie's car disappeared out of the car park.

Chapter 30

Down in Surrey, Scott Harvington decided he was through with Martin Stomes. The phone call had put Emelia within touching distance yet he still knew nothing. How was that possible?

It was fucking simple. He needed to know where the hell she was. She could not be left to run around Scotland all by herself, living it up guilt free, after all she had put him through, he simply wouldn't allow it.

There was no other option. Scott was going to have to go to Scotland himself. His body still shook with anger after the call, and after the little stunt Martin had just pulled, tearing him slowly limb from limb may be higher on the list than finding Emelia right now.

His thumb hovered over the dial button to inform Martin that he could fuck off, but then he paused. No; he wouldn't contact again. If Martin found anything more he would be straight on the phone licking his ass which would make his job easier, until then he was past arguing with him. Let him sit in fear wondering where he stood in the game and Scott would enjoy the look of surprise on his face when he arrived.

He grinned and placed the phone back on the table. Much better.

He looked at the clock. 1.05pm.

Where the fuck has that gone?

Annoyed that he had already wasted so much of the day he dressed quickly and shook the redhead who had spent the last few weeks in his bed. As he watched her pout, he almost shuddered with disgust. She had pursued him doggedly after he had thrown Emmie out, telling him to move on. He had only given in to abate his craving for a woman. Sex, not companionship. He didn't need a relationship, in that sense she was meaningless to him, but sex released tension. He knew there would come a point when he had sampled enough of her, and with Emelia back in touching distance that point had come about now.

'Get up,' he said, 'it's time to go.'

'Aww, baby, it's Saturday, and it's cold out there.' She looked at him, pretty green eyes under thick false lashes as she pushed her lips into a pout. 'Come and see how hot it can get in here.'

She pawed at him trying to lure him back to bed, but he was immovable. He had only one thing on his mind now. Emelia.

He pushed her away, jerking his thumb toward the door.

'Out.'

At the wardrobe, he threw some clothes in a holdall ignoring her pleas, but she was starting to irritate him, and she still wasn't getting out of his fucking bed.

He stalked past her to the bathroom where he washed, brushed his teeth and styled his short dark hair neatly with gel before checking his appearance in the mirror. He eyed the little white pill bottle on the side of the sink. Calcium channel blockers. Maybe he should throw them in his bag as he didn't know how long he would be gone?

He wrinkled his nose. He hadn't taken more than a handful since he had been diagnosed with hypertension three years ago. He knew the diagnosis was bullshit. He was in excellent health. There was no way someone like him had high blood pressure it was laughable. He didn't need the pills any more than he needed a velvet dog turd.

Striding back to the bedroom he picked up his bag, and threw it over his shoulder. Without saying a word he grabbed the girls clothes with one hand, and with the other he dragged her out of bed and down the stairs naked. She pleaded, pouted and moaned the whole way, until he threw her on the settee where she giggled and bit her lip, one hand moving provocatively between her legs. His temper surged as he dumped her clothes on top of her.

'This is not a fucking joke. Get dressed, get the hell out of my house, and while we're at it don't bother coming back. I don't need you, and I don't want you. You're a cheap slut good for a shag and nothing more. It's been fun. It's over. Time to go.'

Shock registered on her face, mouth falling open as tears filled her eyes.

'But, Scott, I … you … I don't understand … I thought this was more! I love you, and you love me I know you do, I can see ...'

Scott laughed, harsh and clipped.

'I don't love you, Amy, I assure you. I'm not even sure I like you. I liked what you had to offer that's all. You can't fill Emelia's shoes; you're a fool if you think I ever thought of you like that. Even being the infuriating, insolent, demented bitch that she is you don't compare. You never will.'

He watched Amy's face crumple. She cried and pleaded as she dressed.

Slowly - making his blood boil.

He wondered how this woman had anything in common with Emelia, how she had tolerated Amy's whining and neediness. Amy looked at him, one false lash now sitting attractively on her cheek.

'You're going after her aren't you? She was never good enough for you, Scott.' She pulled a t-shirt down over her head momentarily hiding her tear-streaked face, 'She messed you around, took your kids, fucked up your god-damn life. Leave her to it if she wants to move away. Why do you need to chase her up there? Why? She's not worth it. She doesn't deserve you. We're good together Scott. I'll change, I promise, I'll give you everything you need and more. I love you, I always loved you, much more than she ever did, remember that.'

He didn't answer. Face set in stone, he watched as she arranged the t-shirt around her waist and pulled on heeled sandals, then he followed her out of the door, throwing his bag into the back of the BMW, taking care not to look at her as she walked down the driveway.

Her speech had set him on edge, dredging up memories he'd rather forget. Climbing into the driver's seat, he shook his head, scrubbing the words away as he tried to think, hands gripping the steering wheel. He needed to calm down. Focus.

Running up to Scotland was all well and good but where did that get him? He had the name of the village and the place that Martin was staying, where Martin had run up a very extravagant bill too, thank you for *that* asshole. But that left him no further forward than Martin, unless Emelia was still at the guest house when he arrived, which he doubted. No, he was sure she would have gone home by now.

Home.

Where is 'home' Emelia?

He could run up to Bracken Hill and sort Martin out sure, and while that would be very satisfying he couldn't stay up there to find her, he would already be in trouble with his boss if he missed getting back for work on Monday, and to jeopardise his job for her was not an option. He wouldn't allow her to take that from him as well.

He placed his head on his hands on top of the steering wheel, eyes closed, jaw clenched.

A thought slipped into his mind, and he looked back up and out through the windscreen with a frown.

The phone call.

He had dismissed the phone call to Amy this morning. He hadn't been aware that Emelia had been on the phone until Amy had hung up, and at his interest she had played coy. She had already told him she had no idea of Emelia's address; lost it she said. Or maybe she was being facetious as any mention of Emelia made her pout. But he *had* got the gist from Amy's side of the call that Emelia had been worried about something, enough that Amy had asked her to call her back.

He kicked himself for not listening harder, and for thinking so little of it that he hadn't forced Amy to tell him before he threw her out.

But maybe he could use what information he did have to his advantage. If Amy wasn't willing to play ball, there was someone else he could play with. She was a tougher nut to crack, but he only had to break her enough and Emelia would be his. He would need to be careful not to arouse suspicion and give her cause to tell Emelia of his visit, but he thought the benefit outweighed the risk.

Scott grinned at his own genius as he got back out of the car. He needed a coffee while he planned his next move, and this time he wasn't willing to come away without information. This time he would push until he had what he wanted.

Chapter 31

As Emmie was driving slowly up the road listening to nursery rhymes, Martin Stomes was fully out of control. He stumbled out of his room and sprinted down the stairs into the main lounge corridor. He used the fire escape into the car park instead of running the length of the pub, the alarm sounding in his ears as the door crashed shut behind him. He sprinted for the road and came to a skidding stop on the path, panting hard.

The road was clear, but he could still smell the exhaust fumes. So close. His battered old fiesta sat in the car park but it would do him no good now, he couldn't even tell which way she had gone.

'Fuck!' He screamed into the misty air fists clenched by his sides.

An elderly lady walking his way hesitated, staring at him before crossing the road, and carrying on up the other side. Something about this act struck him as hilarious.

'Oh, What? You think I'm the bad guy? You wait till you see the bad guy, lady, I'm a pussycat by comparison. You have no idea what's coming to tear up your shitty little village.'

The lady gave a sideways glance and scurried on. Martin leaned against the front facade of the pub and laughed until his sides ached. He was in the shit now, he knew it. Emmie had gone, he had missed her by inches - no millimetres - and it wasn't even his god damn fault.

If Scott hadn't phoned at that instant; if he hadn't answered, as he hadn't the previous twenty-five calls, he would have her now. He could have been tailing her to wherever she was hiding out. Now Scott would be coming up to eat his dick for dinner because Emmie had gone, and there was nothing else Martin could tell him. Nothing he could do.

He needed a cigarette.

He checked his pockets, where he found a ten-pound note, and as he turned to the general store, he remembered there *was* something he could do.

Hell yes.

The little lady could no longer tell him she didn't know who he was talking about. He had seen them together. Watched them drinking and laughing. And now she was about to help him further his investigation.

Adrenaline spiking, he threw the little shop door open with a grin and strode purposefully inside.

Chapter 32

The children had laughed most of the way back in the car, Charlie playing rhyming games with Grace; 'What rhymes with tree?' 'Wee!' Grace had declared reducing them both into fits of giggles. Emmie would have enjoyed joining in with them had she been on her way to anywhere else in the world, but uneasiness had settled in, moving a chill up her spine that refused to leave. If Charlie felt the same sense of foreboding, he didn't show it. He seemed relaxed, full of confidence that Emmie had everything under control.

If only she could convince herself.

'I'm hungry, mommy.' Grace said.

'Hungry?' Emmie joked with forced cheer, 'after all that breakfast you ate? How can you fit any more in your little tummy, Grace, you'll pop!'

Grace laughed.

'Like pig!' She said, referring to her favourite game 'pig goes pop'. Grace loved it but would never play properly, much to Charlie's annoyance. She just wanted the pig to get fat and explode. Such were the intelligent games of modern day. Emmie smiled.

'That's right, Just like pig. Only you'll make more mess.'

Grace wrinkled her nose as Charlie laughed, and then she asked for her 'tunes', which meant singing to nursery rhymes all the way home. Grace insisted. Charlie rolled his eyes, but he carried on singing good naturedly, all the same.

Emmie preferred the chatter, it took her mind off the job at hand.

All too soon their lane came into view. Taking a deep breath, Emmie swung onto the narrow track, driving more slowly than necessary, until Bruadair appeared, ghost like, out of the murk.

The house sat passive, inoffensive, blank windows looking out over the tangled garden. The trees swayed in a firm, gusting breeze and the sun appeared from behind a cloud, giving the landscape a brief cheery tone. Emmie felt something give in her stomach as she looked at her little house. It was stunning up here. She was so lucky.

The comforting sensation of coming home was quickly replaced by a surge of anger.

This was her house, her home. How dare someone step onto her property and make her feel unsafe? Who the hell was this man, and what did he want?

Emmie became aware of Bill's land rover parked on the grass. She could hear Brutus barking over the nursery rhymes.

She rolled her eyes. She didn't know whether she was glad to see Bill or not. He was a strange character, but he was also a big man. Maybe he could help her look around, it would be nice to have his presence should she come across the intruder. On the other hand, what was he doing here anyway? Maybe he *was* the intruder. She hadn't entirely ruled him out yet. He was approximately the right height and build, but then weren't a lot of men? Even her father would have fit the remit.

Dad. A lump came to her throat at the thought of him. He would have been someone she could have called and talked this all through with. Heck, he probably would have been up here by now if she had called him last night. She swallowed the lump, dispelling his image with a quick shake of her head before tears decided to join the party too.

She had no option but to carry on, Bill would have seen her arrive by now. Pulling up next to the land rover, she shut the engine off. Next door, Brutus made a dive to the driver's side of the 4x4, rocking the vehicle on its suspension as he hit the window with his large paws. He quit barking at the house and resumed barking at the car all without pause.

'Right you two,' Emmie said, eyeing the dog as she turned to face Charlie and Grace. She raised her voice above his barks. 'Stay in the car and keep the doors locked. I want to check the house before you come in. I won't be long then we can light the fire and get cuddly warm, okay?'

Charlie nodded watching Brutus through the passenger window, only Grace replied.

'Okay mommy, I want my tunes on though.'

Charlie groaned and turned back to her.

'Gracie these tunes will eat me up from the inside if I have to listen to them much more.'

Emmie laughed and threw the keys to Charlie.

'You heard the girl sunshine, get those tunes on.'

'How come she gets to choose?' Charlie moaned.

'Woman's prerogative, 'Emmie replied.

Grace grinned from ear to ear in the back seat.

'Put them on Charlie.' She said.

'What about a man's perogo-thingy?'

Emmie leaned forward and ruffled Charlie's hair

'A man's prerogative? Honey, there ain't no such thing. Now lock the doors I won't be long,' she shut the door and waited for Charlie to click the locks from the inside.

Emmie passed the land rover, which squeaked on it's suspension as Brutus launched himself and a volley of barks back to the other side of the vehicle.

Bill was facing the front door, obviously not aware of her arrival over Brutus's manic barks. She took time to assess him; he didn't look threatening or like he was up to no good. He was at the front door, not around the back, and he seemed to have a small box of something by his feet. Maybe this was just a neighbourly visit.

The gate banged shut behind her and Bill turned letting out a gruff sound.

'Hmmpft.'

Emmie raised a hand in greeting.

Was she to call him Bill? She couldn't remember but decided to plumb for it anyway. If he didn't like it, he could always take his land rover and go back to his own patch. Emmie was through wasting time. She wanted to check her house and get everyone inside before darkness descended again.

'Hi, Bill.' She said lightly.

Bill dipped his head as he watched her approach. He took in her wet hair and clothes with an odd look on his face.

'Been out lass?'

'Just a walk to the falls with the kids.'

'Aye,' He nodded looking her up and down, 'you'll be taking a bigger coat next time I should think.'

Emmie smiled and hoped it didn't look as sarcastic as it felt.

'I should think so, yes, I didn't realise just how *wet* that mist would be. Are you okay, Bill? Only I would like to get in and get dry, the children are waiting in the car.'

Bill looked taken aback. His massive hands came up next to his chest, palms outward and he took a step away from the door.

'Aye lass, aye. Sorry. I just had some things for you from the farm. We had extra I thought you may be able to use. There'll be no charge. I know you didn't ask for anything.'

Emmie looked at the box again realising it for what it was.

A gift.

He'd come up here with a gift. Emmie closed her eyes briefly, dismayed by her behaviour.

'Thank you, Bill.' She said, 'I'm sorry I snapped at you, I'm wet through and cold, and I have a lot on my mind at the moment. It's no excuse. This is very much appreciated.'

Bill nodded eyeing her carefully.

'Well, it's no problem, lass. Sometimes the hens lay more than we know what to do with and sometimes we have to slaughter more cows than necessary for one reason or another. You get the idea. Either way we end up with surplus, and there's nothing I hate more than waste.'

'Well, thank you, that's very kind. If you hang on a minute, I can give you a little something for it.'

Putting her key in the lock she twisted, but the key jammed and the lock stuck tight. She tried again with more force, feeling panic rise, until she remembered she hadn't locked the door in the rush to leave. Removing the key, she pulled the handle. It turned easily. The door swung open into the cool hall.

Emmie swallowed hard. She glanced inside but saw just the hall. No movement, no mess. With a breath of relief she noted that her bag still hung on the coat hooks along with the rest of their coats and Charlie's jumper. Nothing seemed out of place.

She listened to the silence for a moment before crossing to her bag.

'I said I wanted nothing for them. It's only a bit of butter and milk with a few eggs. Nothing major, lass, 'Bill said from the doorway. She turned, clutching her bag, and nodded.

'Well, if you're sure. I'm very grateful. Thank you.'

She scanned up the stairs as she spoke, straining to see the top of the landing, her eyes falling back to the kitchen doorway where she caught a glimpse of the cupboards before reaching Bill

'Are you okay, lass? You seem a wee bit nervous.'

'Yes … yes, just...' She ran out of words. What in the hell could she possibly be doing other than checking the house? He would wonder why, but here he was, looking at her like she was crazy anyway. Then an idea came to her.

'I'm just checking the house over. Truth is we stayed down in the village last night. You know for the Burns night celebrations at the pub? This is the first time we've been home. I just wanted to make sure the house is secure before I bring the kids in.'

Bill stared at her, mirth in his clear green eyes.

'What do you think would happen to it, lassie? The house has been standing for over a century with no trouble. One night away and you think it's falling down?'

Emmie flushed feeling a little foolish, but now Bill was acting normal she wanted him to stay around until she had finished checking every nook and cranny. She laughed nervously.

'No. No, not falling down. Just making sure, you know, that no one has broken in while we were gone.'

Bill's laugh boomed suddenly out across the quiet landscape. Emmie winced..

'Ach, now I know you've a screw loose, lass, there's no one around here for miles. We can go for weeks without seeing a single soul on the hills. No one has been in your house I'll put my life on it. No one comes this far out unless they're seasoned walkers.'

'Then there's somebody. Maybe someone lost in the hills who needed a place to shelter? Maybe they're still here? There were a couple of broken windows when I first bought the place. It's not so far-fetched.'

Apparently, Bill thought it was. His face crumpled again, and he laughed so hard that a spasm of coughs ignited. He brought out his hankie, coughing and spluttering into it until the fit had passed. Thoroughly embarrassed Emmie felt the need to explain further.

'It's a 'city' thing, I know. Old habits die hard, but I won't rest until I know for sure. It's not a laughing matter to me.'

Bill had a hard time stopping his chuckles, but finally controlled himself enough to wipe the tears from his eyes and apologise.

'Look, lass, I'm sorry. City life is a different ball game, I get that, but there ain't no one broken into this house. Ain't no one been near it except you and I since you moved in. That I will guarantee. But if you feel the need to check, then I can only offer to help. You shouldn't be checking for nasty burglars all by yourself now.'

He was mocking her, and Emmie felt trapped between hell and the devil. Half of her wanted to tell him to stick his help, and his surplus cow and eggs. Stick them right up his jaxie and trot off home. The other half told her to swallow her pride. If anyone jumped her, she had a much better chance with Bill here.

She knew what she had to do; what she wanted to do. She had Grace and Charlie to think about, and they had been in the car long enough. Hell Charlie was probably well on his way to the end of the nursery rhyme CD by now. She needed this done.

'Well, if you have time I guess I'd feel a little better having someone else around while I checked. I would like to get Charlie and Grace out of the cold.'

'Okay lassie, then let's get the place checked.'

It turned out that Bill was a good house checker, and a gentleman. Once he had seen that she was serious, he looked after her well going into each room first and checking it over before standing back and allowing Emmie to search for herself. No one was hiding, from the attic to the living room. The windows were locked and secure as was the utility door and the patio doors from the playroom. Nothing seemed out of place so far.

The sunroom was last. Even with Bill by her side Emmie felt her head spin and thought she might faint. Bill opened the door and checked first before calling her through. If he thought she was been silly he didn't show it. Maybe he too was embarrassed after laughing at her on the doorstep.

The room looked as welcoming as it usually did. Emmie let out a breath, she had thought it might carry some sense of foreboding or a stain of eeriness after the man at the doors, but it looked and felt fine. She checked the windows and finally came to the doors, pulse quickening.

Putting a hand on each handle, Emmie mentally counted to three and pulled.

Locked. Both of them.

Confused, she pulled them again. Locked tight.

She jumped as Bill's voice came from right behind her.

'There you are, lass, all secure, just as you left it.'

'Yes,' She replied thinly.

Looking out at the orchard she felt her stomach churn. She fought the urge to lose what little food she'd eaten since last night over the floor.

'All secure.'

Chapter 33

Edith looked up as the door to the shop flew open and banged shut, the bell tinkled wildly. The man from the guest house stalked in, eyes meeting hers as he entered. He raised a hand and gave a grin that implied he would be quite happy to eat puppies for breakfast.

She swallowed and scanned the shop. There were five people inside at the moment. Three shopping with baskets, one looking at magazines and the other coming toward her with his items. She only hoped that the man from the guest house, who had now stopped in the tins aisle, would get what he wanted and leave before the shop emptied.

Edith served the gentleman, Ned from number sixty-three, and managed to make small talk with effort. She packed his things into his shopping bag and he left.

Four to go, and the new man was still staring at the tins. Picking them up and putting them down again.

Here was one of the shopping basket ladies. Irene, who had recently lost her son in a horrific skiing accident in Switzerland. Again Edith greeted her and made small talk while keeping an eye on the man. Still at the tins.

She knew in that instant, with all her heart, that he was waiting, biding his time, and it worried her. She was old now. She couldn't fight this man on her own. Len was upstairs in his usual chair puffing on inhalers she couldn't count on him to help.

Irene gone, Edith served a young girl called Cara with her Barbie magazine and a few sweets. She lived at thirty-two, daughter of one of only a handful of families who lived in the village. Cara, a sweet girl of around nine years old, said her thank you's and left. That left just two shoppers.

Edith felt her odds disappearing, and the man was on the move. He looked annoyed or frustrated. Definitely on edge and not up for small talk today. He moved to the freezers and appeared to be looking at the ready meals section.

Her heart skipped a beat as the last two shoppers came up to the desk chatting together, No-one had entered the shop, and although she kept both ladies, neighbours at forty-four and forty-six, talking, they were soon finished. Cheery goodbyes said, they left the shop laughing together. Edith could think of no legitimate excuse to ask them to stay.

Now it was Edith and the man, hunter and prey. He grinned up at her over the freezer chests and started around the shop toward the desk. Edith had an inkling he had come about Emmie, and she would hold off telling him anything until absolutely necessary but she wasn't stupid, this man could harm her in an instant. If he wanted information he would get it out of her one way or another, but she wouldn't give it up lightly.

Edith swallowed hard and realised she was starting to shake, heart thudding against her ribs. It took four strides for him to reach the desk grinning and holding her gaze the whole way.

'Hello, again,' He said cool grey eyes locking on hers

She dipped her head at him.

'Can I help you?'

'Oh, you most certainly can. I would like very much for you to help me. First things first, I'll take 20 Benson please.'

Edith looked up. She didn't want to turn her back on him, but the cigarettes were all behind the counter, she had no choice. Turning as quickly as she could, she grabbed the packet and swung back to the desk. The cigarettes flew from her shaking hand and fell to the floor, skidding against the back of the counter. She quickly bent to pick them up expecting a blow to the head, her left knee popping under the pressure.

'Oops, butterfingers,' The man said with a small chuckle, 'I'm not sure I want my cigarettes after they've been thrown all around the floor of the shop. I'd like a new packet please.'

Edith stood, pain shooting from her knee and looked at him.

'They're wrapped.' She said putting them on the counter.

'Well, that's customer service, right there. I'll give you a tip, first rule, the customer is always right. I want another packet.'

Edith looked at him and he stared right back. The menacing grin never left his face. His cold eyes were devoid of emotion. Cold fingers travelled up and down her spine and deciding not to argue she turned and grabbed a second packet placing it on the desk in front of him.

'Thank you.' He said as he picked up the packet, unwrapped the cellophane and took out a cigarette placing it between his lips.

'Oh, there's no smoking in here.' Edith said, wishing she sounded firmer.

The man glanced at her before reaching into his pocket and pulling out a lighter. He kept his eyes on hers as he flicked the top bringing the flame to life and lit the cigarette. Pulling in a drag and letting it back out.

'Ah, now that's better. How are you feeling today? Isn't it nice when you have only one customer in the shop and you can just have a friendly chat?'

Edith swallowed saying nothing. He kept his eyes on hers as he took another drag of the cigarette blowing the smoke into her face, she blinked rapidly.

'I asked how you were feeling,' He said, 'Maybe a little rough around the edges after the big old barn dance at the pub last night? A lovely night for a little get together with *friends,* eh?'

He emphasised the word friends and Edith went cold. It wasn't unreasonable to think he could have been there, last night she hadn't given him a thought, but now it was obvious he had been watching her. And if he had been watching, he would know that she was with Emmie most of the night. Her stomach churned. She said nothing but the shaking increased.

'Nothing to say? Nothing at all?'

'No, I don't. What do you want from me?'

The man smiled and stroked his beard with his right hand, cigarette between the fingers of his left. He feigned innocence.

'Want from you? What could I possibly *want* from you?'

Edith glanced at the door as the outline of a figure passed but didn't enter. She hadn't cried in a long time, but she certainly felt like it right now.

He heaved a loud sigh making her jump and turn back to him.

'Okay, let's stop playing games, I can see it's upsetting you, 'He smiled, hard eyes glinting. 'Let's get to the point. What *is* the point? Well, the point is that you lied to me. *You* lied to me. You might

RUIN

remember that tiny little lie from the last time I was in the shop. You have a good head for names if I remember rightly, which means you must be able to retain a little information. Such as me asking about my beloved sister who you knew nothing about. Remember? Can you remember that?'

Edith nodded, her heart upping from a jog to a sprint. She had a small mobile telephone under the desk. She didn't know how she was going to use it but it was her only hope of making someone aware that she was in trouble.

'Ah, she nods. She does remember indeed.' The man's voice was raising. He was getting angrier with every word. 'So then, you will remember telling me that you had no idea who I was talking about. No-one around here that you could think of. Remember, Remember that?'

He was shouting now and Edith let a small whine escape her lips. She moved her hand down under the counter and onto the phone almost unconsciously. Fear taking over.

'Put both hands on the desk where I can see what they're up to, dear,' He said.

Edith looked up swallowing and slowly placed both hands on the desk. He grabbed both of her wrists in one of his hands binding them tightly together pushing them onto the counter painfully. She yelped and closed her eyes. She started to count in her head. She had read somewhere that giving her brain something to focus on helped with controlling fear, so she would count; on and on until this was over.

'Something needs clarifying.' He went on, taking another drag of cigarette, 'I'm confused. You see you told me you knew nothing of her. Never seen anyone fitting that description or name but yesterday, in the pub, there you are sitting together. Laughing and joking like lifelong friends. Imagine my surprise. Just imagine sitting there after such a lie and seeing you both together. How do you think that made me feel?'

Edith counted. 53, 54, 55.

'Open your god damned eyes bitch and answer my question,' He roared.

Edith's eyes flew open, she yelped. His face was so close and contorted with anger, she tried to move her hands, but he only gripped tighter.

'I... I... I don't know. Please let my hands go, you're hurting me.'

'Hurting you? How about how you hurt me, bitch? Saying you

180

know nothing of her and rubbing my face in it. You were probably sitting there laughing at me, weren't you? So very clever. Ha ha ha, well now, how funny. The joke's on you. You can't deny it now. So you'd better tell me where the fuck she lives before I break the hands right off your skinny little wrists.'

Someone else passed by the shop door and a tear slipped down Edith's cheek. It was like they knew there was a madman in here. No-one would come in to save her. They would be just outside the door as her end came.

'Look at me,' He roared.

Edith slowly brought her eyes to his, fear convulsing her body, shaky legs barely holding her up.

'I'm in deep shit, probably in the form of being left in an unmarked grave if I don't find out where she is by tonight. You are my only link. You know where she is, now spill. I need answers, and I need them now.'

He was so close, face inches from hers, breath spilling smoke in her face. She whimpered, mentally apologising to Emmie. She had held out all that she could. If she carried on, she would die in this shop, either by his hands or her frail body.

'Please, okay. Okay, I'll talk, please, please just let go of...'

The bell tinkled cheerfully as the door swung open and the man made a frustrated strangled sound.

'This is not over,' He hissed through clenched teeth. He gave her hands one last painful squeeze before letting go. He grabbed the cigarettes and walked out of the shop bumping the shoulder of the man who had come in. Edith's vision was blurry, but she recognised Stuart immediately.

'Oh thank goodness, thank goodness,' She murmured, the tears letting go. Stuart looked out after Martin, rubbing his shoulder, then he turned to her surprised and concerned.

'Edie, what the hell is going on?'

Chapter 34

Bill didn't hang around after checking the house, Emmie walked up the path with him, waving him off before calling the children from the car and bustling them inside the house. She locked the door behind them and shuddered, with relief that the ordeal was over, or the cold, she couldn't tell. Probably both.

The damp of the day seemed to have penetrated the walls, and the air inside the house seemed cool. Emmie checked the boiler's thermostat which still sat at twenty-eight degrees, but the chill in the air said less. A lot less.

Sighing she checked the boiler was on and up to pressure before reluctantly turning the thermostat up to thirty.

In the kitchen, she switched on the little radio and made cheese omelettes with the eggs that Bill had given them. The children ate every last mouthful before going their separate ways. Grace to play with her dolls upstairs while Charlie poured out his Lego in the playroom.

Emmie sat at the kitchen table with a hot cup of tea, but she couldn't settle. She hated that they were all in different parts of the house. Far from being satisfied after the search, she now felt even more insecure, just because the damn French doors had been locked.

She tried to focus on the radio but found herself listening for sounds behind the music, She was restless and on edge, shifting in her seat and glancing out of the front window, thoughts drifting as her conscious tried to make sense of the previous night's events.

The doors had been open last night she was sure. She had opened them herself, and she hadn't had the keys to lock them again, even if she had thought to. There was also no reason why she would have thought the man had got inside if the doors had remained locked.

How was it possible?

Only one answer made sense; shadow man must have a key. He had unlocked the door and come in, and he had locked it on the way out. It was the only explanation, wasn't it?

Why would he bother?

She supposed the only other option was that the man was either John Watts, come to claim her children, or Ted from the storm of '99. Neither of them should have any trouble getting in or out through doors, locked or otherwise.

Emmie grinned to herself, but she supposed she shouldn't completely discount Edith's legend. She looked down into her cup, steam rising to warm her face.

Either way, door open or not, both theories led to the same unpleasant fact. Whoever it was they could get in the house at any time. They hadn't been as safe here as she'd thought, and they certainly weren't safe now.

She looked at her watch. 1.50pm. Today was more than half gone and tomorrow was Sunday. Emmie decided first thing Monday after dropping Charlie at school, and Grace at nursery for her first session, she would call a locksmith and change all the locks. She couldn't afford it. She wasn't working properly yet, and her savings were running dangerously low but for peace of mind she had to do it.

She had Stuart to pay too.

She supposed that gesture could be overlooked, he hadn't asked her for anything, but kindness like that at a time when she had been terrified had meant the world to her. She wouldn't ever forget it, and debt could be paid off.

Until Monday she would sleep downstairs and make sure the house was secure as the children slept. She wouldn't scare them anymore, and she refused to stay locked in one room. This was her house, and they were her children, she would defend both to the end.

She downed the last gulp of tea and stood, chair scraping backwards. She took her cup to the sink looking out over the garden briefly. She had intended to check the house and go straight back to Bracken Hill to pay Stuart, but in mere hours the dark and cold would creep in fast. She shuddered involuntarily. She couldn't handle coming back into the house in the dark today. She would have to go to the pub tomorrow morning.

Emmie decided to freshen up before lighting the fire to warm the living room, her jeans were still damp and the cold was already winding it's way around her legs. She could check Grace while she was upstairs too, make sure she was playing alone and not with her invisible friend. She couldn't take another episode with invisible man yet. It may just tip her slightly tilted world right the way over.

Upstairs in the bathroom, she splashed her face with water noting the tiredness that was starting to show around her eyes. She wondered when she had last had a full night's sleep, other than last night in the pub, and thought it must have been before she had arrived here, before the dratted dreams had started again.

She changed into fresh jeans and a jumper and was two strides out of her room to check on Grace when she heard a dull thud from behind her.

She stopped, frowning. She waited. All was quiet.

For god sake Em, if you're this jumpy in daylight, I dread to think what the night will bring.

Taking a breath, she forced herself to keep walking.

It's nothing.

She found Grace playing normally, Emily clutched in one hand, busy telling off one of the smaller dolls for messing up the kitchen.

She shivered as she watched her. It was colder up here than it had been downstairs - again.

'Come on, Gracie,' She said, 'We need to go down now. You can play dolls downstairs in the warm sweetie.'

Grace looked up bottom lip pushing out.

'Aw, don't want to go down, I'm playing here.'

Emmie grinned and stooped down next to Grace smoothing her hair off her forehead.

'It's cold up here Grace, I've turned up the heating so you can come up later when it's warmer if you still want to.'

But over my dead body in the dark, Grace. You'll be downstairs until bedtime but let's put that fight aside for now.

Still pouting Grace put the dolls in her house, keeping hold of Emily and the smaller naughty doll, and stood heaving the sigh of much older person. Emmie offered Grace her hand and they walked together down the landing. At the top of the stairs, she hesitated. The thud had come from her room, and if there had been a thud at all, she needed to know what it was.

Emmie sent Grace downstairs and went back to her room swinging the door inward and glancing around as she did so. Nothing seemed out of place. She let out a small breath.

Jeez Em, you do have the heebie-jeebies. The house is fine, and your imagination is going to pot. You'll give yourself a heart attack over nothing.

But as she pulled the door too, she saw there was something. On the floor next to the wardrobe. A small white box. Emmie frowned and pushed the door again, going into the room. The little white box of photos from the attic was lying open on the floor. Photographs of Grace and Charlie scattered by the wardrobe doors. Mind racing, Emmie stared at them, as if at any moment they might rise in formation and do a jig.

Shit. Right. It's okay Em. It's just the photos. First, you couldn't find them now they appear when you least expect it. It's fine, they just fell.

But they hadn't just fallen. How could they? Just yesterday afternoon she had put them in the desk, up in the attic. No one had been in the house until now so who the hell had brought them out of the attic and put them on top of her wardrobe where they appeared to have fallen from? Shadow man?

Emmie closed her eyes and took a breath running a hand through her hair. That was ridiculous, there had to be a plausible explanation, and there probably was. Her mind was shot, she was jumpy and irrational. She must have moved them herself and forgotten. It wasn't like she was acting or thinking normally at the moment.

Emmie scooped them up and put them back into the box, replacing the lid before putting it on her dressing table. Right now she had to get the fire lit she could think about it later when her nerves settled again.

Chapter 35

Closed sign on the door of the shop, Edith sat in the small living room above, next to a concerned Len who had heard the raised voice down in the shop but hadn't had the breath to get down the stairs. He'd shuffled as far as the top when Stuart had brought Edith up, sat her down, and made her a drink.

Now that Edith had time to calm down she felt foolish. She wasn't a weak lady, frail maybe, but she had never let herself be bullied like that by anyone. She was angry with herself and even more annoyed that she had been so ready to give away Emmie's position to this man. She had no idea why he wanted to find her or what she could have done for him to be chasing her, but Edith had relied on gut instinct all of her life, and her gut was telling her that Emmie needed protecting from this man. She knew neither of them well, but she knew this with all her heart.

Edith sipped at the tea letting the warmth soothe her. Sat on the two-seater sofa, Len's arm was around her rubbing at the top of her shoulder, his breathing ragged in her ear, every exhale letting out a thin whine. She put her hand on his knee giving it a light squeeze telling him wordlessly that she was okay. Stuart brought a chair from the dining table and sat opposite her leaning forward, hands clasped, forearms resting on his knees, concern etched on his face.

'I'm fine.' She said looking at him.

He didn't look convinced, and neither did Len.

'What happened Edie? What did he do?'

'Nothing much. Really. He frightened me, hurt my hands a little, but it was the energy around him that scared me more. He is so full of anger.'

Stuart nodded.

'Aye, I saw him not more than half hour ago, tore out of the back door of the pub like his ass was on fire. Set off the alarms. I was up for having a stern word with him when he came back. I had half the guests down at the front thinking there was a fire drill. He had a lot to drink last night, Edie, I'm sure he just has his demons on his back today.'

Edith shook her head.

'No Stu, it's something more. He's after someone, he wanted information, and he knows I have it. He'll be back to get it. He said if he didn't have it by tonight there would be trouble.'

That had Len worried. He pulled his hand from her shoulders and turned to face her, their knees knocking together.

'Edie, what's all this? What information could you possibly have that this man wants? We have a quiet life running a village shop. How could you know anything?'

His voice was raspy. He was struggling with his lungs again today, and Edith regretted that she had to worry him with this. She and Stuart should have stayed downstairs to discuss it. She leaned over to a small table and passed him his inhaler which he took without a word clearing his throat before he sucked the medicine up.

Edith decided she had better start from the beginning. She needed help, and Stuart was probably one of the best people in the village to get it. His size and solid stance belied his gentle kindness; outwardly he was someone this weedy little man may think twice about tangling with.

'He's been in the shop a few times over the last week, of course, but he never spoke other than to ask for his cigarettes, he must get through a good many I'll tell you that. Not that I'm moaning of course.'

She chuckled mirthlessly, suddenly remembering that he had got away with tonight's, that was money lost from the shop. She had a feeling she wouldn't be brave enough to ask for it either.

'Edith?' Stuart coaxed.

'Yes, well. Earlier in the week he came in and spoke. Small talk. I was surprised and warmed if I'm honest. Thought he was finally letting his guard down. He spoke of how he was a nature photographer or something of the sort. He spends a lot of time at the falls, so I told him of the less used track and the walk into the hills-'

At the mention of the hills it hit Edith that she had revealed the exact location of Emmie's house. Bruadair was remote and isolated but could easily be seen and reached from not far up this side of Bracken Hill. She let out a small gasp putting her hand to her mouth. She felt like someone had punched her in the stomach, all the air sucked out of her lungs.

'Edie, what is it?' Len said leaning back into her, putting his hand on to her knee this time 'What is it you think you know?'

Edith held her hand up to him, settling herself and taking a shaky breath to continue.

'After I told him of the hill walk he said he was looking for someone. His sister, who he hadn't seen for a few years if I remember rightly. He asked if I knew her, telling me her name and description. I didn't know. I couldn't remember, and it matched no-one in the village. He was calm at that point, so I said as much, and that was when he turned.'

Edith took another shaky breath. She felt stifled. The warm collar of her shirt ruffling under her chin seemed to be choking her. She tried to open the top button, hands shaking as she grasped at it, her slightly arthritic knuckles in the way. Len pushed her hands down gently and opened it for her. Teamwork, she thought. I have the lungs; he has the hands.

'What do you mean he turned Edie? Why haven't you said anything about this before?' Stuart said brow furrowed. Edith looked at him steadily. This man was also staying in his guest house. He was probably wondering what kind of man was under his roof too.

'When I said I didn't know, he got angry. Told me she had only been in the shop the day before and that he had seen her. Of course, it clicked what lady he was talking about, but he got angry so quickly. I don't know if I was more scared for her or myself, so I chose to pretend I knew nothing. He went out, and I carried on, forgetting all about it. That's why I didn't say anything. I thought it was at an end.'

Edith's breath hitched, and she thought she might cry for the second time today. Only one tear escaped though, trickling down her right cheek. Len wiped it away.

'Edie,' Stuart said, and she knew he was starting to catch up with her, 'You know this man isn't a photographer, right? I have never seen him with a camera, most of the time he wanders up and down the falls, or the village, or he sits drinking at the bar. I have wondered what he's been here for but as long as the room is paid for it's not up to me to get into peoples business. I shun the gossip as much as you. He never caused any trouble, until now anyway.'

'I know, 'Edith replied, 'I know he's not what he says he is. I knew it in my bones as soon as he turned angry that day.'

Stuart nodded and reached out for her shaking hands, holding them gently.

'And the girl?' He asked, but she saw he knew already, he just needed it confirming.

'Emmie. The one at the pub. He saw us together last night. That's why he was here. He knows I know her, and he said he won't stop until I give him the information he needs.'

'What information does he want? If he saw her why not just ask her himself?'

'I don't know Stu, and that frightens me because he wants to know where she lives. Something is going on, and there's a reason he wants it without Emmie knowing.' Edith shuddered.

'*Do* you know where she lives, Edie? I had no details from her yesterday, and she left around lunch, presumably to go home.'

Edith nodded closing her eyes briefly and taking back a hand to rub the rest of the wetness off her cheek.

'Aye I do, that's the trouble. I know he'll get it out of me, I don't know how long I can hold off if he keeps coming at me. The other thing is, even if I don't, I've already given him the location and a secluded way of getting there by telling him of the walk to the hills from the side of the falls.'

Stuart's eyes met hers. He blew out a breath and rubbed his brow.

'Bruadair. Christ, Edie. it's remote out there. He can't know if he's been asking this morning and we need to keep it that way.' He rubbed at his whiskered chin. Edith waited.

'Okay, this is starting to make a bit of sense. Emmie was troubled yesterday when she came in asking for a room. She didn't want to go home, but if she only lives at Bruadair that's what, Five miles? Six at most, so why?'

'I thought she'd come down for Burns night? Although I wondered about the bairns, I must admit.'

'They were sleeping when you came in. She seemed to need the break, and the bairns were nearby in the room next to the bar, so I didn't see any need to hassle her about it.'

'The room you don't use?'

'Aye, I had nothing else, and she seemed desperate. There were other things too, they had no luggage, and she had no money with her. Not a penny. I can't imagine what happened, but I couldn't just turf them out.'

Len, who had sat quietly listening, cleared his throat.

'Maybe she had an argument at home and didn't want to go back?' he said.

They both turned to him, and Edith shook her head.

'No, she moved here alone with the bairns. She told me as much last night.'

Len nodded slowly, thinking.

'So she was running from the house? It can be the only explanation. The other thing striking me is that she has no knowledge this man is after her, or she wouldn't have run down here to the very place he is staying.'

Stuart frowned.

'Agreed. And if he's the threat why would she run *from* the house?'

Edith paled suddenly feeling queasy.

'It does have quite a history. They say things happen there. I asked Emmie if she was having any trouble at the house when I saw her in the shop.'

There was a moment of silence before Len broke into laughter breaking the mood and setting off a series of wheezes, face creased into a series of lines that had accumulated over the years. Edith thought she must know every one and the year they had appeared.

'And I bet she thought you were batty, woman.' He said through wheezes. 'Local legends are gossip and Chinese whispers that have lasted the centuries and twisted themselves into dark, ugly tales.'

Stuart grinned too, although at least he had the decency not to laugh, that's what thirty-six years of marriage did for you, no secrets and no attempt at humouring her, Len wheezed on merrily. Edith shrugged, she wasn't bothered, she knew they didn't believe in such things, but she did. And there had been a whole heap of talk about Bruadair over the years. Besides, Emmie had been rattled she was sure, although she hadn't called, and she hadn't mentioned it last night. Either way, something spooked her enough to leave with no money and only the clothes on their backs.

Edith looked from one to the other of the two men waiting for their mirth to subside.

'Well, whatever happened or whatever trouble she is in we need to decide what to do about it. We have information that this man wants and I don't want to give it to him. She seems a sweet girl and a caring mother. The bairns worry me. I believe they're only young. If he gets her alone in the house with them, who knows what they may see.'

'I couldn't see them above the bar, 'Stuart said, 'so they're much too young to be caught up in whatever is going on.'

'Could you not throw him out of his room Stu? He set the alarms off causing trouble, it's reason enough,' Len said.

'Aye, I could, but at least while he's here we know where he is and what he's up to. We're also aware of the information he has.'

Edith wholeheartedly agreed.

'Exactly, keep your friends close and your enemies closer. Once he's gone, we won't know if he's found her or not. I won't settle knowing she's not safe.'

'But Edith, 'Len protested, 'He's already assaulted you, what will he try next time?'

Edith waved him off.

'It can hardly be called assault Len, he held my hands down and frightened me a little. Look, there are no marks, he did no damage.'

She held her hands up. They were a little less shaky now, and she was glad. She looked at Stuart who was looking back at her thoughtfully.

'Edie, Can you signal something to Len? Is there anything you can use that won't arouse suspicion but will alert him so that he knows Martin is in the shop and you're worried. If Len can contact me, I can be here before he gets as far as he did today.'

Edith started to shake her head. She put her hand up to her mouth pinching her lips and thought. Then an idea came to her.

'Aye, I suppose I do. I have a batch of twelve ugly ceramic pig money boxes. Had them for years and not one sold. If I open one and put it on the counter, I can pretend to knock it off. The smash could be your cue to call Stuart, Len.'

Len was nodding, Stuart wasn't as convinced.

'How could you be sure Len would hear? And you could get hurt if any of the bits catch you.'

'Len could hear a pin drop in hell, and I'm more worried about getting hurt by this man than getting a scratch from a piggy money box.'

Len was nodding in agreement. Stuart looked from one to the other and must have decided that it was good enough. Edith knew it would be a failsafe, Len had fantastic hearing, and she would put the phone where he could reach it by his chair each morning. She felt the knots of tension in her shoulders loosen a little.

'Okay,' Stuart said, 'So I suppose we've covered everything except what we tell the lass herself. I'm not sure how fragile she is? She was certainly upset last night but seemed to pull herself out of it fairly quickly. To come out to a local bar full of strangers by herself suggests a certain confidence. I'm assuming she didn't know you were coming in at that point, Edie?'

Edith shook her head.

'As I said, I thought she was there for the band.'

Stuart nodded and frowned.

'She needs to know,' Edith said quickly, 'She might even know this man. At least she can assess the threat and protect herself, and maybe we all get to know what the hell is going on. She may even know why.'

'Aye,' Stuart sat back slowly with an odd look on his face, it landed somewhere between irritation and regret, 'She needs to know as soon as possible too. I've just remembered, Connor was speaking to Martin last night at the bar for quite some time. He said he was very chatty which is unusual, and that he was soaked through and drinking like a fish. He told Connor he'd been for a walk and got lost climbing the hills...'

Stuart let the sentence hang, letting its implications sink in. Edith's heart thumped noisily in her chest. The shakes that had been easing off caught up with her again. She rubbed her hands over her face. She looked at Stuart who was rubbing a hand through his hair.

'I don't have a way to contact her, Stu, please tell me you have a number for her.'

He shook his head slowly eyes full of regret.

'I didn't take one, it wasn't a normal room booking. There was no money exchanged I didn't see the need to pester her for information when she seemed upset.'

'So what do we do?' She whispered.

'Well, I could drive out to Bruadair, that's not a problem, but I've given Connor the weekend off, He went off to Glasgow this morning and I'm rushed off my feet this weekend after yesterday, a full house is hectic, it's probably stacking up while I'm here. The earliest I could go is first thing Monday when things are calmer and Connor's back.' He heaved a big sigh rubbing his chin between thumb and forefinger, 'I really wish I had time to go today but...'

Edith covered his free hand with her own patting it lightly.

'I know, we just have to hope it will be alright. At the moment he knows nothing lets hope it stays that way for another day at least, eh?'

Edith sat back and sighed. She suddenly felt very old, and very stupid. If this man had climbed the side of Bracken Hill he had already seen where Emmie lived. Whether he knew it or not, he had already seen Bruadair.

Chapter 36

Tonight's dream had involved no Peppa pig tops and no rustling skirts, only faceless, shadowy men that wanted to get into her house. They batted and swiped at the doors and windows making small taps, arms seemingly boneless, swaying and blowing like paper in a light breeze.

Emmie was trapped in the only room of the house; the sunroom, destined to watch these creatures until it was light and they went wherever shadow men go in the day. The windows would keep them out. Everything was locked, she had double checked before dark. But now one of the shadow men produced something that he was holding aloft with glee. She struggled to make it out in the darkness, and then the moon lit the sky revealing a key and shadow man's face. It was Stuart from the pub.

The relief that flooded through her was immediate. Stuart was going to save them. They could leave and never come back. He grinned as he inserted the key into the lock and turned. The lock clunked open, and he looked at her, grin widening. Only now the grin was sinister, his face had changed, and she knew he was one of them.

This wasn't a rescue. He was coming to kill her. Sat in the middle of the sunroom floor she screamed.

Emmie sat bolt upright in the darkness, gasping for breath and slick with sweat, scream still sounding in her ears. It took her a second to realise that she was in her bed when she had fully intended to sleep on the settee. She couldn't even remember coming upstairs.

Throwing back the duvet she peeled off her wet pyjamas, sweat on her body drying in the cool night air. Pulling more from the drawers at the side of the bed, she dressed and reached for her phone, swiping to light the screen. 3.20am.

Fabulous, too early to get up, too scared to sleep, so what now?

'I'd like tea actually,' She said quietly to the empty room, 'A peaceful cup of tea in my own kitchen with none of your scary bullshit going on. Can you manage that?'

She looked slowly around the room eyes adjusting to the dark. The room didn't seem to think that was out of the question, apparently - no objections here.

All the same, she sat for a moment listening to the faint tick of the grandfather clock down in the living room. All was quiet, and the house felt different. Not as scary in the dark this morning. Like it had surrendered its guns when Emmie had upped her game yesterday and refused to let shadow man pigeon-hole her into sections of the house like a scared rabbit.

Perhaps you changed, honey, did you think about that? Maybe you upped your stance, and the demons backed down.

She frowned into the darkness. She was used to the voice in her head, it had been around so long she couldn't remember a time it hadn't spoken to her, but usually, it was only her voice. It guided her through life's rough patches like an old friend, it had given her gentle nudges through the divorce, nudges to handle Scott's anger, and many nudges when he had been controlling or belittled her. Especially about her work as an artist which he hadn't thought was a valid career path after earning a degree. He hadn't bothered to notice that when she had a good month, she could bring in as much money as he did being an overworked, over stressed, lawyer.

Lately, the voice had been with her continuously. She thought maybe it had to do with the lack of people she could speak to out here as much as the change. This morning, sitting in the dark, two things had subtly altered.

The first was that she had answered it out loud which she had never done before. The second was that this voice wasn't her own. It was her dad's. Which threw her off balance. He had died four years ago and had never visited the realms of her head until now.

She looked around the room making out shapes of the furniture around her.

'Dad?' She whispered

Only the grandfather clock ticked its acknowledgement. The stillness of the house continued, and Emmie suddenly felt comforted. Whether it was a one-off or not, whether she was going insane or not, if her dad was going to join her for the ride she knew she could face anything. Her mind had thrown him up for a reason, and that was just fine.

Okay, dad, it's you and me, fancy joining me for tea?

Getting no reply, she pushed on her slippers and grabbed her dressing gown before stepping out onto the landing. She stopped to listen again, checking her body for responses that she had come to expect in this house. There was nothing. Stillness inside and out. Her heartbeat remained normal, the air remained normal, there was nothing to fear, she knew it as surely as the sun would rise in the east. She padded across to the stairs and peered down over the railing.

Downstairs was dark; shadows clung to the corners. She had no idea if shadow man had let himself in last night.

She waited, allowing her thoughts to run, but there was still no response from her heart, which pumped along steadily.

I do believe a priest must have entered in the night and cleansed this place.

Heck, maybe he has a key too.

She grinned as she stepped downstairs and into the kitchen.

The blinds were open, silvery moonlight flooded the room, and she looked out across the garden as she made a drink. All was still outside this morning too, nothing to see except the outline of vegetation, the fence, her car. No shadows wearing hats. The kitchen was warm and the grandfather clock soothing, ticking steadily along, like the pulsing heartbeat of the house.

Sat at the kitchen table, hands circling the cup, hot liquid warming her from her throat to her feet, Emmie felt a calmness fall over her. It was lovely sitting here in the dark with hot tea, feeling safe after a nightmare. Wasn't this what a home was all about? Maybe it *was* that she had upped her stance, she didn't know, but for now, Emmie Landers and Bruadair seemed to have come to a truce.

The last gulp of tea finished Emmie pushed the cup aside and folded her arms loosely on the table, hands to opposite elbows. She lay her head down on her forearms looking toward the utility and the gentle roar of the boiler. The ticking of the clock lulled her. *Home* was her last thought before she slipped into a deep and dreamless sleep.

Chapter 37

'The beast is dead. We killed it! Get over here quick we need to tie it up, just in case!'

'There are no strings Charlie. I'll use power to check. Hi-yah!'

The blow landed swift and sharp on Emmie's shin. Pain zipped up her leg forcing her from deep sleep to wide awake in approximately half a second.

'Ow! What the hell...'

She shot upright in the chair, one hand going down to rub her leg, the other flying up to her neck as the crick that had set in complained painfully.

'Its awake Charlie get the axe.'

The fucking axe?

'I'll use power to shoot it.'

At the word power, Emmie was up and out of the chair. She circled the table as Grace's second blow hit only air, and saw Charlie grab at her shoulder pulling her back.

'No Gracie, you can't kick mom.'

'She's a monster.'

'I'm touched, I love you too Grace. You shouldn't kick though you hurt me.'

Grace swung round to Charlie, arms still bent up like a kung fu Barbie.

'It's ok Charlie; the monster loves me. Shall we let it live?'

Emmie looked over at Charlie too, pretend pout on her lips. Charlie grinned at her.

'Yeah, we'll need breakfast soon, I'm starving. Leave her, let's get the other beasts before they take over the world.'

Charlie and Grace, protectors of the world, ran out of the kitchen. Charlie with bed-mussed hair and star wars pyjamas and Grace with her pink dressing gown flapping behind her like a cape.

Emmie groaned as she stood by the table, one hand massaging her neck muscles into submission as their shouts faded to the other side of the house. Sunlight poured in through the kitchen window forcing her to squint as she turned to look outside. For a second she thought it had snowed overnight, but closer inspection revealed just a heavy frost. The garden was white over, and everything looked washed clean. The sky a clear blue with not a cloud in sight.

Emmie glanced at her watch, rubbed her eyes and looked at it again, 9.46am?

Wow, nearly a good six hours all in one shot, even if it was at the kitchen table. And guess what Em? You're still here. The kids are still here. No one has been murdered. No-one has got in, you know why? Because there was never anyone in. I think you flipped. Shadow man had you running scared for one too many days, and you flipped all the way over to the tail side and made an irrational assumption.

Emmie thought she might have a point. Shadow man didn't hurt them before they left yesterday, he didn't jump out at them, hell, she didn't see or hear a thing of him. Grace was on her own upstairs for god sake. He had a perfect opportunity to get each of them if that's what he had wanted. Which surely means he didn't want. And on that note, there would be no reason to come in at all. Would there?

Nope, and another thing, toots, your bag was still here fully loaded. Nothing was missing, just in case you throw that one up a bit later in the dark. Nothing was touched anywhere, so he wasn't even a thief. Which makes him a not very dangerous, not very likely, intruder. In fact, not an intruder at all. Your mind slipped, but that's okay. You scared the kids, sure, but it won't happen again.

No, it wouldn't. The last thing she wanted was to pack up and prove everyone in Surrey right. Poor little Emmie couldn't make it on her own up there, cracked under the pressure and started seeing ghouls outside the windows.

Shadow man was real though, Grace and Charlie had seen him too, but she refused to be scared of him any more. She would keep locked down in the dark as she had and ignore him - unless he did turn out to be Stuart from the Grey Lion after all. Then she might just let him in.

Emmie grinned as she placed the empty cup in the sink and glanced outside to where the garden glinted in the sunshine like a fine rug had been thrown over the mess. She could hear the birds through the window, a whole chorus of them chirruping together, and leading the choir a robin sat on a small shrub close to the house singing with all his heart before catching her movement and flying off. The hills stood like majestic white guards against the north side of the property, the sparkling trees like soldiers in line along the border.

Emmie smiled, it was truly beautiful here, and she was making friends. Even Bill turned out okay after that first meeting; he was strange but entirely harmless. He'd even shown he could be a gentleman yesterday.

Looking out at the frozen morning she knew they would be okay, she felt it. They were safe. The house would protect them.

'Mom!'

Charlie skidded into the room making her jump, the crick in her neck waking up again as she turned from the window.

'What?' She smiled at him, looking at his happy face and wide eyes as her hand went back to massage her neck.

'Have you seen outside? It looks like snow.'

'It does, doesn't it. Just heavy frost though, unless we've had a sprinkle overnight.'

'Can we go outside? Grace and I want to catch the snow beasts.'

Emmie looked at him incredulously.

'In your pyjamas? I think you may catch something other than a snow beast, don't you?'

He rolled his eyes and flapped a hand at her in dismissal.

'We'll get dressed and wrap up warm. Please?'

'Tell you what.' Emmie said, 'how about you go and get dressed, we'll have a warm breakfast, and then we'll all go and have a climb up the hill while it's sunny. How does that sound?'

Charlie made a little high pitched screech noise in his throat. His mouth stretched into a grin as he turned tail toward the stairs, grabbing Grace as she came into the hall from the living room. She was about to say something, but Charlie cut her off.

'We're mountaineers today Grace! We're going up the hill in the snow to save the city! Quick, we need to dress in warm stuff. I'll help you.'

Grace didn't have a chance to answer as she was dragged upstairs by the hand.

'I'll take that as a solid yes then?' Emmie called.

She moved into the hall, but the only reply was shouts of strategic plans for monster capture. She shrugged and went back to the kitchen to warm the milk for the porridge.

Chapter 38

As Grace and Charlie were hunting early morning beasts up in Scotland, Natalie Hampton was up and dressed, ready for her shift. It was certainly not a perk of the job working on glorious sunny Sundays, but unfortunately the sick and wounded refused to rest, and as much as Natalie wanted to today, she wouldn't call in sick. She had chosen her profession out of a love for helping sick children. The fact that she was in A&E was frustrating, but she told herself it was only a pit stop on the journey of her career.

She finished the last bite of her toast and glanced at the clock on the kitchen wall. It was just after 9am, and she still had an hour to kill. The kids were in bed, as was Michael. Whether they were asleep, she didn't know, and wasn't going up to check. As soon as they realised she was downstairs, they would follow her down like the pied piper.

No, she was going to put the kettle on and have a last quiet coffee before she left.

Flicking the switch on the kettle movement outside the window caught her eye. A car was pulling slowly up to the kerbside. Not just any car, the showy Black BMW that was most definitely Scott's car.

Puzzled she watched as the car came to a stop. They hadn't seen hide nor hair of him since the fiasco at Emmie's leaving party - for which she would never forgive him - and she had no wish to see him now.

She watched him get out of the car and walk stiffly down to the door, His suit perfectly creased, chiselled face serious, short dark hair perfectly slicked with a small quiff at the front. He appeared solemn, not that he had been much else for the last few years.

Natalie supposed she owed him that, he had been through a lot too, both Emmie *and* Scott were involved in what had happened. It was easy to be one-sided, however, when it was Emmie that had been the hurt, confused, and broken one when he threw her out.

She sighed heavily as the bell rang, and made her way into the hall as that last quiet coffee slipped through her fingers. She opened the door, trying to paste a polite smile on her face but finding that she couldn't.

'Hello, Scott.'

'Natalie,' He said. His polished voice was smooth, dark eyes piercing. 'I wonder if you've heard anything from Emelia?'

Natalie flinched. She had assumed he would be here about Emmie, of course, but she hadn't expected the forthrightness of the question.

'I might have,' She said, voice guarded, 'why would you need to know?'

Scott smirked, the left side of his mouth lifting. He rolled his eyes lightly before setting them on hers. She stood straighter and lifted her chin, arms folded. She refused to be intimidated. She waited, offering him nothing else.

'Come on, Natalie,' He said. He seemed to check himself as he relaxed his stance and held his arms out palms toward her. 'Are we not all on the same side? I only ask as I thought she would call you first if she was having trouble, but it seems not from the lack of response. Maybe you're already helping her out and don't think you need my input but she's my wife Natalie, I deserve to be involved too. I worry about her as much as you.'

Natalie kept her arms folded, face closed, but inside her mind was whirring. Trouble? Surely Em would call her if there was any sort of trouble. Scott was trying to trip her up, but why? There was nothing left that he could possibly want with her, was there? She narrowed her eyes at him, regarding him as he stood in front of her.

His expression was now suitably worried, but that was one of his abilities. He could turn on any emotion to twist a situation to his advantage, Emmie had told her hundreds of small incidents over the years, but the big one, Natalie would never forget.

One night just before he had thrown her out, Emmie let slip that he had thrown his dinner up the wall simply because it had been reheated. He liked it waiting on the table, ready for him, every day, hot and fresh (Takeaways and prepared foods were strictly forbidden). That night he had arrived back half an hour late, without warning, which along with being earlier than planned, was one of his favourite games. In the middle of his angry outburst, his mother had arrived, letting herself in. Emmie said he had turned on the charm instantly, blaming the mess and the shouting on Emmie, who had been too upset to tell her otherwise. She had cleaned up and obediently remade another meal from scratch, for both himself and his mother, at his insistence.

Natalie had been horrified, and it had dawned on her that there must have been many more occasions, just like that one, that Emmie hadn't mentioned at all. She would probably never the full extent of what he had put her through, which had made her secretly delighted when the divorce had come about.

But now there was the wife altercation again too, why couldn't he let that go?

'Natalie? If you insist on making this a stand-off could we do it in the warm? Please? I'm worried for Emelia. Believe me, I really wouldn't be here if I had any other choice.'

'Your wife?'

Scott looked downcast and brought his hands to his head covering his eyes. As he looked up he dragged his hands down as if in prayer. Fingers pinching the end of his nose, thumbs tucked under his chin. Natalie tried to assess whether this was for show. He finally brought his hands back down away from his face.

'Ex ... Ex-wife. Is that better? Does it make you feel better, Natalie? Because it makes me feel like a shit.'

'Doesn't matter Scott, the law says you are divorced. You sorted the paperwork yourself, didn't you? Got yourself the best deal? Oh, I know you were working under the premise that one of your colleagues dealt with it but that was just a signature right? Funny how Em ended up with a crappy settlement but you're still living in the house, with all the furniture, and driving your flash car around. You didn't worry about how she would cope with what you let her have, but you're *really* worried about her now are you?'

Natalie had pushed his buttons. His face hardened, hands clenched into fists. He did anger spectacularly fast when you poked at him. Natalie carried on, pleased she was breaking the soft shell and getting to the real man. Maybe then she could asses if the trouble was worth bringing him inside. She would ring Emmie herself as soon as she could anyway.

'It's your fault she's as far away as she is, Scott, isn't it? What did you expect her to buy around here? You were intent on seeing her in the gutter that's what I think. But you know what? She went and got herself a palace in the highlands. Backfired, didn't it? You didn't see that one coming. None of us did. And whatever anyone says, I now directly blame *you* for the loss of my sister.'

Natalie stabbed her finger at him, breathless and red in the face. Had she been asked she would have said she hadn't got much to say to him, but now she had started, it seemed there was no stopping. Scott had stepped two paces back in shock, but a sharp glint appeared in his eyes as he steadied himself and moved back up to her. They were almost nose to nose now. Natalie could smell his aftershave and mint from his toothpaste. His voice became low and menacing through his clenched teeth. A flyaway string of spittle landed on his chin.

'And *I* directly blame *her* for the loss of my children.'

Natalie gasped and stepped backwards catching her foot on a carrier bag of paper recycling that she had put ready for the bin. She watched the bag tear open spilling paper into the doorway as she felt herself falling. She grasped at the door for balance, only succeeding in swinging it wide as she landed with a bump on her backside, the wind forced from her lungs. The door hit the wall with a thump and swung back to hit her thigh adding insult to injury.

Scott watched, passive as the scene played out. It was only when a neighbour passing by with a newspaper under her arm asked if she was okay that he seemed to spring into action.

'We're okay thank you, ' He shouted over his shoulder to her as he bent to help Natalie up. Natalie slapped his hand away and turned onto her knees using the telephone table to help herself up. When she turned, Scott was cleaning up the recycling, putting the paper bag into the bag as he glanced over his shoulder and smiled at the lady.

Natalie shook her head. It was disconcerting how far he would go to keep up appearances, which only made her more glad that Emmie was no longer with him. Who knew what she had really endured being married to this man.

As she stared at him, it dawned on her that he had stopped replacing the paper and was having a good look at a coffee stained piece with a staple in the top. It took her a second to whip it out of his hand and place it on the telephone table while kicking the rest of the paper back into the hall to tidy when he had gone.

'Go.' She said pointing past him back up the driveway, 'Go, and don't darken my door with accusations about my sister again. You know she would never have chosen this path if she had been given a choice. There was nothing she could do.'

He stepped back from the doorway, hands out toward her again. His eyes held a trace of humour although she couldn't think what was funny unless seeing people hurt was his amusement.

'I'm going. And don't worry Natalie, I shall never have to *darken* your door again. Thank God and hallelujah for that. Amen.'

With that, he wheeled around and was up the driveway in four long strides. In the car he turned, tipping his fingers to his right temple in salute at Natalie, a big grin on his face, before driving away, wheels spinning on the frosty tarmac.

Natalie stood in the doorway watching the car as it disappeared down the street. His salute and grin chilled her more than the morning air. What was going on? He came worried about Emmie, although clearly not as much as he'd said as he left with a smile and a wave after achieving nothing.

'Whats going on, hun, I thought I heard voices?'

Natalie turned to see Michael standing behind her looking puzzled.

'That's what I'd like to know,' She said, bending to put the few bits of paper strewn around the floor back into the torn carrier bag, she stepped outside and put the bag into the bin before shutting the door. 'That was Scott saying that Em is in some kind of trouble. I didn't find out what though, I tore a strip off him and told him to leave. I mean, Em would call me if there was trouble right? She sounded fine a few days ago.'

Michael put his hands on her waist and looked down at her.

'Honey, Emmie would most definitely call you. Stop worrying. Scott is an asshole, we all know that. You have a direct line to Emmie, get the news from the horse's mouth before worrying, please.'

'But he smiled at me as he left, it was … weird.'

She shivered, cold fingers walking down her spine.

'People smile all the time, Nat, even Scott, why do you think it was weird?'

She shrugged as he continued.

'We're all aware of the games Scott likes to play. So we're not going to let him play this one, right? Call Em, sort this out, and stop worrying.'

Natalie sighed nodding. She stepped out of his arms and walked down the hall.

'I will. I was making coffee before Scott came, do you want one?'

Michael turned to face her, picking up the paper from the telephone table.

'Go on then, please. Was this for recycling?'

Natalie glanced back at him, nodded, and turned to the kitchen.

'You do realise it's ten to ten, babe.'

'Yeah, well, I need this one.' Natalie murmured as she disappeared into the kitchen. She felt the cold draught of air circle her legs as Michael opened the front door, and heard the bin lid bang as he threw the paper away.

Chapter 39

Emmie lay in bed, cosy and warm, a contented smile on her face. It had been the kind of day that she had imagined when she decided to move to Scotland. A day in nature, up on the hills. She couldn't remember the last time she'd felt so carefree and the children had loved every second. This evening they had roasted marshmallows over the fire and drank hot chocolate. It had been the perfect family day before Grace started nursery, and with them both at school in the morning, she was looking forward to concentrating on getting some work done.

She mentally checked off the things she needed to do as she lay in the darkness. Website updates, social media, advertising and writing a pitch for an article idea to submit to a national art magazine. If that got done within the three and a half hours Grace was at school she would go on to the bit she actually loved; painting.

With the contented feeling that life was moving forward, she slipped into a deep sleep.

She had expected to sleep soundly, but she was awake and on edge after what felt like five minutes. It was cold. Her nose felt like ice, and she was sure she would be able to see her breath before her had it not been dark. She snuggled down further under the duvet but sleep wouldn't come and the more she closed her eyes against the darkness, the more she felt there was someone, or something, in the room with her.

The air was thick and stagnant. Emmie squeezed her eyes closed and rolled onto her side adopting a fetal position. Her heartbeat thumped against her legs.

Then; a soft step, from over by the doorway.

She pulled in a breath, the hairs standing up on the back of her neck, goosebumps breaking out over her arms and legs. She waited, holding her breath, ears straining for the smallest of sounds.

Nothing.

Emmie released her breath chastising herself.

This is ridiculous! We decided to stick two fingers up to shadow man and instead get rendered a shrivelling mess by the invisible man. Roll over and hit the lamp lets see who this bugger is.

Another soft step from inside the room. Emmie whimpered involuntarily as she tried to tame the shakes. The light had to go on fast. She didn't want to take the chance that anything would grab her in the dark.

Ok, Em, ready? We can do this. 3 ... 2 ... 1 ... go!

With the speed of a whippet, she threw back the bedclothes and flung her hand toward the touch-sensitive lamp. She missed twice, banging the cupboard before hitting the base. The room came to life with a glare that immediately made her cover her eyes against the brightness. Blinking into the light, she slowly opened her eyes and looked around the room.

There was nothing to be seen, no unearthly creature was stepping toward her bed to grab her in the dark, but the feeling of a presence and deep unease stayed with her, in spite of the light. A shudder ran through her. She raised a hand to wipe the hair from her face and it came away with a film of sweat. She sat back against the headboard and closed her eyes fighting every childhood urge to fling herself under the covers where she would feel 'safe'. The pressured feeling increased until she could feel the static energy of someone very close to her, every hair on her head seemed to stand on end.

Snapping her eyes open she surveyed the room, which looked completely normal.

What now? When the light doesn't work, what's next?

She sighed shakily. Was it worse to see, or not to see? There was no relief either way. Emmie decided to take the route she often took in childhood after all. She would leave the light on and hide under the covers. If nothing else she hoped the saying 'What you can't see won't hurt you' was recounted for a reason.

Pulling herself down under the duvet she curled into a fetal position. She lay, shivering in a cold sweat, waiting to see if the feeling would die away. Lamplight penetrated the cover, casting dull orange light under the duvet, where Emmie could see her breath clouding over her shaking knees.

There was another step.

Soft and light, further in the room this time. Emmie didn't know where to put herself, she was beginning to feel half past scared, going on terrified.

The next few steps came quickly in a series of thumps right up to her side of the bed. She held her breath, every nerve in her body tingling. Sensing the thing that would be standing just on the other side of the duvet.

There was another step. How much closer was it going to try to get? She pushed out a shaky hand running it down the underside of the duvet pushing slightly as she leaned forward to peer at the floor via the triangle gap.

There were feet.

Toes turned toward the bed, pointing at her. Emmie jumped and let out a strangled noise throwing back the duvet ready to take the thing down out of sheer terror.

She came face to face with Grace who was looking at her expectantly. Emmie stared at her before grabbing her shoulders to make sure she was actually there.

'Grace...?'

'I'm scared, mommy. I had a dream.'

Emmie wished the damn elephant in the room would disappear so that she could concentrate.

'You had a dream?'

Grace nodded and climbed onto the edge of the bed, tucking her knees up to her chest, her toes pointing down to the floor. Emmie thought she looked pretty scared. She wondered if she looked as terrified as she felt to Grace.

'You want to sleep with mommy until morning now?'

Grace nodded again and scrambled over her to the other side of the double bed. She picked up the duvet and slid herself underneath pulling it up to her chin.

'I'm just changing my pj's sweet and then we'll snuggle, I guess mommy had a nightmare too.'

'Okay.'

Emmie sat on the side of the bed and stripped out of her damp pyjamas finding a new nightdress to slip back on. She was pulling the nightdress over her head when she heard Grace.

'Mommy? ... Can you fix this? It's broken ... Help me.'

Icy hands placed themselves up and down Emmie's spine. It was a trick. It hadn't been Grace at all. It was the other Grace, the one from her dreams. The presence in the room was now so intense it was forming a pressure like hands pushing on each side of her head, a high whine settling in her ears.

Emmie was frozen. She couldn't turn around for she knew what she would see. Grace would be in her Peppa top, torn and battered, left arm broken, and heart in her right hand. She had seen this Grace many times in her nightmares but had no desire to sleep with her in bed, with the light *on*.

Her skin prickled. She shimmied the nightdress down her body and slowly looked out of the corner of her eye turning toward Grace. Grace was still there, pink and alive and snuggled in bed with the duvet up to her chin exactly as she had been. Sensing Emmie looking at her, she turned.

'What mommy?'

'What did you say, Grace?'

'Nothing mommy.'

Grace looked puzzled

'A ... Are you sure? I thought I heard you ask me to fix something?'

Saying it out loud brought the gooseflesh out again, she rubbed her arms and swung her legs into bed, trying to claim some warmth.

Grace wrinkled her nose perplexed.

'Fix what?'

Just your heart, darling, no biggie.

'I don't know Grace, never mind. Let's sleep. I think there's someone who starts big girl school in the morning.'

Grace grinned.

'Me.' She said.

Emmie dropped open her mouth in mock horror.

'No! Really? Is it you? Are you that old already?'

Grace nodded, eyes wide, lips pinched together as she grinned.

'We'd better get to sleep then, or you'll be snoring through the whole thing tomorrow.'

She tickled at Grace's sides making her giggle as she lay down next to her until they were almost nose to nose.

'Get off mommy we need to sleep.'

Emmie smiled and planted a kiss on Grace's head, closing her eyes. The presence seemed to have dissipated, she realised with relief, she no longer felt the room was in the realm of another universe. It was as if someone had flipped a switch.

She lay her head on the pillow and closed her eyes. A murmur drifted up from beside her.

'Turn the light off then, mommy.'

Reaching her hand back, she knocked the base and turned the light off. She tensed, holding her breath, but the room felt passive again, warm and homely.

Chapter 40

The morning of the first major school run went with considerable ease. The alarm went off at 7.30am with two chipper children raring to go. Grace was keen to get to big school with Charlie, and Charlie was eager to show her where she had to go. The day had dawned fine and bright again and Emmie felt a little bounce in her step, the events of the night seeming light years away under the cheerful sunshine drifting through the front windows.

At 8.20am Emmie drove to the school, dropping Charlie at the gate before taking Grace to the nursery. Grace had been fantastic; quiet, but there had been no tears as she had hugged her goodbye with a cheery smile.

Driving back, Emmie shed plenty of tears for both of them. She almost missed the turn to the lane as her vision swam in and out of focus, and was just pulling herself together as she passed Bill's farm. When Bruadair finally came into view she saw another vehicle parked on her patch of grass.

Frowning, she slowed. It was a nice car, a white Audi, one of the big four wheel drive ones, and not very old by the looks of it. The problem was that it wasn't a car she recognised, and she really wasn't in the mood for visitors.

Rolling her eyes with a sigh, she pulled up next to the Audi turning the engine off and grabbing another tissue from the pocket of her coat. She quickly dried her eyes and blew her nose before grabbing her bag and getting out of the car.

She saw him immediately, leaning against the boot of the Audi, hands in his pockets, an easy smile on his face as he watched her.

'Oh ...?' Emmie stopped short puzzled.

Stuart? What's he doing here? ... Oh shit, I'm crying again ... How does he know where I live? ... please stop looking so damn hot ... I didn't pay him for the room ...

'Oh!' She said slapping both hands up to her forehead. How had she forgotten? 'Oh shit, I meant to come to the pub yesterday to pay you. I forgot. I mean … I just … I guess I just got lost in what we were doing. I am *so, so* sorry.'

He took his hands out of his pockets, standing taller. He was a big man, easily as tall as Scott had been but definitely in much better shape. He held his right hand up, palm toward her, as he shook his head.

'No, no, I told you I wanted nothing from you, and I meant it. I certainly haven't come up here to bother you for that, Emmie, please, forget about it. Are you okay?'

Her heart gave a little skip as he said her name.

'Okay? Yes, I'm fine.' Then she remembered she must look like a puffy-eyed Rudolph from crying all the way home. She sighed and rolled her eyes, 'Oh, you mean I'm crying again. I don't make a habit of it, really, it's nothing.' She waved a hand at him. 'Grace's first morning at nursery. She's probably having a blast while I'm busy breaking my heart. I'll live.'

'Ah, the joys of parenthood.' He said with a smile.

'Indeed. So, anyway, if you didn't come to string me up for not saying thank you and leaving without a word, on top of not paying then...'

He chuckled at that, a deep soothing sound that sent tingles through her body.

'Emmie, really, stop beating yourself up about things no ones accusing you of. I'm here because we need a chat. I'm glad the bairns are at school to be honest. I'm not sure how much of it you'd want them to hear.'

She paused, searching his eyes for information. He smiled, holding her gaze but offered nothing else. She heaved a sigh.

'Looks like my day is about to hit a new high then. It's cold out here, would you like a tea or coffee?'

'Aye, tea would be nice, lass.' He gestured at the house. 'I'd like to see what you've done with the place. It was a wreck last time I was out here, didn't look much worth saving, although it's looking good and secure from the outside now.'

Emmie nodded.

Oh, it is. All the demons are on the inside, how about that?

They walked to the little gate together, and Emmie led the way down through the tangled path.

'It's a work in progress,' she said, 'I didn't come up here with much, so it's basic, but it's starting to feel like home.'

'Aye and it's looking like a home again too, You've done a grand job externally. I'm just wondering, why a mother with two young bairns … single?'

She looked back over her shoulder.

'Divorced.'

'Right, so what made you take on a derelict building in rural Scotland all alone when you've come from the south of England, if my accent assessment is any good?'

'Surrey,' She threw back, 'Kent border really.'

'All the way from the bottom? What made you run so far from home?'

They reached the door. Emmie turned her back to it, folding her arms over her chest and looking up at him.

'Who said I was running?'

He backtracked immediately.

'I'm sorry, Emmie, I didn't mean any offence. Tell me to butt out if I'm going too far. I love to hear a good story, and yours is intriguing me so far that's all.'

'It's pretty average, really.'

He gestured at the house smiling as a puzzled frown flit across his face.

'What can be average about what you've achieved up here on your own? And the lady that came into my pub Friday night after a room? There was nothing average about that either.'

Her heart picked up pace, her eyes were locked on his and her palms were starting to sweat. She tried to look away but couldn't. She was on the cusp of letting everything go. It would be a relief to tell someone, at least about the man watching. Maybe the invisible man stuff could wait, she didn't want him to think she was a complete lunatic just yet.

Could I tell him everything? Would he believe me?

He seemed kind and genuine, but she knew appearances could be deceptive. Scott had taught her that. Stuart seemed different though. His eyes held a warmth and kindness that Scott's rarely had. And he was here, holding her gaze as much as she held his.

She wondered whether his heart was racing as much as hers, she had the urge to reach out and press her hand onto his shirt to find out.

Stop it, Emmie, what is the deal? You only met him two days ago he could be a blessed serial killer.

She tore her eyes away and turned to the door unlocking it.

'Tell you what,' She said, going into the hallway - warm, which was good news. 'Tell me your news first, and if I'm still standing, I'll show you the house and tell you my *very* average story.'

She turned to hold the door as he stepped into the hall and looked around. He nodded slowly. Emmie couldn't tell if it was in answer to what she had said or approval of the hallway. She locked the front door behind them, immediately regretting the instinctive action at the bemused look on Stuart's face. She shrugged.

'Old habits die hard, okay?'

'I didn't say anything.'

'The look on your face said it all.'

She turned toward the kitchen, and he grabbed her arm gently, stepping toward her. Electricity zipped through her as she looked up at him.

'Emmie, I'm not here to judge you, you know that right?'

She nodded not trusting herself to speak. He was close, so close she could smell the heady scent of his cologne, see the shape of muscle through his fitted shirt. If she slipped her arms around him now her head would nestle just nicely under his stubbled chin.

'Good, then let's get tea.'

He broke the spell, giving her one of his dimpled smiles before letting her arm go and moving into the kitchen. Emmie took a couple of breaths. She was shaking, and her legs wouldn't move to follow him. She looked down the hall at her appearance in the mirror. Not wonderful but at least her eyes looked normal, and there were no black mascara streaks from crying. She ran her hands across her cheeks anyway, fingers brushing the dark circles under her eyes, on the whole she looked okay, she just needed some sleep.

Come on Em, stop this crap. You're a grown woman, and one with no need of a man. Control yourself and listen to what he has to say without being stupid, please?

Nodding to herself in the mirror, she turned to the kitchen where Stuart was filling the kettle.

'Thought I was having tea with myself for a moment there.'

'Sorry,' she mumbled. 'Just checking I didn't have mascara streaked all down my face, we can't have a serious conversation if I look like a clown can we?'

He laughed at that, so much so that Emmie had grinned and finally laughed along with him. She pulled the cups out of the cupboard and made the rest of tea motioning for Stuart to sit down.

'So, we need to talk?' Emmie brought the cups to the table and pulled out the chair to sit opposite him.

Stuart glanced at his tea momentarily. When he looked back at her his face was grave. Emmie felt a stab of worry slice through her, what on earth was this about?

'Aye we do, lass,' He said. 'I don't really know how to tell you without worrying you, so I'll just start from the beginning. Edith was attacked Saturday in the shop.'

Emmie's hand flew to her mouth in genuine shock and worry for the lady she had come to like a whole lot.

'Attacked? Oh god, is she hurt?'

'Shaken, but not physically hurt. The man has done it before. She thought he wouldn't come back, but he did, and he'll be back again unless we can figure out why, and put an end to it somehow.'

Stuart stopped and sipped his tea. Emmie swallowed hard, horrified that this had happened to poor Edith and equally as worried about how it involved her.

'What makes you say he'll do it again?'

'Because he didn't get what he wanted, but he knows damn well she has it, and now I do too.'

He looked at her and sighed heavily, running a hand through his hair.

'I don't want to tell you this, especially not after whatever happened to you Friday, although it could be linked.'

Emmie's heart was pounding now. She steeled herself sitting up straighter in her chair turning her hands in her lap.

'Just tell me, please, what does this have to do with me?'

'This man wants to know where you live. Edith lied and told him she didn't know who you were initially and he left, but Friday night he saw you together at the pub. Saturday he's straight back at the shop putting pressure on her. I presume, as he saw you but he's still harassing Edith, that he doesn't want you to know. He fed a story to Edith that he's your brother?'

Emmie reeled. She looked at him shocked and incredulous.

'I don't have a brother, and why would anyone be bothered about where *I* live? I don't know anyone around here which was kind of the whole reason for moving here in the first place. There's nothing anyone here could want with me. Look, are you sure you got the right person?'

Stuart nodded his face serious.

'He called you by name, Emmie, there's no mistake. And he saw you Friday that's why he went back for Edith on Saturday. He told her as much.'

'By *name*?' She felt like she couldn't breathe. 'How would anyone know my name? And if he saw me Friday night why the hell didn't he come and ask me himself? Why let me drive off and then go attack someone else? It doesn't make sense.'

Stuart shrugged raising his eyebrows as he shook his head.

'Your right it doesn't, unless it's innocent and he only wants to surprise you, but given that he attacked someone for information that seems unlikely.'

'Right.'

Emmie sat back and sighed. Why did this keep happening to her? Hadn't she just said that she would take no more crap from shadow man? She already felt like a tightly coiled spring, any more tension and she would crack. She thought about Grace and Charlie. Why did she seem unable to provide a secure place for them to grow up?

Resting an elbow on the table she rubbed at her forehead lifting her dark fringe.

'Okay, so what info have we got about him? Do you have anything at all I can go on?'

Stuart sat back in his chair.

'Oh, aye, that I can help you with. He's been staying at the Grey Lion for just over a week. Been causing quite a stir in the village as he just seems to be wandering around. People come to the guest house mainly to see the waterfall or walk the hills. They never stay more than a few days, Bracken Hill isn't big enough to keep them entertained. He's drawn attention to himself simply by the length of time he's been here … ' He trailed off and took another sip of tea before continuing. 'Anyway, he's a tall fellow, skinny. Blonde hair, fairly long and he has a full beard and moustache.' He frowned. 'Come to think of it he has a southern accent too.'

Emmie tried to piece together what the man looked like in her head as Stuart got up and reached into his pocket pulling out a small yellow post-it note.

'He says his name is Martin …' He checked the paper, 'Stomes. If that means anything? Of course, he's lied about what he does and why he's here up until now so he could be using a false name.'

Emmie stared at Stuart as he words registered, mouth dropping open. Did she hear that right?

'You know him?'

'Martin Stomes?'

Stuart gave a nod, and she felt uneasy laughter rising from her stomach. Was this a joke? Martin the fucking Martian was up in Scotland beating up old ladies? Jeez, he had come up in the world. But it didn't compute, he wasn't violent, she had known him get into boozy brawls but nothing serious. To think that he was attacking people for information about her was downright weird. She looked at Stuart who was watching her, waiting.

'Yeah,' She said, 'I know him, but it doesn't sound right, he's never been a thug. He's a drunk and a layabout. Never done anything with his life except sit at the pub. I can't imagine why he's up here asking for me, or why he didn't come and talk to me last night. We're not friends now, but we were once. Come to think of it, I hadn't seen him for years, and then he turned up at the party …'

She trailed off, her mind busy clicking things into place and coming to a conclusion she really didn't like when Stuart spoke again.

'Well he can certainly drink, I've seen that over the last week. And if he doesn't work it also makes sense that he isn't the one footing the bill. It's a strange set up I don't often get people asking if someone so far away can pay for their boarding in full. Including his bar tab-'

Emmie held her hand up signalling Stuart to stop.

'Let me guess, Scott Harvington is paying. Am I right?'

'Exactly right, lass. I'm guessing you know him too?'

Emmie chuckled lightly at the absurdity. Did she know him? Once, she had known him better than anyone. Now she wasn't sure who he was, and she didn't like that he was bringing minions to Scotland to stake her out either.

'Oh, I know him alright. You want my average story? I was married to the idiot until early last year. He's a divorce lawyer conveniently, and although he instigated the separation, he got nasty and took great pleasure in telling me he was running the show.

'I fought him for a while, but he knew the strings to pull to twist everything to his advantage. It was stressful and expensive, and I had the kids to think about so in the end I dropped it and took his crappy offer. He made sure he got the house, car, everything of value. The kids and I got a small pot of money to start all over again with.'

'He sounds like the kind of guy you're better off without. So, why this place? Revenge?'

Emmie felt her defences flare up, but his eyes held only interest. No judgement, as he had promised. She sighed.

'No, I don't see the point in revenge. I lived with my sister and her family for a while until things calmed down, but when it came to moving on I couldn't afford to buy anywhere suitable in Surrey. I've always loved it up here so I took the opportunity to start over completely. Since the divorce was finalised I've barely seen or heard anything from Scott anyway, so I didn't see there being an issue.'

Stuart frowned.

'What, not even for contact with the bairns?'

Emmie met his eyes and shook her head.

'I moved here to start over, that's all, there was nothing to keep me down there. I tried for months to get Scott to see them but he refused, he doesn't want contact with them.'

His frown deepened in disbelief.

'What kind of man wants no contact with his own bairns?'

'Not the kind I thought I'd married, that's for sure. I guess after that I didn't want to risk running into him with them, so here I am. That's the story, and that's all this is.'

She shrugged, and Stuart smiled. His eyes narrowed as he leaned forward to rest his arms on the table.

'All it is? You didn't want to run into him in Surrey, so you brought this place? Derelict and abandoned in remote rural Scotland. All by yourself.'

A grin spread across her face, as she realised how ludicrous it sounded.

'Extreme, huh?'

He grinned back at her.

'I'd say average. Very average, indeed.'

She rolled her eyes as he threw her own words back at her.

'You're a risk taker?' He continued.

'No, I wouldn't put it like that. I just wanted to make sure I was far enough away that I never saw him again,' Emmie paused and wrinkled her nose, 'I don't think it worked.'

Stuart chuckled, catching her humour and playing along.

'No. Maybe you should have gone further up.'

'The Orkney's?'

His narrowed eyes twinkled.

'Much too close to Surrey. The Shetland's for sure.'

Emmie clicked her fingers.

'Of course. I need to get the house on the market.'

'Well, maybe you should wait, he could just want the shed key back.'

'Not a chance, that was all he gave me in the divorce settlement.'

They both laughed loudly and for so long Emmie's jaw and sides ached in a way they hadn't for far too long.

She was glad to notice it felt a lot less formal in the kitchen now too, unfortunately, it wasn't doing much to ease her feelings. Stuart was proving as easy to get along with as he was on the eye, even under these circumstances.

As the laughter subsided, Emmie picked up her cup and stood, scraping her chair back. She motioned to his empty cup.

'You want another or do you need to get back?'

Stuart nodded as Emmie flicked the kettle switch.

'Aye to both,' he said, 'I do need to get back, but I'll have another. I want to hear this story first, make sure you're okay, and then have the royal tour of this lovely house.'

'Okay, but there's not much to see I'm afraid. I don't even have much furniture.'

'Something else Scott didn't want to share?'

'Not so much as a footstool.'

Stuart chuckled, and Emmie grinned as she made the tea. She was not only enjoying his presence, but his dry humour also broke the tension of the question at hand; Why couldn't Scott just let her go, why did he have to keep messing with her head?

'Thanks, Em,' Stuart said, looking a little more relaxed as she brought the tea over to the table, 'So, you think you know why Scott would be looking for you?'

'Yep, he's an arrogant, controlling git, and he needs to hold the reins at all times.' She sighed looking down at her tea before meeting his eyes again. 'After he threw us out he took great delight in ringing me, at any time of the day or night. I hated seeing his name come up on the screen but he had me cornered, I had to answer in case he wanted to see or speak to the children, which he never did. It broke their hearts and that broke mine. Every damn time. I changed my number just before I moved up here, so I suppose his nose has been put out of joint because he has no way of controlling us now.'

Stuart looked at her, puzzled.

'Controlling you? Seems a strange choice of words.'

'Not really, He has to have tight control of everything in his life, even me and the kids.'

'But *he* divorced *you*, surely he relinquished control at that point.'

'Nope, he was exercising control even then, and with the settlement, and then the phone calls, even his appearance at the party just before I left Surrey. We got to have our last chat about the kids in front of sixty odd guests. I think it was his last ditch attempt to control the situation, but I left anyway. I think he's mad as hell down there, and that's his problem.'

Stuart gave a small nod, one hand rubbed his whiskered chin.

'What was his take on you bringing the bairns up here? Could this be about them? I know you said he didn't want contact, but when they're around the corner, he can change his mind. Now you're up here, he's completely cut off. Maybe it hit home.'

Emmie shook her head.

'I doubt it, he wasn't bothered. He said they were dead to him. He was more interested in getting my wedding ring back before I left.'

She stopped to take a sip of tea letting it warm her as Stuart sat back in his chair and blew out a breath linking his hands behind his head before bringing them back to his face looking incredulous.

'Emmie, that's appalling, I'm so sorry.'

She shrugged.

'It's done now. We're getting on okay up here. It's been good for the kids and me. I just hope whatever he wants it involves me and not them.'

'I'm not sure I like the sound of it involving any of you. He doesn't sound like the type to come up for a friendly chat.' He took a breath to say something and then closed his mouth pursing his lips. Emmie waited. He looked at her narrowing his eyes before carrying on. 'Forgive me, I have to ask, do you think he'd hurt you or the bairns?'

Emmie frowned and looked out the window toward the front garden. It hadn't crossed her mind that he could. He'd been controlling sure, but all of it had been mentally. Other than grabbing her arm a few times and *that* final slap that had propelled her into the coffee table as he told them to leave he'd never touched a hair on her head, but if Martin was staking her out for him then he was going to great lengths to find them.

Stuart touched her arm across the table bringing her attention back into the room.

'I'm sorry, I didn't mean to pry. You don't have to answer that. I was just trying to assess what kind of man - '

'No, it's fine,' she said, cutting him off. 'I mean, our marriage was mostly mind games, he's a manipulator. He likes to think he's clever, he made me test my faith in myself all the time, and I think he enjoyed watching that. That's not to say he hasn't changed though. He has the most atrocious temper. The kitchenware bore the brunt of it over the years, but he was never physical with us. So I suppose the honest answer is ... I'm not sure. He probably has the potential, but past experience would suggest not.'

Stuart frowned.

'Temper, control, manipulation, and emotional games? Doesn't sound like a harmonious marriage. Was it always like that?'

Emmie heard the insinuation in his voice.

You spent all those years with an asshole by choice?

'No,' She said quickly, 'Well, I suppose it was always there, but it was never a problem at first. He got worse over time, and his demands got bigger as his insecurities grew. He vetted my friends, clothes, where I went, what I did. Eventually, he forced me to quit a job that I loved, amongst other things. We were married for ten years which were up and down I suppose, but the last few years he seemed to go into a downward spiral, and things just got worse until we split up.'

Stuart shook his head, eyes on hers. His hand also found it's way to hers encompassing it in warmth.

'That must have been hard to live with.'

'Not really, I learned how to deal with him, what I could say or do that would calm him when I could see the signs that he was winding up. It became second nature.'

'It shouldn't have to.' He said quietly

He was still holding her gaze, still holding her hand and she found she couldn't speak. The silence swelled, and her heart thumped in her chest. She wondered fleetingly if he felt the way she did, and then he broke eye contact. He took his hand away looking at his watch before placing it back on his cup and looking back at her with a sigh.

'Well, it sounds like you're sure Scott is the driving force behind this. you've no other ideas what Martin could be up to?'

Emmie shook her head vigorously. There was no doubt in her mind. Martin wasn't clever enough to mastermind anything.

'So, where does he fit in?'

'He doesn't. I think Martin's here to stake me out, simply to feed Scott information because he's too busy to come up here himself. I don't know where Scott found him. They were close at uni, but Martin dropped out before he finished. I think he ended up doing something with computers, but I heard he got fired some time ago. The thing is, Martin was never violent, I couldn't imagine him purposely hurting anyone. If he's attacking Edith then Scott is obviously putting pressure on him. Hell, I know what *that* feels like, I should have walked right up to him and reeled off my address, helped him out a little.'

Stuart chuckled, warmth lighting his face and eyes.

'He drank so much Friday night he wouldn't have remembered it in the morning anyway. We'd still have been here today.'

He winked at her and Emmie smiled as her stomach flipped over.

'I think I'll pop down and speak to him,' she said, 'If I tell him I know what's going on and tell him to go home, I think he'll go.'

Stuart raised his eyebrows.

'You think it'll be that easy? Scott is paying for everything remember. Scott also has the temper.'

'I know, but I think Martin will have had enough. If he's had a week of Scott on his tail but isn't getting anywhere, he'll probably be getting annoyed and bored by it all now. If I know Martin it probably started as a bit of fun and a chance to prove his worth to Scott. He wouldn't be thinking about the end result. If I speak to him it makes me real again, and that might help make him back down and go home.'

Stuart rubbed a hand over his mouth and chin, sighing.

'I'm not liking this Em, not at all. He's already hurt someone -'

'He is no criminal, Stu, not even a petty one, he has no idea. Call his bluff and he'll run a mile, I guarantee it.'

Stuart was looking at her with an odd expression. A mix between fear for her and awe at what she was suggesting.

'I'll only agree to this on one condition.'

'What's that?'

'You do it in the Grey Lion, under my roof, in the bar where I can keep an eye on you. I don't want him up here, and I certainly don't want you in his room. If you want to confront him and you think it will work then at least do it where I can get to you if you need me.'

Warmth spread through her, and she had the urge to get up and throw her arms around him. She was so grateful to have someone looking out for her up here she could have cried. Thinking she had cried on him enough already she gave him a big grin instead.

'Thank you,' she said, 'I wouldn't have it any other way.'

He gave her a relieved smile before finishing his last sip of tea and putting the cup down on the table.

'So how do you want to play it?'

'Does he have any routine in the morning? If anything does kick off, I'd rather the children weren't around. The nursery does wraparound sessions so I could book Grace in for a whole day but it's expensive - and I don't really want to this early on.'

'Well, he's down for breakfast right as it closes every morning. 10am, sometimes five past, he doesn't eat in the dining area, prefers the quiet of the bar so that would be perfect. After breakfast, he always has a couple of pints before he goes out or back to his room. As I said, he mainly wanders around the falls and the village according to gossip so he shouldn't be too hard to find. In the evening he's back in the bar from around seven, and there he stays until the bar closes.'

'Predictable.' She looked at her watch, 'It's after ten now, and I have to get Grace soon so I'll have to aim for ten in the morning I suppose, I can't chance evening with Grace and Charlie. I'm just worried about leaving it too long after Edith.'

'She'll be fine. We've got a little system in place if he comes in and she feels threatened. I'll go and see her at some point today and fill her in, and I can keep an eye on Martin while he's around. One final thing, I do need to make you aware that he may have seen the house already, although he doesn't know you live here as far as we know so be extra careful, especially tonight.'

'How would he have seen the house?'

'Edith told him of a walk past the falls and up into the hills before he got nasty. The route she gave him would have been straight past the back of your orchard so any climbing of the hill would give him a view of the house.'

'Okay, but we don't know -'

'Aye, we do. That's where he'd been Friday before he ended up in the bar, he spoke for a fair while to Connor about it.'

'About the house?'

'No, not the house, but he did climb the hill, and you'd have to be blind not to see it from even halfway up there. Get past the tree line, and Bruadair is in full view.'

Emmie felt her heart skip. To think she'd felt safe surrounded by the trees and orchard when all the time she was so exposed. She thought of shadow man. Could it be that Martin had already found her and was scaring her? It would seem like a Scott kind of game. Get Emmie scared out of her mind and then step in to finish off. Martin would certainly be tall enough, but the bulk of shadow man was more than Martins unless he'd put on weight. Stuart had said he was skinny though, and it didn't fit with him attacking Edith for information if he already had it. Scott wouldn't be interested in scaring the locals. He would be focused directly on her.

She was pulled from her thoughts as Stuart lightly touched her hand. He didn't hold it this time, and she was a little disappointed.

'Alright?'

She nodded.

'Let me give you my number, Em.' He said, 'I'd feel better if you had it just in case you run into trouble. And I mean *any* trouble, even just changing a tyre or putting up a shelf, but especially trouble that might make you want to rent a room at the last minute with no money. While we're on the subject if you feel you need to get out of here tonight with everything going on, I've plenty of room now, don't even bother to call just come down, and I'll sort you out. It won't be any trouble.'

Emmie smiled.

'Thank you so much. I don't know how I'll ever repay you for all this.'

They exchanged numbers, and he reached over and grabbed her hand across the table squeezing it and then letting go.

'Stay safe. It's all the repayment I need.' He looked at his watch and stood up tucking the chair back under the table. 'I really need to get back, Connor will think I've abandoned him. Let's do the tour another time, I still want to see this house.'

'I'll hold you to that. It's the least I can do.'

Emmie placed the cups on the drainer and followed him to the front door.

'Do you want to come over for dinner sometime?'

The words were out of her mouth before she had a chance to think about what she was saying, and looking at Stuart, she wanted the floor to swallow her up.

What was she playing at?

Her heart pounded as he hesitated.

'It's okay if you don't, I just feel like I should be doing *something* to thank you that's all.'

He looked at her, but she couldn't read his emotion. His face was guarded, and it puzzled her after his openness. She put her hand on his arm. He looked down at it and back at her, but didn't brush her off. He was tense though, she could feel it through his arm, and he was working his jaw too.

'Emmie, thank you,' He finally said, 'It's not you, it's the guest house, it takes a fair bit of work through the day. I've already left Connor this morning. The evenings are busier, I can't ...'

He trailed off, and she swallowed confused, taking her hand away. She wasn't sure what signals he was firing at her. He'd seemed open and friendly enough as they were chatting for an hour over tea, so why had dinner just shut him down? Maybe it was the idea that it was a date, which she regretted. Dinner did sound formal, but in all honesty, she just wanted his company. She would settle for friendship if he wanted nothing more. In fact, it would probably be for the best.

'Don't worry,' She said trying for lightness but not sure she was finding it. 'It was a silly idea.'

'It wasn't silly, Em. It sounds great, I just ... I love running the place, but it doesn't leave much time for anything else, I'm afraid. I'm sorry. I really am.'

'It's okay, I understand.'

He unlocked the door and stepped outside before turning back.

'Keep the door locked.'

'I always do.'

He nodded.

'You do. I'm sorry about dinner, and for whatever look I was giving you earlier, I didn't mean to make you feel defensive.'

He did look genuinely sorry, but she couldn't help herself.

'It's okay. I didn't mean to snap. My character judgment is

obviously all over the place.'

He stared at her before stepping back and momentarily placing a hand gently on her cheek.

'It's not. I'll see you in the morning.'

'You will.'

She shut the door as he walked down the path and then turned, pressing her back toward it. She rubbed her temples as she slid to the floor and sat knees tucked into her chest.

Christ Em, you sure know how to drive a man away.

And then the tears came, and she wept. For everything.

For Grace being at school; for the house not being secure; for shadow man outside; for the disturbances inside; for Scott coming after her; for Martin who was beating old ladies to get to her; for the fact that he had seen her house already; for Edith who had been scared on her behalf, and for Stuart and his rejection after he had been so nice.

She wept for her whole sorry life up here, sobbing until there was nothing left to come and she was left limp and cold against the door, breath hitching.

Chapter 41

Martin was in hiding out in his room. Or at least that was how it felt, although he was aware that this was the first place anyone would look if they wanted to find him. He lay on his back on the bed, phone off, hands tucked behind his head.

After the little 'to do' with Ma Hubbard he had been in a state of constant tension, sure that at any moment the Landlord would be up to throw him out. Not only had he set off an alarm, but he had caught him red-handed upsetting the old lady. At least he hoped it looked like he had upset her. If he had been seen to be hurting her, it could be a job for the police, and that scared the hell out of him.

As time dragged on, he started to breathe a little easier, but the landlord had been involved on both occasions, and now Martin was feeling more than a little uncomfortable.

Too uncomfortable to sit in the bar chatting with young Connor, and he had felt so uneasy at breakfast yesterday that he had missed this morning's altogether. Instead, he had scurried down to his car and drove a few miles to the next village for supplies of food, drink and cigarettes which he had smuggled back into his room.

Whichever way he looked at it, he couldn't go on with this investigation. The old lady knew he was after Emmie, the landlord also probably knew he was after Emmie. Hell, by now, Emmie may even know he was after Emmie. She had seemed friendly enough with the both of them.

She had been friendly enough with him once too.

He frowned.

What are you doing here, Stomes? Why does she deserve to be stalked as she starts a new life? What right does Scott have? His ego will swallow him whole one day. She always made time for you. This is just wrong. You need to get out of here.

Martin's temper flared as he thought of Scott. How far he had let himself go in pursuit of Scott's approval. Beating up old ladies? He would never usually have done such a thing. Passed them in the street as they struggled with their shopping bags? Hell yes. But to intentionally hurt someone? Never.

And yet, Scott had managed to panic him to such an extent that he had grabbed the ladies hands.

Hard.

Her whimpers and the pain in her eyes had haunted him ever since. What had he become up here?

He ran his hands over his face. He knew the answer to that one.

Desperate.

Which was also unlike him.

He sat up and reached for the phone by the side of the TV table. He held the button to switch it on and swiped at the screen when it came to life. No missed calls.

Martin hadn't dared call Scott with no information after his threats, so he had sat tense, waiting for a call until 2am Sunday morning. Then he had switched the damn thing off and gone to sleep. It had been off ever since, and now, on Monday evening, there were still no calls?

A stab of fear passed through his gut. In Scott's case, no news was definitely *not* good news. Either he was sitting in Surrey thinking up ways he could kill and dispose of a body leaving no forensic trail, or he would be planning a trip to Scotland, and probably writing exactly that into the trip itinerary. Martin thought the latter would probably be more Scott's style.

It was time to move out of the heat or get third-degree burns.

Energised, he got off the bed and packed what little he had brought with him into his bag, before he noticed he was losing the light. Outside he saw the long drawn shadows of a dipping sun across the car park. He pulled a cigarette and the lighter from the pack on the window sill and lit up, pushing the window open further and letting the cold air fan his face. He had an eight-hour journey ahead of him, and that was without traffic and pit stops along the way.

It was also assuming that the car got him all the way back after it had whined all the way here. It had moaned even more at going out this morning after not being used for the last week, and if he were going to break down at all, he would rather it not be in the dead of night. He would also need to pull over and have a nap in the car at some point. It was pure logic that told him, as tall as he was, he wouldn't be sleeping peacefully in a tiny Fiesta, and he had no money for motel rooms.

If the worst happened and Scott got here tonight, he wouldn't see him anyway. He had no intention of going down to the bar, so what was to gain by going now as opposed to going first thing tomorrow morning and taking the day to get home?

If he stayed, he could crack open a can or two, watch TV and sleep in a proper bed for the night. First thing tomorrow he would be out the door.

And this time he was going.

Martin thought about sending a message to Scott telling him that half the village knew what he had been up to, and that he had bullied an old lady (oh, yes indeed), but he decided against it. If Scott called, he wouldn't pick up, he could walk straight into a pile of his own shit. Right where he belonged.

Martin grinned for the first time in days. He flicked the stub of the cigarette out into the air and closed the window. Picking up a can of Carling and a packet of Walkers crisps from his little shopping bag, he switched on the TV on his way to the bed. He settled down ready for one last night in this shitty room before he finally went home.

Chapter 42

As Martin settled down with a Carling for a night of lousy television, Edith sat at her dining table pushing homemade chilli around her plate. Len sat opposite, watching her, his plate empty, his hand encircling a half empty glass of cranberry juice (to keep the waterworks in tip-top condition).

She chased some rice with her fork, unfocused on the plate, her mind littered with thoughts.

'Edie, are you going to chase that around your plate all night, or are you planning to eat it? You haven't taken a mouthful yet.'

'I'm not hungry. If you want it, feel free.'

She pushed the plate toward Len who reached over and took it, scooping a forkful into his mouth. Edith let a small smile play on her lips. He'd always had a big appetite, and chilli was their favourite dish. Tonight, however, her stomach was busy turning over, and she knew one mouthful would be sending her to the toilet to bring it back.

It had been a long time since she had felt nerves like this and pain was starting to throb again at the front of her head. She got up slowly and limped to the counter where she had left the paracetamol she had been popping every four hours, for either her head or her knee, sometimes both.

The last couple of days had drained her mentally and physically. Not knowing whether Martin would turn up and have another play for information was terrifying. She'd had to open the shop, or admit that something was wrong which her pride wasn't willing to do.

Len couldn't do much to help, and she didn't begrudge him that. He had been down to the shop and pottered around a little today, he had struggled, but she knew he sensed her apprehension. A marriage didn't get to thirty-six years without knowing a little of the person you were married to. She hadn't had to say she was scared of Martin, Len knew her well enough to be ninety percent accurate at mind reading. She loved him for trying, and being able to mind read right back, she knew he wouldn't leave her until he absolutely needed to sit down. She did worry what would happen to him if Martin made an appearance though; torn between wanting him with her and wanting him out of the way of trouble. He was so breathless these days she wasn't sure it would take much of a jab to bring him down, and certainly not much more to bring him down indefinitely.

As if that hadn't been enough Stuart had been in to see her this morning to fill her in on his visit to Emmie. To add to the list of worries, she now knew there were two threats, in the form of Martin and Scott, and it appeared that Scott was the big bad wolf of the story. Edith had been scared enough by the mouse not to want to see the wolf at all, but no one knew if he would be turning up to join the story anyway.

The uncertainty was driving her to such distraction that a customer had dropped a can of peas this morning and she'd had to stuff a hand into her mouth to stop herself from screaming out loud. If things were this bad for Edith, she couldn't imagine how poor Emmie must be feeling up there alone, not only wondering whether Scott would be coming up, but also that she was going to have to confront Martin tomorrow too.

Edith sighed and gripped the counter top as she swallowed the pills without water. This headache was a clanger, but she knew exactly where it had originated. The discussion with Stuart had become quite heated when, as Len had told her, she had tried to stick her nose where it didn't belong. Edith had only stuck her nose in out of concern, and she hoped Stuart would understand and come around. She rubbed her head and reached for the red wine pouring herself a small glass.

She patted Len on the shoulder as she hobbled over to the settee and sat down. Tomorrow, one way or another, things would change. She hoped it would be for the better, or the general store in Bracken Hill may not be open for business much longer, the shop owner veering dangerously toward becoming a frightened recluse.

She took a sip of wine, tasting the dry fruitiness on her tongue and decided tomorrow she would go and make her apology. It didn't matter if she thought she was right or wrong, whether she had said it out of the goodness of her heart or not, Stuart was one of her closest friends. He didn't stand for the gossip of a small village any more than she did. He was one of the few people, Len aside, that she could have a decent conversation with about everything but the inhabitants of Bracken Hill.

Decision made, and headache dulled by the painkillers, she put the half-finished glass of wine on the table and told Len she was off to bed while the going was good. She fell asleep before Len had finished with her chilli, but it wasn't long before the dreams returned, keeping her awake and restless through the night.

Chapter 43

As Edith was drowning her sorrows in a small glass of red, Emmie was busy drowning her sorrows in a bottle. The children finally tucked up in bed she went into the living room with the wine and a glass, shutting the doors and curtains for shadow man's benefit, and curling up on the settee opposite the roaring fire. For a while she sat listening to it pop and snap, letting the smell of burning wood and pine remind her of campfires, holidays, and her father. She thought of Natalie and herself, sat roasting marshmallows, giggling as the ghostly orange light danced on their faces in the darkness. She remembered the old guitar their dad would use to sing the campfire songs that they learned to join in with as they got older, the stories he used to tell, scaring them until they shook with fear. And then the last story, that would have them holding their stomachs with laughter, right before they went into the tent and slipped into their sleeping bags. The funny story always took the edge off the fear by the fire, but in the darkness of the tent, it would be the scary stories that would come back to visit Emmie in the night.

The familiarity of the sound, smell, and the memories lulled her so much she almost didn't hear the little tap and scrape. She turned, glancing over the arm of the chair and saw a rectangle of white paper sitting half underneath the door, poking into the living room from the hall.

Eyebrows drawing together Emmie got up off the settee. She was so focused on the strange paper that when her phone chose that moment to buzz and sing it's merry tune she physically recoiled before letting out her breath in a half laugh.

Okay, Em, panic over, it's just a phone.

Oh jeez, I gave a very hot, very uninterested, male my number earlier. If it's him I may just die of embarrassment.

She grabbed the phone looking at the caller id, and was a little deflated to see Natalie's name lit up across the screen. She answered quickly, her heart still thumping.

'Hey Nat, I was just thinking about you.'

'Oh really? All good I hope.'

'Of course! I was thinking about our camping trips when we were little, and how dad used to scare the hell out of us around the campfire before bed.'

She chuckled lightly but trailed off when she realised Natalie wasn't joining in.

'Why would you be thinking of that, Em?'

'Well, I don't know. I'm here sitting by an open fire. It just brought back memories, that's all.'

'Of being scared?'

'No, Nat, of camping holidays ... that just happened to include scary stories. Why on earth would you think I'd be sitting here thinking of being scared?'

'I don't know, Em, is there anything you need to tell me? Anything at all?'

Emmie pulled the phone away from her ear and stared at it. Natalie couldn't know about shadow man, or the fact that she thought she wasn't alone in the house, nor even the fiasco with Martin and Scott, could she?

She put the phone back to her ear and heard Natalie calling her name.

'I'm here. I don't know what you want me to say, Nat. I'm not scared, should I be?'

Natalie harrumphed down the phone. Emmie waited, not sure what Natalie had meant by the sound.

'So I'm not good enough to be told of anything worrying you, is that it?'

'Nat, where is this coming from? I'm not worried. There are a few teething problems, sure. Certainly, nothing I would bother you with.'

And nothing I'm going to worry you about until I need to - if I need to.

'Something you might bother Scott with though?'

'Scott? I don't even have his number anymore, and he changed the house number last year. How could I suddenly call Scott, and why the hell would I want to?'

Natalie didn't reply.

Emmie sighed, if Natalie thought there was an issue with Scott she was halfway there, she was just coming at it from the wrong angle. Maybe it would be a good time to come clean after all.

She rubbed a hand over her face.

'Listen, Nat, if you want the truth, Scott may be *the* problem.'

'What do you mean *Scott's* the problem?'

Her voice came down the line harsh and clipped.

'No Nat, you first. You called me with accusations, so what got your goat?'

She heard Natalie huff.

'Fair enough. Scott came to see me yesterday before work spouting that you were having some kind of trouble and he was worried about you. He didn't elaborate, but the whole encounter was just weird. I have been going out of my mind with worry.'

Emmie frowned in confusion. What would Scott want with Natalie? And then her stomach lurched.

My address. He has no luck with Martin, so he has a shot at getting the information from Natalie.

'Em? You still there?'

'Uh-huh.'

'Did you hear -?'

'I heard you Nat, and there is no need to worry, not yet anyway. Please tell me you didn't tell him anything?'

'As if I would! We didn't talk for more than a minute before he left. What is going on?'

'I believe he is trying to find me for some reason, although I can't figure out why.'

'What? He didn't speak to you for months down here, so why would he need to contact you now?'

'How would I know?'

'That's ridiculous Em. It doesn't make sense. Where did this come from?'

'Martin is up here. I'm not sure if you remember Martin Stomes from my Uni days?'

'Martin? I'm not -'

'Martin the Martian we called him.'

'The guy who dropped out? What does that have to do with Scott?'

'It appears Scott has hired him to chase me up here and find out where I am. He's staying at the guest house in the village nearby. He's been hassling the people who live there for information about me.'

'What?! Are you serious? Because this isn't funny, Em. What do you mean he's hired him? Scott hasn't seen him for years has he?'

'It would appear that he has, and made enough contact to make him chief investigator. It must have been going on way before I moved here too, because Martin somehow sneaked himself into my leaving party. I saw him before Scott turned up, and he followed on his tail as he left. Scott is apparently paying for his room here and all his living expenses. I presume he couldn't get the time off work, or he would surely be here himself.'

Natalie was quiet, and Emmie could almost hear her cogs working.

'Are you completely sure, Em? How did you find all this out?'

Emmie quickly ran through the events of the last few days, starting with Edith's first visit from Martin and the information she had got from Stuart this morning, finishing with the plan to talk to Martin.

'There's no mistake, Nat, I'm on Scott's hit list. Maybe he can't stand the fact that I'm so far away and making a good go of a life up here, he wanted me kept down there under his thumb. It's either that or he wants to take Grace and Charlie back. I can't decide which, but he's not getting his hands on the children, they're happy here. If he wants a fight, he'll most certainly get one.'

'He didn't mention Charlie and Grace, just the fact that he'd heard you were in some trouble and he wanted to help. It seemed like he had partial information he wanted to clarify. Em, are you sure there's nothing you're not telling me?'

'I promise, Nat. The only problem I have is Scott, and the way he's going about this. Why the secrecy? He knows you worry, He probably thought he would use that to get he info he wanted. Thank God you gave him nothing.'

'I promise you I sent him away with his tail between his legs. Do me a favour Em, promise you'll keep in contact if you're worried, upset or any other emotion you need to share. I don't want to be caught off guard like that again. I didn't know what to believe. I could have given him everything he needed if he hadn't switched from worried to angry so quickly that it made me suspicious.'

'Of course I will Nat, but I'm okay at the moment, especially knowing that Scott is still in Surrey. I'm looking forward to getting a clearer picture tomorrow after Martin sheds light on his part in all this.'

Natalie gave a hefty sigh on the other end of the phone.

'God Em, I don't like this ... make sure you call me straight after, and please be careful. If he is attacking people he may not be as harmless as you remember.'

I must hold the record for the most times being told to be careful in the last two days.

'I will, Nat, but I'll be fine. As I said, I'll be in a public bar, and Stu is way bigger than Martin. He promised to be around while I talk to him, if anything happens Stu could probably knock him flat with a flick of his finger.'

Natalie laughed surprised.

'Oh, you managed to get doe-eyed about someone up there already?'

Emmie smiled.

'No, not really. He's got a kind soul, and he's certainly very nice to look at, but I'll have to stick to dreaming. I'm busy making an idiot of myself, and he's not at all interested. I think I've cried on him one too many times. He probably thinks I'm an emotional wreck.'

'What?! Back up, I need details.'

Emmie quickly filled Natalie in on how she met Stuart, only mentioning that she was staying over for the burns night celebrations, nothing about shadow man at the doors. She went for humour rather than horror and Natalie was laughing at the end of the tale.

'Oh my god, Em,' she spluttered down the phone, 'Only you can get emotional begging for a room and then have no money to pay and still manage to work it to your advantage.'

Emmie laughed too. The sound filled the warm living room. This version was working out a lot better than the real one, if only the ending were a little different.

'I don't know if I blushed more through embarrassment, being plied with free wine, or when I thought he was going in for the kill asking me my name. I was a mess, Nat.'

More laughter down the line.

'I wish I'd have been there. I'd have told him you were a mess, and spared him the effort of finding out.'

'Thanks, I always wondered what big sisters were for.'

Emmie and Natalie laughed together, by the time their laughter had died away Emmie was wiping the tears from her cheeks again. Good tears this time.

God, it's good to speak to you, Nat.

'So, are you seeing him again?'

'Tomorrow obviously, with the Martin business.'

'Stop being coy you know exactly what I mean, are you *seeing* him?'

'Nope. I did invite him to dinner, but he turned me down.'

'Right.'

There was a pause and then Natalie sighed. Not one of those little huffs, this was a full-on exhale, out of pity or relief Emmie couldn't tell, but when Natalie spoke again, she seemed to be choosing her words carefully.

'Em, it may be better that way you know, you have a lot on your plate. Don't go chasing him, let it lie, Concentrate on getting yourself on your feet. Take some time to be by yourself up there.'

From anyone else that would have stung but Emmie knew that Natalie was a born worrier. Anyway, she was doing just fine up here alone.

Although that's not entirely true is it Em? Not at all. And she's right you do have a lot on your plate.

'Don't worry Nat, I know what I have to deal with, and this stuff with Scott has to be figured out. I'm not chasing him, if it's meant to be it will happen in time. I'm just going to be happy to have him watch out for me as a friend, and god knows I can use a couple of those up here right now.'

'It's for the best at the moment, you know that right, Em?'

Em chewed on a nail.

Maybe I do, and maybe I don't. All I know is I've been on my own for a long time, and he makes my head spin, is it so wrong to want a little company?

'Yep,' She said lightly.

'I hope so Em, I really do. Listen, I've got to go,' Natalie said with a yawn, 'I haven't managed much sleep with two such close shifts, and I'm back on tomorrow afternoon. Call me before then and let me know what's going on okay?'

'Will do. Bye Nat.'

'Take care, Em.'

The phone clicked cutting off the connection, and Emmie turned to put it back on the table. From the corner of her eye she caught sight of the small piece of paper, still half under the doorway to the hall. She frowned, more curious than concerned, as she picked the paper up and turned it over.

The smile slowly slipped from her lips as she took in the photograph.

It was one from the box, and that was okay, she had left it on the dressing table, the kids could have been messing with them this afternoon.

What made a shudder run through her was the picture itself. It would have been from around 1996, when Emmie had been fourteen, and Natalie seventeen. It had been the last holiday they had been on together as a family, camping in the Cairngorms. The photo depicted Natalie, in Jeans and a black ski jacket, a huge smile on her face. Emmie sat next to her, in a parka with fur around the hood, head thrown back in laughter. Both girls sat on a log, orange light playing over the front of them, shadows slinking behind. At their side, also smiling, their father played the guitar next to the campfire.

Holy crap, that's some coincidence!

Emmie's hands shook, and the photo fluttered from her grasp, twirling down to the floor and landing picture side up.

Chapter 44

Natalie woke early Tuesday morning with a thumping headache. She lay in the dark staring at the shadows on the ceiling but sleep just wouldn't come. She turned toward Michael, propping herself on an elbow, enviously watching as he slept, chest rising and falling with each loud snore. She'd had two hectic shifts almost back to back over the last couple of days, getting back over an hour late from each one. Michael had promised her last night that he would deal with the children this morning, allowing her to sleep in for as long as she wanted before her shift at 2pm this afternoon.

And yet, as sod's law would have it, here she was, wide awake at some ungodly hour after a night of unsettled sleep, listening to the snores of someone who was obviously sleeping very well.

She got out of bed before she gave in to the urge to place a pillow over his face and hold it there until he was quiet. Feeling her way down the stairs she only turned on the light when she got into the small kitchen. She filled the kettle and switched it on before leaning back against the counter, rubbing her face with both hands.

A little knot of worry worked it's way into her stomach as she waited. She glanced at the clock.

4.30am. Great.

Her shift finished at 10pm tonight, and she didn't think she had a hope of staying awake that late. Conversely, she knew there was no point going back to bed, any chance of sleep had long gone. She decided she would go into the living room, pull the blanket over her and read a book, see if she could sleep downstairs. If nothing else at least it might take her mind off Emmie until she called later.

She was at the sink, staring at the little pile of washing up from the night before, looking but not really seeing, when a clatter from behind made her jump, almost making her scream out loud. She swung around in time to see a fluffy tail disappear out of the kitchen door in a streak of grey. The dog, Minnie, padded in from the living room where she had been curled up in bed and looked at Natalie, head cocked on one side inquiring.

'Don't look at me I didn't wake you, go see Snoop. Damn cat nearly gave me a heart attack.'

Minnie cocked her head to the other side listening but didn't move.

'Bed!' Natalie said as firmly as she dared without waking the house. Minnie turned tail and padded out.

She turned to the sink to pick up the spoon, and arms clamped around her waist. She flinched, spoon clattering to the floor and bouncing across the tiles. She opened her mouth to scream, and a hand found it's way quickly from behind and over her mouth. She muffled a scream anyway and was about to bite the hand when a voice whispered in her ear.

'Shhhh, Nat, it's me! Christ, you're so jumpy. What on earth are you doing out of bed at ten to five in the morning?'

All of her muscles turned to jelly with relief as she heard Michaels voice. She turned to him thumping him lightly with both fists on his chest.

'Good God Mike, what do you expect when you creep up on me in the dead of night? I thought you were …'

She stopped, knowing she was going to say Scott but that was ridiculous right? Scott had never shown any tendencies toward breaking into peoples houses. Had he freaked her out so much that she thought he was going to stalk her in the night until she told him Emmie's address?

'Were who?' Michael pressed, looking amused.

'No-one, I don't know. A murderer or something. Just don't creep up on me in the dark okay? Coffee?'

'Coffee? Did you hear me? It's ten to *five*. What I want is for you to come back to bed. You've hardly had any rest for the last two days. You asked me to sort the kids to let you have a lie in and here you are up drinking coffee before the crack of dawn.'

Natalie stooped to pick up the spoon and turned to rinse it under the tap before adding sugar and stirring her coffee.

'I can't sleep.' She said.

'No kidding.' He said, hands circling her waist again. 'What's the matter, honey?'

'I think you'd better have a coffee. It's a long story.'

Settled on the settee, coffee in hand, Natalie filled Michael in on the phone call with Emmie the previous evening and of her worries about both Martin and Scott, and ultimately Emmie's safety. She left nothing out, reiterating how Scott had seemed strange on Sunday. When the tale was complete, Michael sat quietly, watching her.

'Well?'

'Well, I'm not sure what to think Nat, but I do think you're over worrying. I can't believe Scott would be thinking about chasing Emmie all the way up to Scotland, especially when he's had the chance to say what he wanted for the last year while she has been living on his doorstep.'

'But Emmie knows that Martin is after her address, do you think he wants it for himself?'

'Maybe. They're old friends. He may just want to get in touch again. It's not out of the question is it?'

'He hurt someone, and Scott was after information Sunday when he said Emmie was in trouble. He got mad when I wouldn't give him anything. He was after her address, Mike.'

'Did he say that directly?'

'Well, no. Not in so many words.'

'So it's supposition.'

'He was acting weird. He was after something.'

'Maybe he was actually worried? He's been through as much as she has, it's only natural when you share so many years to still be concerned about the person you shared hardships with.'

'Hardships? For god sake Mike! He was the problem, at the beginning of the relationship and at the close of it too. Bloody hardships! He wasn't worried a squat I'd bet my life on it.'

'Yes, he was a problem, but he was *half* the problem. Maybe I'd give him a little more than half of the share, but Emmie was the other half wasn't she?'

'Mike!'

'It takes two legs to win a running race. The end of the marriage was down to both of them, as is any marriage breakdown. It's a tale of two halves.'

'I can't believe you just said that after all she's been through, after all he put her through!'

'Keep your voice down Nat. I'm not trying to start an argument. You know I love Em as much as you, and yes I know what she has been through, and I know that it's been tough for her, but you also know that she is prone to diving off into the deep end without learning to swim first.'

'So I should just ignore everything I've heard because she is obviously not checking facts, is that it?'

'No, I'm not saying ignore anything, and I'm not saying don't worry. I *am* saying you shouldn't be losing sleep over something unconfirmed and which, to be frank, sounds like lunacy to me. If Scott had anything left to say or do, he would have said and done it by now. I don't understand why he'd bother Nat, really, do you?'

'The children, Mike...'

'Like I said, he'd have said and done it by now, wouldn't he?'

She looked at him, searching his eyes before looking away sighing.

'She seemed so certain though, and what else could he want? She's speaking to Martin this morning remember, can we wait to see what's said before we go dismissing it? If she needs us and I let her down, Mike, I'll never forgive myself. And thinking of that horrible smile Scott gave me Sunday gives me chills.'

Michael looked at her, concerned, but not for Emmie, he was concerned about her. She knew that, but she couldn't help it, until she knew what was going on she wouldn't stop worrying. If Mike and Emmie weren't concerned about all of this then she would worry enough for all of them, it was the way she was made.

'Was it as bad as you thought it was? Was he actually just smiling as he left?'

'At me? I very much doubt it, don't you? No, one minute he was asking to come in to discuss Em and the next he was driving off smiling.'

'Okay, so what happened in the middle?'

'Middle of what?'

'After getting here and before driving off.'

'You mean aside from saying he blames Em for the loss of Charlie and Grace? Which is unforgivable, by the way.'

Michael reached out for her hand with one of his and rubbed at her shoulder with the other.

'I agree but that's not giving us anything, there must be something else.'

Tears well up in Natalie's eyes. She forced them back trying to think.

'I fell over my own bag of recycling, and the blessed door gave me a bruise on my thigh. Maybe he was laughing at that as he drove off. I wouldn't put it past him.'

Mike wasn't listening. He was looking past her, frowning, eyes glazing as he thought.

'Hang on. There was something Nat. The paper on the side table in the hall, the one you asked me to throw out? Did he see it before he went back to the car?'

'Yes, but that was just rubbish Mike, there wasn't anything in that bag that could possibly interest him.'

'I wouldn't be so sure. I put that paper in the bin, and I saw what it was.'

He stopped, licking his lips. Natalie stared at him, not breathing, waiting for him to continue.

'Nat, this could be coincidence, I don't want you to freak out on me alright?'

'For god sake, Michael, tell me what the hell it was.'

'It was the estate agent particulars for Em's place.'

Natalie's hand flew to her mouth, and she uttered a thin cry.

'I … I thought we had thrown them ages ago?'

'Me too, how long has that pure paper recycling bag taken to fill?'

'A month or so, I think'

Michael nodded and she got it immediately. Just about how long Em had been in Scotland.

Natalie covered her eyes and let the tears come.

'Oh god, Mike. I … I … I told her Scott hadn't got anything. But he has everything he wants, doesn't he? No wonder he smiled at me. What do we do?'

Michael moved closer, enveloping her in his arms and rubbing her back as she cried into his shoulder.

'We wait to see what Em comes back with from this Martin fellow. If it matches …'

Natalie looked up at him finishing his sentence.

'If it matches then we need to get up there, she can't deal with whatever Scott is up to alone. I'm booking the week off when I get in this afternoon.'

'Woah, woah. Nat don't be hasty, let's wait and see what she says first. But okay, if it matches maybe we could both get a couple of days off and go up there. See if we can figure this out together. I'll see if Lana could have the kids for a couple of days when I drop them there this morning. If not I'll try my parents. As long as they're okay, then yes, we'll go up there alright?'

'Thank you. I've got a bad feeling about this Mike, everything is about to blow up, I can feel it, I need to get up there to her.'

'Calm down Nat. We have nothing concrete yet. The other thing is there's supposed to be a big storm moving up the country tomorrow. I'm not sure we should be running anywhere just yet. Maybe we should wait a few days, let it pass -'

'No!'

'Nat, if anything happens to us we won't be there for Emmie either way. And, let's face it, if we can't get up there then neither can Scott. Everyone is in the same situation here.'

'He may already be well on his way Mike. He could already be there.'

'Well then Emmie will say so won't she, and if he is we'll get going straight away. I promise, okay?'

Natalie nodded amongst the shakes of her sobs holding onto Michael as if her very life depended on it.

Chapter 45

Tuesday morning in Scotland dawned clear and bright, frozen and heavy with frost, but pleasant, as the last few days had been. If the little radio in the kitchen was to be believed, however, the good weather was about to turn into one almighty storm. Over the next few days it would head up the country from the south, and by Friday the whole of the UK would be hit. Up here heavy snow was predicted to fall for a few days, along with strong winds, which would mean drifts. Emmie thought there might be a chance she could get snowed in, and she was sure the snowplough wasn't going to be in operation up her little lane.

For now, she made breakfast basking in the sun's warmth as it streamed in through the kitchen window, but she made a mental note to pick up extra food and supplies while she was in the village, just in case. She wanted to see Edith anyway. It would be an opportunity to check how she was holding up.

When breakfast was through, and with Charlie and Grace ready for school, Emmie went upstairs to get herself ready. She surveyed her wardrobe remembering a saying her mom always used.

'When you have a job to do, dress well, and you'll perform well.'

God knew she could do with putting in a stellar performance today and although the meeting with Martin didn't need to involve shirts and suits she wanted to feel confident.

She chose Skinny jeans with knee-high fur trimmed boots and a cream long sleeved t-shirt topped with a powder blue cardigan that perfectly matched the colour of her eyes and contrasted her dark hair. She pulled out a long, camel coloured, woollen coat from the wardrobe, hanging it over the bannister as she went into the bathroom to apply a light layer of makeup and sort her hair. The wavy curls seemed to be falling right today, so she clipped the sides up leaving the rest to hang loose down her back. Finished, she rubbed her lips together smudging out the rose coloured lip gloss and surveyed herself in the mirror.

Not bad Em, even after such a crappy inning you still scrub up well. Let's go and knock his feet from under him, eh?

She smiled as she grabbed her coat and headed for the stairs.

If it were a good day, she would be able to do precisely that; but she thought a great day would involve knocking both Martin *and* Stuart's feet from under them simultaneously, for very different reasons.

A bad day didn't bear thinking about.

The first flutter of nerves hit her as she was strapping Grace into the car, just a ripple around her midsection but there all the same. The real nerves, however, started after dropping them off at school and turning the car toward Bracken Hill. Her heart set up a steady fast rhythm behind her ribs, and a bead of sweat gathered on her top lip. She was also shaking she noticed as she changed gear, not just her hands either, her whole body was doing a shake from the inside out. Her stomach clenched, she was barely breathing as she neared the village.

Slowing and indicating she pulled onto the side of the road, bumping the car up onto the verge. The clock on the dashboard read 9.10am, plenty of time.

Turning the car off she folded her arms over the steering wheel and pressed her head into them.

Come on Em, you can do this. Breathe. If you go in like a bag of nerves, he'll sense it. Confidence is what you need even just for the next half an hour, plenty of time for falling apart later.

She took deep breaths in and out but only succeeded in making the car spin and the walls close in at the side of her vision. At the point she thought she might actually faint she turned on the ignition and lowered the driver's window all the way down. Freezing air poured into the car, rushing up her nose with the smell of wet earth bringing her world back steady. She looked out at the road and lowered her head back onto the steering wheel looking out of the driver's side window shivering from cold or fear, maybe a bit of both.

You know you've built Scott into a monster, don't you? You've made him larger than life and given him a power he doesn't possess. What was his worst trait as a husband Em? Throwing a few things, Shouting and twisting words. Twisting your thoughts. Controlling a few actions. That was it.

'Isn't that enough dad?' She told the car unperturbed that her father had appeared in her head from nowhere again.

Oh, sure it is, honey, but the saying goes sticks and stones may break my bones but words ...

'... will never hurt me.' She whispered.

He has as much power as you let him have. The moment you take control and choose to believe in yourself is the moment he loses power. He's a bully with a big mouth and a bigger ego - don't let him be any more than that and he won't. He can't be. His power comes from you and your reaction to him.

She thought that he probably had a point. How much of what Scott had done and said during their ten-year marriage had been compounded by what she had let him get away with. She hadn't wanted to rock the boat, hated the confrontation, so she had agreed with almost all Scott had to say. All of the time. Even to her detriment. The worst thing was, she had known what was going on and had let him get away with it. She had let him beat her down.

'It was all my fault, wasn't it dad? It was all me. I was too weak.'

Her father's voice was gone, whether he agreed or not, he wasn't going to say.

She felt a surge of anger rise from her gut and lifted her head banging a fist on the steering wheel.

Damn Scott. She was doing alright up here (aside from the little issue of the something watching and the something co-habiting) what right did he have following her up here anyway? Why couldn't he let it go? And Martin - why would he want to come up here and help to make her life hell? She had done nothing to him. They had been friends before they parted ways.

After the divorce she had said she was done with self entitled, angry, men controlling her, she had been *determined* a man would never treat her like that again.

And yet, here they were; both of them.

She lifted her chin and looked into the rear view mirror. Her eyes were deep pools, fearful and uncertain, and that wouldn't do.

'I will not be bullied by these men.' She said aloud, looking herself in the eye.

'Did you hear that? I said I will *not* be bullied. I'm *through* with the fucking bullies who the hell do they think they are? Let's go kick Martin's ass, and if and when Scott decides to have a go, I'll be ready and waiting. How dare he think he can violate my territory, and scare us in my part of the world. Fuck you, Scott.'

She grinned at herself. That sounded good out loud. She tried it again.

'Fuck you and your stupid fucking ego you arrogant bastard.'

A giggle escaped her, and she realised she was no longer shaking.

'And Martin?' She continued into the empty car, 'You can stick your shitty detective skills where the sun doesn't shine, you slimy piece of shit.'

Now she laughed aloud.

'And yes, I'm aware I'm talking to myself. Maybe I'll finish my days in Broadmore asylum, and you boys can see if you can find your way in there to brighten your fucking days.'

She nodded to herself in the mirror her eyes no longer held fear just a steely reserve. It was now or never. There was still a niggle in the pit of her stomach, but she didn't think that was up for shifting. That one was in it for the ride, and it was okay, she could squash that one down when it came to it.

She switched the engine on, pulled back onto the road and headed for the village pressing the button to raise the window as she went.

Chapter 46

As Emmie was giving herself a little pep talk in the car, Martin Stomes was rubbing his eyes in bed. He had planned to be on the road by 9am, but it appeared he had overslept, which could have been something to do with the five cans of Carling littered on the floor. He couldn't remember the end of the film he had been watching. For that matter, he couldn't remember what the film was.

He sat up, stretched, and got out of bed swinging his arms in a wide arc. He went to pee and splashed water on his face before getting dressed and placing the cans in a line next to the television. A little going away gift for the landlord.

Opening the top of the packed holdall that served as his luggage, he reached for a packet of crisps and a Snickers for breakfast, but paused halfway to opening the chocolate. They might be useful for the journey. He wasn't going to waste time driving back to the other village today, and he couldn't shop next door now. He replaced the snacks and zipped the bag shut. It seemed this morning he would be having a full English and a pint, on Scott, as a last little farewell gift to him too.

Martin grinned as he snatched the packet of cigarettes off the window sill, lighting one and stuffing the rest into his pocket. What a generous mood he was in this morning. He was feeling good. Maybe it was the going home vibe. He wondered what he could leave for little ma Hubbard next door and thought that a large shit on her back stoop would have done nicely if it had been dark outside.

Shame.

But he wouldn't be going to the shop to cause any more harm. That was the end for him. The lady may have been awkward, but he had done enough, scared himself even. From now on it was back to World of Warcraft for the fighting and the Frog and Toad for the watering. He needed no more excitement in his life.

Taking one last look around his room, he grabbed his bag and coat and went downstairs.

He had expected the same coldness he'd felt over the last few days from the landlord, but although it was clear they weren't about to become best buddies, the man was polite and courteous. He seemed neither surprised, nor relieved, when Martin handed in his key and said he was on his way. He even offered to serve him at a small table by the bar where it was quiet, as Martin himself had often requested when the dining area had been too full for his liking.

The food was excellent, and he set about it with more vigour than usual, having eaten only crisps, biscuits and chocolate for the last couple of days. The smell was divine, that classic full English smell of beans and bacon, even the toast tasted sweet and melted on his tongue. He washed it all down with the finest cup of tea he had ever tasted and ordered a pint as his plates were cleared.

He was sitting back in his seat feeling more than content when the young woman walked into the bar. He eyed her approvingly, taking in her confident stride and slight figure under the long coat, which flowed behind her.

Where were all the women like that in Surrey? He grinned, unable to help himself as he watched her come closer, and then he faltered as she made eye contact with him.

He knew that walk, those eyes, that face. The confidence was new though, and it was sexy as hell, he hadn't gotten that vibe on Friday night, but then he had been pretty drunk, he supposed.

Now he understood why Scott couldn't let her go. Martin wouldn't have let her out of his sight, and a glance at the bar, where the landlord had stopped wiping down the pumps and straightened up to watch her enter, told Martin that the man was as taken with her as he was. Call it guy vibes.

Scott wouldn't like that at all.

He swung his head back to her, heart picking up pace.

What the fuck was he doing here? Scott was an idiot, for losing her and for being an arrogant shit, but Emmie was clearly at her best, broken out from under him and looking all the better for it.

He mentally shook himself, breaking the spell. He needed to move, but it was too late, he was in a half crouch, neither sitting nor standing, when she pulled out the chair opposite him and gracefully folded herself into it. She smiled keeping her eyes on him as he tried to shrink back into his seat wishing it would swallow him up and spit him out somewhere very far away. She leaned forward and rested her head on her clasped hands, elbows on the table.

'Hello Martin,' She said, 'I think we need a little chat don't you?'

Chapter 47

Scott was pacing the living room. The phone clamped to his ear so hard it was starting to hurt. He let it. He was shaking with rage but unable to let it go, the pain helped a little.

'You have Mrs Munroe at 11.30am and Mr Foster at 2pm. You know how I feel about messing clients around Scott. Butler and Tranter have a reputation to uphold. I cannot have my staff dumping clients willy-nilly. I will grant you three days leave from tomorrow, but today I expect your clients to be well served, and the paperwork complete before you go. I don't need to tell you how busy we are at the moment, Scott. Mrs Hibble will get your appointments rearranged from Wednesday through Friday.'

Scott closed his eyes and clenched his jaw holding the phone tighter, knuckles white.

'But this is an emergency, sir. I have never asked for short-term leave before, and I'm rarely off work sick. Please, could you not take that into consideration? I need to leave today.'

'You haven't told me what the emergency is, Scott?'

'Emelia, my wi ... ex-wife. She moved to Scotland last month, she's having some trouble coping, and she's all alone. You know how fragile she is, please sir, after everything we've been through, I'd like to be there for her. She needs me.'

'Yes. I remember Emelia, a lovely girl and such a terrible shame how events played out for the both of you. Of course, the noble thing is to go to her; I appreciate that. Unfortunately, Scott, if no one is dead or is dying, god forbid, I'm afraid tomorrow will have to suffice. I am truly sorry, and I do wish Emelia all the very best, but we need you here today. Do you understand?'

'I do, but sir, if you could just -'

'I *said* do you understand?'

'Yes, sir, of course I do. Thank you very much, sir.'

'Good. I will see you here within the hour.'

The line disconnected before Scott could reply which only fuelled the flames which had started to make his vision red. He unclamped the phone from his ear and glared at it breathing heavily. How was she being so damn protected? He was so close he could almost touch her, and yet there was always something in his *fucking* way.

He was shaking. The suppression of anger had taken enormous control. So much *effort*. His vision wavered. The pressure in his head was immense. If he didn't let it out, it would explode like a grenade. The phone dropped to the floor as his body tensed every muscle shaking violently. His arms raised up to his chest, fists clenched so hard they had turned white. He threw his head back looking up at the ceiling and *roared*, long and loud, tendons in his neck threatening to snap under the strain. His face turned red, and then purple, until his bulging eyes finally glazed over, seeing, but unseeing.

He started with the settee as the nearest thing to him. He bent, grasping the underneath and pulled upward, flipping it right off the floor and spinning it over. It crashed into the nest of tables shattering the legs of all three in a single blow. The back of the settee cracked loudly as it hit and skidded slightly to the right.

Next was the TV. A wall mounted 52-inch which he ripped from the wall complete with brackets like he was taking a book from a shelf. Wires and ariels pinged and whizzed by him as they let go of their hold with the sockets. He held the screen aloft before bringing it crashing to the ground. Glass was still rebounding from the wooden floor as he shot out his left leg and kicked at the little cabinet in the corner.

Emmie had liked to line photos of the family along the top and had stored the glass-wear used for entertaining in here. He had not touched anything on or in this cabinet since she had left. He touched it now.

His foot connected with one of the wooden doors, forcing it inside the housing as it's twin swung out and knocked on the wall before bouncing back with a thud. Glass shattered, and photos flew from the top like birds taking flight. The little cupboard rocked once, twice, bouncing off the wall, before finally losing grip and toppling forward with the high pitched crash of breaking glass.

In one swift motion Scott was out of the way of the cabinet debris and had swung his other foot toward the freestanding chair of the suite. It connected squarely, and he pushed at it with a guttural growl. It didn't topple, but scooted back unsatisfactorily, rocking on its feet.

Ragged rattles came from Scott's chest and up through his throat with his breath, and a small pain was waking up behind his ribs. He absently scrubbed at the area with the knuckle of his thumb as he moved into the dining room heaving over the large table. It hit the wall taking a large chunk of plaster with it as it removed the legs of two chairs and the back of another. Two of the remaining chairs he picked up one by one and hurled them through the doorway into the living room, where they bounced off the far wall and joined the other destroyed furniture, snapping obediently as they crashed into the debris.

Leaving the remaining chair intact and alone, he stalked into the neat kitchen. He flung open the cupboard doors one by one, ripping some right off their hinges as he swung his arms in wide arcs. He emptied the contents of each one to the floor in an explosion of glass, shattered plastic and colourful spices, tins and packets. The last cupboard he removed from the wall complete with contents, throwing it to the far end of the kitchen, packets smacking at his chest and arms as they flew from the doors.

He turned back toward the dining room with a roar, eyes bulging as he swept his arm across the counter top sending the toaster, microwave and kettle skidding across the edge of the worktop. The plug ripped right off the kettle and sat in the wall socket wires hanging torn. He pulled each drawer from its runners one by one and hurled them backwards. Cutlery flew. Knives, forks and spoons shot across the room like arrows hitting their targets as they came to a stop. Two knives embedded in a cupboard door so deep that, later, they couldn't be removed.

The last few cupboards held the plates, bowls, cups and glasses which all met their demise accordingly, smashing into a mosaic of crockery on the floor.

He stopped, hands on his hips, heart pounding, muscles fizzing, and fighting in each ragged breath one by one.

The pain was more than niggling now, cutting through the rage, and he was struggling to draw a breath. He vaguely remembered leaving the demolished kitchen before he blacked out, which was good as he probably would have impaled himself on the destruction that was the kitchen floor.

He came round in the middle of the living room, muscles bulging, shaking from exertion and drenched in sweat. He stood tentatively, holding the arm of the chair for balance on his unsteady legs, and surveyed the destruction with a certain amount of awe and satisfaction.

God, he was strong. Sometimes it impressed him just how strong he was.

The downstairs looked like it had been done over but it was a small price to pay for the sheer exhilaration he felt right now. Pulling a big breath in and out he noticed there was no trace left of the pain that had come out of nowhere. Maybe he had imagined it.

Now he could start the day in good form. Endorphins were racing around him, he felt on top of the world.

He went upstairs and showered quickly, putting on a clean shirt, tie and suit. He did his hair and brushed his teeth, checking his chin for stubble and deciding he didn't need a shave but splashing on aftershave anyway. He looked at himself in the mirror and marvelled at how normal he looked.

He was a machine. He had blitzed through the three downstairs rooms like a whirlwind approximately ten minutes ago and yet the only outward sign that anything unusual had happened was his slightly bloodshot eyes.

He felt calm now, spent even, all anger diminished. Emelia wouldn't be moving house within a day. It would just give him more time to figure out how he would play it when he got up there.

He had most of Emelia's address from the papers he had found while tidying Natalie's rubbish.

Such carelessness on her part leaving them lying around in the hall. She had snatched them away before he got a proper look at the name, but he knew it started with 'Bru', and he knew it was specifically 5 miles from Bracken Hill, the village where Martin was staying. It couldn't be hard to find the place.

He decided to use the day wisely. He would pick up an OS map on the way home tonight and mark out a five-mile radius seeing what buildings he hit before he got up there. From the pictures on the front page it was a stone built detached house, and a fucking mess too, but it looked isolated, and that was a good thing.

No, he corrected himself; it was a *great* thing, he would really be able to get things off his chest without restraint.

Whistling cheerfully, he left the house and got in the car, a smile on his face and a spring in his step. Today was going to be a great day.

Tomorrow, he thought, would be even better.

Chapter 48

Things were substantially calmer in the Grey Lion although the emotion was running as high as it had been in Surrey. The little knot in Emmie's stomach had slowly been growing until she walked into the pub, where it threatened to unravel and swamp her completely. She saw both men simultaneously, but decided she needed to deal with Martin before he recognised her fully, and before she decided she couldn't go through with it. She lifted her chin, setting her jaw as her father had taught her to do when she had felt intimidated by Scott, and strode to the table not letting herself pause to think. By the time she reached Martin, she was starting to tremble again. She pushed it back as much as she could as she sat down, clasping her hands together and leaning her chin on them to stop the movement.

'Hello Martin,' She said thankful that her voice sounded in a lot better form than she felt. It was steady and strong, 'I think we need a little chat don't you?'

He looked like a rabbit stuck in the glare of headlights. Unsure whether to speak or run. He opened and shut his mouth a few times saying nothing. A memory surfaced. Scott at the party.

Well? A simple answer would suffice, the whole acting like a fish thing is getting us nowhere.

She tried not to grin as she watched him. His reaction was good, it was settling her nerves and reinforcing the knowledge that he was as dangerous as cotton wool. It also reminded her of dads voice in the car.

Your reaction gives him power. You can choose to take control.

How true this was from the other side. It was a lot harder to see as the victim, but then maybe that point of view was just as dangerous as the reaction. She had *thought* she was the victim, and she had dutifully acted like one, bending over backwards to give Scott the response he required to reinforce his power and hold over her.

Martin was doing precisely the same right now, and it was giving Emmie the upper hand. This, in turn, gave her the courage to carry on, squashing the nerves, not entirely, but almost completely.

'Well?' She said, 'You have nothing to say? Really?'

Martin sighed, looked over at the pub door and then back at her, shoulders slumping as he gave in. He looked at her.

'I don't know how much you know, Em, but I'm sorry, I really am. I'm on my way out of here this morning, ask him.'

He jabbed his thumb towards the bar, keeping his eyes on her. Emmie glanced at Stuart, who nodded confirmation, before she turned her attention back to Martin.

'So? ...'

'So, I want nothing to do with this anymore. It's sick, Scott should just leave you alone. You look good by the way.'

'Thanks,' she said lightly, 'So what exactly are we talking about. Let's get some facts straight before you go shall we? Especially if you're going to leave me here alone with the outcome of whatever it is you're hunting me down for.'

He had the sense to look both surprised and hurt. He swallowed hard.

'Em, I ... I'm sorry. I wasn't hunting you down, really. I got caught up in his whole stupid game, and it's gone too far. All I was supposed to do was find out your address and pass it on to Scott. As far as I'm concerned that was it, and I would be on my way back to Surrey. I know I've done stupid things while I've been here. I would never have hurt you though.'

'So you think passing that information on to Scott *wouldn't* have hurt me? Or still won't? Surely he hasn't given up, so you've either given him what he wants, or your conscience is catching up with you, and he's going it alone. Either way, the outcome will be the same. Which ultimately *will* hurt me. Don't you think?'

He nodded, but barely, as he looked down at his hands.

'So which is it, Martin? You've played your part, or you've had enough?'

'I'm done. I've told Scott nothing. I *know* nothing. He's a grade A psychopath, and I realise that now. Hell, I guess I knew that he had it in him before, you must have seen it in him too.'

Emmie glanced over to the window. His voice pulled her attention back.

'I always thought he was a little dangerous, it was fun then, back in Uni. I can't say I wasn't pleased when he sought me out. I thought we could get back to the way things were, liven things up again, you know. I didn't realise just how deep he had gone under. I don't know what happened Em -'

'He was a shit, and we got divorced.'

Martin looked at her, his mouth falling open.

'The long and short of it.' She added shrugging.

His mouth snapped shut.

'He never mentioned divorce … Well, if that's what it is, it's flipped him a hundred and eighty degrees, he's a fucking fruit-loop. He's *raging* that you're up here, Em, *really* raging. I think he's also digging me a shallow grave back in Surrey after I told him I had nothing on you. He actually threatened to kill me, Em, and honestly? I think he'd fucking do it. The anger in that man is beyond scary. I don't know how you lived with him. He needs locking up.'

Emmie frowned. Through all of his outbursts she had never seen Scott angry to the extreme that he had threatened to kill someone, although when he passed the thumb digging stage and really zoned out, she was sure he could do it, accidentally or otherwise. This stage was something she had only seen once and she had run before it was over, after a knife had embedded itself into the wall inches from her arm. He had apologised profusely afterward and agreed to have anger management counselling, which, of course, had never materialised. He had apparently dealt with it himself.

Emmie searched Martin's eyes, which held hers evenly, waiting for a reaction.

'He threatened to kill you?'

Martin nodded, visibly shades paler than he had been when she sat down.

'He meant it too, I'm not hanging around to find out if he could follow it through.'

Emmie felt a chill encompass her.

It scared her to hear any more but she needed to know just how bad this may end up, and although death seemed a little extreme, ignorance could get you hurt. As far as she was aware Scott had never threatened to kill anyone before Martin. If his controlling streak had declined to such an extent, she needed to be able to prepare, to defend herself and the children.

Houston? I think we have a problem.

She smiled wanly.

'Em?'

'Yep, just thinking. What do you think he's angry about, Martin? Is it the children or …'

Martin's eyebrows shot up.

'The children? No, he never mentions them. I can't remember a single time he's brought them up, other than to check the schools for their names to see if you were in the area … Shit, what the hell did I do? I didn't think … I didn't connect that the children would be involved.'

Emmie nodded. She didn't know whether to feel immensely relieved or immensely hurt. She did hope it meant that he was coming for *her* though, and that was more bearable than thinking he would take Charlie and Grace.

'So what *is* he after then?'

'I don't know. He's never told me. My initial thoughts were that he was trying to get you back.'

Emmie shook her head quickly.

'No, he instigated the divorce. He was nasty with the proceedings too. There's no way he wants a reconciliation. More like he wanted to watch me suffer but now I'm too far away, and he doesn't like it.'

Martin dropped his eyes examining his hands but nodded agreement. After a pause, he looked back up at her.

'You might be right. I have no idea. He certainly craves control I've found that out the hard way over the last few days. I can't deal with him anymore.'

'All very well for you. So, you're up here to find me as an 'adventure' on behalf a 'psychopath'. Your words. And you didn't even bother finding out what his motivations were? You were going to happily feed me to the wolf for a bit of fun?'

She watched him visibly squirm. Letting him feel the weight of her words before she continued.

'Why Martin? What did I ever do to you?'

'Nothing.' The word was barely audible.

'Not really good enough is it? Do you want to try a little harder?'

'I can't … I just … I don't know, Em. He's persuasive. I got caught up in the fever. I thought it was a harmless game, I had no idea that he had gone so far under. It's like the old Scott isn't even in there anymore. It used to be fun, but now I'm scared shitless, running for my fucking life. I didn't think of you at all, if I had - '

She waved a hand at him cutting him off

'Yeah, I know. Easy to say right? But you were thinking of me as you attacked the lady in the shop next door though, want to tell me what that was about? Because if we're talking about people changing, Martin, then I want to say I never thought you were the type to beat up old ladies, or anyone else for that matter.'

He reddened and closed his eyes briefly rubbing a hand across his brow. His hand was shaking a little. He was breathing heavily too, getting distressed, she thought. Well maybe that wasn't so bad. She waited him out, a good twenty seconds of silence passed between them sitting heavy in the air, before he finally spoke his words coming out fast and jumbled.

'I don't know. It wasn't me … It's not me. I didn't mean to hurt her. I mean … it *was* me I know that, but it's not me. I don't do that sort of thing.' He stopped to rake a hand through his hair, taking a ragged breath. 'I was desperate. Scott was threatening to kill me if I didn't have info that night, he was beyond furious, and I panicked. I knew that she knew you, but I didn't know if she had what I needed and she wouldn't give me any sign. I got frustrated. I hurt her, I know, and I am sorry. I'm sorry I had a part in any of this, I didn't see it for what it is, you have to believe me. I'm not a bad person Em, you know me, please. How can I make it up to you?'

She ignored his question and continued calmly wanting him to feel the force of what he'd done.

'She could have called the police, you know. You owe her for not pressing the button or where would you be now. Did getting arrested figure in your little adventure when you came up here?'

He paled in front of her, eyes pleading.

'No, nothing like this. Scott's a madman, and I panicked. It went too far I know, and I'm so grateful she didn't call them. I really am. It was the jolt I needed. I'm not this person, I'm so, so sorry.'

Emmie knew he was. The shame and relief were evident in the way he hung his head and stumbled over his words, and his panic at mention of the police spoke volumes. She also noted two other things.

One was just how utterly scared he really was, and Martin had never been someone who scared easily. What made him think he had no option to walk away from Scott? Unless he was being candid about fearing for his life, which was also unlike him.

The second was that she had been right about his reasons for hurting Edith which meant she was also right when she had thought he wasn't a threat.

Looking at him now, she thought he might start bawling if she so much as raised her voice. He had been stupid and got caught up in something way bigger than him thinking it was all a game. It didn't excuse him or his behaviour but it was time to let up on him, she had got as much as she could from him anyway.

'I take it Scott doesn't know you're leaving?'

'I … I haven't heard from him since the threat on Saturday. I turned my phone off for a while expecting him to call. After the … the … you know, shop thing, I couldn't deal with him, so I shut the phone off. When I turned it back on yesterday, he hadn't called, and I haven't called him. I just need to get out of here.'

Emmie stared at him.

'You haven't heard from him since *Saturday*?'

'Nothing.'

'That's not good news.'

'No,' He mumbled, 'that crossed my mind too, it's another reason I want to get out of here, like right now, and you really should too, Em.'

He lurched across the table and grabbed her hands. She jumped a little, the look in his eyes was sheer fright as they bored into hers.

'Get the fuck out of here before he arrives, I'm not asking you, I'm begging you, please. He's not sane, and I'm not sure what he's planning to do, but it's not going to involve a reunion tea party is it?'

The intensity of his speech pumped her heartbeat up a few notches. She took her hands away, sitting back in her chair, regarding him. How could Scott be this bad, really? She had left him little more than a year ago, and he had been perfectly sane then. He had his issues, sure, but he hadn't seemed capable of really hurting someone physically, never mind killing them. And why should she need to be worried? He had left her, for Christ sake, she hadn't divorced him by choice.

Martin picked up his bag from the floor and placed it on the table in front of them. He was sweating even in the cool air.

'Please, Em, I'm scared … for us both.'

She shook her head slowly straightening up.

'I can't, Martin, where would I go? Back to Surrey? Right back down to his doorstep? I don't think so. I have Grace and Charlie to think about. I can't keep running. I'm just going to have to wait to see if he turns up and find out what he wants.'

'Please don't do that, I don't know who he is anymore, I mean it Em, fucking run.'

She felt a smile curl at the edges of her mouth. The whole situation had got so serious that it suddenly struck her as absurdly funny. Here she was, sitting with Martin the Martian, who she hadn't seen for at least fifteen years, miles away from the town they met, discussing both of their demise's at the hand of their ex-best friend and husband. It was quite frankly just absurd, and his brilliant idea was to *fucking run*? She could have been sitting in a bad movie right now. She held her hands out gesturing at the pub.

'Martin look around you. I ran all the way to another bloody country, and he followed me.'

The terror resounded in Martin's eyes as he nodded at her.

'Yes, he's going to great lengths to follow you … great lengths to get to you, and to what end?'

He stood up scooting his chair back and put his hand on the strap of his sports bag. He travelled lightly, Emmie noticed, he didn't have enough luggage for even a couple of days. She stood too out of an ingrained courtesy. He paused, heaving a breath, and then he surprised her, stepping around the table and folding his arms around her. It was the quick, tight hug of old friends. Then he stepped back and looked at her.

'I'm not sure what I was thinking, and I don't know why I'm here. If I could take it all back and start over, I'd do everything differently. I just needed *something*, an adventure I suppose. I can't tell you how sorry I am.'

'It's done Martin, it doesn't matter what I say it won't change anything. Just go, at least one of us will be out of the line of fire, and I should think when Scott's finished with me you will be very much forgotten.'

'I fucking hope so.'

He started to walk toward the door and then stopped and turned.

'If you decide to stay, be careful, won't you? He can go off like a bomb, and without warning, I was only on the other end of the phone, and he damn near made me shit my pants. More than once.'

Emmie nodded shivering a little. Had the bar got colder or was it the thought of Scott? Martin turned to Stuart.

'While we're at it I'm sorry about setting the alarm off too. I know you're probably glad to see the back of me but could I just ask one more thing?'

Stuart was standing rod straight, arms folded over his broad chest, hard gaze set on Martin. He didn't reply. Martin carried on regardless.

'You saw what I did when she walked in here I'm almost sure of it. If I'm right, I know you won't need asking, but I'm going to anyway, just in case. Please look out for her. She won't be able to tackle Scott alone, she'll need someone with some muscle around, and you're at least a match for him. Em isn't going to stand a chance if he kicks off.'

Emmie was about to contest that idea, she had managed quite well for sixteen years, but the words stuck in her throat as Stuart looked at her softening.

'Aye, I fully intend to, you have my word. Not that you deserve it, mind.'

Martin gave a curt nod before turning back toward the door. In six strides he was through it and gone. Emmie wondered if she would ever see him again, and then she turned to Stuart, who gave her a smile, and her pattering heart pushed out all thought of Martin. She rolled her eyes inwardly and stepped around the table to join him at the bar.

Chapter 49

Emmie was shaking. The build-up, the nerves, the relief, and now the fear of what she had learned coming together in one huge overwhelming emotion. It was as if her body didn't know how to respond to the mass of stimuli, she shook from head to toe, inside and out.

She was also cold. From shock or the freezing weather she couldn't say, but she hadn't been this cold all week. The temperature in the car this morning had said only minus two degrees, yesterday had plunged to minus six, and she had been just fine. Right now she needed a hot drink to warm her up, and something to stop the shakes.

She pulled herself onto a bar stool and put her hands flat down on the bar to try to stop them from moving. That wasn't working so she clenched them into fists instead, squeezing hard, making her knuckles white. Stuart watched her momentarily before moving down the bar to pour a shot of something pale which he placed in front of her.

'Here, get this down you.'

'What is it?' Emmie said trying to stall picking up the glass and showing him just how shaky she was. He probably already knew, he wasn't blind, and he had already proven to be perceptive.

'Whisky. It'll help with the shakes, and then I'll make you a hot drink. There's a fire going in the back room. We can go in there if you like, it's a bit more comfortable.'

Emmie nodded and picked up the glass taking a sip. The liquid was harsh and tasted bitter, but it burned all the way down pleasantly warming her insides.

'Okay?'

Emmie finished off the Whisky in one big gulp acutely aware that she would soon need to drive to school to pick up Grace. She wrinkled her nose shutting one eye as it hit and burned.

'Yep.'

Stuart grabbed the empty glass and motioned for her to come around the curve of the bar. He lifted the bar counter for her and held the door as they went into the living area.

A large rug covered most of the wooden floor. Two patterned settees skirted the edge at right angles to one another, one facing the fireplace and one to the side. A large window split into many small square panes of glass looked out onto the street. In front of the window was a desk, with paper stacked neatly, and a large television. Along the back wall was a floor to ceiling bookshelf which was neatly filled top to bottom.

The warmth hit her immediately, and she thought there was nothing quite like a roaring fire to draw you in on a cold day.

Stuart put a hand lightly on her shoulder.

'What would you like to drink? I can set you up with pretty much anything you fancy.'

She looked up at him trying to smile.

'Anything? Well, a large hot chocolate with cream and marshmallows would go down a treat, but I'll settle for tea. Anything hot will do really.'

He smiled back at her unperturbed and gestured to the settees.

'Make yourself at home. I won't be long.'

Just as she thought she had been holding her own as friends reasonably well he dropped her a wink that sent her insides to mush. Still, it beat the shakes which were finally starting to subside.

Choosing the settee closest to the fire, she sat leaning forward to warm her hands. There was the steady tick of a clock and voices from somewhere else in the building, but mostly it was the crackle and roar of the wood that comforted her. She felt safe and cosy as the warmth penetrated to her bones.

She glanced around the room taking in the furnishings, everything was mismatched but seemed to go together perfectly at the same time. Taking off her coat and laying it over the back of the chair, she smiled.

I could live here. It has a homely feel to it. It's warm. This place has happy memories, not memories of people fried on the patio and hanging from the wood. It also has the bonus of coming with a stupidly handsome man I could happily see myself spending lots of time with.

Except that he very graciously let me know he wasn't interested, and he's probably married.

Emmie Looked back into the fire and grinned as it warmed her face. Oh well, she was here with him now, she'd have to make the most of sneaked glances and fantasy.

'Here you go, Em, I hope that's to your satisfaction.'

She turned from the fire and nearly fell off the chair with shock. Stuart had two mugs on a small black bar tray, the larger one filled with what must have been hot chocolate as it was topped with cream and followed by marshmallows to boot, small ones on top of the cream and large ones on the large saucer at the bottom where they sat with a spoon.

He placed the tray on a little table that sat between the right angle of the two settees, joining them together, and sat down on the settee opposite the fire, picking up the smaller mug. Emmie scooted up and stuck her head over the mug with the cream inhaling and popping a marshmallow in her mouth. It dissolved on her tongue leaving a trail of sweet stickiness that she swallowed.

'Oh my god, really? He killed me, didn't he? I must be in heaven.'

Stuart chuckled.

'I'll not have murder in my bar, but hot chocolate I can do for you.'

'Hot chocolate you can do for me any day.'

The words were out of her mouth before she could stop them and she cringed inside. As her cheeks coloured she quickly picked up the cup sucking the chocolate up from below the cream.

In Surrey, she had spent many an hour at Costa Coffee with Amy supping chocolate with cream. She had thought they did the best hot chocolate in the world, but she was wrong. This was better.

'That is absolutely divine. What chocolate is that? There's a hint of something else in there too, isn't there?'

He tapped the side of his nose with a finger and winked.

'Secret recipe. I could tell you, but then I'd have to kill you, and I'd rather you just come and drink it.'

She laughed, surprised and delighted. It didn't seem to take a lot to please her these days she thought. If only Scott weren't on the rampage things would be just about perfect right now. Bastard. She sat back with the mug in her hands warmed and comforted.

'Better?'

She nodded.

'Much better thank you.'

'Good. Let's see if we can't figure this situation out then.'

They went over the details Martin had given her and whether he could be trusted. They discussed Scott, the implications of him coming here, and his possible reasons. They also went through what Emmie could do to make herself and the children as secure as possible when she was alone.

Stuart wasn't only an attentive and patient listener; he was logical too. Where Emmie was prone to want to crawl under the bed and hide until the situation went away, Stuart was good at keeping his feet on the ground, breaking things down and providing a more sensible solution. Emmie found herself pouring out all of the ideas she had, whether they sounded crazy or not. Stuart explained most of them away with an ease that settled her flighty mind.

Once they had explored all the avenues she could think of, and all of the scenarios Stuart added, she felt calmer, stronger and more able to take Scott on.

The only thing Stuart hadn't been able to remove was the fear of seeing him again, and not knowing what he had become, or what to expect. The unknown was the scariest thing in life, she thought, and she had learned a good deal about that just living with Scott.

They sipped at their cooled drinks in comfortable silence. Emmie watched the flames in the fire and thought about how utterly consumed the wood was. It had no chance of survival. Was this to be her fate too? Would Scott continue to consume her until there was nothing left?

Maybe, but she would fight him. She wouldn't let him control her again. There had to be a way to break free from his grip.

'How are you feeling, Em? I mean really feeling, don't sugar coat it. I want to help you, but I need to know what you're thinking about all this and how you feel it will play out. When you said Martin would be ready to quit, I had my doubts, but he did exactly that. As you said, you know him, and I don't. It's going to be much the same with Scott. I don't know the man. I can only follow your lead. What's your take on it?'

She looked at Stuart and chewed her lip.

'Honestly? That I'm in trouble. Martin was right about one thing if he gets me alone and starts anything physical I won't have a chance. I know he's manipulative, and I know how he's brought me down that way in the past. I'm not familiar with this angry streak that's so bad it's got Martin scared for his life. I'm not entirely sure who or what Scott has become over the last year and that scares me a little. I'm also scared that he will catch me when the kids are around. In fact, I'm just plain scared, does that about cover it?'

'Aye,' He said softly, 'I'm not liking it either, and I'm not liking the fact that you're so isolated up there. Listen, can I not convince you to come and stay here for a while? I've plenty of room. Just until we know what he wants?'

Emmie shook her head and looked back at the fire.

'He's already on his way to winning then, isn't he? Driving me out of my house before he's even got here? I can't let him do that. I need to stay, the children need their own beds. He's pushed me around too much already, and if I can help it, I won't allow it to happen again. Anyway, we still don't know for certain he'll come up here.'

'We've been through this, Em, what else would he do with your address?'

'I don't know, but I definitely think he already has it …' She frowned and shook her head, 'It must have been my sister. Scott paid her visit on Sunday, which is strange as they don't get on, but she said he was convinced I was in some sort of trouble. She was adamant she told him nothing, but she's the only person he could have got information from. Something took him to Nat's in the first place though, and why would he say I was in trouble, where would he get that from?'

'A play on words to get what he wanted from her?'

'I agree it was for that reason, but he has the imagination of a gnat. He must have heard something from someone.'

'Okay, so who could he have been speaking to?'

'I don't know. I haven't spoken to anyone down there apart from Natalie, and it was only when she gave me a roasting for keeping her out of the loop that I told her what was going on. I haven't spoken to anyone else down there at all.'

'You're absolutely sure?'

She nodded, hands circling the warm mug, smelling the chocolate as it floated up from under the melting cream. An uncertainty was tugging at her stomach, she had spoken to someone hadn't she? An answer ran just short of coming into her mind. It sat at the edges nibbling. She took a sip of chocolate, the chocolate that reminded her of being in Costa with …

'Amy!'

Stuart flinched a little and looked at her eyebrows raised.

'Who's Amy?'

'A friend, I called her from the falls on Saturday morning before I went home.'

'To say you were in trouble?'

'Not as such no, I just told her about staying the night here because I hadn't wanted to go home. She could have got the impression I was in trouble from that I suppose.'

Could have got the impression? No doubt about that is there? You're hilarious Em. A barrel of fucking laughs.

Stuart watched her, puzzlement crossing his face. She knew he wanted to know what had gone on Friday night but she just wasn't ready to go into the spooks in her life. Deal with the living first. If I survive, then I'll get to the dead. When she offered no more, he carried on.

'So she could have spoken to Scott about it?'

'Well, no, I can't see why she would, and she didn't even seem to be listening, she was a little preoccupied. She wouldn't have anything to do with Scott after we split so …'

She shrugged and trailed off remembering the phone call. Amy *had* seemed preoccupied. She hadn't sounded like herself at all now she thought back to the conversation. The not wanting to answer when Emmie had asked her who she was with, those giggles, and Scott having information he could never come by was starting to form a horrible little circle in her mind.

She wouldn't, would she?

Amy would chase anything with a penis so she supposed yes, it could happen, and there would be no other reason for her being so coy about who she was in bed with would there? Emmie had heard first hand, and in great detail, of all of Amy's conquests since she'd had her first sexual encounter at fourteen. She left nothing out, and certainly never who it was, whether Emmie knew him or not.

She felt winded, as though she had taken a punch to the stomach. Why would Amy do that to her though? And Scott, who had said there was no-one else? He had never seemed interested, he always called Amy the local bike and joked that when Emmie couldn't get hold of her, she would be on her back in someone's bed. Emmie had largely ignored him, but the comments had hurt, with Amy being her oldest and closest friend. And now Scott himself was having a go on the bike? Seeing what all the fuss was about obviously.

She closed her eyes and brought a hand up to her head chuckling softly.

'Emmie? Whats the matter?'

Stuart had sat quietly letting her gather her thoughts, now she looked at him, a rueful smile on her lips.

'I think … I think maybe they're sleeping together. Unless I'm adding two and two and getting five, but I … I don't think so.'

Stuart placed his cup down, turning to face her fully, forearms resting on his knees. He shook his head confused.

'You've lost me. Who are?'

'Amy and Scott. I'm pretty sure that's where he's got it from. When I called Amy she was distracted and obviously with someone, in bed, you know. She would normally give me chapter and verse, who, what and where, whether I wanted to know or not, but she wouldn't elaborate at all. It was a bizarre phone call if I'm honest, but I think I understand why now. If I'm right, Scott would have been there the whole time, and that means I just gave him a helping hand all on my own.'

Stuart raised his eyebrows and rubbed a hand across his brow.

'You're certain you're not putting things together that don't fit?'

'Well, no. But Amy is the only person I spoke to. I don't believe I'm too far off the mark, but it's just a feeling.'

She paused finishing her chocolate. No longer even lukewarm but still as tasty.

'God, I manage to have the most fantastic bad luck, don't I? I think I must have been a serial killer in a past life. Karma is royally kicking my ass.'

She laughed and rolled her eyes, shaking her head a little as she turned to put the empty mug back onto the table. As she turned back, Stuart caught both her hands in a gentle grip. Her breath caught as his hands engulfed hers, warm and protective. He looked at her steadily. She didn't dare breathe, and she knew she wouldn't be able to speak, so she gazed back at him. The air seemed to crackle with chemistry.

How was he not getting any of this? Or was he? She thought she had seen something in the way he had looked at her at the bar, and he was obviously happy to help her, but he wouldn't allow any more. She wondered why he had shut down at the mention of dinner. She wondered what his story was, the hell with her own, which was getting worse by the minute.

If he didn't let go of her hands soon, she was afraid the shakes would be well and truly back.

'Stu?' She whispered.

He smiled at her then, not sadly and not out of pity. A full, light up his face, eyes shining kind of smile. It was infectious, and she found herself smiling back.

'What?' She said.

'You're going to be okay, Em, I think you've got this more than you realise. You handled Martin perfectly, and I think you'll do the same with Scott. I was just thinking how wrong I had you. You're vulnerable, sure, but you're not weak.'

'Not weak? I'm terrified of my own shadow at the moment.'

'I don't doubt it, but you hide it well. Outwardly, even with Martin, I'd never have known.'

Emmie gave a small shrug.

'I'm working on pretending my life is a movie. It takes the pressure off me having to be the lead character in my own version of 'Psycho'.'

He chuckled, and she was aware that he was still holding on to her hands. She felt an enormous pull in the pit of her stomach. It felt like they were pole ends of a magnet, she just wanted to 'attach' to him and never let go. She briefly imagined climbing onto his lap and throwing her arms around him but thought it might not go down too well. His voice cut back into her thoughts.

'You have an infectious way of seeing things, lightening them up with humour. You seem to just go with your heart and experience the moment. It's not a bad way to be, Em. I'm sure everything will work out.'

She nodded at him. Wondering if he was still with her or trying to convince himself. He looked down stroking his thumbs over the backs of her hands. Another jolt of electricity shot up Emmie's arms and landed in her stomach. She wanted to lean across and kiss him but didn't dare move. She closed her eyes briefly instead fighting the urge.

When he spoke, his voice didn't sound as sure as usual, missing the usual note of confidence.

'If the offer is still open, I'd really like to have that dinner with you, Em.'

She started, snapping her head up to meet his eyes with her own.

'Oh, I thought you said -'

He gently let go of her hands, which still tingled from his touch, and sat back further in the chair, running a hand shakily through his hair.

'I know what I said, and I didn't mean it quite so harshly. I panicked that's all. I need to stop thinking so much and learn to go with the flow. You are very quickly teaching me that.'

Emmie felt a little lost. She had no idea what he was talking about. He was the most confident, open, friendly and kind person she had ever met. She would be happy to half of what he was. What could she possibly teach him?

'It may be better to stick with your head, Stu. Keep thinking. Sometimes I drive myself nuts.'

'But you're *living* Em. Even after all you've been through, and with everything that's going on, you're still living, still going forward. I think following my heart is exactly what I need to do right now.'

She was stunned into silence, not knowing how to answer him. She searched his eyes and only came up with a brief flash of pain. Whatever had happened he was good at closing it off. She shook her head slightly in confusion.

'What is it?'

He sighed and looked up at the clock.

'It's a long story and I know I owe you the short version at least, but right now we're running out of time, you have to get Grace, and I have a guest house to run. Agnes is already working overtime. She normally clocks off just after 10am, but I asked her to stay and help Connor until I had been through things with you.'

She nodded looking at the clock.

11.40am? Where did the time go?

'Okay, so dinner? I'd like to tell you I have to fit you in a social calendar, but there aren't many people to have over in the middle of nowhere. You choose, all I ask is that we aim for an evening, about 8.30pm? I can get the kids up to bed first then. If you come round before, they'll be up all night making you play on the x-box or sit through re-runs of 'guess who'. I'll never get them to bed.'

He grinned, looking more like himself again.

'I think I'd quite like that.'

'It's fun for a while. It gets boring quickly when Grace thinks it's hilarious to ask if your man has a 'tosh' every time it's her turn. Charlie and I were ready to sneak out the door and head into the hills after she had asked for the fiftieth time last night.'

Stuart chuckled softly, eyes back to lighting the world.

'Well, how about tomorrow? I couldn't let you cook tonight, and I'm not sure I could get someone to take over here that quickly anyway. I've also missed getting the paperwork done this morning so I could probably do with being here -'

'Okay. Stu, that's fine you don't need to explain further. Tomorrow is good.'

Emmie pulled her coat off the back of the chair. She knew outside would be cold enough to get to her bones in minutes, so she decided to put it on even in the warmth of the room.

Stuart stood, helping her into it, rearranging the collar as she smiled up at him. He finally stood looking down at her, hands on her shoulders.

'Call me if you need anything.'

'I will.'

'I mean it, Em, anything at all.'

She nodded.

'I will, and thank you for listening, and helping me out, and making *really* good chocolate. I didn't intend to waste your whole morning.'

He rolled his eyes and grinned at her, dimples appearing.

'Aye, what a waste of time it's been, please don't make a habit of it you'll run my business into the ground.'

He smiled, and she suppressed the urge to slip her hands around his waist while he was close. Instead, she grinned and stepped past him toward the door to the bar.

'See you tomorrow, Stu.'

'I'll look forward to it.'

'Me too,' She said as the door swung shut behind her. She lifted the heavy counter and waved to Connor, who waved back with an easy smile.

Like father, like son.

How was it that each day up here seemed to be getting better as it simultaneously got worse.

Ironic, really.

Chapter 50

The clouds that had gathered over the morning were full and threatening but holding back their deluge as Emmie strapped Grace into the car. The radio warned of the rain to set in this afternoon and of further bad weather over Wednesday, gradually worsening through the night when the storm and snow would finally move up from the south.

Emmie let it slide over her head. Grace was full of cheerful babble about the morning's events and her favourite teacher *ever* Miss Willsburn. Emmie glanced at her daughter with a surge of love as she chattered. She was so cute, even covered in red paint from her picture.

But just minutes later the chatter stopped, and Emmie looked into the rear view mirror to see Grace, head flopped back onto her car seat, eyes closed and rosebud mouth open. School must be tiring her out. It had been a good few months since Grace had needed a daytime nap.

As she rounded the bend which brought Bill's farmhouse into view, she slowed. In the middle of the lane was Bill himself, leading a big shire horse by the forelock toward the open gate of his driveway. Another stood chewing the hedge at the side of the road a few yards up. Emmie brought the car to a stop as Bill held up his hand to her. She lowered the window and leaned out.

'Fence down in the paddock.' He shouted to her. 'There's another one further up, I'll have to get them in before you can pass.'

Shutting off the engine Emmie looked back at Grace, who was still catching flies with a light snore. Smiling, she got out of the car and headed for the gate which was slowly swinging shut. Bill was saying something illegible at the horse as it plodded next to him. Emmie swung the gate open fully and placed a house brick that was sitting nearby in front of it stopping its movement.

Bill grunted and pulled on the horse's forelock, tugging gently, leading it through the gate.

'Thank you,' Emmie said heartily as he passed.

Bill grunted again.

'I'll thank you when I have three horses in three stables. They get out so often I think they go at the fence on purpose to piss me off.'

Bill lead the horse slowly down the left side of the house toward a small stable block and Emmie turned her attention away from him looking at the horse near the hedge.

She hadn't so much as looked at a horse for the last twenty years but before that, she had been a volunteer at some local stables. She had loved horses when she was younger. She didn't know what had changed.

No, she did, it was boys. One boy to be exact. Scott Harvington, a tall, dashing, chisel-jawed, future divorce lawyer. She had fallen in love, and that had overridden everything.

She walked slowly over to the horse clicking her tongue and holding out a hand. The horse eyed her tearing chunks out of the hedge with huge dips and pulls of its head. She took a few steps closer, and the horse took two steps away before turning back to the hedge still eyeing her.

Emmie thought of a pony at the stables. A small Welsh called Cherry. She had been wise to every trick in the book when anyone tried to get her in from the field. Emmie had eventually learnt that putting her hand out when calling had done nothing, but putting a hand in her pocket as though for treats, and of course giving her one now and then, had always brought the pony over.

Emmie eyed the horse. This one looked a little over 17 hands, no comparison to little Cherry at 13 hands, and this one was a bulky shire, but then size made no difference did it? If a horse wanted a treat, it would come anyway.

As the horse watched her, chewing, Emmie dropped her hand and began feeling around in her pocket, pretending to look for a treat, no longer looking at the horse at all. Emmie dug deeper, turning side on to the horse. Nothing happened for a while and then she heard the clip of a hoof coming toward her. She grinned and took a few steps away turning her back on the horse altogether. Another clip, and then another. Emmie didn't look back but stopped, digging into her jeans pocket wishing she had a mint she could give to the horse if this actually worked. The horse took a few more steps until it was close and she could feel the huff of its breath on her hair.

Then the horse's nose hit the left side of her with such force she stumbled forward. When Cherry had butted for treats, Emmie had barely felt it. This horse nearly knocked her flat. She staggered and spun to the right gasping, as the horses head shot up into the air, eyes rolling as it took a step back.

Emmie gathered herself quickly and held her hands up to the horse.

'Shhh, shhh, it's okay, you scared me that's all, come on.'

She put her hand back in her pocket, and the horse came forward. Emmie moved forward slowly too until the horse was blowing at her pockets and she could rub its head between the eyes. She was entranced for a while. Caught by the beauty of such a strong beast brought down by the temptation of a small mint or carrot, all the love she'd had for these creatures came surging back in torrents.

And then it tried to nibble at the edge of her coat.

'Woah, not the coat gorgeous, I don't have a treat, it's more of a trick, sorry about that, but we need to get you in the stable so I can get home. I promise if I see you again I will bring a treat for you okay?'

The horse butted her pocket again, knocking her back a few steps. Regaining her balance she grasped the horse's forelock as Bill had done and, holding it with her right hand while patting as close to the front leg with her left as she could manage to get the horse moving. She lead it toward the gate where Bill was returning from the side of the house. He caught sight of her, or the horse, and stopped dead. He watched for a few seconds before nodding and walking over to them.

'This is Clover, the biggest we own and a pain in my ass. I see you have her covered. Round the back second stable from the left. Give the bolts a whack and push them all the way down over the latch. This mare can undo them given half a chance. I'll get the other in.'

Emmie nodded and led the horse around the side of the house and into the stable. She took a moment to give her a pat before shutting the stable door, fully shutting the bolts down as Bill had said. Clover moved to the stable door, hanging her head over as the final horse was lead up the driveway.

Bill locked the smaller gelding into a stable and checked the locks on all the doors. Giving each one a bang before looking up at them.

'Done yourselves a hardship now haven't you? No more paddock until I can fix the fence, you'll be staying here for a day or two at least. Hope your efforts were worth it.'

The first horse stood over the door ears forward and nickered at him.

'Aye Daisy, I'm sure it wasn't your fault, pet. Daffodil has the strongest intent to leave, but Clover is the mastermind I know it.'

Clover chewed hay over the door watching him quietly, and Emmie watched him too with a smile. It was hard to believe that she had thought he was watching her just a few short nights ago when it was becoming more apparent that he was nothing more than a gentle giant, just like the horses really.

Bill turned to Emmie with a nod and a grunt that she could only think was appreciation before he confirmed it.

'Good work lass, that didn't take too long. Last time they took the sheep with them too, that was a whole different level of fun I'll tell you.'

Emmie grimaced.

'I can imagine.'

'No, lass, not until you've been there. The imagination is not half so powerful as to imagine the chaos of three shires and forty sheep on the same lane with only one man to get them all in. It was the stuff of nightmares.'

Emmie gave him a half smile and glanced toward the car wondering whether Grace had woken up yet.

'Are you alright lass? You look a little on edge. Come to think of it you've looked a little on edge since you moved here. Sometimes you city folk don't get on in the rural quiet. City-jitters I call it. Or is it something else?'

Emmie looked at him chewing her lip. She was sick to death of covering up her feelings and hiding her fear from all but the empty house, and she was sick of hearing Bills insinuations that she couldn't handle it out here. Gentle giant or not he was as sarcastic as a carload of teenagers when it came to her 'belonging' out here.

She could tell him of shadow man, but dress him up a little as the man she hoped hadn't got here yet. She rubbed her chin and looked at the hills. Bill followed her gaze.

'Hills worrying you are they? Nothing coming over there for you lass I told you that when we searched the house. It'll be the open space getting your goat.'

'Nope, you could be wrong Bill. There may very well be

something coming over the hills for me any day now. Or some*one* anyway.'

Bill didn't flinch. He stood watching her amused.

'Aye, and pigs may fly.'

Emmie looked back at him. He stood, hands in the pockets of his open coat, watching her like he'd seen a bunch of 'city folk' go mad up here over the years. Watched them come and watched them go.

'I've got problems in the form of an unstable ex-husband. Remember the other day you helped me check the house?'

He tipped his head at her, one nod. She took this as confirmation that he did.

'I stayed at the pub because I had seen someone at the back doors Friday evening. When I checked again, he had gone, but when I tried the doors, which should have been locked, they were open. I thought maybe he had got in and so we left. The thing is when we checked the doors together they were locked again. It sounds crazy I know, and then I learned Scott was after me.'

Bill watched her quietly. She couldn't tell whether he believed her or whether he thought she was just plain crazy. He was giving nothing away.

'So, yes, I suppose you could say the open space worries me in that respect.'

'Someone was at your door?'

'Friday evening, yes, the sunroom doors.'

'And that someone had a key?'

She pulled her coat around her and stuffed her hands in her pockets. She half wished she had said nothing.

'Right lass, so let's get this straight. A man was at the sunroom doors, he used his key to get in. You didn't see him because you ran. Next day he left before you got back and locked the door behind him? Aye, he sounds like a very dangerous and conscientious unstable ex to me … Oh, wait! he's a city boy too, knows the importance of locking a door against the dangers outside.'

He held her gaze for a moment before his face crumpled, eyes twinkling and guffawed then as if then he had just told the funniest joke in the world. Out came the hankie as he laughed, long and hard, through the hankie and through the coughs. Emmie watched him silently until he had finished.

'Well, I guess I'll be going now the roadblock has been shifted.'

She turned to leave a lump rising in her throat.

Don't you dare, don't cry until you get in the car, and not even then if Grace is awake. Hold it Em. He's not worth it.

'Wait, wait.' His gruff voice came from behind her. She stopped and inhaled a big shaky breath of air. She waited for the apology, but it didn't come.

'So you think it was your ex-husband?'

She couldn't do this. Wouldn't be intimidated or laughed at anymore. Hadn't she had enough of that over the years with Scott? She was on her own now, and no-one was going to use her as the butt of their jokes.

She turned to look at him, tilting her chin up and giving him her most sarcastic smile.

'Goodbye Bill. I'm sorry you have to fix your fence again.'

'Now, now, lass don't get precious. I can see you're rattled and maybe something scared you up there but your city boy walking the hills in the dark and dead of night? It would be suicide for someone used to the hills and winter temperatures. You have to see where I'm coming from.'

'No Bill, I don't. I may not be from around here, and yes, you know the place better than me, but I know this man better than you. He has already gone to great lengths to follow me here, and someone has already been hurt in his attempts.'

Bills face was finally verging on serious. He wasn't quite there yet, but he was getting it.

'The bairns?'

'No, thank god, not them, but someone just as unable to defend herself and I'm not in the business of having people attacked because of me.'

Bill looked over at Emmie's car where Grace was hopefully still sleeping and not frozen solid.

'Anyone I know?'

'Yes Bill, very well.'

He grunted.

'Aye, Edith?'

Emmie nodded and glanced down at the floor. She still felt
horribly guilty that Edith had got caught in the crossfire. She also felt
guilty that she hadn't had a chance to see her since Friday and tell her
how sorry she was. She looked up as Bill continued.

'Jumped like a horse with a whip on it's arse when I went to the
store yesterday. Wouldn't say what had happened exactly, just that she
had been threatened by a man in the shop. She said it was nothing, but
her eyes said different, I could see the fear.' He pursed his lips looking
over at her car again before feeling in his coat pockets for his
cigarettes. He plucked one out and lit up, coughing at the first inhale.
Emmie wondered why he bothered.

'Here you look like you could do with one.'

He offered the packet to Emmie complete with lighter. She was
about to tell him that she didn't smoke for the second time when she
stalled.

She had never been a smoker, Scott would never allow it for one,
but she had a few here and there over the years, usually when out with
Amy, nothing that would class itself as a habit, and nothing at all since
Charlie was conceived. Now she suddenly found herself with an urge.

*I look like I could do with one? Does anybody ever really need
one?*

She decided she might see if she did. She pulled one out of the
pack and lit it, feeling the acrid sting of nicotine hit her lungs. She
handed the pack and lighter back to Bill who pocketed them. They
smoked in silence for a while before Bill spoke, blowing a breath of
smoke into the cool air.

'So you think this man was your ex-husband?'

She puffed out her own smoke before she answered.

'No, it wasn't, it was someone he had hired to look for me. As it
happens he appears to have found me now anyway, so even if the man
at the door Friday wasn't him, it very soon will be. And that, Bill, is
why I'm 'rattled' and why I'm behaving like a city girl. I'm sorry if I
look pathetic to you.'

'I didn't say that lass, did I? No need to get defensive.'

'You didn't need to say it.'

'Look, I was brought up in this house, I know the hills like the back of my hand. I know their pleasures, and I also know the dangers, and of all the dangers I've seen up there in my life, lass, I've not seen one in the form of a city man faffing around in the dead of night. By morning, at this time of year, he would be lost or dead. Right? I know the hills, lass, you don't. But I am aware you know this man, and I don't. Tit for tat. But, if he's coming for you, I'll bet my ass and tackle he'll be driving up this very lane and coming in through the front door. He won't be walking from anywhere. Keep your eyes on the front of the house you'll see his car or his lights before you see him.'

Emmie let her shoulders drop and looked at the cigarette in her hand watching the smoke curl up from the tip. He had a point, and it was glaringly obvious. The man at the door hadn't been Scott that was for sure, but neither had he (it?) hurt her or taken anything. The genuine threat would probably do exactly that but from the front entrance. Scott had never been a walker, let alone a climber. He wouldn't tackle the hills, no sir. His arrogance would bring him through the front door.

Bill ground his finished cigarette into the earth with his boot.

'If you like lass I'll keep an eye out. If I see any unfamiliar cars pass I can come and check you're okay at the house if it would make you feel better.'

Emmie smiled, the patronising tone was creeping back, but she'd take whatever help was thrown her way. And let's face it, Bill was a damn sight nearer to her than Stuart.

'Thank you, Bill. I would appreciate that.'

He nodded slowly, staring into the distance.

'Aye.'

She took the last puff of her cigarette and ground it into the earth as Bill had done, feeling nothing. Not better, not worse.

So much for looking like I could do with one.

Now all she had was a mouth that tasted like stale bug-shit. Smoking was definitely not her thing.

'If anything is amiss Bill, would you do me a favour?'

His bushy eyebrows raised revealing those clear green eyes.

'Would you call Stuart at the pub for me? He said to let him know if anything happened, but I'm not sure in that instance I would have a chance to call him.'

Bill looked at her momentarily and then burst into his spontaneous shoulder-shaking laughter. She waited until it had died away unsure what could possibly be funny.

'Right lass,' He leaned toward her, turning his head to spit on the ground before he continued, 'I'll tell you now, many a damsel in distress would like Stuart to be the big hero, and many would be sorely disappointed. Oh, he's a big man, easy on the eye too, but a fighter? Not a chance lass.'

'I don't want him to fight for me Bill, I want him to be there that's all.'

'Aye, well, 'being there' may be a problem for him too. I've seen some things down in that pub late at night. Get a few drinks in them, and I've seen women almost throw themselves over that bar. He's had more than plenty of opportunities to 'save' women, but he's not interested, lass. I've not seen that man with a single woman since Judith died, not even for a drink over his own bar. He can't let her go, and he seems to do pretty well alone. Sometimes a man just needs space … eight years is a lot of space mind.'

Emmie felt a blush rise, not only at what Bill had thought she meant but that he was correct in thinking it all the same. She would have run for the car embarrassed if this new information hadn't piqued her interest.

'I didn't mean I *wanted* him, Bill. I simply meant he's asked me to call him if anything happens. The man who attacked Edith was staying in the guest house, and it was Stu and Edith between them who figured out what was going on. He was offering to help if he could that's all. Nothing more.'

'Ah well, that sounds like Stuart, aye. If that's the case, I'll be sure to call him if I suspect anything.'

'Thank you.'

A little disappointed, Emmie started toward the car with a shiver, hoping Grace wasn't blue with cold.

Aware that Bill was keeping pace with her, she could keep it in no longer.

'Who was Judith, Bill?'

He let out a huff.

'Ah there it is, the billion dollar question, eh?'

Emmie glanced at him sidelong.

'You don't have to answer, I'm only making conversation. We have approximately thirty steps left to the car. I can go in silence if you like. Your call.'

Bill laughed again and pushed her left shoulder, almost knocking her down as the horse had earlier.

'I like you lass, straight as a die. Look, it's none of my business what you're up to with Stuart, he will tell you he's not interested if it gets that far, and that's his call. But because I like you, I'll tell you a little story if you're interested?'

Emmie nodded, and Bill continued

'In 1998 a young couple, not long married, brought the Grey Lion from its elderly owner, Samuel Beet. Sam could no longer keep it going, and truth be told, there weren't many who even drank there at that point; it was big, old, and very cold in the winter months. I couldn't even say the last time old Sam had cleaned or done any maintenance when he put the place on the market. He was a surly fellow, born and raised in the village; he was well known, but not well-liked, and he left the place a big mess for this young pair. But, they had optimism and charm, they were friendly and open, and soon had themselves accepted as the village's own. Even before the place was complete, more people were drinking in there than had the previous ten years, and they had more volunteered help to clean the place up than they could shake a stick at.'

They arrived at the car and Emmie peered in. Grace was exactly as she had left her a few minutes ago. She looked back up at Bill and nodded at him to continue.

'Judith was the one with vision. It was her idea to turn the place into a guest house, and she had all these grand designs for the place believe me. Stu told everyone he was much more interested in looking after the finances, and keeping her in check, so she didn't bankrupt them. It was the subject of much banter over the bar; we all knew Stu would have given her anything she damn well wanted.

'Between them, they made the place a success, had their son Connor, and should be living happily ever after. They were very much in love, a perfectly matched couple if ever I laid eyes on one, I don't think anyone in the village would contest that. We were all wrapped up in their bubble with them and good company they kept too.'

Emmie forced a smile. Pretending to be unconcerned with Stuart's perfect relationship. She knew she couldn't ever offer him the same, She had a psycho ex and a couple of kids, and that was just for starters.

'So what happened?' She asked quietly.

Bill held his clear eyes on hers and rubbed his beard slowly.

'It was 28th May 2010. I'll never forget that date. Judith had made a run down into Perth for a few supplies as they did once a month or so. They usually went together, but the guest house side of things had picked up, and Stu had stayed back home with Connor who was just a wee ten year old at the time. It's a decision that's haunted him ever since, he's told me himself on more than one occasion. On her way back up the A9, a timber lorry with a full load lost control.'

Emmie's hands covered her mouth, and she closed her eyes briefly a shudder ran up her spine as she anticipated what Bill was about to say.

'It took Judith's car and three others clean off the road with it down an embankment and into the trees. All of them rolled, including the Arctic who came to a stop on its side on top of two of the cars, one of them Judith and Stu's. There were no survivors. As the first car to be hit, they said Judith's death would probably have been instantaneous. If she had been travelling just 5mph faster, they said she might not have been involved at all.'

Bill heaved his big shoulders up in a shrug and Emmie felt a surge in her stomach and thought she might be sick, the ground swayed under her feet and she broke into a cold sweat. She could almost hear the squeal of brakes as the lorry careened toward the car, the sickening crunch of metal on metal, the banging as the car rolled. She could see and hear it all in vivid 3d and stereo sound. The after effects of surviving a bad accident she supposed.

Come on Em, get yourself together. Breathe.

'Are you okay lass? You've gone white as a sheet.'

She leaned against the door taking deep breaths until the feeling had passed.

'I'm okay, that's just … it's just horrible.'

'Aye, it was. We all tried to help Stuart, but he was knocked off his feet for a long time. When he could finally function he obsessed over that guest house as the only thing he had left of Judith. It crushed him to stay, and a few of us tried to get him to sell, but he wouldn't leave. In all my years I've never seen a man broken like that. I think something in all of us broke over that time watching him try to get it together and bring up young Connor without his mother. It devastated all of us, but it damn near tore Stu apart.'

Bill stopped to light another cigarette, this time with shaking hands. He offered them to Emmie who shook her head. She fought back her tears. If she'd had any idea just how much he had been through she wouldn't have put him through her own crap, or put her silly infatuation at his feet.

He loved his wife whether she was here or not. It was better they stay friends, she couldn't compete, she didn't have the strength or the energy, and frankly, she didn't want to.

Bill exhaled smoke watching her.

'So, lass, now you know the reason he won't be saving anyone, any more than he could have saved the woman he loved that day. As I said, I've not seen him so much as glance at any lass who gave him the eye. He humours them and banters, of course, his good nature is all natural, but it'll take a very special someone to break down those barriers.'

Emmie didn't know what to say. She ran a hand over her head feeling a little shaky herself. It was Grace who broke the atmosphere calling for her from the car.

'I've got to go, Bill,' She said, 'Thanks for listening and watching out for me. And thanks for telling me about Stu. It's a heartbreaking story.'

'It is. Always happens to the nicest people, but that's life eh lass?'

'That's life,' She repeated as she got into the car and started the engine. She put her hand up to Bill as she pulled away feeling for the world like she was on a roller coaster. In the clouds one minute, rock bottom the next.

She felt like crying for the umpteenth time this week. Only this time she felt like crying for Stuart.

She was confused about the morning too when she thought she had seen something in him, the way he had held her hands and held onto her shoulders as they said goodbye. If that was just his good nature, she understood why so many women had fallen at his feet over the bar.

She wondered what it would be like for him to love if this was just concern and friendship, she also wondered what it would be like for him to want to give her the world, as he had done for Judith.

She pushed the thought away before she started bawling again at the loss of something that had never even begun, Grace was asking for lunch through chattering teeth, better to concentrate on that and calling Natalie for now.

Chapter 51

Scott finished work at 6.30pm. Paperwork done, clients served, bullshit completed. Now he could think about getting to the real work. He swung by the petrol station on the way home filling up the tank of the BMW, getting in every drop he could for his journey tomorrow, and then stopping at the Chinese for dinner. He wasn't a fan of takeaways, but he was ravenous after missing his entire lunch break while the incompetent staff at Waterstones, a full five of them, had hunted down a copy of a large scale OS Explorer map of Perth and Kinross.

It was as if they knew they were pushing his buttons.

No, sir, it doesn't look like we have one in stock ... I'll ask my colleague to check the computer. Yes, sir, there should be one, I'll go and look again for you ... No, sir, it's not on the shelf, I'll ask my colleague to look out back for you ... We don't have one out back I'm afraid ... I saw one on the shelf just yesterday I'll look for you ...

And so it went until his blood was boiling and he was ready to shake someone. He very nearly decided to resort to Google, but he wanted a good old-fashioned paper copy he could draw on without all the printing and faffing. He wanted the whole of Bracken Hill and the surrounding five miles in black and white as he made his way up to her.

The map had eventually turned up on the damned shelf it was supposed to be on, cue polite laughter from the incompetents. Scott paid and quickly left before he gave them something to laugh about.

Pulling up onto the drive he felt a rush of adrenaline. He could finally see just how many houses were likely to be within that five-mile radius of the village and narrow it down to one or two if he was lucky.

He grabbed his briefcase, opened the front door, and reeled back.

The house was trashed, had someone broken in?

Then he remembered the surge of anger this morning. His heart pumped as he surveyed the damage. Had he really managed to do all this himself? Sometimes the level of his rage was something that both

RUIN

disturbed and impressed him in equal measure, but he couldn't help it, it was the way he was made.

His father had been the same, not with the furniture, he preferred to vent using his fists on Scott's mother. Scott, often being a witness to how much his mother had suffered, had never been a wife beater, he was a house wrecker though, that was for sure. Even so, it was all anger, and he thought it was inherited just the same.

He stepped over the mess, retrieved a fork from the floor of the kitchen - which looked like a bomb had ripped through it - and took everything upstairs.

Sitting on the bed, he took the map from his briefcase and laid it out, surveying it as he ate Sweet and sour chicken and rice from the foil tubs. He found Bracken Hill, quite a way above and to the left of Perth. It was small, consisting of what looked like around fifty or so small houses centred around the roads surrounding a triangle of green. There was a church in the middle of the green area, of course. All small village folks needed faith. It gave them something to do with their time, either that or poke their nose into everyone else's business.

Pulling a ruler and pencil out of the front pocket of his briefcase he measured the scale and ruled lines five miles out from the village at half-inch intervals, he could have done with buying a compass, but it was too late now. He joined the top of the lines together in a rudimentary circle and studied the area narrowing his eyes.

There were a number of houses dotted around the countryside along the lanes just outside the village, but these got fewer and fewer as the miles went by, at the five-mile mark Scott thought his ship had come in. There were only five houses on or around the mark enough to matter.

Pushing the empty packets of his dinner aside he pulled the laptop from his briefcase and started it up, punching in his password. He opened up Google maps and searched for Bracken Hill.

Using the map, and the computer together, he located the buildings he needed. Three of them he could use street view and drive 'virtually' right by, but none of them looked to be the one he had seen on the papers at Natalie's. One was too tall, three stories, instead of two, with pitched attic windows. Another had a block paved driveway, and he thought there hadn't been a driveway at all at the front of the one Emelia had purchased. The other had too many trees around the front, the picture he remembered had seemed a lot more exposed. So far so good three down and two to go.

A rapid tapping on the window caught his attention in the quiet, he turned to see a sudden downpour hissing outside. Wet streaks poured down the window pane highlighted orange by the street lamps outside. The wind was gusting too, blowing the rain to slap angrily against the window before easing off again in succession. He remembered the storm that was rolling in slowly and climbed over to the bedside table to set the alarm for 4.30am in the morning.

The worst of the storm was supposed to hit at some point tomorrow before making its way up the country. He hoped to be out early enough to miss the worst of it here and beat it up into Scotland where the heavier snow was expected.

Alarm set, he pulled the bag he had packed out of the wardrobe throwing in a couple more jumpers and jeans just in case he got cold or wet. He removed his ski jacket from its hanger and lay it on top of the bag, putting it next to the door ready for the morning. He wanted to be out as quickly as possible.

Satisfied, Scott went back to the bed and checked the final two houses. These were almost together up the same road. Unfortunately, Google hadn't seen fit to drive up the small lane, so street view was out of the question. He zoomed in as much as he could on the houses.

Both were small rectangles of around the same shape. He couldn't tell how many stories there were, but he could see other buildings around the one which looked very much like a farm. He looked closer and saw the deal breaker.

This house only had one bay window at the front where the one on the estate details was double fronted. He moved on to the house at the end of the lane and saw the two bays rounding out from the front. There was no drive after the road ended, and the front of the house was open. Aerially a hedge ran down the left-hand side of the road and continued past the property ending down at a field. To the right was a small, slim wooded area running parallel to the hedge and alongside the foot of the hill until it opened out into a more substantial wood toward the bottom field where the hedge ended.

He stared at the house. Is this where she had been all along? He found himself marginally impressed. It was quite a lot of house and a generous plot of land she had acquired. How in the hell had she been able to afford a place like this? He had obviously been way too lenient with the money he had let her have.

A stab of anger ran through him. He was working his ass off as he climbed his way up the ladder of his profession. An honourable profession, albeit with long hours and a backbreaking amount of paperwork, but which paid him good money. And yet, here he sat in this poky detached with a postage stamp of land while she fiddled around with her paints up there with double the size of house and a field of her own.

He pulled up his briefcase from the floor and rummaged around for a red pen. He drew a large red ring around the place that he was almost sure was the one, nearly gouging a hole in the map as anger forced pressure down the pen, and then he stared at it.

So, you think you can take my hard earned money and live it up in the country like lady muck? You really think you can take everything I have and make a fool of me? I don't think so, sweet pea. I should be watching my back if I were you, Emelia, because daddy's coming to knock you down a peg or two and by the time I'm finished you'll be begging me to bring you back home where you belong.

Chapter 52

Around the time Scott had circled a big red mark around her house Emmie was playing hide and seek with Grace and Charlie. Wardrobe cupboards were strictly off limits and, of course, as the adult player, Emmie had to be the seeker.

Always.

As she counted to one hundred for what seemed like the thousandth time she poked at the fire moving the wood around trying to get it to burn.

The logs were damp. They had got wet stacked at the side of the house and with no chance to dry today, getting the fire going was proving to be a chore. The damn boiler just wasn't seeming to cut it lately, the house always seemed to go from degrees of cool to cold.

Once she had found the children this time, she was going to enlist their help bringing as many of the logs as they could fit into the small utility where they would be dry. After turning the logs, Emmie put the poker back in its holder at the side of the fire and stood back before calling out.

'One hundred, coming ready or not!'

She started with the sunroom. The one place she didn't like to be in the dark after the incident with shadow man. Keeping her eyes off the doors and windows as much as she could she checked behind the chairs skimming her eyes around the rest of the room quickly before moving into the playroom, also empty, and the kitchen.

The kitchen wasn't empty. It was full of the stifled giggles of a three-year-old trying to be quiet as she hid underneath the table. Emmie heard her first and saw her foot a little after, sticking out from under the chair. She grinned and pursed her lips looking behind the utility door and in a couple of empty cupboards, all the time keeping a running commentary.

'Is there anyone in … here!' She joked as she flung doors open. 'Hmmm, nope. Where could they be? Maybe in the … hall? Nope not here either. Where could they have got to?'

She kept her attention firmly inside the house, blocking the outside but still hyper-aware of it, just on the edge of consciousness. She felt it pressing, inviting her to look outside ... go on look outside the window. Look a little harder, can you see a shadow? Is he around tonight? Is he watching?

She ignored the voice and kept up the cheerful chat as she searched the hall and, finding no-one, went upstairs.

She found her father in the middle of the landing, grinning at her face up on the floor where he lay. Frowning slightly she picked up the photograph and stuck it into the pocket of her cardigan,

Who the hell keeps leaving these around the house? I think it's time for another talk with the kids.

Except you know it's not the kids don't you, Em? How would they have dropped the one of dad at the door the other night? They were both in bed when you heard it fall.

Sighing, she pushed it to the back of her mind and carried on searching until she came to Charlie's room.

She found Charlie under his bed. She hadn't expected it to be quite so easy, so when she lifted the covers off the floor and saw the eyes looking out at her she gave a yelp and then nearly cried with laughter as he flinched, knocking his head off the slats on the underside of the bed. He scrambled out of the confined space laughing, and she rubbed his head kissing the spot he had bumped.

They laughed their way down the landing, Emmie's arm around Charlie's neck, his arms around her waist. He stopped to use the toilet as Emmie carried on downstairs to pretend to find Grace under the kitchen table.

Halfway down Emmie nearly stepped on another picture, also face up, this one depicted Charlie at six months old. He was only recently sitting unaided, and this was one of the first photos they had managed to snap before he fell over. He had a big grin on his face, drool hung in a line from his mouth to the floor. One hand balanced in the middle of the wide stance of his legs. She smiled stopping to pick the photo up and adding it to her pocket with the other one. She wondered how she hadn't noticed it on her way up the stairs only moments ago.

Charlie passed her on the stairs pretending to look for Grace, although her giggles could now be heard from upstairs. She caught up with him in the kitchen and went back into game mode. She could think about the photographs later.

'Well Charlie, that's the whole house searched. I just don't know where she could be.'

Charlie grinned, his hazel eyes shining with glee.

'She's too good at this game. We'll just have to leave her hiding until she comes out on her own.'

'I think you may be right Charlie, I just hope she doesn't stay all evening, she'll miss her hot chocolate before bed.'

'Well, I'll have to drink it for her tonight … '

'Nooooo! I'm here sillies!'

Grace flew from under the table throwing one arm around Emmie's leg and another around Charlie's. They both yelled pretending that she had scared them.

'You big meanies won't have my chocolate, naughty Charlie,' She batted at his feet with her little hand.

Charlie groaned and put his head in his hands as Emmie laughed at them.

'Another game!' Grace shouted.

Emmie put her hands up in front of her and took a step backwards.

'No, no Gracie, I'm through counting to a hundred, I must have counted a thousand times tonight. I'll tell you what, I'll make the chocolate early and we can play a game in the living room where it's warmer.'

Grace pouted a little and Charlie closed his eyes shaking his head in feigned resignation.

'Mom can't cut it, Gracie, we're too good for her.'

'Yeah, mom sucks!'

Sucks? Where the hell had she got that little beauty from?

She wrinkled her nose.

'Thank you, Grace.'

'Your welcome.'

Emmie shook her head smiling as Grace took off towards the living room tugging Charlie's hand.

'We'll play 'guess who' Charlie, come on.'

Charlie groaned as he was pulled and made noose actions with his free hand, head to the side. Emmie didn't have to see his face to know his tongue would be lolling out of his mouth and to the side.

She laughed and made the drinks without giving in to the temptation to look out into the dark (If Scott were to appear she would see headlights as Bill had said, and she wouldn't wind herself up looking for shadows) she turned to put the milk back into the fridge and stopped dead.

Sitting in the middle of the floor was yet another photo, this one face down, and this time she was sure that it hadn't been there before.

This is impossible, what is going on?

She set the milk back on the side and bent down to pick up the photo. This one was Emmie and Grace in the hospital. Grace had just been born, and both of them could have looked a whole lot better. Emmie looked tired, hair slicked back with sweat but smiling all the same. Grace's face poked out from the yellow cellular blanket, on her head was a tiny white hat. She was in full scream, mouth wide, little eyes closed into slits her face beet red.

Emmie looked around the kitchen, she couldn't understand who, or what, was throwing the photos in front of her and what on earth for. She placed this one with the others in her pocket, and continued to put the milk in the fridge with a sigh.

'Ok whoever you are. I'm not at all sure what you want me to do with the photos or why they keep appearing in front of me. I'm not moaning, I'd rather that than you hide my mobile phone or car keys but if you're trying to tell me something I'm not getting the memo.'

She shut the fridge door, leaning against it, and listened to the house. There was no reply, just the ticking of the grandfather clock. The house was calm and silent. She felt uneasy but couldn't place why. There were no ill feelings tonight, inside the house felt homely and safe, the Grandfather clock ticked away companionably.

The Grandfather clock?

Her stomach plummeted as she realised what was wrong. It was too quiet.

'Guess who' was particularly loud when Grace was playing and full of her giggles when it was in full swing, Charlie usually moaned loudly over Grace's laughter too, but there wasn't a murmur now.

Shit! Scott?

She pushed off the fridge rocking it on its feet as she stumbled into the hall, crossing it in three strides to fling wide the partially open door of the living room.

Grace and Charlie sat on the rug by the fire, guess who between them, and it was as if a switch had flicked the sound back on in her brain. Their laughter and shouts died away only as they swung to look at her. She stared back at them.

I heard the ticking clock but not Charlie and Grace in the same room?

'Mom? What's up?' Charlie asked.

Emmie tried to back peddle quickly not wanting to scare them again.

'Nothing. Nothing, I was running in to sit down, but I realised I forgot the chocolate as I pushed the door that's all.'

Grace blinked, and Charlie wrinkled his nose at her.

'You're weird, mom.'

Grace swung her head to look at Charlie who was still looking at Emmie like something that had walked out of the deep. Emmie looked back at him mouth starting to quiver, and then they were all laughing. She held her hands up at them.

'I'll get the chocolate and be back without the drama, sound good?'

Charlie nodded, but little miss chatterbox had to be more vocal.

'Noooo drama!' Grace yelled, 'That's my best words! Nooo, drama!'

Charlie grinned at Emmie, who shrugged and left to get the cups from the kitchen. She hesitated, listening. Grace and Charlie were coming through loud and clear now. She couldn't hear the clock over their noise. Emmie half wondered if she had imagined the whole thing but the jittery feeling was still with her, as was her pounding heart, which had almost wrenched out of her body with fear. She wished Scott would hurry up and get here so the weight of him looming over her would disappear, and she could get on with her life.

She took the chocolate into the living room suddenly remembering the wood pile.

Well, enough drama had gone on tonight, it could wait until

tomorrow, there was no way she was going out there in the dark now. Not a chance.

Chapter 53

The knock at the front door came at just after 8.45pm. Emmie was curled up on the settee in the living room, radio on quietly as she flicked through an art magazine.

She paused, frozen, as the knocks came again. Knocks in the middle of nowhere at night were never good news surely, and there was only one person that she was expecting to chance a call tonight.

Scott.

Her heart drummed against her ribs as she sat, unsure what to do.

She picked up her phone ready to press Stuarts number but paused over the green call symbol. He would be getting busy at this time of night, and she didn't actually know if the person at her door was Scott.

She groaned inwardly. She was going to have to find out who the hell it was. If it were Scott then she would dial Stuart before opening the door. And she *would* open the door to save Scott from breaking it down or causing a commotion when the kids were asleep.

The door rapped again. Emmie got up from the settee, legs like jelly. Her heart rate accelerating and breath coming in short gasps as she moved to the solid front door. Goosebumps crawled down her arms and legs as she leaned down to the letterbox just below her waist and with trembling hands pulled up the flap and pushed the outer bit open slightly.

'Who is it?'

Her voice shook almost as much as her hands. As she peered out she suddenly had a vivid image of the barrel of a gun appearing and shooting her through the head. She let go of the flap with a bang and scurried back into the hallway on her backside, legs scooting in front of her. The flap of the letterbox rattled and moved inward before clicking back down and then pushing back up.

Violent shakes took hold of her body, and she was aware of the whimpers that were escaping her unconsciously. She hugged her knees up to her chest as the flap came all the way up now and a hand, not a gun, appeared.

'Who the hell is it? Answer me.'

She was shouting now, not thinking of the children through her fear.

'It's me, lass, Bill.'

She stared at the door.

'Bill?'

'Aye, I didn't mean to scare you, I need to speak to you.'

Emmie got up and brushed herself down swallowing hard, vision darkening at the edges. She went to the door on legs made of rubber and keeping the chain on the door, she opened it just a crack.

'It's really me, Emmie, only me.'

'Bill? You scared the freaking shit out of me. Couldn't it wait until the morning?'

'No, I figured I need to speak to you now, it's not late. Can I come in?'

Still unsure, Emmie hesitated. What could Bill possibly want at this time of night?

'Fine, we'll speak through the crack of the door chain. Another city thing, eh lass?'

There he went again. Patronising bastard. She shut the door taking the chain from its hook and opening the door for him.

'Come in then, let's see what couldn't wait until morning. After what I told you today you couldn't wait to scare me to death in the dark is that it? Hilarious.'

Bill stepped into the hall and she motioned him into the living room where they could sit down, she followed him through on legs that didn't seem to want to hold her up.

'Drink?'

'No lass, I'll not take up too much of your time.'

Emmie sat back on the settee curling her cold feet back underneath her as Bill took the chair by the grandfather clock. She looked at him.

'So what couldn't wait?'

'I've been down to the village this afternoon, got some bits and pieces in for Maggie and had myself a bit of a chat.'

Emmie blinked at him wondering why the hell he had needed to scare her half to death just to share his shopping trip with her.

'I had a chat with Edith while I was in the shop and then I went round for a pint and had a chat there too.'

Emmie froze and narrowed her eyes at him.

'You checked up on me you mean?'

'Well, I only had one side of a story, and that will never do now, will it? It never hurts to find out the facts.'

'So did the 'story' check out for you?'

'Aye, mores the pity. I had hoped you might be exaggerating a little -'

'Hoped it was city girl nerves, eh Bill?'

He eyed her shrugging his nonchalance.

'I hoped so, for your sake. It appears though that I may have got it wrong. Edith is still in a state even though she knows the man is gone now. She admitted what had happened though and confirmed your story just as you said. She asked me to keep the details between the four of us. She's worried about you, and worried that she hasn't seen you.'

Emmie sighed and looked down at her hands in her lap.

'I should have gone earlier I know. I have to take a trip to the store before the storm moves in so I'll be there tomorrow morning after the school run. I'll speak to her then.'

'Good, she'll like that.'

'And Stu? I suppose you spoke to him too while you had a pint?'

Bill shuffled in the chair and heaved a sigh.

'Aye, and he confirmed what you said too. He also agreed that I should call him if I thought anything was going on.'

'Thanks, Bill. You really told him I said that?'

Bill shrugged.

'You said you wanted him there. I was just making sure he was in the same boat. No point calling the man up here if he didn't want to be called.'

Emmie rolled her eyes.

Thanks, Bill old pal. I have to have dinner with this man tomorrow. How awkward is that going to be now?

'And?'

'And, aye, he's worried about you too. He says this Scott may well want to harm you or the bairns and that he doesn't like you being alone out here. He seems to think there's a fair amount of danger and that you could be hurt.'

Emmie nodded and swallowed. She thought it was probably a fair assessment.

'Well I hope not, but I haven't seen Scott properly for a good while, and I've been told he's changed. I also had news from my sister this afternoon that he saw the estate agent details at her house Sunday so he knows full well where I am now, he could be on his way as we speak. I should think the visit is imminent. Which is why I was scared out of my mind at you knocking the door at 9pm when I wasn't expecting anyone.'

'Aye, and it's also the reason I had to see you straight away. I have something that may be of use to you.'

She frowned as he pulled his bulk out of the chair and felt around and under the back of his coat. His hands came back with a small revolver. Emmie gasped, jumping to her feet and backing away with her hands in the air. Her heart accelerated at the ease with which he had just pulled out a gun like it was a serving spoon.

'Bill! Please! Bill, no, no, no. I can't have a gun in the house. Why did you bring that here? I have small children. They could be killed! Put it away, please, I have no use for it; I couldn't hold that up to Scott any more than I could bash his brains with a hammer. Someone could really get hurt. Thank you. but I have no use for it, really.'

Bill was watching her reaction with amusement, a small smile playing on his face.

'It's not funny Bill. Shit, you told me it was safe out here, and you have a gun? What are you doing with a gun?'

'I have several, including a rifle.'

Emmie's jaw dropped, eyes wide. She started to speak, but he cut her off.

'Mainly I use it to scare predators off the land, foxes, wild cats, anything that may hurt the animals. Don't worry I have never had to use it to scare off a human. This little revolver hasn't been used for quite some years now it's a -'

'I should hope not! Put it away for God sake. I can't use it, Bill. Even if I wanted to, I have no idea how to hold a gun let alone use one safely. I can't take the chance with the children around, what if I accidentally shot and killed one of them, or Scott? I couldn't live with myself - '

'Emmie stop,' Bill raised his voice and she stared at him. His face was serious, and he was still holding out the damned gun.

'Do you think you could gather yourself together enough to shut up and listen for a minute. As I said earlier, get the facts and weigh up the options before you run out the starting gate when the gun hasn't even gone off … excuse the pun.'

Emmie licked her lips quickly and stared at the gun. She looked back up at Bill and gave him a quick nod.

'Right, hear me out then make your decision, if you still don't want to use it I will gladly take it home and never mention it again. Always listen before you look a gift horse in the mouth, lass.'

Emmie sat back down on the settee, heart still pounding.

'Okay, I'm listening. You have five minutes, and then you can take that thing away.'

He sat himself down shaking his head, laying the gun in his lap, barrel toward him, where it could quite happily blow his nuts off if triggered. She stared with horrified fascination.

Please don't blow your ass and tackle off in my chair Bill I may just go insane, and I could do without the mess.

'Ok, lass. Now we're calmer let's take a look at what I'm offering. The gun is completely useless. It won't fire, and even if it could I have no cartridges for it anyway. It's a real gun. It's a .38 Smith and Wesson Victory model revolver, newer varieties are known as the model 10. It was possibly last used in world war II, mostly by United States forces I should think. This one is a collector's item deactivated in 1996. It has a steel pin welded into the chamber entrance of the barrel. The rest of the gun has a fully working action, even so, it's days of firing were over a long time ago.'

Emmie took in the information, turning it over in her mind.

'So it won't kill anyone?'

'A gun never killed anyone lass. It's the people on the end of them
do that. But no, this gun isn't dangerous, it's a collector's item. It's like
a dick that won't stand to attention; it's useless. What I'm offering is the
chance to scare this man of yours with a very real gun, which will pose
no danger to you or the bairns while you have it here. I'm presuming he
has no knowledge of guns of course?'

Emmie shook her head. As far as she knew anyway.

'Right, so all you need to do is practice a stance where you look
fairly stable and like you know what you're doing, and anything you
say will suddenly carry a lot more weight. Even a big, strong man will
think twice staring down the barrel of a gun.'

Bill paused and looked at her. She looked back at him.

Could this actually work?

She sat forward and held her hand out for the gun. Bill rose and
came to sit next to her on the settee. He passed it to her holding it by
the barrel. She took it noting its weight, heavy but not overly so,
probably little more than a bag of frozen peas. She ran her hand over
the wooden handle, or grip as Bill corrected her, and the long smooth
steel of the barrel which was soft and cold under her touch. Bill calmly
went through the parts of the gun with a thorough knowledge pointing
each one out working backwards from the muzzle. Front and rear sight,
ejector rod, he opened the cylinder showing her where the six
cartridges would have been loaded before closing it back up and
showing her the hammer, trigger guard and trigger. Enough detail to
give her an insight but not overwhelm her.

As her heart slowed she tried the gun for size, fingers white as she
tried to control her shaking hand with the weight of the gun. She held
the grip, pointing the muzzle toward the fireplace. Her hand shook, and
her forefinger involuntary squeezed the trigger giving it a light click.

Bill chuckled big shoulders heaving.

'And that, lass, is why I would never be stupid enough to give you
a live gun. You'd have just shot a hole in your fireplace. Try holding it
this way instead.'

He leaned in front of her placing the forefinger of her right hand
over the trigger and folding the others and her thumb around the
bottom of the grip loosening her fingers so that the pink came back into
her knuckles.

'Rest your finger lightly on the trigger letting the weight of the gun lean into your palm. If you're shaking and you pull the trigger, the game will be up quicker than a naked man sat on a tack. Never take the weight of the gun into the finger that's resting on the trigger, that's what the rest of your hand is for.'

She nodded and did as he said. She held the gun a little steadier but the weight concentrated at one end of her arm was making the muscles in her arm and shoulder ache. The gun wavered up and down.

'Use two hands but put all of your fingers around the grip. Only one on the trigger. Keep your arms straight out in front and lock your elbows. It helps to hold the weight and looks a whole lot meaner than a shaky gun.'

She did as he said, the weight distributed between both hands and arms felt a whole lot easier to handle. The gun was steady and straight. She felt good; even having a go at lining up the sights.

'Much better, now you're looking like you're in control. You want to feel like it's an extension of your hands, not a foreign object. The more you practice with it, the more you will be able to pick it up under pressure and feel like you own it.'

Emmie lowered the gun back down into her lap and turned to look at Bill.

'What if the police are called at any point? I'm hoping they won't be, but I don't want to be carted off to jail for having a gun on the property without a license.'

'Won't happen, lass, anyone over eighteen can own a gun without a license if it can be proven to have been deactivated. I have the paperwork should it be an issue.'

Emmie nodded running her fingers lightly over the side of the gun.

'So what's the verdict then lass? Want me to take it back or are you happy to use a harmless piece of equipment as a deterrent in a situation that might prove to be more dangerous than the gun?'

He looked at her, bushy eyebrows raised in question. She smiled back at him.

'Well, now I've listened to the facts, I think I probably owe you an apology. It's the best defence I have, and I certainly feel like I have a better chance if he does bring his violent streak with him.'

Bill nodded, she expected him to say 'I told you so' but he stayed silent, surprising her.

'No rubbing my nose in it?'

He huffed a laugh

'If you hadn't reacted like you did lass I'd have thought you were crazy. Anyone with an ounce of sense having a gun pulled out on them would have done the same. I knew that was coming. I didn't know you would be quite so easily persuaded. I expected more of a fight.'

'Right, here it comes. Let it all out, Bill. I'm used to you already.'

She braced herself for the onslaught.

'It tells me two things about you lass. One, It tells me that you can listen to reason and show some sense when you get down from your high horse and your mouth stops running away with you. And two, it shows me how scared you really are, and how much you believe he may hurt you. I know we grate on each other wrong, that goes both ways, but I like you lass, and I wouldn't want to see you or the bairns hurt.'

Letting her shoulders drop she sighed and softened.

'Thank you. And for the record I like you too, the patronising and condescending bit of you is an ass -'

'Aye, there you go again just when I was starting to think you may have learned a lesson.'

'I don't need to learn a lesson, Bill.'

'Then carry on lass,' he said standing up and pushing down his coat, 'I have to go, Maggie will think I've got lost.'

Emmie rose too leaving the gun on the settee as she walked him to the door. He stepped outside and turned to her.

'Take care. I'll be looking out for you as much as I can.'

She shivered pulling her cardigan around her as cold air and rain blew inside. The wind was starting to pick up.

'If you need anything, or any more help with the gun, you know where I am.'

'I can't thank you enough for helping me out and thinking of such a brilliant plan. Thank you, it means a lot, really.'

He dipped his head and started to turn around as she stepped forward and grabbed him around the waist in a big bear hug. He was huge, and her hands didn't connect at the back of him so she squeezed as hard as she could and then let him go stepping back.

He looked shocked as she grinned at him.

'Hey, hey lass, we'll have none of that, people will talk.'

'Who's going to talk around here, the mountain goats? Don't worry. I have a reputation to uphold too, I'll never hug you in daylight or public, and we can still throw sarcastic remarks at each other if anyone is looking.'

Bill laughed loudly and she cringed thinking of the children asleep upstairs.

'You know what lass? I think you'll be okay, just a feeling I get but I reckon I'll be right. You'll do just fine.'

He turned and walked away coughing into his hankie as he laughed. Emmie shut and locked the door smiling. If faith was anything to go by she had the situation covered. Bill was the second person to tell her she would be okay now. They obviously saw something in her she couldn't see herself, or it was just that they didn't know Scott. Which one it was remained to be seen.

Emmie made her way back to the living room looking at the gun still sat on the chair. She picked it up, looking it over again before holding it out in the stance that Bill had told her to use. She flicked the end up lightly as she pulled the trigger three times.

Bam, bam, bam. Take that Scotty boy.

She chuckled to herself as she lowered the gun and took it through to the utility where the children didn't go too often. She put it on top of one of the cupboards before changing her mind and placing it on top of the fridge behind the kitchen door. It seemed more central there and a little easier to get to if she needed it. Stepping back to check it couldn't be seen she went back into the living room and sat on the settee picking up her magazine again.

A rectangle of paper flew out of the pages and fluttered down to the floor. Emmie stared at it.

Another? Christ give me a break.

She fingered the other three photos still in her pocket and then leaned down to pick it up, calm until she turned it over. Then she almost screeched, clamping a hand over her mouth to hold in the sound.

The picture was a close up of Scott, head and shoulders. He had a blue suit jacket and white shirt. His hair was impeccable, slicked just right with gel. His mouth was a hard line with no sign of stubble on his set jaw. His eyes were what scared her though. They seemed to bore right out of the photo into hers with piercing quality.

She quickly screwed the photo up, her heart pounding. She was getting quite used to the photographs moving around and the memories they brought back when she found them, but she would have bet her life on there not being a single one of Scott in that box. She had searched through them purposely, taking every one of him out after they split up, and she would never have missed such a close up of that look he gave her when she had done something he thought was out of order.

She shuddered and stood to throw the photo onto the fire. Stomach churning she placed her hands on her thighs breathing heavily watching the ball of paper curl and burn until it disintegrated into nothing.

Chapter 54

The alarm clock pulled Scott from a deep sleep. The radio show hosts were blathering on about the forecast snow and what they would be doing in it if it stuck around. UK weathermen were skilled at getting the forecast wrong so the four inches of snowfall planned, followed by a week or so of deathly cold, could all just disintegrate on the wet floor after all the rain that had hammered down overnight.

Scott leaned over and banged the off button to shut them up, listening instead to the howling of the wind at the window. It was going to be a fine day today, yes indeed, storm or no storm.

He sat up yawning, rolling his shoulders and stretching his neck putting one ear to his shoulder and then the other before getting out of bed. He dressed quickly before going into the bathroom where he took a leak, washed, brushed and flossed his teeth and took time over his perfectly styled hair. He checked his teeth in the mirror, biting them together and pulling his lips back exposing all but the sides where he lifted the cheeks up and down for a better view. Perfect. He wanted to look his best when he walked back into Emelia's life later.

He grinned as he thought how shocked she would be when he turned up to bring her home, where penance for her actions would start immediately with tidying downstairs. It was a shit-tip down there, and he had found it tough being cooped up in the bedroom all evening with no TV and only himself for company.

He had almost called Amy and invited her over.

Almost.

But she hadn't stopped calling since he threw her out Saturday evening. She was a good fuck, but a royal pain in the ass in every other way, and she had taken the crown for whinging. Amy wasn't his style, and he was done with her, it was time to focus on Emelia now. It was time to bring his wife home. That would put Amy's nose out of joint for good.

His phone buzzed on the sink next to him, and he glanced at the screen. Apparently, a new voicemail was waiting for him.

Too late Marti-boy, I've already found her. Your services are officially obsolete.

He grinned as he called the service and listened to the first few seconds of Amy's pathetic pleading before deleting it, frustrated. It would appear the one person he wanted to hear from was running scared.

Come to think of it …

He frowned and swiped his phone, opening his bank app and confirming his suspicions. No money had left his account for the guest house at all yesterday.

Bastard. So Martin had left without a word? That little fuckwit was going to leave him *hanging?*

Anger surged up from Scott's stomach. He wouldn't be made a fool of. His hands shook as he put the phone back on the side of the sink and looked at himself in the mirror, breathing hard.

Get it together, Scott, if you fuck over the bedrooms as well as downstairs you'll have nowhere for Emelia to come home to.

He clenched his jaw, taking deep breaths, knuckles white as he gripped to edge of the basin. He got control of his breathing and felt himself slowly getting calmer. He smiled at himself in the mirror. It was taut and strained.

He turned, shooting an arm at the bottles that sat on the corner of the bath. They flew into the air, bounced off the wall, and scattered into the bathtub with a loud clatter. One jumped out of the tub and skid across the floor towards his foot. He kicked it away and looked back into the mirror.

That felt better. There was less strain on his face now. He needed to focus on Emelia. He could sort out Martin when she was back at home.

The divorce had been a mistake. Scott knew that now, he had panicked as she had lost control, but that wasn't his fault. She had no idea of the extent of what she had done or what she had put him through, what she was *still* putting him through. He would tell her though, in no uncertain terms, it was time to stop pissing around. He needed his family back together. He was strong again now, ready to deal with her shit.

We'll be remarried within the year, and everything will be perfect again, as it used to be.

He nodded at his reflection and checked himself over in the mirror once more, assessing himself appreciatively. Damn, he was a good-looking man, he knew that Emelia would be grateful to hear he wanted to try again. She had been devastated when he had suggested divorce, as she should have been, he was a catch, and she was lucky to have him.

She had always loved the smell of his aftershave too. Reaching over, he undid the top and splashed a good amount of it over his chin and neck before putting it back into position on the side of the sink. Label outward. He grinned.

I'm all yours, baby.

Totally calm, he picked up his bag and ski jacket from the bedroom doorway and was halfway downstairs when he realised he had forgotten to open the curtains. He could have left them, it didn't matter, but he knew within the hour it would bug him to within an inch of his life. He didn't need an excuse to turn around when he had got halfway to Scotland.

Going back to the bedroom, he crossed to the window flinging open the curtains in a brisk motion. He paused and blinked.

Street lights were orange, weren't they? So why did the world look white?

It took a moment to register. Snow. It had snowed overnight. At some point, the rain had stopped, and the snow had started falling, fast enough to stick too. There wasn't much, just a few centimetres but it would be enough to grind Britain to a halt as people flailed about in their cars trying to get to work in a few hours time, and he knew the rear wheel drive BMW would have trouble too if much more fell.

He looked at the light shining from under the street lamp and saw just a light flurry of the tiniest snowflakes getting tossed around in the wind. Good. At the moment he should be okay as long as it held off enough for him to drive up the country and hopefully out of the snow altogether.

He switched off the bedroom light, strode downstairs and straight out of the front door. No point hanging around here to get stuck, with any luck he would be through the M25 by 7am. If he was really lucky he could be past Birmingham by 8am and then he would allow himself to stop for breakfast. Hopefully, the worst of the motorway traffic would be behind him in the Midlands, and he could get a clear run up the M6 to Scotland ahead of the storm.

Chapter 55

Wednesday started much earlier for Emmie than she had intended. After a restful first half of the night, she had awoken at 4.30am with a jolt and a looming sense of dread that wouldn't shift. When falling back to sleep had proved futile she had got up and gone down to the kitchen to make tea.

Outside the weather was giving a prerequisite to the impending storm. The wind gusted and raged, and heavy clouds raced across the sky covering and uncovering the moon in quick succession.

Filling the kettle and switching it on she had glanced out of the window. Other than the photo's things seemed to have calmed down over the last few days and she hadn't seen shadow man himself since last Friday when he may, or may not, have stayed the night.

She saw him now though, up by the fence where she had first caught a glimpse of him in the storm just over a week ago. Her heart lurched, and she jumped back from the kitchen counter with a gasp. She stared at him, and he stared back - at least she got the impression he was staring back - she had never seen his face, she didn't even know whether he had one.

The kettle clicked off loudly as the water boiled making her flinch again in the quiet of the house.

Shit. Get a grip, Em.

She looked back outside thinking the spell would have been broken and that he would be gone, but he was still there, unmoving, watching.

'Who are you?' She whispered, sending goosebumps crawling up her spine as her voice broke the silence around her. She gripped her biceps with her hands crossing her arms over her chest.

There was no reply, but the brim of the hat seemed to tip just a little, barely noticeable, to the right.

Emmie cocked her head to the right in unconscious imitation, heart pattering behind her ribs, wondering if this was a real person or some sort of spirit. Did she believe in ghosts anyway? The photographs came to mind, and she decided she believed more than she had when she had arrived here a few short weeks ago.

She thought of what Bill had said about the reaction of a person who was staring down the barrel of a gun. She went to the fridge, reaching it off the top.

This would show her whether he was human or not, wouldn't it? If he turned away, hid, twitched even, she would know. If he carried on acting like a statue, then there was a possibility he wasn't real.

Stepping back into the view of the window she saw he was still there, still unmoving. She held the gun in two hands pointing it down below the counter and set her hands up as Bill as suggested, her right finger on the trigger, the rest around the grip. She kept her eyes on shadow man.

In one lunge she stepped her left foot back and pulled her arms up quickly keeping her elbows locked and aiming the gun straight at him. She pulled the trigger, because she could, and made to shoot him like she had Scott the evening before.

Bam, bam, bam. Take that shadow man. I'm armed, and I'm not afraid of you.

She smiled at her reflection in the window but then she noticed something else in the moonlight. Shadow man was on the move.

He was coming down the path through the garden at a rate of knots. If he had been a man he would have been sprinting but there was no movement other than a rapid glide, and he was growing bigger by the second his mass heading for the window. For her.

Reeling back, Emmie screamed and threw herself down onto the floor. She scrambled on all fours, fear propelling her into the hall where she pushed her back into the right angle of wall between the front door and the kitchen door, legs pulled in to her chest. The gun was still in her hand knocking against her shins as the whole of her body tensed and shook. She waited for the clatter of the window or rattle of the door.

It didn't come, but Emmie didn't move.

She sat shaking in the corner until her alarm went off upstairs at 7am and the children had to be woken for school. By 8am it would be almost fully light, and she knew she would count the seconds until daylight arrived.

Two hours later, assessing shadow man in the relative safety of the car after dropping the children at school, she concluded that he wasn't real. It wasn't possible that he could be real, and yet her brain wanted to tell her that it was impossible that he couldn't.

Even so, the fact remained that nothing human moved that fast without the jerk of a running motion, and it was equally impossible for a man to 'glide' smoothly through a mass of brambles, never mind the fact that he had seemed to be looking right at her as he'd done it. A man would have gone under without any grace in seconds.

So who the hell was he? John Watts? Ted? And what the hell did he want?

Having him watching the house was almost as bad as waiting to see when Scott would show up. It was intense. The only saving grace was that although he had scared her a number of times, he had never physically hurt any of them, whether that meant he wouldn't over time she didn't know.

As she entered Bracken Hill, she forced her thoughts to the more pressing question of what to buy in case she ended up snowbound, and what to cook for dinner tonight. She had meant to plan a meal, but that had gone by the board with this morning's encounter. She wasn't too bothered, she was a skilled cook, Scott had made sure of that.

He had insisted all of their meals were made from scratch. Nothing was allowed in the cupboards unless it contained single wholesome ingredients. No jars of bolognese sauce, no packets of cheese sauce, no curry sauces, the list went on. Everything was made with fresh ingredients on a daily basis. As time went on, she started to think it was less about preservatives and hidden e-numbers, and more about keeping her on her toes. It had been stressful, and testing, but it had set her up perfectly for a situation like tonight.

Thank you, Scott, this is the one good thing to have come out of our marriage, other than the children.

She huffed a laugh. Funny how those days seemed an age ago now.

Pulling up between two parked cars outside the shop she got out, pulling her coat around her against the raging wind and bitter cold. She half jogged the few paces to the shop door, the bell tingling as she entered.

Looking right she saw Edith, noting the lady's hand fluttering up from the counter to her chest. Emmie took in this immaculately presented lady, in a frill collared shirt and pale yellow cardigan, glasses hanging from her neck, and felt a sudden surge of respect. She was a small lady, a good few inches shorter than Emmie, and a lot older. She had been hurt and threatened, but here she was, carrying on in the face of fear, as she had done each day since Saturday.

'Oh!' Edith met her gaze and stepped around the desk with her arms out, a look of such worry and joy mixed in her features that Emmie couldn't tell which was at the forefront. She gave a small smile and stepped into Edith's embrace, holding onto her, smelling soap and hair solution, tears welling from nowhere, and thinking she had never meant the feeling in a hug more than she did at that moment.

It was like holding onto her mother. Paradoxically she wanted to keep Edith safe, and yet she wanted Edith to tell her it would be okay and keep her safe. It was a strange emotion and one she had to bite back, or she would have broken the tear bank, and the crying wouldn't have stopped for some time.

Breaking the embrace and stepping back she wiped at a stray tear and realised Edith was doing the same. Emmie left a hand on Edith's arm looking down at her.

'I'm so sorry for everything Edith, I'm sorry Martin attacked you, and I'm sorry I haven't been in to see you earlier. I just …'

She broke off. What had she been doing? What could be the excuse for not coming in and seeing if a lady who had been attacked was alright? Even just for five minutes? She took her hand away and looked at the floor struggling for an answer.

'You have things to sort out, I know. You must be so worried, in fact, I can see in your eyes that you are.'

'It's no excuse. I should have come down. I can't control this and in the end what will be will be, until then I have to carry on as normal with the threat on the horizon. It's a hard place to be, but I guess you know that.'

'I couldn't have put it better myself.'

'And that's why I should have popped in. I feel so guilty.'

Edith's hand found her arm squeezing gently, comforting Emmie, but her eyes were fearful.

'Don't, it's not your fault, dear. I'm glad you're here now though, I was getting worried. The only information I've been getting is from Stuart, and I'm certain that he's only telling me what I need to hear.'

Emmie smiled, and her heart warmed at the thought of him.

'Well, tell me what he told you, and I'll tell you whether he's right.'

'He said that Martin left the pub after you spoke to him, and he won't be back to bother me, and that's great, but how can he know he's gone for good? I liked that Martin was next door, I felt a whole lot safer with him there under Stuart's gaze than not knowing where he is at all now.'

'He's gone Edith, and no, he won't be back. Scott, my ex-husband, has what he needs, it's up to the big boy himself now. Martin as good as apologised as he left. It's not an excuse for his behaviour, but he did look very sorry, and it isn't his usual approach at all. He was scared to death that you would call the police. He won't be back, and that's an absolute guarantee.'

Edith placed a hand over her heart and blew out a shaky breath.

'You're sure?'

'One hundred percent. He's probably back in Surrey by now.'

She placed a hand on the counter and rubbed her brow visibly relieved.

'So, it's just you that we have to worry about then.'

'Nope, I don't want you worrying about me either. I have some good backup in Bill and Stu, and my sister and her husband are coming up after the storm has calmed a little. It's supposed to be at it's worst down south today, so they could be on the road by tomorrow. I'm hoping if they feel it's dangerous driving through it then maybe Scott will too.'

Edith nodded.

'I hope you're right, dear. The worst here is supposed to run through the early hours of tomorrow, but we could get snow for a few days yet, or so they say. If we have lots of snow, your lane will drift. Bill will help *you* with that, he has the land rover, but at least there won't be many people able to get up to the house. Of course, the weather is changeable here from one minute to the next. It's far too cold for snow this morning.'

Emmie smiled.

'Well, I hope that changes, I haven't seen decent snowfall since Charlie was a baby. The children haven't ever seen enough to make a decent snowman, it would make their day, and make my year.'

Edith chuckled and then paused, thinking.

'You know, I have a sledge out back that Len and I have no use for. Sometimes the local children borrow it, but I think it would be better used at your place if you don't have one already.'

Emmie's mouth dropped open, eyes widening.

'Really? That would be fantastic! I was going to stick with snow angels and snowmen but a sledge? And a hill to run it down next to us too? That would be amazing! Thank you so much, Edith.'

'It's my pleasure. When you've got your things, I'll pop out and bring it inside. It's a large sturdy wooden one that Len made himself when our daughter was small. She had no use for it, screamed every time he brought it out of the shed. It may get all of you together on it if you're game.'

'All together? I'm so excited I'll be on it when the kids are in school.'

'Aye, because these things are children's toys after all.' Edith laughed delighted. 'Len would say the same, he gave up on Karen and took the sledge out himself every snowfall. He'd be up on the hills all day, damn near scared me to death. You'll have to come up and say hello when you have time. I think you'd get on like a house on fire.'

'I would love that. Remind me I need to ask him which part of the hill is the best to come down.'

They laughed as the door tinkled open and Emmie noticed that Edith didn't flinch at all this time.

'Don't come running to me when you break a leg dear, Len is not my responsibility where sensible sledging instruction is concerned.'

'Morning, ladies.' The now familiar soothing deepness of Stuart's voice made Emmie swing around smiling, and Edith raise a hand, still laughing.

'Morning,' They said together.

'It's the wrong time of the morning for you to be in here Stu,' Edith called as he disappeared around to the back of the shop and reappeared with three boxes of eggs nestled neatly in his hands. He put them down, feeling in his pocket for change and placing it on the counter as he gave them both a smile.

'Eggs. Everyone seems to want extra eggs with their breakfast this morning.'

'Aye, I bet those lassies need a decent breakfast after the amount of alcohol they put away last night.' Edith turned to Emmie shaking her head in disdain.

'If I was their mother, Honestly! I've not seen a show like it since I was out in the clubs of Edinburgh when I was just a wee lass. Four of them, draping themselves over the bar offering things that made my toes curl. How you have the patience for these things Stu is beyond me.'

'They line my pockets, simple as that. Any bunch of women with alcohol usually end up the same way in my experience.'

'Yep, seen it a million times.' Emmie said as nonchalantly as she could manage.

What exactly had they been offering?

A sharp stab of jealousy plunged into her stomach. That was an image she didn't need to think about. Stuart smiled at her.

'They checked in for an extra night too, obviously up for another go later.'

Emmie tried to keep her expression neutral as the feeling twisted itself up to her heart, and then he managed to smother it in an instant as he picked up the eggs and started for the door.

'I won't be there, though, I'll be spending my evening with someone far more interesting, and with a cartload more decorum.' He looked back winking at her, making her flush, 'eight thirty, Em?'

She grinned.

'Yep, well, anytime after eight, whenever you're ready.'

'Alright, Sweetheart, see you later. Bye Edie.'

He disappeared out of the door leaving it to shut with a tinkle of the bell and Emmie stared at it heart swelling.

Did that actually just happen?

Obviously, Edith felt the same. She reached out, putting a hand on Emmie's left arm, staring at the door.

'Oh my goodness, what just happened?'

'I'm not sure.'

'What's happening tonight?'

Emmie turned to face Edith, feeling flushed and a little off balance. She placed her hand on the counter to steady the ground.

'Nothing, just dinner, as a thank you that's all.'

'That's all?'

Emmie frowned, not understanding, and Edith continued.

'He told me you'd asked him to dinner, and he also told me he turned you down. How on earth did you manage to change his mind?'

'I didn't. He said he'd changed his mind yesterday and asked if the offer was still open.'

Edith stared back at the shop door.

'Well, I'll be. I knew there was something there, I just knew it.'

'Edith, what are you talking about?'

Edith looked back at her a small smile playing on her face.

'Have you heard about Judith yet, dear?'

'Well, Bill told me a little about the accident yesterday.'

Emmie felt uncomfortable discussing such a private and painful thing for the second time before Stuart had told her of it himself, but Edith didn't seem to notice, or to be surprised that Bill had said something.

'Aye, it was a nasty affair, and for a while, I didn't think we'd get Stu back from it. It was the longest few years I've ever spent watching someone in that much pain, but he slowly came round, except that he wasn't interested in moving on in the form another relationship. Perfectly acceptable in the beginning, but as time has gone on I've said to him countless times that he has to stop thinking about Judith and start moving forward. She loved him dearly, and she would have wanted him to find happiness again. He's a good man in the prime of his life and not short of offers. It's such a terrible waste.'

Edith stared off into the distance, going quiet for a moment, and then she was back.

'So when he said you had invited him to dinner and he'd said no, I'm afraid I snapped at him a little.'

Emmie raised her eyebrows.

'Oh don't worry, he snapped back dear, as people are liable to do when you hit a nerve. We had quite a to-do about it. But I knew from the moment he was bringing us wine at the table that there was something around you both, and I know damn well he's been fighting it. I've not known him to serve anyone at tables in the evening he's always stayed behind the bar at a professional distance from the customers, and I told him so. I've never seen him react to anyone he was attracted to, and there surely must have been a few in that time, but you shifted something in him that night dear, I saw it, and I know very well how he makes you feel.'

Emmie flushed again and rolled her eyes.

'That obvious huh?'

Edith chuckled and patted Emmie's hand.

'I think you're a breath of fresh air. You could teach him a thing or two about moving on. You'd be good for him. You wear your heart on your sleeve dear, right out there for everyone to see. If you want my take on it, I think you scared him. He could deal with feelings going one way, but not being reciprocated. He wants to help you because he genuinely is that kind of man, but because of the things he's feeling he doesn't want to get too close, understand?'

Emmie thought of the way he had shut down at the mention of dinner and thought that, yes, she understood. But something else niggled at her.

'I'm worried I may have pushed him into dinner if it's that obvious how I feel?'

'Impossible, he's had countless women making it obvious how they feel, especially when they get alcohol inside them. He's never been interested in taking anything further. Professional banter, a bit of a giggle, and goodnight. That's all he's ever given before he shut them out.'

'Are you sure you're not making too much of this? It's only a thank you dinner, he probably just felt bad about my situation getting worse.'

Edith looked at Emmie incredulously.

'I'm just saying, as someone who's known him for twenty years, that he's being different with you, not much, but enough to get an old lady's radar working again. You can't have missed the massive compliments he gave you just then, and dear, if I'm not mistaken, he called you sweetheart?'

Emmie nodded, stomach swirling warmly, she could get used to that too.

'Aye,' Edith said. She nodded to herself, smiling, 'Just little things to you, but enormous steps to me. I didn't think it would take quite so long mind.'

Emmie smiled and enjoyed a little of the warm feeling climbing up from her stomach, but she wouldn't allow what Edith said to penetrate too far. She already knew she was climbing to the top of the roller coaster again and by tonight something would probably bring her crashing back down to the ground. Either Edith would have gotten it all wrong, and Emmie would be the one crushed, or maybe Scott would come and crash the party, he was making a habit of that.

As Emmie shopped, they chatted about what to cook, what to drink and what she would need for the snow and how many days she would possibly need to buy for. Finally finished, and with bags full of food and supplies in the car, Emmie came back into the shop for the sledge. Picking it up she said thank you and goodbye to Edith who was now serving an elderly gentleman. Edith looked up.

'Good luck tonight, dear.'

'I don't need luck, Edith, it's just a friendly dinner.'

'Aye,' She said, 'and I'm a monkey's uncle.'

Chapter 56

Grace came out of school cheerful and chatty, as she had every day since Monday. They listened to her tunes, singing *Humpty Dumpty* and *The Grand old Duke of York* with vigour until Grace suddenly trailed off and went quiet. Emmie tried to chivvy her along, but Grace continued to look out of the window in silence. Confused by the sudden change in mood, Emmie glanced in the rear view mirror at her daughter.

'What's the matter, Gracie?'

Grace caught Emmie's eyes in the mirror.

'Can't say.'

Emmie's stomach dropped if Grace couldn't say it was usually because her invisible friend was involved.

'You can tell me anything, Grace, you know that. Why can't you say?'

Grace looked back out of the window.

'Do you think you will be in trouble?'

Grace shook her head, and Emmie frowned.

'Then what?'

Grace chewed her finger and finally let out a small sigh. Emmie glanced at the road and then met her eyes again.

'Mommy has been naughty, not Gracie.'

'Me?'

Grace nodded, and Emmie floundered, wondering what on earth she could be talking about.

'Well, if I have I didn't know. What did I do?'

'The man says you have.'

'What man grace? Your friend, the funny man that I can't speak to?'

Grace nodded again and stared back out of the window.

'Okay, well, I'm sure whatever I did wasn't that bad.'

'It was really bad, mommy, super duper bad.'

Emmie sighed. If Grace wasn't going to elaborate, then she would try just apologising so that they could get on with the day without this strange mood hanging over them.

'Okay, well, tell the man I'm very so-'

Grace cut her off, eyes serious as she met Emmie's gaze in the mirror.

'He says you *shot* at him, mommy. With a real live *gun*.'

Grace put her fingers together in a two-handed gun hold, just as Emmie had done with the real gun and flicked her fingers up and down in shooting motions.

'Bam, bam, bam, I not afraid of you shadow man.'

Emmie lost the bottom out of her stomach. The world seemed to spin, darkening, and she lost her grip on the steering wheel momentarily, Knocking it with her hand as it dropped. The car pulled to the right crossing to the other side of the road, and a horn blared.

Grace screamed, and Emmie saw a car bearing down on theirs, front end down and braking hard. She yelled, grabbing the wheel, and pulled it hard to the left. The other car flew past, missing them by inches. Emmie stamped on the brake and the car spun on the smooth surface, two full revolutions before coming to a stop facing the wrong way on the verge, smoke curling from the tyres.

The car who had blared its horn sailed on into the distance as Emmie flung open the driver's door, the acrid smell of burnt rubber reaching her nostrils. She leaned out and lost her breakfast on the grass, heaving and retching until there was nothing left to come up and she thought her stomach might just break. Then she leaned back into the car and pulled a tissue from the glove box wiping her mouth with shaking hands. She was drenched in sweat and shaking violently.

Grace was howling in her child seat but otherwise looked unharmed. Emmie shut the door to keep the warmth inside, but couldn't stop shaking enough to drive.

The screech of brakes, the car out of control and the smell of burnt rubber had propelled her straight back to the accident two years ago as though the car had been through a time machine. This time there had been no crunch and squeal of metal against metal, but she heard it all the same.

She folded her arms over the steering wheel and lay her head on them closing her eyes trying to control her ragged breathing and calm herself down.

'Mommy! Mommy! I'm sorry, are you hurt?' Grace yelled between gulping sobs.

Emmie lifted her head which seemed to have gained several tons of weight in the aftermath, and turned giving Grace the best smile she could manage. She was sure it looked more like a grimace, but it would have to do. Looking at Grace was putting her on edge after what she had just said and done.

'No Gracie, I'm fine, just a little scared. Are you hurt sweetie?'

'No, I'm scared too,' She wailed, dragging out the oo in too.

Emmie unlocked her seatbelt and climbed shakily into the back, unlocking grace and pulling her to her, smothering her in the folds of her coat and brushing the tears from her little face.

'I'm so sorry, Grace. It's not your fault.'

'It's shadow man's fault, he told me!' Fresh wails left Grace and Emmie hugged her closer.

'How does he tell you Grace? How does he speak to you if I can't hear him?'

'He ... he puts words in my head, I don't want to, but he does it anyway.'

'Okay,' She kissed the top of Grace's head, 'It's okay sweetie, don't worry.'

'He made you crash!'

'No Grace, mommy made the car crash because what he said shocked me. Maybe we should just talk about him at home in future.'

'Okay.' She said nodding, tears finally subsiding to hiccups, 'Mommy, he says you have a real live gun.'

Emmie thought about how to answer.

'I don't have a live gun, Grace, where would I get one of those?'

'Well, a dead one then. It won't work.'

Emmie reeled back shocked and looked at Grace, searching her scared little eyes. Where could she get hold of such information? Had she heard Bill when he brought it round?

Grace had called her invisible friend shadow man too, she had never called him that before, and did that mean that the entity in her bedroom was also shadow man? The implications of shadow man being her invisible friend were too significant to think about right now. And did that mean the entity that visited her bedroom in the night was also shadow man?

Emmie rubbed a shaky hand across her forehead feeling disjointed and unsure.

'How can you know all of this?'

'He tells me.'

'Okay, honey, how does *he* know all of this?'

Grace shrugged and started to cry again.

Emmie folded her arms around the little girl burying her nose in her soft hair. Grace finally quietened and looked back into Emmie's eyes sniffing.

'Mommy?' She whispered, 'I'm scared. I'm scared he is going to take Charlie and me away, and I don't want to go, mommy, I don't want to!'

Emmie looked into her daughter's scared eyes and fear prickled through her. Was this a shadow man threat or was he telling Grace things about Scott that she was getting confused with? Scott could well be coming to take them away, but shadow man couldn't harm them, could he?

She didn't know. She wasn't sure what could or couldn't happen anymore.

She knew one thing though, whether the threat came from Shadow man, or more likely the impending arrival of Scott, no one would be taking the children away unless it was over her dead body.

'Grace, sweetheart, no one will be taking you and Charlie anywhere. I absolutely won't allow it. Don't be scared, honey. Shadow man is just that. A shadow. He can't hurt us.'

'Promise?'

'I promise.'

And as Grace clung to her, Emmie only hoped it would be a promise that she could keep.

Chapter 57

Scott outran the scattering of snow that had fallen in Surrey but not the buffeting wind or dull murk as he headed up the country. The journey had been uneventful, and by the time he had stopped for a small break in the Midlands at 11.30am he was in good spirits. The services were empty, and he managed to eat, drink, and be back at the car within half an hour, even grabbing a chance to scan the newspaper.

The headlines screamed the oncoming storm, large weather maps showing how it would progress over the UK, nowhere would be safe from a battering of heavy winds and snowfall. The paper urged people to stay inside through the worst with the usual media scare tactics of dangerous conditions and risk to life, but he had driven out of the start of it with ease, and would get up country before it had finished blowing it's worst down south.

He had still been chuckling at his good fortune when he got back into the car. There was a good chunk of the journey to go, but he thought he was through the worst of it.

He was wrong.

As he drove into Manchester, the snow started falling, lightly at first, and then heavier the further North he drove. The motorway had turned white quickly as he hit Penrith slowing traffic to 20mph with just two snowy lanes, and it was getting worse as he traveled at a snail's pace toward the Lake District. Darkness had descended fast an hour ago, making the road seem harder to navigate, and a pain had started up in earnest behind his left eye with the concentration.

Static filled his ears and he grimaced as it ground against the pain in his head. He fiddled with the radio, which had lost more signals than it found in the last five miles, the only thing coming through loud and clear now was the cheesy pop that Emmie loved. He decided it would have to do, at least it would get him in the mood for her.

Eyes back on the road his heart gave a jolt as he saw the car in front had come to a stop. He pressed the brake hard, and the car slid, he turned the wheel to cross into the snowier, but empty lane next to him and the front end rotated too far right so that he was now sliding sidewards toward the stationary vehicle. Heart in his mouth he pressed the accelerator hard spinning the wheels madly. By some miracle, they managed to inch the car forward into the fresh snow before the cars collided. He eased off the pedal using the engine to slow the car allowing him to gain control.

As he passed the idiot who had stopped, he looked into the car. A young lad sat with both hands on the wheel, staring out of the windscreen, looking for all the world like he was driving but going nowhere, and then Scott saw the wheels spinning madly and realised he was stuck. The youngster glanced at Scott as he passed, making eye contact. Scott used the opportunity.

'Fucking dickhead, get off the road!' he shouted, gesturing up and down with his left hand at the window. The lads face passed out of view, and Scott pulled back into the clearer lane in front of him, his heart still pounding as the car's headlights diminished slowly behind him.

Fuck, that was close.

The snow fell thick in front of him and with a grunt of irritation, he decided it was time to call it a day. If he didn't find somewhere to stop he would be sleeping on the motorway as the weather worsened, or crashing into the idiots who couldn't drive in it.

Anger bubbled low in his stomach, Emmie would just have to wait another day if she could stand the suspense, he wasn't sure he could, but sometimes life just threw a curveball. He would have to live with it.

Clenching his jaw, he turned off at the next junction and crawled up to an island where he stopped, drumming his fingers impatiently on the steering wheel.

He scanned the area and was relieved to see a small retail park with a Holiday Inn lit up like Blackpool Illuminations a few hundred yards to his left.

Halle-fucking-lujah, and that right there is fate in action.

Scott felt a weight release from his shoulders. His head hurt, he was tired, hungry, and pissed off. It would be good to get out of the car again, and if he had to stop overnight at least a warm bed in a hotel was the best way to go.

Pressing too hard on the accelerator the engine revved as the back wheels spun trying to grasp something substantial. Easing off the gas a little the car crawled down the road, and Scott squinted out into the darkness beyond the windscreen, the car's headlights only serving to illuminate the thick blanket of flakes flying toward him. The vehicle felt weightless, wheels slipping and sliding, making the car weave as it tried to gain traction.

His knuckles were white on the steering wheel, he hated being out of control, it was uncomfortable on his chest, but the hotel wasn't far now.

Concentrating on keeping the car steady he turned into the road to the complex with no problem, but the right turn into the car park of the Holiday Inn sent the car sliding to the left down the slight incline.

Scott's heart pumped seeing everything slide sideways through the windscreen, and then it came to a stop bumping heavily into the curb, rocking the car, the engine stalling.

Well, here will have to do, I'm not driving any fucking further today.

He leaned over to grab his bag from the back seat of the car and walked the short distance to the hotel reception, leaving the car abandoned where it sat.

Chapter 58

Natalie looked out of the front window as she paced the room waiting for Michael to return home. He was working late, and as the wind howled and the snow blew, sending the world white over again under the yellow street lamps, she knew she would worry until he made it home.

Worry.

It was all she seemed to do at the moment. All she had done since Emmie had moved to Scotland, but right now it was ramped up to a degree where she felt she could cry at the drop of a hat. She could cry right now wondering where Mike was, where Scott was, how Emmie was, knowing that there was nothing she could do about any of them.

She had called Emmie a couple of times through the afternoon checking she was okay, and again at 5.30pm when she had got home from her shift and sat the kids down for tea. Although Emmie sounded tired and distracted, she had said she was fine and that she hadn't heard anything from Scott. From the tone of her voice, Scott didn't seem to be worrying Emmie too much; he bothered Natalie though.

Since Sunday she had been keeping an eye on his movements via a friend, Lana, who lived a little further down his street. She had said that his activity had been normal until she had seen his car gone when she had got up this morning.

By all accounts, his car still hadn't returned, and Natalie worried that he had made his move. She had Lana on hold until tomorrow morning, when she could say if his car had returned overnight before she would hit the big red emergency button, and tell Emmie he was probably on his way.

She felt wound up like a spring, and just as she thought she was as tight as she could go, worry would twist her a little tighter. She wondered if there was a point when she would explode, shattering into a million pieces.

She paced, half listening to James and Nathan fight over the play station controller, and then Michael's car pulled into the driveway. She felt her body let go of some tension, shoulders dropping as she opened the front door. She leaned against the frame, the freezing wind pulling and tugging at her hair and clothes.

She was anxious that he had booked the flight, but after calling him twelve times before 10am this morning, he had snapped and told her in no uncertain terms that it would be done before he got home, and that she shouldn't call him again before he did.

Mike took his time getting out, folding his coat over his arm, and clutching his briefcase on his lap before struggling to open the door against the wind. He just managed to get out before the door was snatched out of his hand and slammed shut with a bang.

As he came inside Natalie shut the door behind him, leaning against it. She looked at his back as he put down his briefcase, shook his coat, and hung it up. She waited until he turned to her. With a small sigh and a look of resignation, he pulled her into his arms and kissed the top of her head.

'It's done, flight to Glasgow booked for 3.10pm tomorrow. We should be there for half four, and I've hired a 4x4 to meet us at the airport when we land. It's an hour and a half to Em's so, depending on the storm, which should have passed over by then, we should be there for around half six. I've asked Lana if she will drive us to the airport, and I've organised for mom to have the kids for a few days. It's the best I could do. And I'm sorry I snapped at you.'

Natalie looked up at him heart swelling. She smiled, he really had taken care of everything. She had booked a few days off work, so she was able to sort the kid's suitcases, get them to his moms tomorrow, and pack a couple of bags for Mike and herself too.

'Thank you. I've been so worried. At least now I can call and tell Emmie we will be there tomorrow. It will be a weight off my mind if we can get there before Scott.'

'I know. The scenario you haven't considered is what happens after our four days leave are up, and he still hasn't arrived? We can't stay up there waiting forever, Nat.'

Natalie thought of Scott's missing car and hoped that wouldn't be an issue. She needed the whole business over with, or she would drive herself crazy.

'Lets cross that bridge when we get there. Right now we just need to get up to Em's before Scott. Whatever he says is going to break her. She'll need support. If he gets there first and starts throwing the truth around, she'll be confused and devastated. I know she needs to know, and maybe we were wrong to protect her the way we did, but I couldn't bear to see her hurt Mike. She was hurting enough. If everything is going to come out in the wash, I need to be there for her. I won't live with myself if I'm not.'

'I know Nat, but listen. If Scott doesn't say anything, if that isn't his plan, when this is all over promise me we will tell her anyway. Whichever way you want to play it, but this needs to stop, honey, it's gone on long enough.'

Natalie nodded, tears spilling silently down her cheeks.

'Okay.' She said. 'But she will need to come back here.'

Michael lifted her chin wiping her tears.

'I didn't say she had to leave, Nat.'

Natalie nodded and leaned into his embrace sighing heavily. She had a feeling that these were going to be the longest and hardest few days she would ever have to endure, but it would be a whole lot worse if Scott got to Emmie first.

Chapter 59

The phone rang a little after 8.10pm and Emmie jumped, nearly throwing the casserole dish across the kitchen, her heart pounding.

This is it Em. He's canceling. It's too much to expect him to come up here and spend time alone with you after all he's been through.

She glanced over at the screen and saw it wasn't Stuart, but Natalie. She rolled her eyes, heart slowing as she placed the dish on the side.

Again? Really?

Natalie had managed to fit in calling four times since Emmie had got home after picking up Grace.

Grace had been on the quiet side most of the afternoon and Emmie knew how she felt. She was in a quiet mood too, unsettled from the accident and nervous for the evening.

It had run through her head more than once that she should never have asked Stuart over in the first place. Emmie didn't know what she intended to get out of it. She could be friends, but she was fooling herself if she thought she didn't want more. At the same time, she knew that any relationship with him might be entirely out of the question and to that end she didn't need to complicate the situation.

But it was done now. She would just have to ride the wave until the end.

She swiped to answer the call, balancing the phone between her ear and shoulder so that she could carry on stirring the mince mixture in the wok and add the chopped coriander. The sweet, meaty smell rose to meet her nostrils and her mouth watered. She couldn't remember the last time she had eaten so late. She was ravenous.

'Nat? What is it now?

She transferred the meat to the casserole dish, topped it with mashed potatoes and threw it into the oven shutting the door and setting the timer. The wind whistled past the kitchen window, and

Emmie noticed the first flakes of snow slide down the glass.

'Hi, Em. I just wanted to let you know that we will be with you tomorrow evening. Mike and I both have a few days off so we can stay with you for a while until we know what Scott is up to.'

Emmie smiled feeling her spirits rise. It had been a month since she had seen them, and if they were here maybe the photo situation would stop and shadow man would piss off, especially as he was now scaring Grace who hadn't wanted to go up to bed tonight for the first time since moving here.

'That's great Nat, shame it's not under better circumstances, but it will be good to see you both.'

As Natalie chatted and Emmie watched outside, she saw lights come up the lane, snow falling across the bobbing yellow eyes.

Glancing at the clock she saw it was just after quarter past eight. She chewed her lip. She had told Stuart anytime after eight, but it could just as easily be Scott. Natalie's voice faded to muffled tones as her attention wavered; this would either go one way or the other, good or bad, either end of the spectrum but nothing in between.

She swallowed, wishing she had a light up at the gate so that she could see the car. It didn't help that both men were a similar height and build. She walked into the hallway to wait, maybe she would be able to tell by the knock, but she was finding it hard to focus with Natalie wittering on in the background.

'Nat, there's someone here, I need to go.' She cut Natalie off mid-sentence and immediately regretted her choice of words. Natalie went into panic mode as there was a knock, and Stuart shouted through the shut door.

'It's okay, Nat.'

She opened the door to let him in, wind and snow swirling, as she indicated that she was on the phone. She didn't want to let Natalie hear Stuart or she would be in a pickle. Natalie had made her feelings on that subject very clear last time they had spoken. He smiled, nodding, and she caught a whiff of his heady cologne as he passed her. She shut and locked the door.

'Don't answer the door, Em,' Natalie was saying, 'If it's Scott pretend you're not in.'

Emmie grinned at the absurdity of the statement.

'The lights are on, and the chimney is smoking, Nat.'

She placed the phone between her ear and shoulder to take Stuarts coat and hang it up by the stairs.

'What does that matter? Don't open the door.'

'I already have, it's fine, but I really need to go.'

'Well, who is it? Someone you know?'

Emmie rolled her eyes.

'No, Nat, I always let strangers in off the hills, it passes the time.'

Natalie huffed.

'I'm worried Emmie, tell me who it is.'

Emmie turned to Stuart and took the bottle of wine, mouthing thanks, and motioning him into the kitchen.

'Trust me, it's fine, really, Nat.'

'Excuse me, miss high and mighty, for being concerned.' Natalie snapped.

Emmie sighed, being around a worried Natalie for the next few days may not work out so well. She had forgotten just how wound up she got, and there was nowhere to escape the tension here.

'You don't need to be concerned. I need to go now, Nat, please.'

'Well, I am. You don't know these people Em. It's eight in the evening who the hell is at your door? Is it even safe to open your door at that time of night?'

'Well, do you think I can judge that for myself?'

'I'm not sure, Emmie, can you?'

Emmie rolled her eyes skyward at Stuart who leaned himself up the kitchen table watching her. Christ, he was a beautiful man, and here was her sister eating into her time with him. Who knew whether this would ever happen again after today, or even after she was through with Scott and he had no reason to be with her.

She pursed her lips.

'Nat, I'm hanging up, don't be mad please.'

'Emmie, that's rude! If you hang up on me-'

'I'm not trying to be rude. I'm trying to get you off the phone.'

Natalie huffed on the other end of the line.

'Which is plain rude! Are you listening to yourself?'

'No, I'm putting the phone down. See you tomorrow, Nat.'

She pulled the phone away from her ear catching Natalie's rant as she grimaced and pressed the end button. She put the phone on the side before turning back to Stuart who was looking bemused.

'Sorry, Stu, shall we start again?'

He chuckled. 'Your sister?'

'The one and only. Four times she's phoned today since I picked up Grace. Four. She's driving me mad.'

'She's worried about you ... and you just hung up on her.' His voice held mild amusement.

'I did, but I gave her warning. She can rant at me properly when she gets here tomorrow.'

He frowned.

'She's coming up tomorrow? I hope the storm runs through by the time she gets here or she may be getting stuck.'

'I know, I told her that earlier, but she's too worried about Scott, she's flying up with her husband Mike for a few days.' Emmie let out a sigh unable to stop it.

A puzzled look crossed his face.

'That's not a good thing?'

'No. I mean, yes, it's a good thing ... Yes, I suppose so ... It is, isn't it?'

He smiled.

'You won't be on your own if Scott turns up, that's a big bonus in my eyes, Em.'

Emmie nodded.

'I know, and I am grateful, I just ... I cope better when Nat isn't flapping over me, I guess. She means well, but she makes me uneasy when she gets wound up. I don't mind the phone calls, I can put it aside afterward, but I literally have nowhere to get away from the tension here.'

Stuart raised his eyebrows.

'Well, you're always welcome at the pub. You can do the alternative of putting the phone down and just slam the door in her face.'

Emmie caught the grin playing on his lips and rolled her eyes.

'That depends whether there's a hot chocolate involved or just a sarcastic landlord.'

He laughed, eyes twinkling with humour.

'I can provide ample of both whenever you feel the need.'

Emmie grinned and threw the tea towel at him. He caught it deftly in his right hand. She smiled as she watched him fold it and place it on the table still chuckling. Maybe it was all the small talk he had to make at the pub because if he was nervous, he didn't show it. Even in this situation, that had rung his alarm bells, he was holding his own well. He looked calm and relaxed.

'What are you thinking?' He said gently pulling her from her thoughts.

'That I'm a crappy host, I haven't even offered you a drink.'

'Crappy's a wee bit strong. You took my coat.'

'One point to me.'

'I'll give you two; something smells really good.' He said with a smile.

'That's generous. I should wait until you taste it before you go dishing out points.'

'Aye, and that's a good point.'

Emmie laughed and shook her head as she grabbed a couple of glasses letting Stuart open the wine, she was appallingly useless at removing a cork from a bottle. He was an expert, however, and had it removed in seconds with a satisfying pop.

She persuaded him to have a glass with her, and poured out two small measures, feeling guilty for slugging the bottle when he couldn't drink. She checked the cottage pie and looked up to find he had filled her glass anyway, and was taking them over to the table.

He laughed when he saw her expression.

'You don't have to drive, stop being polite and have a drink.'

He pulled out a chair for her and took a seat opposite as she took a sip of wine, the smooth and fruity taste hitting her tongue with a glorious hint of sweetness before giving way to that leathery aftertaste.

They chatted easily about their respective days, although Emmie left out the earlier accident. The mood was light and relaxed, the company good, and she wanted it to stay that way. In all honesty, it was a relief to have the spotlight shared and to learn a little more about Stuart.

He was attentive, chatty, and friendly, looking relaxed as he sipped at his wine. His passion for the Guest House, and his interest in people evident as he told her about the pub and what it took to run. When talk turned to the falls and his fortune at being so close to them she could only nod her agreement.

'We climbed up there Saturday morning. It's such an idyllic spot. Shame the weather wasn't more accommodating I should think the view is amazing on a clear day.'

Stuart nodded.

'Oh aye, it's beautiful. And it's so peaceful up there. Judith had the bench installed at the top just after we bought the place. She said it was sacrilege that no one could sit and enjoy the view after the walk it took to get up there.' He huffed a laugh, 'It's funny how things work out. That bench became my salvation after she died, it was the only place I could truly be alone, and I always felt a part of her there with me. I still run up to it every morning, more now for fitness than Judith, it was a habit that stuck, there's something about the air up the top of those falls that sets the day up right.'

Emmie let the reference to Judith hang, although she was surprised he had brought her up without prompting.

'You run up there *every* morning? Doesn't that sign say it's two miles.'

He smiled.

'Aye, and two back again.' he looked at her shocked expression and laughed. 'Impressed?'

She wrinkled her nose as she pinched her thumb and forefinger together and held it up to him.

'Just a little.'

He sat back in his seat laughing openly, and she grinned before taking a sip of wine as she watched him. His mention of Judith intrigued her. She found herself wanting to know more about the woman who had stolen his heart. She was also surprised how he was handling it for someone who was supposed to be still hurting, and wondered if he felt as calm as he looked after what Edith and Bill had said. The butterflies in her stomach fluttered as he held her gaze, open and relaxed.

'Go on,' he said, 'I can see you're brewing something. Ask away. I'm ready for it.'

The reference to the accident was obvious, but suddenly it seemed wrong to bring it up, she didn't have the heart to ask him the question, so she plumbed for the second most intriguing subject.

'What was she like, Stu?'

He frowned, nonplussed.

'Who, Judith?'

She nodded, resting her chin on a hand. He rubbed a hand across his mouth, taking a moment to think.

'She was everything, Em, everything to me. A great wife, best friend, companion and mother. She was warm and funny and loving. She had a great way of making people feel at ease around her. We were both born and bred in Glasgow, but she always liked the idea of living in a small community, so after we were married we decided to find somewhere more rural to start over which was one of the reasons she chose the Grey Lion. I'd say we, but she was the one that fell in love with it. I was less than impressed with the shape it was in. It may as well have been as derelict as this place. I tried to talk her out of it but she was taken, and the falls won her over completely. She loved being up there whatever the season.'

He smiled dropping his gaze and swirling his wine in the glass slowly. Emmie let him have the moment waiting for him continue.

'Anyway, as it turned out her instincts about the place were bang on, and it came together well. We had a good life and a perfect few years, especially after Connor was born. I don't think there was anything else I could have asked for back then. I was lucky to have her, even for a short time.' He paused and smiled at her, 'And I know you're skirting the issue, you want the story, but you're too polite to ask.'

She shrugged her shoulders.

'I don't want you to feel you have to tell it, although I am intrigued, and I do want to know what changed your mind about coming to dinner. You've had all the crap I can throw at you. Throw some back.'

She took a sip of wine, and he looked at her thoughtfully. She thought he might back out and change the subject, and she wouldn't have blamed him. Instead, he threw her off balance.

'What do you know already?'

The question was asked lightly with no insinuations, but it still shocked her. She regarded him puzzled.

'It's not a trick question. Small villages talk Em, I won't believe you've heard nothing, especially all the chatting you've been doing with Edith. I don't want to bore you with what you've already been told. I'll just give you the correct version; amend the bits they conveniently alter to aid gossip.'

'You're sure?'

He nodded at her to carry on, and she filled him in on what both Bill and Edith had said. She stuck only to the facts about the accident and how devastated his and Connor's lives had been afterward. Stuarts version was the only one she was interested in so she skirted over their personal opinions, but he quickly caught on.

'You're filtering.'

She looked at him exasperated.

'Of course I'm filtering! The rest is just assumption. It doesn't matter how close they are to you it still didn't happen to them, and they can't pretend to know how that feels, can they?'

Stuart gazed at her. Finally, he shook his head.

'No,' he said quietly, 'And I hope to god they never have to find out how that feels.'

He sighed, playing with the bottom of the wine glass before continuing.

'Aye, the accident happened pretty much as they told you, it was devastating, and trying to deal with Connor's grief as well as my own was the hardest thing I've ever had to do. But in fact, devastation doesn't even come close to describing that kind of pain. It hurts like a bastard, all day every day, like someone is twisting knives into you and won't let up. You can't see the end, and it feels like it won't ever end because the only person who loves and understands you enough to be able to take some of it away isn't there anymore. That pain and emptiness - it's indescribable.'

Emmie's heart lurched, but he smiled calmly as he looked at her.

'But it does come to an end with time. The feeling of loss takes longer to go and I sometimes still miss her for little things she would have liked, or found funny. It's not the same emptiness though, it's more comfort, like sharing a moment while she's somewhere else. I know she's up there cursing me for not tucking the corner of a sheet, or polishing the glassware enough.'

Emmie smiled.

'I think you've done well to continue with it. I'm sure Judith is more than happy just with that.'

He dropped his gaze nodding lightly.

'It was hard trying to carry it on after she died, and I'm still not certain I'm getting it right sometimes. It's a massive juggling act, and she was much better with the details than I am. I do worry I'm not doing the place justice.'

Emmie felt a tug of emotion and reached over to touch his hand, pulling his gaze back to hers.

'Stu, the place is thriving, and that's not down to details, that's down to you. I've never stepped into a local pub, in any small village, and felt so welcome. I'm sure the guests remember the experience much more than a shiny glass,'

He pursed his lips, nodding and she smiled.

'Bill said some of the villagers tried to get you to sell after the accident. Did you ever think about giving it up?'

'No. I couldn't give it up, it was one of the only things keeping me going, along with Connor. I knew Judith's vision, and I wanted to achieve it for her. It was hard to live with reminders of her around me, but it seemed easier than selling up and having to leave them. The memories in that place killed me and comforted me at the same time. Maybe it took longer to deal with the grief that way, I don't know, but the only real healers, in my experience, are time and space.' He paused huffing a breath through his nose, 'Ironically, everyone thought I needed constant company and to move forward. A lot of folks think I still need to do that now.'

Emmie grinned as she thought of Edith and her need to get him married back off while he was in his prime.

'What do you think?' She said.

'I think … no, I *know*, I'm perfectly fine. Judith is dead and buried, god rest her soul, I'm perfectly aware of that, and I'm not holding on to her.'

He stopped and took a breath.

'Truth be told, Em, I'm too busy. There's been no one I've wanted to get to know any more than a short chat over the bar. No one has piqued my interest enough to bother, and I'm not going to waste time trying to make something of every tiny spark, it has to be more than that. I'm not adverse to having another relationship but I've learned life is short, and I'm going to choose that person myself for the right reasons, not let the locals dictate who would be 'good for me'. Its been a long time, sure, but I can't jump into bed with any woman who walks into the bar to keep folk thinking I'm normal. Judith may want me to be happy, but I think she'd have something to say about that when I meet her in the afterlife.'

Emmie laughed.

'You know, both Bill and Edith make you seem like a lost soul who isn't interested in moving on, but that's not the impression you're giving me at all.'

Stuart looked down at his wine swirling it before he took a sip and looked back up at her.

'What are they saying?'

'Bill said you'll likely be alone forever, and that you're okay with that. Edith wants you married off but thinks you're too scared to let anyone in.'

Stuart met Emmie's eyes and shrugged.

'They could both be right. I am okay with life at the moment, I get to chat with plenty of interesting people through the day, and when the bar shuts, I read. I'm okay with my own company, yes. Edith is probably touching a little on what I said to you yesterday. I overthink, and I can talk myself out of doing something within seconds because it's more comfortable to stay as I am. I suppose letting someone in is an element of that uncertainty, born of a need not to get hurt again.'

Emmie thought she understood.

'So when I asked you here it was a little too far out of your comfort zone?'

He huffed a laugh.

'Way too far out. It was leaving the pub, which is my security, and stepping into a place where I'm alone with a woman who intrigues me, and whose company I'm enjoying a lot, even under the circumstances. Aye, that scared me a little. Maybe more than a little.'

A warmth swirled in her stomach at his words, even if this was just a blossoming friendship and nothing more she was pleased that it wasn't Scott that was binding them together.

'Well, Edith got it wrong. You're still here.'

'Aye, but she strung me up after I told her I'd turned you down, and she said some things that made me think. I still wasn't ready to change my mind until you spoke to Martin. If you could do that with the level of confidence you did, when I knew you must have been nervous, I decided giving dinner a go was child's play in comparison. I just needed to get over myself.'

Emmie smiled as he looked at her, pale blue eyes calm and steady. She was floored and impressed by his honesty.

'I'm glad you did.'

'I am too. It beats watching those four lassies cavort on the bar.'

Emmie saw the opening she needed to lighten the mood.

'That's good news because I'm not about to cavort on the table for you.'

She laughed as Stuart groaned.

'Thank god for that.' He said.

Emmie wrinkled her nose and pouted.

'I don't know whether to be insulted. I can cavort quite well when the mood takes me.'

He snorted, laughing.

'I don't doubt it. Did you not say you had a jealous ex-husband?'

'I did, but when he wasn't around, I had to run off a little suppressed steam.'

He shook his head in mock chagrin.

'This may have been a mistake. I thought I was having dinner with a lady.'

347

'Oh. Well, I've never cavorted on a bar, making suggestive comments, wearing little or nothing. Good enough?'

'It will have to be.'

A sly grin crossed her face.

'I've danced on a few bars in Surrey though, back in the day.'

Stuart shook his head, but his eyes twinkled with warmth. He sucked a breath through his teeth.

'As a barman that fills me with horror. I know how heels can wreck a bar.'

They laughed.

'I can take the shoes off. It's not a problem.'

'Oh, no, there'll be no dancing on my bar.'

'Only cavorting?'

'I don't like that either. You ladies need to keep off my bar altogether.'

'You're a spoilsport. You have the only bar for miles. Let us have some fun.'

Stuart raised his eyebrows.

'Aye, and it's a bar in a village with a healthy gossip vine, they'll think I'm running a brothel.'

Emmie laughed, then a thought crossed her mind.

'Oh, no, do you think that gossip vine -'

He cut her off instinctively knowing where she was going.

'Aye, it'll be going full steam tonight. I can't even have dinner in the middle of nowhere in peace.'

'Do you really think they're that interested?'

'Interested? I'll bet they're keeping scores on how well you're doing getting me a life.'

'I got you to dinner. They must be getting excited by now.'

They both laughed loudly, and Emmie tried to shush Stuart as she smothered her own laughter. They were both getting a little too loud, and she didn't need Grace waking and coming down.

'Sorry,' He said, and she shrugged to tell him it didn't matter drinking the last mouthful of wine, 'You realise we'll be the talk of the village tomorrow. Maybe we should just go to bed, get it over with for them.'

Emmie spluttered, damn near spitting her wine back into the glass. Choking as it went the right way but down the wrong hole. He laughed leaning over to slap her back. When she could finally grab some air into her lungs, she looked at him.

'I can't. I have a cartload of decorum remember.'

'You're right. I should have had dinner with one of the 'fracas four'.'

He was so deadpan she had to put her hands over her mouth to stop the laughter escalating again. She managed to smother most of the noise, but tears rolled down her face. She tried to talk through the gulping laughter.

'I think they may have skipped the dinner altogether. And they weren't good for you on the Edith meter. You'd attract attention for all the wrong reasons. I'm crying. Again.'

Stuart laughed at that.

'Well, at least that's for the right reasons.'

She nodded and wiped her tears as the beeps went off on the oven. Still giggling she got up to remove the pie and drain the vegetables putting it on plates as Stuart filled her wine glass and grabbed water for himself, rinsing his glass and filling it up.

The chat was a lot more in line with a friendly dinner as they ate, touching on Grace and Charlie and Connor who was going off to university in September. He asked her about her business, listening attentively and with a keen interest that Scott had never shown. The conversation flowed, and Emmie sent up a silent cheer as he finished his plate, enjoying it so much he cleared the casserole dish of the remainder.

She made him tea as he filled her wine glass again. She was already feeling light-headed, if she weren't careful she would be well on the way to being drunk, or blootered, as Stuart had told her was a more popular Scottish word.

He asked to see the downstairs, and she showed him around. They discussed the state each room was in when she moved here, finishing up in the living room which was toasty with the fire she had made earlier crackling in the hearth.

'Oh, this is my kind of room, very cosy.'

'Yeah, it's my favourite too, we spend most of the time either here or the kitchen. Usually, the evenings are spent in here by the fire - playing guess who, or pig goes pop.'

She crossed her eyes, and Stuart chuckled as he sat on the settee opposite the fire and patted the seat for her to join him.

The wind battered this side of the house. The chimney made an eerie whistle as the wind found it's way down causing the flames to dance, sending orange light licking around the room in the low lamplight. Emmie was glad Stuart was here, with the two of them it was cosy, if not a little romantic. Alone it would have been the stuff of horror movies.

They chatted for a while about the house and what it had taken to put it right. They laughed over her first encounter with Bill and how he had told her of Ted on the patio, and then how she had thought he would murder them all in their sleep. Somewhere along the evening, Stuart had poured the last of the wine into her glass, and they had ended up pulling the little side table out and setting up scrabble between them.

It was a game Emmie loved, and she usually played well, but Stuart was better. He knew words she hadn't heard of, but the Oxford dictionary confirmed their existence. After losing the first game, fuzzy headed and with wine-induced confidence, she decided to make up her own words, from her own dictionary, which he wasn't able to check because it was inside her head. For some reason he had declined a third game, and Emmie had grinned as she rose to put the game away. The room spun now she was on her feet, wine catching up with her head after sitting for so long. She tried to walk to the cupboard as Stuart went to the side window and took a peek outside.

'How bad is it?' Emmie said.

'Come and look.'

She shut the cupboard and went over to him, taking a wide birth around the small table, on legs that seemed to pitch the room to the left. Her head seemed to be hanging around the cupboard area, taking its time catching up as she looked out onto the dark garden. She blinked a few times to clear her vision. There was no moonlight tonight all that she could see was what was illuminated from the windows of the house, but she could make out that it was white over and that the snow was still falling, battered around by the relentless wind and pressing it onto the pane.

'Yes!' She whispered making Stuart blow laughter out of his nose.

'You're happy about the snow?'

'Oh god, those kids faces. I may have to wake them up to show them.'

'It'll be there in the morning. We've got this all night yet, at least.'

'Will you be okay getting back?'

She swung round to him a little too fast, and the room followed at a slower rate, she held the window sill for stability.

'Aye. Take it easy if you plan to get the bairns to school tomorrow though. There'll be drifts up your lane by the morning if this carries on.'

She smiled and nodded, peering back at the window to get a better look outside as Stuart checked his watch.

'It's twelve thirty? I hope to god Connor has locked up okay, I told him I'd be back by eleven-ish.'

'Oops,' She grimaced, 'I'm sure he'd have called if he'd had any trouble.'

Stuart looked at her warmly. Or was that just the wine?

'Aye, I would think so. Well, I'm going to have to go but thank you for a lovely evening, we should do this again sometime, Em.'

'It's been fun.' She said nodding.

'Fun for *you*. You cheated your way through scrabble do you know how annoying that is?' He said laughing.

'Well, you helped a whole bottle of wine find it's way into my glass. I play fair when I'm not ...,' She clicked her fingers, 'what was it again?'

'Blootered?'

'Blootered! What a wonderful word.'

He chuckled.

'You're far from blootered, sweetheart.'

As the words left his mouth she turned to move away from the window too quickly, and the room tilted, pushing her off balance. He grabbed her arm until she was upright although the floor still seemed to want to lay off kilter slightly.

'Well, maybe halfway there.'

'Over halfway, definitely.'

Emmie finished the last mouthful of wine in the glass and Stuart took it off her placing it safely on the side table they had used for scrabble. She hadn't meant to drink quite so much, but for the first time since she had moved here, she was feeling relaxed and warm, comfortable and safe.

He was right she wasn't drunk, just warm and fuzzy ... and a little off balance.

'Come on then, let's see if I can manage to let you out.'

She went ahead of him into the hall and handed him his coat. He put it on but didn't zip it up, feeling in the pocket for his keys and phone automatically. He stood with his back to the door looking at her more seriously than he had all night.

'Lock the door behind me. I'm going to wait until I hear the click, Em, so if you don't, you're going to find me frozen on your doorstep in the morning.'

She nodded, trying and failing to smother a batch of giggles at the image he had conjured up for her. The world tilted again, and she inadvertently stepped forward into him. He caught her arms, but she had already put her hands on his chest to stop herself. Far away, in another world, she was aware that she should step back and let go, but she felt pulled in. The heady scent of cologne, the warmth of his skin under her hands and the hard shape of muscle under his shirt.

She was so close that she felt a little woozy and detached, wanting only to be in his arms. She tried to drop her hands but found the wine had given them a mind of their own. She ran them slowly down to his firm stomach before circling them back under his coat at his waist. The thin shirt fabric shifting, the only layer between her hands and the warm softness of his skin. He held her arms gently at the elbows where he had caught them, not stopping her. Even so, she didn't dare look at him and break the spell.

Then he took his hands away, and she prepared to step back, but he caught her by surprise, cupping a warm hand under her chin and lifting her face to his. She met his eyes feeling like she was in a dream as he ran his thumb under her lower lip lightly and then the world spun as his lips met hers. The kiss was gentle and soft. He ran a hand into the hair at the back of her neck as she pulled herself closer to him, hands climbing up his back toward his shoulders. He wrapped his free arm around her waist deepening the kiss, and she felt her legs buckle. Maybe it was the wine, but she couldn't remember the last time a kiss had felt so magical.

His hand was still in her hair when he broke away, and she kept her eyes closed, holding onto him as he leaned his forehead against hers, knowing she was trembling and feeling him shake too.

And then it hit her what they had done.

'Oh shit, Stu. I'm so sorry. I've had far too much wine.'

He pulled back, lowering both hands to her waist.

'Aye, and what was my excuse?'

She shook her head, feeling this was all a bit unreal. A dream she would wake from at a crucial moment.

'Are you okay?' she said.

He smiled moving his hands from her waist to hold onto her hands.

'I'm good, Em. I've waited a long time for that, I just never found the right person.'

She took in the weight of the comment, and broke into a grin.

'Not one of the half-dressed fracas at the bar then?'

He chuckled putting a hand up to her face pushing her hair behind her ear gently.

'God no, I prefer a fully dressed, emotional wreck.'

She narrowed her eyes and wrinkled her nose laughing at him before growing serious.

'You don't have to take this any further you know.' She whispered. 'You can stop right here. I won't hold it against you. I know what you've been through.'

'I wish I had a choice, Em, but I can't stop thinking about you, and believe me, at first I really tried.'

She nodded.

'I've been the same.'

He gazed at her interlinking his fingers with hers. He moved slowly, and she wondered how he managed to set off the most explosive fireworks in her just from the touch of his hands. The room spun slightly and she wasn't sure if it was the wine or his touch that was making her dizzy.

'I wasn't certain I was reading you right. It's far easier to know if someone is interested when you're not, or maybe that's because it's been so long that I'd forgotten the emotional stakes.'

'Well, some things you didn't forget.'

Oh, for fuck sake Em, really?

She cringed inside, but Stuart only smiled the big warm smile that made his eyes dance and her stomach flip.

'Em, I know you've a lot on your plate right now, and I'll be here for you whatever your answer so you're welcome to tell me to back off, but I can't leave here knowing you feel the same and doing nothing about it. I won't have the courage tomorrow, and it's been eating me up, so what do you think? There's no harm in taking things slowly if we're on the same page is there?'

She shook her head heart soaring.

It looks like Kate Winslet didn't go down with the ship, after all, she broke the surface and gasped the cool sweet air, how about that toots?

She felt giddy. If they were going anywhere together, going slowly was exactly what both of them needed, and it was a thousand percent better than not going any speed at all.

Still shaking, Emmie did what she had imagined doing from the moment she set eyes on him. She stepped into his arms and hugged him, her head nestling exactly where she had thought it would, just under his chin. He wrapped his arms around her gently, kissing the top of her head, and engulfed in his warm hug, she thought she had never felt so safe.

Chapter 60

Scott sat in the warm hotel room watching the light appear slowly outside the window as the wind howled and moaned around the building. The clouds were an ominous grey. Low, and dense. Snow was falling lightly onto the six inches that had accumulated on the ground. He watched the small flakes get tugged in the turbulent air, as he finished the call to the fourth rental company he had spoken to in the last twenty minutes.

Putting down the phone, he let out a small sigh of satisfaction. Of the previous three companies he had called, two had stated they were closed due to the 'adverse weather conditions', and the other didn't have a four-wheel drive car worth renting. This last one, however, had a year old Range Rover that would be perfect.

It was overpriced at a hundred and sixty pounds per day, but he took it without a quibble, asking for it to be delivered to the hotel. As he had expected, this service wasn't rendered; especially during the worst storm of the year so far. Scott had pointed out that it was only January of this particular year, but it hadn't swayed their decision.

Money had swayed the manager of the firm, however, as Scott found it usually did, and he managed to get someone to drop it at the door for an extortionate cost. The manager promised to get the car to him as quickly as possible, but it was over ten miles to the hotel, so he couldn't guarantee when that would be. So now all Scott had to do was wait. And he didn't like waiting. He had to do something besides sitting in this room, or he would wind himself up.

In the dining area he ate a full English Breakfast, with extra toast and coffee, while he read the paper. When the dining room closed for breakfast, he reluctantly went back to his room, taking the newspaper with him.

At 11am he was forced to leave his room or pay for an extra night so he relocated to the small waiting area in reception. If one chair, and a plant could be called a waiting area anyway. He passed the time watching the young girl behind the desk pretending to work while scrolling on her phone. Did no-one have a work ethic these days? With a sigh of frustration, he fought the urge to snatch the phone out of her hand and beat it about her mindless head.

Around midday, he started to get annoyed. It was only three and a half hours to Emelia's house from here under normal circumstances, but he thought it would be closer to five in the snow. And that was providing it didn't get much worse as he got further into Scotland where, according to the little TV behind the desk, the storm had decided to stick around a little longer than just overnight.

To top it off another weather front was due across central Scotland later today bringing little relief from last nights storm, which still appeared to be raging outside the window. This new storm was coming across from the Atlantic bringing with it even more snow and gales.

Agitated, Scott started to pace, and finally the girl's attention left her phone as she nervously snatched glances at him. He breathed heavily as he clenched his jaw and noticed the pain was back niggling behind his ribs. He rubbed his chest as he paced.

I need to get going where the fuck is the car? And what the fuck is this pain?

And then it arrived, like a silver stallion, sure-footed and capable. The grey Range Rover cut through the snow like a boat on water, right up to the door. The Nissan behind, who was probably the drivers ride back, was having more trouble, he stayed off the car park altogether, parking at the side of the main road and walking to the hotel across the car park. Scott grabbed his bag, meeting the two men just outside the doors.

There was paperwork to sort before he could leave. The world was full of fucking paperwork; clauses to sign and bank details to give, just in case he should decide to run off and not bring the car back. It was all bullshit, and Scott waved them on as they went through details and then through the buttons and dials on the car, which was also bullshit. The car was automatic. Foot down and drive, right? What was so fucking hard?

The most useful thing he learned was the terrain response mode for driving in the snow and how to flick the gearbox to manual if he needed to select a higher gear in the event of unlikely wheel spin. After that, he was on his way. Bag thrown in the back, heaters on, he pulled out of the car park easily, glancing at his abandoned BMW as he passed.

Perfect, he thought, turning up the radio and relaxing back into the warm leather seat, heated seats were a very welcome function in this weather. Nothing would stop this car getting there tonight. Emelia was in for a shock, yes indeed.

Here I come, Honey. Hope you're happy to see me.

He grinned as he turned back toward the motorway heading for the Highlands. The niggling pain had all but disappeared again. He was back in control, and that was just how he liked it.

Chapter 61

As Scott was pacing the reception of the Holiday Inn, Natalie and Michael were loading their luggage into the boot of Lana's car.

Natalie was in good spirits as she lifted a suitcase into the boot. It was clear and bright. The snow lay thinly on the ground, sparkling in the sunlight, the last of the storm blowing itself up the country by yesterday afternoon. The clouds had dropped around two inches of snow in the end, which had mostly cleared from the main roads already. It was just the ice that would be treacherous now as the temperatures plummeted.

Michael shut the boot, and Natalie got into the back of the warm car, smiling at Lana as she said hi. It had been fate that had chosen the flight time for them she was sure of that now.

All flights to Glasgow had been cancelled overnight and early this morning as the storm battered the city. As the wind and snow had slowed, flights this morning had been back up and running, but there was another storm to follow this evening, and Natalie thought that their flight had been perfectly planted between the two storms.

They should be landed and on the road by the time the second storm hit, which wasn't ideal, but far better than being stranded down here if the flight was delayed or cancelled. Michael, ever organised, had called the rental company and asked for snow chains to be applied to the vehicle at their discretion if they thought that they would need them driving up into the highlands.

With all eventualities covered, there was nothing else to do but wait once they got to the airport, and Natalie felt herself relax for the first time in weeks. As the car pulled away a weight seemed to lift from her shoulders. They were due to land at 4.30pm, and it would be an hour and a half, at least, to Emmie's from there, but they would still be with her in just a matter of hours. By early evening she could finally concentrate on nothing but looking after her little sister.

Chapter 62

The howling wind woke Emmie just after 6am Thursday morning.
Which was a change from the early hours of the morning when she had
been woken by the 'thing' stepping into her room, after the nightmare
of all nightmares about skidding off the road, and what might have
been, as opposed to what had actually happened.

She supposed it was because she had bottled it up and put the cork
in tight. Which in turn, was because she didn't want to admit the reason
it had happened, even to herself.

As for invisible man, he still wanted to walk around her room in
the darkness trying to scare the hell out of her, for whatever his reasons
were. She hadn't even bothered to look this time, she pulled the covers
over her head and lay shaking in a cold sweat, heart hammering, eyes
shut tight.

The footsteps had come to the side of the bed, just as they had the
night Grace had gotten in with her. She waited, and when it had done
nothing else to announce it's presence - other than fill the air with
oppressive static energy - she had quietly told it to fuck off.

It must have worked because she had now woke back on her
pillow as she usually slept, although she had no memory of getting
there or of falling back to sleep.

She lay listening to the wind for a while, head throbbing, thinking
of last night, of Stuart, how easy he had been to spend time with, and
how much she had enjoyed herself. How much she had -

Her heart gave a jolt, and she suddenly sat upright, making her
head swim and throb over her eyes.

Shit, Did that kiss actually happen? Or did I dream it?

It seemed real, and she did remember being very close to him by
the door, the calm energy and warmth he had omitted. She put her
fingers to her lips as if that might reveal the answer, but nothing
concrete came back. She wished she hadn't drank quite so much last
night.

Pain throbbed in her head, God, she needed paracetamol. A bracing gust of wind tore past the window as she swung her legs from the bed. The outline of a tree bent and swayed at such an extreme angle in the murky half-light that her heart began to thump.

It's okay Em, this house and these trees have stood here in worse since long before you were born.

The gust died down, and Emmie let out a breath putting her head in her hands and closing her eyes, elbows resting on her knees, letting her heart slow.

Better get used to these Ems, that's two big storms already, and you've been here less than a month. No point being a wuss about them.

She opened her eyes and switched on the lamp. A familiar rectangle of paper caught her eye, halfway under the bed about where the footsteps stopped in the night. She hesitated, not sure she wanted to pick it up after the picture of Scott had appeared in the living room.

She was more than aware that the pictures wouldn't be confined to the photos that were in the box, which was still sitting on top of her dresser, unmoved from where she had put it after last time it spilled its contents.

A little shiver ran up her spine as she bent to pick it up and turned it over to look.

It took only a moment to process the picture of Grace, grey and bloody, holding out what looked like wet red meat to the camera.

Fix it, mommy.

Another gust of wind battered at the window, and she gave a stifled yell hurling the paper back to the floor as an almighty crash blasted like a shotgun through the silence. Snapping her head toward the stairs, she jumped up, heart hammering against her ribs. She ran out on to the landing, leaned over the bannister, and peered into the darkness. Grace and Charlie thudded down the hallway to her, Grace in tears. Emmie gathered her in her arms.

'What was that mom?' Charlie said, fear in his eyes.

'I'm not sure, honey, stay here with Grace and I'll go and have a look.'

Grace tightened her grip on Emmie's neck.

'No! No, no, no, don't go down there mommy it might be the bad man.'

Emmie hugged her tight and kissed her soft hair.

'What bad man?' Charlie said

'There's no bad man, Charlie. Grace sweetie, Charlie will look after you, I have to see what's happened. Sit on the stairs at the turn where I can see you, and you can see me as I go down, okay?'

Grace mithered. Charlie took her by the hand and sat on the top step of the turn facing the front door. Grace hunkered next to him snivelling softly, one hand linked in his, his other arm around her shoulders.

Emmie put a hand on his head as she passed them in silent acknowledgement of the fact that he was scared too but had set that aside to look out for Grace.

At the bottom of the stairs, she felt a cold breeze sweep past her, lifting her hair as she glanced into the living room.

She flicked on the light. Everything was as it should be in here. She turned, the kitchen looked okay from across the hall too.

Grace and Charlie were sitting like scared little orphans halfway up the stairs. Heads almost touching, identical fear in their eyes.

'All good. I'm just checking in the kitchen. I won't be long, sit tight.'

'Get the dead gun mommy!' Grace shouted.

Emmie stopped in her tracks, fear prickling at the back of her neck. What if Grace could actually sense something that would need the 'dead' gun? She had known about the shadow man incident, maybe she knew about other things too. She pulled in a breath.

'It's okay, Grace. I'll be back in a little while.'

She swallowed hard as a large gust battered the front of the house rattling the front door. Another cold breeze lifted her hair, and a low scrape came from the kitchen. The hairs on the back of her neck stood up, but aware of the children watching her Emmie pushed down the swirling in her gut and crossed to the kitchen.

The scraping diminished to a light scratching, a rustling such as a mouse or a rat would make, except it would be neither of these pests this morning, there had been no evidence of them before now.

Goosebumps littered Emmie's arms as she reached a shaking hand for the light switch, flooding the kitchen and the utility with light and immediately discovering the source of the noise.

The small tree at the side of the house had been uprooted placing its branches through the little utility window. The branch lay across the small counter area scraping as the wind tugged and pulled at it.

Letting out a long breath, Emmie closed her eyes and leaned against the door frame.

When the dizziness passed, she moved shakily to the utility and tried to push the branch back outside so that she could patch the little window up. It wouldn't budge. There was glass all over the counter and the floor, and she didn't want to risk getting cut, plus it was still dark outside.

She huffed a frustrated sigh and closed the utility door. It would just have to wait. She decided to check if the school was open and get Charlie and Grace sorted before tackling the tree. She had to concentrate on traversing the snow with no more accidents first.

Three hours later Emmie renegotiated the snowy lane back up to the house. The road itself had turned out to be worse at the right side where it had drifted up to the hedge. She had kept to the left, edging the car slowly in as high a gear as it would take without stalling. She stopped twice to move snow where a couple of the drifts had fallen or spread out into the lane, but after Bills farm, it was easier. He was already out with the land rover, so she stuck to his tyre tracks and the compacted snow beneath them.

The route to school had been nothing compared to the lane, but driving back up it now she felt as though she had been out for hours. Her arms were tired from gripping the wheel. Legs from the effort of dipping and holding the clutch and feathering the accelerator. Her mind was tired from the concentration, but at least the paracetamol was doing its job and her headache seemed to be easing off.

Grace had got on well at school this week, and as she was scared of shadow man, Emmie had paid for the wraparound session today meaning that Grace could stay for lunch and the afternoon nursery session until Charlie came out. At least that meant she would only have to drive up and down this lane once more today.

Parking in the clear patch that the car had sheltered during the night she got out and looked at the front of the house. In the light she could see the offending tree and realised that it hadn't been uprooted at all. The trunk had split and peeled leaving one side to snap away and hit the window.

Wading down to the side of the house she inspected the damage. Jagged bark protruded where the trees tendons had stretched and let go; only a few peels of bark held the section of trunk to the tree. She tugged and kicked her boot at the them, but for all their small size they wouldn't give. Fingers frozen through her gloves already, Emmie decided to give it another go from inside the house.

Kicking fresh snow before her, she made her way to the utility where she took in the branch; long, and only a little bigger than her forearm this far from the trunk.

She grabbed it and tried to push it back out of the window, but driving it into the tree, which was still rooted to the ground, was proving futile. She tried to pull it instead and got minor movement but nothing that was making a difference in the little peels of bark outside, the biggest of which was no bigger than her hand and like a thin flap of skin.

Irritation growing as she got colder she gave one last pull, as hard as she could into the kitchen. The wet branch bent downward, and she thought it was finally going to give. All it gave her, though, was its bark.

With a wet crunch, it came away in her hands, and she sat down hard on the kitchen floor. The branch whipped back into the air grazing past her ear, and painfully pulling her hair. Her hand flew up to her head. She threw the bark across the room and slammed her hand down to the floor.

'Ow! For Christ sake, how can this be so bloody hard?'

She deduced that the only way this was going to happen was from the outside. And with a saw.

Except that she didn't have one.

Bill would have one but she hadn't seen his land rover at the farm when she drove past so he probably wasn't back yet. She opened the door to go back outside and was nearly knocked off her feet as the wind gusted and battered the door, swinging it back into the house.

'Give over!' She shouted at the house as she steadied herself. 'Are you trying to bloody kill me?'

The house remained passive as she stomped back out of the door, following her footprints back through the snow, wind buffeting at her face.

God, this is so annoying. How obvious is it that I'll need tools when I live alone? Jesus Christ, Em, how could you be so stupid?

She seethed. The wind was bitter, she was freezing, and she was too tired after the restless night for this tree's crap. She crossed her arms over her chest, hugging her cold hands into her armpits and stared at the tree, breathing hard, trying to think how to wage war and coming up with nothing.

From behind her came a low whistle.

'You're lucky it wasn't the whole tree, or you could have been fixing the wall too.'

She turned, anger quickly dissipating to relief at the sight of Stuart. She couldn't understand what he was doing here, but she would take it.

'Being lucky hadn't been in my thoughts, to be honest.'

She turned back to the tree as Stuart moved past her to assess the damage. He pushed onto the split of the tree. There was a splintering of bark and the branch shifted, moving against the trunk. She grinned as she shivered.

Tree, you are about to be toast.

He pushed at the split a little more and then turned to her.

'Do you have a saw?'

She shook her head.

'I kind of didn't think about tools when I moved here. Dumb huh?'

He winked at her smiling.

'Not to worry I've got a shovel in the car, I'll give that a go.'

Emmie stepped back to the tree as he went to the car. Turning her back to the bitter wind, she looked at the window. She supposed she had been lucky when she thought about it. A hole straight through the middle of the glass was probably the least amount of damage that could have resulted from the tree falling.

Then Stuart was back, attacking the largest peel of bark using the end of the shovel like an axe. The bark gave, and there was a splintering of glass as the heavier end fell and the branch in the house rose up like it had been filled with helium. Throwing the shovel aside, Stuart pushed at the broken trunk moving it out of the line of the tree.

Emmie watched him, marvelling that he was managing all this with only a shovel when she hadn't been able to budge it at all.

'Come round the other side, Em, I'm going to need help pulling it out.'

She rounded the back of the tree and grabbed the broken end from the side as he showed her.

'I know it's heavy. Just try to lift it off the floor a little, and I'll try and guide it back from the window rather than scrape it across the frame. If it's too much just say and we can try something else.'

She nodded and tried lifting. It was like holding a small car, and her cold muscles screamed. She put it down to try to get a better grip. This shitty tree was not going to beat her. Stuart looked back at her.

'Okay?'

'Yep, just getting a better grip.'

And breaking my weedy arms in the process.

She lifted again, and he turned back toward the window. She was thinking that maybe this way was just going to pull her arms right out of her sockets when he took the weight of the branch midway down which eased things considerably. Now it was like lifting a couple of wheels instead of the whole car. Bad enough but she could hold it for a short time.

'Let's get this out as quick as we can then. Shout if I'm going to fast or you need to stop.'

'Go for it. I'm ready.'

She held the end walking backwards slowly, breathing shakily as her body trembled with effort, but focusing on the snow and her next step rather than the weight in her arms as he guided the smaller end out of the utility. When her muscles started to shake as well as scream, and her back and legs started in on the moaning too, she had to give up.

'I can't do anymore, Stu, it's killing me,' She shouted over the wind.

He looked back nodding.

'Just drop it and move back.' He shouted.

She didn't need asking twice although she did try to put it down instead of dropping it to lessen the effect on him. He swung the front end out past the wall as the back end dropped and threw it onto the ground. It rolled toward her, and she stepped over it as quickly as she could on numb feet and rubber legs. Her body still shook from the exertion, but the tree was out, and she felt a rush of exhilaration.

Stuart took her hand, helping her through the snow and up to the slightly more sheltered wall of the house. She stood against the wall, hands on her thighs, heart hammering.

'Well done, Em, I wasn't convinced we'd be able to manage that. You're stronger than you look.'

Charming.

Emmie wished she could throw something at him, but she was shaky from exertion and breathing hard, so she only nodded. He put a hand on her shoulder squeezing briefly before retrieving the shovel and using it to remove the remaining glass from the window. She watched him, simultaneously wondering why he had come up here, and feeling giddy from being with him again.

When her breathing settled, she looked back down at the snow and found she had the perfect thing to throw at him for that crappy comment. She gathered some snow as quietly as she could, frozen, but feeling like a big kid and thoroughly enjoying it.

She stood with her arms behind her back, holding the snowball lightly in her wet gloves, and moving away from the house. She shivered in the wind letting him finish and move away from the window and broken glass before challenging him.

'Do you always hand out such crushing compliments. I'm starting to think I've got you all wrong, Stu.'

She couldn't help grinning as he looked a little confused.

'Stronger than I look? Kind of a backward compliment I suppose.'

She brought the snowball forward aiming it.

'Any apologies?'

He broke into a grin, and then frowned and shook his head, lips pursed, laughter in his eyes.

'That may be something you regret, sweetheart. I have much bigger hands than you, and there will be no mercy.'

She pretended to think, flicking her eyes up to the sky before launching the snowball getting him squarely in the chest. She shrugged.

'Whoops.'

Stuart was as good as his word, he didn't spare her. She got in a few good hits, but he was fit and moved deftly away from her awkward shots, usually taken from the floor where she fell repeatedly.

After he pummelled her with five consecutive snowballs, leaving her on her knees unable to get up, she had to admit defeat. She flopped on her back in the snow breathing hard. She had snow down her back, was soaked through, hair hanging across her face, and was beyond cold.

What she was though, she thought, was gloriously happy. She was having fun like she hadn't had for years. Scott would never entertain a game like this so she would be confined to 'going easy' on the kids. Which was fun, but this was better. She felt free on a level above anything she had felt for the last ten years.

'Okay, okay, I quit,' she said still lying on her back.

Stuart stood over her, snowball in his hand.

'Oh, you quit? Is that what you said? Whoops.'

He let the ball go, getting her in the stomach. She yelled and doubled up rolling onto her hands and knees.

'Hey that's cheating, I said I quit!'

'Well if you can cheat all night at scrabble…'

He let the words hang, and she laughed.

'Wine induced cheating doesn't count.'

'All cheating counts.'

Stuart picked her up out of the snow and threw her over his shoulder carrying her inside out of the bitter wind both of them laughing.

The house was almost as cold as outside but felt a hundred degrees warmer without the bitter wind chill as Stuart shut the door behind them. Emmie was shaking as he set her back on her feet, and now she stopped to think about it about the cold in her hands and feet was actually painful. Her teeth wouldn't stop chattering.

'I don't think I've ever been so cold that it hurts. I can't even feel my hands and feet.'

He moved closer rubbing his hands up and down her arms.

'Maybe I was a little hard on you, I'm sorry. Have you got the fire going yet?'

She shook her head.

'No I'd only just got back from school, I was trying to sort the tree before getting warm. And you weren't too hard on me I haven't had that much fun in ages.'

He chuckled.

'I can't say I have either. Let me make it up to you; I'll start the fire, and we'll have a quick drink, warm you up a bit. Then I'll pop down to Bill and see if I can borrow some bits to get this window patched up. Sound okay?'

'Perfect.'

He set about the fire as Emmie went into the kitchen, flicking on the kettle before looking at the mess in the utility. She used a dustpan and brush as best as she could to get the glass off the floor and the countertop. Stopping only when the pain in her hands got too much, and the wind blowing through the hole where her window had been chilled her to the bone. She shut the utility door and reached for the cups as Stuart entered the kitchen.

'All done, you go and sit down. I'll make us a drink. My hands are warm.'

She smiled.

'Alright, thank you.'

She went back to the living room where the fire was starting to take nicely. She sat on the edge of the settee feeling the warmth on her face. She watched the flames lick and dance until Stuart returned with the tea which he put on the small table. She reached for it, but he stopped her.

'Let's get these gloves off first and get some circulation going.'

He sat next to her and peeled them off slowly causing her to wince. He looked at her fingers before rubbing them and moving her joints gently with his now warm hands, his touch causing the now familiar fluttering in her stomach, juxtaposed with crucifying pain. After a few minutes rubbing pins and needles reached her fingers, and when feeling started to come back, he allowed her to have the tea.

She sipped, feeling the delicious warmth run all the way through to her stomach as the fire started to warm her slowly from the outside, and pins and needles returned to her feet. She wiggled her toes getting the circulation going down there too because there was no way he was rubbing her feet no matter how good the hand rub had been.

'Better?' he said as they sipped their tea side by side.

'Much better, especially now that tree is out.'

'You should have called me, I'd have been up sooner.'

'You were next on my list, but it didn't seem like that big a deal, I thought I could manage.' She huffed a laugh, 'You know that branch wouldn't budge an inch, but it still managed to pile drive me into the floor, smack me upside the head and pull my hair. I was bloody furious by the time you got here!'

He grinned at her, pushing her wet fringe gently out of her eyes.

'It's inanimate.'

'Yes. Well, it still managed to put its inanimate ass through my window. Anyway by some miracle you appeared when I was about to give up, what was all that about?'

He chuckled.

'I wanted to check you were still standing. The wind managed to do a little damage in the village in the last night. We're in a valley but you're so exposed here it must have been like a hurricane. I was worried about you.'

'It did keep me up a little, but the tree didn't come down until this morning. I think the wine knocked me out.'

He smiled, but his eyes showed concern.

'I probably shouldn't have plied you with the bottle, you were a little unsteady by the end of the night. I'm sorry, it's a habit to keep filling glasses I suppose.'

She looked at him eyebrows raised.

'It's not a habit. It's your job.'

'Even so, it wasn't my intention to…'

He turned to the fire shaking his head a little seemingly unable to convey what he wanted to say. She thought she knew where he was going though.

'To get me drunk and kiss me?' She said.

He turned back to her quickly frowning a little.

'No, that was absolutely *not* my intention. You just ...' he took a breath, 'I haven't kissed anyone like that for a long time Em, and I don't know where it came from. I don't properly know you, and yet, I'm so comfortable with you I feel like I've known you forever. I can't explain it.'

He looked so unsure she thought his feelings had come out of the blue as much for him as they had for her. She put her hand on his feeling the electricity as he moved his to link his fingers with hers. She hadn't believed that such a strong attraction between two people who didn't know each other was possible, especially from both sides.

She had been attracted to Scott, but it had still taken time to fall in love as he courted her. But this was different. Stuart didn't have to promise her anything she felt head over heels just being in the same room with him. It was both a bizarre and beautiful feeling, and she was glad he felt something of the same or he may have driven her insane.

'Please say something Em.' He said quietly putting his cup on the table and taking her other hand in his. 'Look, I know you had a lot to drink, and I know what you said, but I want you to be sure you meant it, and you still feel the same this morning. If you don't, I need you to be honest with me, Em, because I...'

He trailed off, the pain back in his eyes and Emmie couldn't say anything. The pull was back that made her want to attach to him and let the rest of the world melt away. She allowed it to take her and met his lips kissing him softly at first, and then as fully as he had kissed her last night. He responded without hesitation, letting go of her hands to wind his arms around her. It left her breathless and wanting more, electricity flooding through her from her head to her toes. The feeling so intense she felt that she was floating, not anchored to anything but him. Reluctantly, she pulled back looking into his pale eyes.

'I feel the same, Stu.' she said, 'I said that, I think, and I meant it. I don't know where this came from, but I can't stop it. The intensity scares me a little.'

'It scares me too, sweetheart, more than you know.' he whispered.

She scooted up, pulling herself closer to him. He wrapped her in his arms and she buried her head in his neck thinking she could see herself spending the rest of her life alongside this beautiful man with his big, kind, protective soul.

She didn't know how long they stayed locked in each other's arms, but she knew it wasn't long enough before he loosened his grip and pulled back. She looked up at him, and he kissed her forehead lightly.

'As much as I want to stay right here, we have a window that won't patch itself, and I have a pub that won't run itself.'

She smiled, reluctantly letting him go.

'I don't want you to go home, but I suppose we need to fix the window.'

Stuart got up with a chuckle, but Emmie thought he looked as shaken as she felt.

'Stick some more wood on the fire and keep warm while I go see what I can borrow from Bill.'

Chapter 63

Stuart came back with a couple of sheets of thick plywood, some nails and a hammer and they fixed the outside board first. Emmie held it still and handed him the nails as he drove each one home into the frame with just a couple of good blows. It was an easy job after the tree and they completed it quickly, mainly because standing so still in the bitter wind rendered her bone-cold and shivering within a few minutes.

Back inside it was already warmer with the hole covered, and they got straight to work putting the other piece of wood over the inside, Emmie sat on the countertop, handing him nails as they chatted idly. It was comfortable until Stuart brought up a subject she was desperate to forget.

'Can I ask you a question, Em? Tell me to shut up if you don't want to answer. I'm just intrigued to know what happened last Friday, when you first came to the pub. What scared you so much you brought the bairns away from here, on a cold evening, to stay in a guest house. That's what happened isn't it?'

Emmie looked at him. She knew she owed him an explanation, but she wondered how deep to go. She hesitated looking down at the nails in her hand. Stuart watched her quietly.

'It was stupid really, nothing at all. Bill says I've got city jitters and that's probably the extent of it. I just got rumbled in the country. It's not that interesting.'

'I'm all ears.' He said.

Emmie rolled her eyes handing him a nail.

'Okay, fine. So, we were all in the living room, Grace, Charlie and I, just chilling before I got them some tea, when there's a knock at the door. I know this is going to sound weird, but you need to be aware that I thought someone had been watching the house.'

He hammered the nail in and looked at her amused, taking another nail from her hand.

'Out here?'

'Yeah I know, Bill laughed like a loon when I told him, but at the time I just made sure everything was always locked and that way I knew we were secure.'

Stuart nodded slowly.

'Hence, locking the door when I came up on Monday, right, I'm with you. I called you defensive, I think, for that? I had no idea. I'm so sorry.'

Emmie smiled, it was water under the bridge three days later. How had things changed so fast?

'It's okay,' she said, 'I didn't really take any notice. I was busy feeling sorry for myself after some guy I liked turned down a dinner invitation.'

Stuart hammered the nail home, looked at her with amusement and then shook his head playing along.

'He sounds like an eejit.' He said taking another nail.

'Yeah.' She agreed.

He laughed as he hammered.

'So someone knocked at the door?'

'Well I thought so but I was already jittery, it was dark, and I didn't want to scare the kids. I went to the door, but the knocking turned out to be coming from the kitchen window. Then it came from the living room window, and then Grace screamed from the sunroom saying there was a man at the doors. I pulled the kids into the living room and went to look, but he was gone, and that's when I noticed the doors were open.'

Stuart had stopped hammering and was listening intently with a frown.

'Obviously, there was no-one to be seen by then, but I didn't know whether he was inside or out, so I panicked, threw the kids into the car and drove down to you.'

'Which is why you had no money or luggage. I wish you'd said something. Christ, I came so close to turning you away.'

'What could I say? I didn't know you then, it took everything I had just trying not to appear a crazy idiot.'

Stuart sighed and hammered another nail into the wood before he answered.

'You came across more terrified than crazy, sweetheart. I should have done more for you, I knew it then, I just didn't know what I *could* do.'

'No, you did more than enough for us that night. I thought you were going to throw us out anyway when I realised I hadn't picked up my purse, that's why those tears suddenly came from nowhere. Frustration, and fear I suppose. I didn't want to have to come back here. I was too scared to come home.'

Stuart sighed laying the hammer on the side and rubbing at his forehead.

'Aye, and that's why I should have done more for you. I put you all in that poky, noisy room. It didn't sit well with me then, and I don't like it now.'

Emmie smiled at him.

'Don't beat yourself up, that was the best nights sleep I had in ages. I completely shut off. It was glorious. And if the children had been sleeping anywhere other than next to the bar, I would never have left them in the room alone. It was only because I could watch the door from there that I felt I could get out and enjoy the band, relax a little and take my mind off what was going on here. So it was the perfect room. And I felt thoroughly looked after with the food and drink too. There wasn't anything else I wanted or needed. You were perfect in my eyes Stu. I still owe you so much for that night.'

He smiled at her, picked up the hammer and took the last nail hammering it in.

'You don't owe me a thing. So what happened Saturday, you came back here with the bairns alone?'

'I had no choice, but it didn't turn out so bad. Bill was already at the door when I pulled up, so I roped him into staying with me until I had looked around. Thing is when I checked the sunroom doors with Bill on Saturday they were locked again. Weird, huh?'

'How can they have been locked if you were in the village. Are you sure they were open in the first place?'

'I've been over it a hundred times, there would be no other reason for me to grab the kids and run. I had been living thinking he was outside anyway. It was the unlocked door that provided the panic to run, I'm certain.'

Stuart nodded as he checked the boarded window.

'All secure.' He said turning to her.

An involuntary shudder ran through her. This house always felt anything but secure, and yet Bill had said similar on Saturday.

'Let's have a look at that back door as well while I'm here then.' He said

He helped her off the counter top and she told him to carry on through while she grabbed the keys.

In the sunroom, Stuart was holding something in his hand, and Emmie felt her stomach disappear through the floor as she caught sight of the small white paper.

Another photo? Really? You couldn't wait until I hadn't got company?

She swallowed hard, heart pumping, hoping it wasn't another one like this morning's, but Stuart was smiling as he turned to her.

'They're bonnie bairns Em, Grace is the image of you. Did you say they were eight and three?'

Trying not to shake with relief, she nodded as she stepped over to his side and looked at the picture. It wasn't one that she had taken, but at least it seemed normal and relatively recent too. Charlie and Grace together, sitting slightly sideways on the settee in the very living room she had just walked out of, perfectly posed like a school photograph.

The living room? How is that possible?

She looked over the photo. Charlie wore a brown jacket with a red, brown and cream striped scarf. He grinned out at the camera happily, hair flopping into his hazel eyes. Grace was more serious smiling only with her big blue eyes, her rosebud mouth and full lips straight, dark hair brushed over to one side. Her rough ringlets were fastened with a pink flower hair clip.

Emmie's heart swelled and she couldn't help but smile, they were pretty cute, even if she was biased. They had done so well up here, fitting in without an issue, and without moaning. She took the photo from Stuart.

'Where did you find this?' She said.

'On the floor by the chair.'

He pointed to the wicker chair next to them, and Emmie nodded.

'The kids must have had them out again, I find them all over the place.'

She handed him the keys and glanced at the photo again thinking this was one she would add to her little box. Apparently, invisible man had no need for throwing the box around now he was busy snapping his own pictures.

She thought of the one of Grace this morning. Some were better than others. He could really do with a crash course in photography.

She put the photo on the small table and followed Stuart to the doors. He tried the handles, and she was relieved to find they were still locked from last night. He put the key in, locked and unlocked them a few times, and then opened them checking the lock while he could see it and pulling on the handle.

'The lock seems to be working okay, but I'd get a couple of bolt locks to be safe. Wooden doors with one point of entry are easy enough to get into even if they are locked.'

'Okay, But the handle turned, it was unlocked, and when I came back, it was locked again.'

He shrugged and shook his head.

'I can't see how that would happen without a key.'

She sighed heavily as he locked the door and passed her the keys.

'I'm not saying it didn't happen.'

'Just that it's impossible.'

He put a hand on her shoulder.

'Nothing is impossible. I didn't say that, and remember, I'm not a locksmith. There is one in the village though I can ask him to pop up and have a look if you'd like.'

'Thank you, but I can't see what good it would do now. It was probably me, I wasn't in the best frame of mind at the time, and nothing has happened since so…'

She held her hands up in resignation.

Stuart wasn't arguing with her as he pulled on the handles again, which probably meant he had come to the same conclusion.

Fantastic.

And for the record, she didn't believe that version any more than she believed in the tooth fairy. She had spent the last sixteen years living on precision intuition and instinct just to get through the day, and her alarm was on red alert about those doors.

'Well, if nothing has happened since I'll bet your man was a walker that misjudged time and weather. He probably saw he had scared Grace and went away again as you hadn't answered the door.'

Except he didn't knock the door, sunshine, and I'd seen him before that too. If you excuse those things, I'd be at the same conclusion.

'Probably.' She said quietly.

'Right,' he said, 'If you're happy then I suppose I'll get back home and see if Connor has managed to deal with breakfast.'

Oh, I'm not happy. Not at all. That door was unlocked which proves that someone may actually have a key.

But if she had witnessed shadow man being very inhuman as he glided down the garden then why the heck would he need a key? And if it wasn't him then who had unlocked the doors?

The wind, which had seemed to be dying down as the last hour had passed, suddenly got it's breath back and the French doors rattled slightly as it hit. Emmie frowned, another noise to add to list she would have to remember in this old house, add that to the stuff she couldn't explain, and she was going to be living on tenterhooks forever.

She nearly jumped out of her skin as Stuart touched her arm pulling her from her thoughts and back into the room.

'What's the matter, Em?'

She shook her head slightly.

'Nothing - Everything - I'm losing it, Stu, I can't take the constant tension, it's driving me mad. Everything is an unknown here. I'm going to end up hanging from the orchard like ...' She struggled for his name, clicking her fingers and then it came to her in a flash. '... John Watts.'

'John Watts?'

'The bloke who built the place. His wife died not long after they moved in and he hung himself from the orchard. Edith told me last week.'

'Charming. What on earth made her tell you that?'

Emmie shrugged.

'Same thing that made Bill tell me about Ted getting struck down on the patio just the day before I suppose. You Scots have a thing for stories about the dead.'

Stuart chuckled making Emmie smile.

'Aye legends and ghosts, It's all the bloody battles we've fought.'

'Which are interesting, but not when they involve my house.'

The French doors blew open with a bang so loud it seemed to shake the windows of the sunroom. Emmie yelped Stuart grabbed her back away from the doors. The strong gust of wind sent snow flurrying inside from the patio as it moaned around the building.

Stuart grabbed at the right-hand door and began pushing it shut, but Emmie was rooted to the spot. A chill was escalating up her back, and it wasn't the chill of the cold air and snow, which was now swirling around the room. She felt as if the door to hell had opened and was letting the spirits through into her house. The moan of the wind sounded for all the world like the moan of the dead and right here outside was where Ted had met his final moments. She needed to shut out the damn sound before she began accompanying it with her own screams.

She made herself move on stiff legs, and grabbed the other door pushing it to meet Stuarts with as much force as she could. They got the doors together but the tongue of the lock prevented them from being shut completely.

'We need the keys,' Stuart said over the noise of the wind.

Emmie turned her back to the door so that she feel for them in her pocket when her dads' disjointed voice appeared in her head.

Try the handle first, Emmie, let's get to the root of the problem, shall we?

Emmie stopped searching shocked by the urgency in the tone of his voice. She also thought that for a voice inside her own head she had no idea what the hell it was talking about or where it had come from. She turned to face the door quickly putting one hand back on the glass to stop it from flying open again. Stuart looked at her confused his own back against the other door keeping it shut flush against the frame.

'What are you doing, Em?'

'I just need to try something first.'

She put her hand on the cold handle and pulled downward. It turned easily pulling the tongue of the lock back into its frame. The door banged the last few inches into the frame meeting the other with a click.

It was as though someone had pressed the mute button, all was very suddenly still and quiet, the only sound coming from the Grandfather clock which ticked the seconds unperturbed with its perpetually steady heartbeat.

'I guess you have a broken lock.'

Emmie nodded relieved. It was the best piece of news she'd had all day. It meant that no one had a key, the lock came open of its own accord under pressure. She fished for the keys in her pocket and handed them to him. He locked the door, tried the handle, and looked at it.

'All the wind did was move it so…'

He pulled at the handle a little and tried it again. Still locked. He frowned and pulled harder. There was a click, and the handle fell downward in his hand, and the door came open. He shut and locked it again before standing up from his crouch.

'Guess you'll be needing that locksmith after all. I'll bring you a couple of slide bolts over later and get them fixed onto the doors, so you're safe for now.'

Emmie wasn't listening she was staring out at the orchard where not a single tree was moving. She narrowed her eyes, hands coming up to opposite biceps in a self hug. It looked peaceful out there, and there were no creaks and groans from the house. The wind had disappeared as quickly as it had changed direction and built up pressure just a few minutes ago.

'Look outside, Stu.'

Stuart looked at her and then outside.

'How is it that still when we just struggled to shut the blessed doors.'

'I don't know. That is a little strange, the weather up here changes on a dime from minute to minute, but I've not seen anything happen that fast before I must admit.'

'Stu, this is exactly what I mean. Shit like this happens here all the time.'

'It's an old house, these windows and doors are wooden, they'll expand and contract with the temperature and damp. The lock is old, it's just broken. At some point, these things will give, and we'll get them fixed, it's not a problem. And weather is just weather, nothing you can do about that. Are you okay?'

Emmie nodded, and he put an arm around her shoulders, pulling her close.

'I really need to get back, but I'll drop those bolts in for you later.'

They went to the front door together.

'It's okay, Stu, I'll pop down for them after I've picked the kids up, I can't expect you to come out again today you have work to do.'

'I don't mind.'

'I know you don't, but I'll be out anyway so I'll come to you.'

'Alright, will you be okay fitting them?'

'Yep, I'm not completely useless - although, I'll have to borrow a screwdriver - and some screws.'

Stuart grinned shaking his head.

'No bloody tools.'

'I'm such a woman, I know.'

'You sure you don't need me to fit those locks?'

She aimed a playful swing toward him and he stepped back laughing, hands out in front of him.

'I'll take that as a no.'

'Even if I did have trouble Nat and Mike should be arriving in a few hours anyway. I'm sure we'll manage it together.'

Stuart stepped closer and circled his arms around her. She stepped into his hug smiling happily. He kissed the top of her head.

'I'm glad they're coming.'

'I'm not.'

He stepped back a little so that he could see her face.

'You're really not?'

'No. Nat thinks I'm far too fragile for a relationship after the divorce. I don't want to argue with her, so it means I get no time to be with you. And I want to be with you more than anything at the moment.'

'Ah. Well, okay, it's not forever though, Em, they have to go home eventually, and we have all the time in the world. Does this mean I don't get to meet them?'

'If you do we're friends. Period. Got it?'

'Aye, and suddenly I'm back to being fifteen again.'

She laughed as he leaned down towards her.

'There'll be none of this then.' He whispered as his lips met hers, sweeping her feet from under her for the second time that morning.

She looked at him flushing.

'Definitely none of that.' Emmie whispered.

He chuckled and opened the door that she had managed to forget to lock somewhere in the events of the morning. A blustery, icy breeze joined them in the doorway.

'Wind's back,' He said smiling.

Emmie sighed. That wind had seemed to come and go just to prove a point to her, but she also knew that was crazy. Stuart put a hand on her shoulder looking down at her.

'Don't read more into things than there is, it's winding you up, keeping you tense. The house will make noises, and things will break, it's nothing more sinister than that. Edie and Bill should never have told you those stories. But listen, I've already told you if you need a break from being up here with everything that's going on, come and spend a few nights down in the pub, I've plenty of room now, the house will still be here when you get back.'

'Stu, I-'

'I know what you're going to say, and I'm just saying the offer is always open. Anytime you need it. And you can call me anytime, for anything, alright? Especially if the man of the moment turns up.'

'You're the man of the moment, Stu. He's the arsehole of the south.'

'Emmie.' His tone was serious, but his eyes twinkled, and a grin played around his mouth.

'I know, and thank you.'

He curled his fingers under her chin, stroking her cheek with his thumb.

'I don't need thanking, I just need to know you're doing okay, and if you're not, I want you to tell me. It's that simple. You aren't alone up here, don't ever think that you are.'

There was a dull thud from upstairs as if the house wholeheartedly agreed. Stuart looked at her a frown crossing his face, but Emmie shrugged. She had a feeling she knew exactly what it was - the little box was back on the move. She hoped whatever was right side up wasn't going the same way as the last few photographs had gone.

'It's okay, I left a box of stuff on the edge of the dressing table this morning, it probably gave up trying to hold on.'

He smiled, and she stepped back in for one last hug in those protective arms. She held on to him for longer than necessary feeling the warmth of him close to her, drinking him in with all of her senses. She didn't know when she would get another chance once Natalie and Michael arrived.

Chapter 64

After Stuart left Emmie spent an uneasy few hours rattling around the house. She went upstairs to find the little box had indeed 'slipped' off the dresser. Photo's of Grace, Charlie and her dad littered the floor. She frowned as she rifled through trying to find her own photographs, the ones she remembered being in the box, but they were gone. There was only a single photograph of each one of them, duplicated over and over. With a sigh, she put them back into the box, and stuffed it in a drawer of the dresser.

After making arrangements for the little window to be replaced, Emmie tried to work, but she couldn't shake the feeling that something was waiting for her downstairs while she was alone up in the rafters. When the atmosphere got so intense that she couldn't look at the hole leading down onto the landing, she finally packed up, switched the little radio off, and shut the loft up without a single brush stroke taking place on the canvas.

There *had* been something waiting for her on the stairs - always the damn stairs - another photo. This was like the one of Grace in her bloodstained Peppa top, but it showed Charlie instead. Just as grey, Left eye puffed closed, his mouth swollen with a single trickle of blood running back toward his ear. His beautiful floppy hair was missing along with the top of his head.

Emmie yelped, heart pumping and hands shaking as she screwed it up, adrenaline pushing her into the living room to throw it onto the fire as she had with the one of Scott.

As she watched the photo curl and burn, she couldn't shake the feeling that a storm was brewing. She knew that a real one was on the way, and she was a little apprehensive after the storm last night, but this felt different.

There was nowhere in the house that felt safe to relax. The kitchen was dark and cold, and she didn't like the view out of the window, where she had now seen shadow man twice, and once hurtling straight toward her.

Thinking of shadow man, she went to the fridge to check the gun, giving it a click on the hammer and practicing her grip. She didn't pretend to shoot anything, Grace's comments had thoroughly wedged themselves into her brain providing ice from the top to the bottom of her spine, but she did carry the gun with her as she walked the rest of the ground floor.

The feeling that something was accompanying her was intense. Like pressure in the air, pushing down on her shoulders.

The playroom was cold and lifeless. It had never been a comfortable room, Emmie didn't know how Charlie managed to stay in here on the playstation for hours, the hairs on the back of her neck rose just stepping inside the doorway. She wasn't aware anything had happened in the room, but she would bet her life something had gone down here at some point in the past, it had too much of a 'haunted' feeling.

With an involuntary Shudder, she crossed the room quickly to the sunroom, which was cold, but didn't have the same eerie feeling as the kitchen and playroom.

Strange, really, as this was the room that had had most of the unexplainable happen, from the dream, to shadow man, and the unlocked door, not to mention the doors flying open today in a freak wind.

Emmie stood, feeling the cold in the room travel up her nose with each inward breath as she looked at the doors.

Those doors bothered her.

So block them up, drag something over, honey.

The voice was her dads, and she briefly wondered if he was the one following her around the house.

Okay, it's not a bad idea until I can fix the bolts on.

She scanned the near-empty room and decided the two seater settee would do. It wasn't particularly heavy being made of wicker, and she lifted one end, dragging it over with ease. Not ideal, but there was nothing else in the room worth putting there. At least the wind wouldn't be able to blow the doors open again unless they took the chair with them, alerting her. She checked the door handles.

Locked tight.

Not completely reassuring, but better than nothing.

She turned to the living room. It was still warm in here, but the fire was getting low. She put on a couple of extra logs from the small pile Stuart had brought in earlier and perched on the settee, chewing at her lip, wondering when Natalie and Michael would arrive. She knew their plane didn't land until 4.30pm so she supposed it would be dinner time. They would be starving.

She decided to plan a big meal for them and have a shower before she had to pick up Grace and Charlie. It would give her something to focus on instead of sitting around with a 'dead gun' feeling thoroughly hunted and watched.

Mid-afternoon the wind picked up again and small snow flurries joined it, dancing in the biting cold air. Emmie picked up the children and drove into the village to get the door bolts, leaving Charlie and Grace in the car as she popped into the pub. Stuart was busy with a customer, so when he retrieved them from under the bar complete with screwdriver and screws, she took them, mouthed a thank you, and left with a wave.

She gladly listened to the nursery rhymes CD, both herself and Charlie singing along with Grace. She felt she had been waiting forever for their chatter and laughter to come back home, after the gloomy, depressing feel of the house today.

She drove carefully, the vibe in the car relaxed and happy until they got to the house where she and Grace fell quiet. Never had a feeling of such desolation and gloom hung around her shoulders as it did now. Only Charlie seemed unaffected. He carried on to the door with his bags while Emmie and Grace were slower, holding hands as if they knew what was to come.

Chapter 65

It was just after 6pm when Emmie heard the thud over the roar of the wind. She turned down the little radio she had placed in the kitchen to accompany her as she prepared dinner on the kitchen table.

Natalie and Michael had been in the hire car and on their way by 5pm, their plane landing perfectly on schedule, but Emmie knew the journey was a couple of hours under normal circumstances so they would be a while yet.

It was dark outside, although the falling snow gave the impression of a solid grey just outside the window. She glanced through the open door into the hallway, listening. Charlie and Grace had retreated upstairs to play and she was back on edge being alone downstairs, but she knew with all the bumps and bangs in this house the thud could be anything. She didn't even think she wanted to check.

She waited, and hearing nothing more, picked up the knife to carry on cutting carrots.

Another thud and then a scrape.

A trickle of relief ran down her spine, and she blew out a breath.

The damn wicker chair.

She glanced at the bolts on the counter-top, and regretted not fitting them when it was light.

Conscious of losing the warm air from the fire, and what little heat the boiler seemed to pump out with the broken window, she strode out of the kitchen, across the hallway, and into the living room.

And came face to face with Scott.

He stood by the fire, warming his hands. He turned as she entered the room, seemingly unsurprised.

Feeling like she had hit a physical glass wall, Emmie stopped abruptly taking in his size and those piercing eyes that had looked at her from the photograph only a couple of nights ago.

Adrenaline surged and her heart started to pump. She struggled to keep her composure while looking at a man of whom she knew every inch, but after all that had happened and how far he had gone to track her down, it seemed she hardly knew at all.

He smiled, not his patronising sneer, but his most charming smile, the one he had used way back when they first met.

'Emelia, it's good to see you. You're not an easy woman to hunt down.'

Somewhere in the back of her mind, she wanted to tell him she hadn't been anywhere, and that his detective hiring skills sucked; but the front of her mind was screaming with abandon. Her throat was dry, and she had to clear it a couple of times before she could speak. She tried to keep her voice level, but it wavered with fear all the same.

'W... what are you doing in my house, Scott?'

Scott looked about him innocently, Gesturing back to the sunroom.

'I knocked on the front door, no one answered, but I knew you were here I could see you in the kitchen. The back doors were open, so I let myself in.' He leaned toward her, lowering his voice. 'Got to tell you, your wicker security sucks.'

He leaned back and laughed like he had told the worlds funniest joke and she watched him unable to gauge whether it was genuine or condescending.

She felt a flutter of panic. Too long out of his company and unable to read him, she felt out of her depth. She floundered for the confidence she had managed to fake for dealing with Martin but failed to grasp it. When Scott saw she wasn't laughing with him, he stopped abruptly and pushed her arm playfully.

'Joking, just joking. Where has your sense of humour gone, darling?'

She smiled, pasting it on her mouth instinctively, out of a duty she no longer had, but with a need to keep him on side while she worked out what to do.

'What are you doing here, Scott?'

'What am I doing here? Well now, that is the million dollar question isn't it?'

Emmie found herself trembling as she took in his chiselled good looks, perfect hair and baby soft shaved face. It was disconcerting; if he hadn't instigated the divorce she would probably still have been with him, and yet, she realised she felt almost nothing in his presence. There was no nostalgia, no rush of love, no longing. Nothing.

He sighed and took her hand. She was shaking too much to take it away from him. She swallowed, the sound washing past her ears.

Come on, Em, keep it together.

'And the million dollar answer is, I'm here for you, Emelia.' He smiled showing his perfect white teeth. 'I'm here to take you home, where you belong. I realise that I was wrong, I shouldn't have shrugged off your pain, but I was hurting too, you have to understand that. I proceeded with the divorce out of frustration. I didn't actually think it would go ahead to completion. I love you. I was wrong. You can't stay up here by yourself, it's ridiculous, come home sweet pea. Please.'

Emmie gaped at him. He was holding onto her hand, looking at her with concern and regret, and longing. She felt a flicker of uncertainty. She saw the man she had married in his face and felt a brief pang of regret. She pushed the feeling down, taking her hand away from his, and shook her head which finally started to click into gear.

She thought of the children playing upstairs, oblivious, and knew she had to try to get him out as quickly and quietly as she could. The hard part would be not rousing his anger, especially after Martin's warnings.

She wanted to get a message to Stuart, too, just in case trouble arose, but she couldn't remember where her phone was.

Scott was giving her no leeway under that stare. As her thoughts came fast and furious, he scrutinised every flicker of emotion she gave away. She swallowed hard.

'I … I can't go back, Scott. You chose this route for us. I wasn't happy at the time, but I'm happy now. You can't just decide that you want everything you threw away and come to claim it back, people move on. I've been through hell to get here. I can't just walk away.'

He worked his jaw, and she hoped she hadn't said too much. She was starting to acquire a thin layer of sweat on top of the shaking.

'You've been through hell?' He said, 'What about me? I've been through hell and had to make the tough decision of divorce to try to shake you back up. I didn't think you would walk. I thought our relationship was worth more than that.'

'Walk? I didn't walk Scott. You told me to leave, and then you put me through a nightmare with legalities. None of this was me!'

Scott clenched and unclenched his jaw running his hand over his mouth and back up his jawline. He huffed, and she saw him trying to control himself. When he spoke, it was level and even.

'Okay. Look, you're saying you didn't want it, I'm saying I'm sorry. That makes us even. Let's go home, Emelia, please. I don't want to argue. I miss you. Let's put this horrible business behind us and get back on track.'

Emmie stared at him, wondering how in the world they were 'even' after everything he'd done.

Scott was clearly trying to control himself, she could have sliced the uneasy tension around him with a knife. She took a shaky breath.

'What am I supposed to do with this?' Her voice sounded whiny and pleading as she gestured to the house around them. 'I've worked my ass off to get here and make this place home for the kids. They love it here, heck *I* love it here, and they love their school. I won't uproot them again. They were up-heaved enough when you shut us out. They're doing good for the first time in ages. I've made a life here Scott, and I won't let them suffer anymore.'

To her surprise, Scott laughed, smooth and controlled.

'You've made a life here? Are you sure about that? Clearly, your life still isn't what you think it is honey. We need to go home.'

He moved toward her, and she automatically took a step back heart pumping.

'What is the matter, Emelia?'

Emmie looked at his serious, hard face and thought about all the times he had asked her that question over the years with that same damn look.

'Well?'

His mouth was a line, eyes boring into hers and she realised she had stepped back further.

'Nothing, Scott,' She said, forcing herself to step toward him again to keep him calm. It was coming back to her, the little tricks to keep him from flying off the handle. She was stepping back into the 'good wife' role again as though she had never left.

Except you're not his wife, and he has no right to be here.

No, she wasn't, and he didn't, but she had no idea where he was going with this come home stuff. It worried her, and she didn't know how to get him out.

'I just … I'm confused.'

Scott's shoulders relaxed a little as she stepped closer, and she saw a softness appear in his eyes. A morsel of weight slid off her own shoulders with relief.

'I know you are, and I was hurting before, but I can help you now. Let me help you.' He smiled.

Emmie stared at him.

'Scott, I'm not sure what you want to help me with. I'm okay. Really. I appreciate you coming up here, but-'

He changed instantly. He kept the smile but his cold eyes belied his emotion, and his voice raised a few notches as he spoke.

'Oh, you do? Do you know what I've had to go through to get to you? Not only with locating you but getting here in this fucking storm. I've lost money left and right trying to reach you. Lots of money. And you're just going to tell me to fuck off? I don't think so, honey.'

Reeling she stepped back again involuntarily, and he grabbed her arm closing the gap.

'Scott, you're scaring me, please.'

He looked at his hand on her arm and immediately let go. The softness was back in his voice.

'I'm sorry darling, I don't want to scare you. I want you to come home, I've had a rough month not knowing where you were and how you've been. I've been worried sick about you.'

Emmie stared at him stomach swirling.

'Look,' he said, 'I know our last few months together weren't the best and I know I was hard on you. We need to talk, and I was going to do that on the way back, but if you feel more comfortable, we could sit down and work this out here instead of running off straight away. Would that be better?'

Emmie nodded. She had no idea what he wanted to say, but if he wanted to talk calmly, she would let him and hope that Natalie or

Stuart would appear so that he could leave. She thought of her phone again, and it came to her where it was. Upstairs. Where she had got changed out of her wet clothes this morning.

Stupid, Em, just bloody stupid.

Now she was going to have to think of a way to get up there without alerting him that she was up to something. She sat on the settee opposite the fire and Scott sat down next to her, his thigh and arm touched hers, but she didn't dare move. The powerful scent of his aftershave made the hair on the back of her neck stand up.

'So, what do we need to talk about?'

Scott looked at her with a tenderness she hadn't seen in years, and her heart fluttered involuntarily.

'You and the children. I think it's time we all stopped skirting around the issue and told you some facts.'

She looked at him puzzled, heart thudding. She hadn't expected a story; she had expected excuses and lies. Stories weren't Scott's forte. She thought of the children upstairs playing quietly. She hadn't so much as heard a murmur out of them for an hour or more.

Please god, let them stay quiet.

He sighed, hands in a prayer position, forefingers to his lips, eyes on hers.

'Okay darling, let's start at the beginning. you remember the car accident a couple of years ago?'

She blinked. The accident? What the hell did that have to do with anything?

'I don't see-'

'Honey, just answer the question all will become clear I promise you.'

'Well, of course, I remember the accident, it won't be something I forget in a hurry, Scott'

'How much do you remember?'

She shook her head, heart starting to pound.

'I remember as much as I could before. I remember the van that hit us …'

The words seized in her mouth. Her heart was racing now, and goosebumps prickled at her arms. She heard the screech of tyres as the car in front failed to stop. She saw the lorry's trailer jackknife out into the carriageway. She heard her own typres screech and the scream on her lips as she realised that she wouldn't be able to stop the car. She remembered screaming at the kids to brace themselves just before impact and the sickening thud as the car ploughed into the one in front pulling her hard against the seatbelt before throwing her back into her seat.

A moment of silence and clarity had ensued as she saw the car behind swing out to the left of her stopping on the hard shoulder, and the one behind that managing to stop too. She remembered a moment of relief that the worst was over, even though the crunch and screech of twisting metal and locked brakes remained evident around her.

And then she saw it.

Both Grace and Charlie screamed as the lorry's trailer, which was still kicking out, knocked the van sidelong into the car.

She remembered the van looming toward them, seemingly in slow motion, as she tried to start the car. It was only after looking at photos of the accident and seeing the car that she realised how foolish that had been. The front of the car had all but disappeared, squashed into the boot of the car in front. It wouldn't have moved anywhere even if she could start it.

The inevitable happened and the van collided with the rear section of the car with such force that it was pulled out of the wreckage and spun. At that point, Emmie must have hit her head because the memories stopped and didn't start again until she was hooked up to all sorts of monitors in the hospital with a leg that was broken in five places, a collapsed lung and a fractured skull. The fluid was drained off her brain three times, and it was touch and go for a while, but it was the leg that kept her in hospital for weeks as she underwent two operations to mend the shattered bones. Emmie remembered the doctors saying it was a miracle she hadn't sustained worse injuries, and that she was fortunate to be alive, but she hadn't felt it lying in that bed in excruciating pain. Her lung was the only thing that hadn't seemed to give her much trouble after it had been re-inflated, but she had thought that might have been because of the other injuries.

Emmie looked at Scott, breathing hard, covered in goosebumps and a thin layer of sweat. She felt sick. Scott brushed her fringe out of her eyes in much the same way Stuart had only this morning, she wanted to knock his hand away, but she had no energy left to move. He put his hands over hers and looked at her.

'It's going to get harder, Emelia, but I need you to stay with me. You remember the van, and you remember it hit the car, yes?'

'Yes I know it hit the fucking car, Scott, I was there, can we stop talking about this I'm doing fine. Driving doesn't bother me anymore. It's like the therapist said I'm in control and I go as fast or slow as I like. If I need to stop, I can. There's no reason for me to panic. It worked. I've done enough driving since buying this place to know I'm absolutely fine. I just needed to get back on the horse. It's over.'

Scott pursed his lips and inhaled deeply through his nose, letting it go before he spoke.

'I know you're alright driving, and I know you worked hard on that, sweet pea, but I want to know if you're alright with the children.'

'Charlie and Grace? They had nightmares for a while sure, but kids deal with these things better than adults. They had more nightmares about not seeing you for months. They are both good in the car now.'

'No, Emelia, they're not. That's just the point.'

She frowned at him, shocked to see his eyes were watery. She had only ever seen Scott come close to crying once, just after the accident, and with Martin's assessment of how psycho he was, she hadn't expected tears in her living room. It unnerved her, and she tried to brush him off nonchalantly.

'How would you know? When was the last time you were in a car with them anyway?'

Scott looked away, working his jaw, before looking back at her and taking a breath.

'Before the crash was the last time either of us was in a car with them, Emelia. They didn't survive the accident. Either of them.'

Emmie nearly laughed out loud.

'What the hell are you talking about, Scott? They're right here, upstairs, where they've been since you got here.'

He shook his head face downcast.

'No, they're not. This has been the problem all along. You won't accept they're gone. I had to deal with the loss, the process of burying them, the grief, while you carried on chatting to them as though they were in the *fucking* room. Do you know how hard that was?'

Emmie blinked..

'They're right upstairs, Scott, I think maybe it's you that needs therapy. I can call them down.'

Scott put his head in his hands, elbows on his knees. She thought he was crying for a moment, but when he spoke his voice was even.

'Go ahead. Be my guest.'

Emmie left him on the settee and went to the stairs. Dread fell over her like a cloak. She hadn't heard them playing for a while now, and usually, Grace's chatter could be heard from any part of the house. She stood at the bottom of the stairs listening to the ominous lack of noise.

The wind gusted and moaned around the front of the house, and the letterbox rattled, reminding her that the front door was locked. With the most significant threat now inside, they may need a quick escape. She slipped over to the door and turned the key, unlocking it, before putting the bunch of keys in her jeans pocket. Now they could get out without hesitation, or at least Nat and Mike could get in.

She remembered she had to get a message to Stuart too, and finally faced the stairs. She had to go up like it or not. She could hear nothing from the living room, it was as if Scott had vanished, but she knew that was just wishful thinking.

Swallowing hard, and taking an unsteady breath, she climbed up shakily. Her legs were like jelly, blood pumping in her ears as her heart pounded. At the top, the silence chilled her more. She decided to get her phone and text Stu and Nat before looking in the children's rooms. Scott could interrupt her checking on the children, but she had a feeling he wouldn't like her calling for back up.

She found the phone on her dressing table and swiped it unlocked. She typed in a quick message:

Scott's here. Don't rush. I think I can keep him calm, get here when you can. Drive carefully.

She sent it to both numbers simultaneously as Scott called up the stairs to her.

'Coming, I just had to pee.'

She crept to the bathroom and flushed the chain as she clicked the phone onto vibrate and stuffed it into the other pocket of her jeans thankful that these were boyfriend jeans and not skinnies.

'Have you found them?'

'I haven't looked yet.'

Emmie frowned, every hair on her head seemed to stand on end. They would have come running at her and Scott's voices by now, wouldn't they?

She hurried to Charlie's room and threw open the door. It was empty. She checked his wardrobe, under his bed and the nook beside his cabinet but he wasn't here. Concerned, but not quite at panic level, she went next door to the little room she had used as a studio. This room was now empty aside from a set of drawers. No one was hiding behind them. Her phone buzzed, and she sneaked a quick look while she was in the room. It was Stuart.

Please be careful, on my way.

She breathed a sigh of relief. The storm was bad, and would slow him a little, but he could still be here within fifteen to twenty minutes. She didn't need to hold on much longer by herself. As she put the phone back in her pocket, it buzzed again. She whipped it back out quickly. This time it was Nat.

Be careful Em. We're on the A9 sat nav says 30 mins but it's awful out here in the blizzard, we'll be there as soon as we possibly can. Love you, honey. X

Emmie felt herself relaxing, help wasn't far away now.

Scott's voice floated upstairs, and she heard him starting to climb them. Pushing the phone into her pocket, she stepped out of the little room and across to Grace's bedroom. She pushed open the door thinking she would see them together huddled on the bed or on the floor, but this room was empty too.

Panic finally swelled in her chest. She caught Scott coming down the landing out of the corner of her eye as she entered the room checking the wardrobe and bed as she had done in Charlie's room.

Scott stood in the doorway with a small smile on his face.

'Find them?' he said.

As he spoke, with that smile on his face, it hit her what was going on. She glowered at him, anger meeting the panic that was chorusing through her.

'What the fuck have you done with them?'

Scott had the decency to look shocked and back out of the doorway, but she knew it was fake. He could fake every emotion in the book.

'No, darling-'

'Where are they, Scott? What have you done with them?'

'Emelia, please, I haven't done anything, why would I? I was their god-damn father. I loved them as much as you did.'

He was still composed, not flinching at her accusations. He even had the audacity to roll his eyes at her. She flew at him banging her fists on his chest and arms. He took it with the indifference of windblown leaves batting off him.

'Where are they,' She screamed, 'You can't come up here and mess with my mind again Scott, I'm through with your shit. Get me the children and leave, before I call the police.'

'Mess with your mind? I-'

'Bring my children back, now!'

He lost some of his composure and grabbed her arms, eyes hard.

'Emelia, control yourself. I told you I don't have them, and neither do you.'

She struggled against his grip, but he was strong.

'They were right here. I picked them up from school just hours ago. They were as real as this house. Whatever you've done you'd better undo fast because if you've hurt them, Scott, I *will* kill you.'

Scott laughed fingers twisting into her elbows as she struggled against him. Pain shot up her arms.

'Oh, *I* didn't hurt them, Emelia. You did that all by yourself, sweet pea. I told you what happened.'

'No, Scott, I saw them. They were at the hospital. They were the *only* thing that made me want to get well and come home.'

Scott lost his temper, face going red as he spat at her.

'How the fuck do you deduce that they were fine? Look at the state you were in after they pulled you from the wreckage. The van hit the rear of the car. You were shown the pictures. There was nothing left of the back. There was nothing left of any of it. Even you were lucky to be alive.'

Emmie faltered. She had seen the pictures, and he was right. She hadn't been able to tell the front end from the back at first. The metal had seemed twisted into such a mess that it might never have been a car at all.

'But ... But they were there. I saw them. They were okay … they are okay. Stop it, Scott, please. Just get them and let me carry on with my life. I'm begging you, is that what you want? If you want me to beg, Scott, I will. Just please stop this.'

He tightened his grip on her arms again shaking her. She gasped, and tears pricked at her eyes.

'No, you stop it. I've been through hell while you've been in la-la land for the last couple of years. We were parents, Emelia, but it was me who had to deal with the fallout. Alone. You will never know what it's like to have to identify you're own children when they're so fucked up you're looking for any excuse that it's not them at all. You have no idea how fucking hard that was.'

His grip was painful and she tried to peel his fingers off but he was too far gone to notice. She whimpered, shaking.

'Scott, please-'

'Charlie came out of it the worst. The van hit his side of the car and he was black and blue. From the chest down they said there was barely a bone intact. But the worst was his face. It was so swollen and bruised I could hardly tell it was him. He only avoided being identified by his dental records because he had turned his face away from the van. The back of his head was missing. Completely fucking gone. I didn't see that, thank god, but I knew it was true from the angle and lie of it. He had a sheet over the top of his head. It had been ripped right off Emelia. Only Grace's car seat stopped his face from going with it.'

The picture she had found on the stairs flashed into her mind of Charlie with the top of his head missing. Emmie fell to her knees arms in the air as Scott still held them. The tears spilled over. She shook her head pushing the image away.

Scott was playing with her, wasn't he? How long had he been here? Weeks? Planting the photo's, driving home his game, plotting seeds for when he finally faced her? Anger surged.

'What the fuck is up with you? This is bullshit. They would never have told you that. You're a liar, Scott, you always were, and I hate you. Do you hear me, I hate you!'

He bent down so that he was on her level and let go of one of her arms forcing her chin up, thumb and forefinger pressed hard into each side of her jaw, so that she had to look at him.

'Some of it is deduced because when you look at an image like that, your mind makes up the rest. Fills in the blanks, whether the fuck you want it to or not. You were spared that image, darling, be fucking thankful. And Grace? Grace was worse in a way. Her face had been spared mostly, other than some missing teeth where she had hit the side of her car seat -'

The ground shifted, and Emmie thought she was going to faint. If Scott hadn't been holding her chin, pain forcing consciousness, she might well have done so. Instead, her stomach roiled and she threw up, Scott must have seen the signs. He let go of her chin and moved away in the nick of time, standing with his back to her. Everything came up and out over and over as the picture of Charlie and the wrecked car flooded her mind along with the squeal of the brakes and the looming van. And Grace? Emmie had a feeling she knew what had happened to Grace in Scott's game.

Or was it real?

What he was saying was resonating on a subterranean level deep in her consciousness.

Was this the truth?

She shook her head trying to hang on to her sanity.

No, this was a game, all a game. The children had been here just hours earlier. This was Scott. She knew how hard he played. She just needed to keep herself one step ahead, get the kids back safely and get him out.

Breathe, Em, breathe. Keep it together.

Her stomach hitched, but there was nothing left to come. She wiped at her mouth unsteadily and crawled away from the mess slowly and shakily. Her energy seemed to have drained away

'Finished?'

She couldn't answer him. He turned to her anyway grabbing her arm and forcing her to stand on her shaking legs, facing toward the stairs so that he didn't have to look at the mess. He hadn't been able to be in the same room as the children when they had been sick, even as babies. She leaned into him unconsciously for support and got a whiff of his aftershave and hair gel. Her stomach rolled again, and she retched. Nothing came up, but Scot jumped back angrily.

'For fuck sake, Emelia. You know I hate that. I asked if you were finished, are you or not?'

She nodded lightly as her stomach relaxed, still bubbling, but staying down for the moment.

'Good as I was saying-'

'Please Scott, I don't want to hear any more.'

He stepped back to her.

'Oh, I'm sorry darling, you don't? Let me see, did they offer that option to me when I was having to identify them? Look at their little faces, grey and lifeless, and decide if they were my children or not. Did they tell me I could stop? Did I have a choice? I don't think so. It was all good for you though, wasn't it? Sitting in denial as I sorted everything. So do you think I should stop Emelia? Do you think you should be spared what I went through? You need to wake up and face facts, darling.'

The shudders that went through her were violent, and the tears came again. Scott ignored her carrying on.

'As I was saying Grace was a little better to look at. Her face anyway. It's funny when you think about it; Grace only had a broken arm where the car seat had trapped it against the car door. She had more of Charlie's blood on her face than her own. They said her car seat could possibly have saved her life if it hadn't have been for the vans A-frame. It went through the window as the metal twisted, ripping it from the van, and forcing it through the car. It missed Charlie, sliding past him, but it penetrated Grace's seat with such force that it went straight through her chest. The upper part of her body would have been a mess. Luckily I didn't have to see that part.'

Emmie thought he might have been spared that part, but she certainly hadn't. She thought about the photos and the dreams, Grace in her Peppa top, heart in her hand.

Fix it, mommy.

Jesus Christ, Grace, how was mommy supposed to fix that?

And yet, as a mother, the thought killed her, she knew she should have been able to fix everything for her little girl and keep her safe. She gulped at air that seemed thick and stagnant.

'She had the Peppa Pig top on.' She whispered.

'Oh, you remember something then? She went mad for that top in Sainsbury's just two days before remember? Wanted to put it on straight away in the shop, we had to bring her out howling as we paid. Remember?'

Emmie nodded, and he laughed lightly.

'That Peppa top was as fucked as she was.'

However insensitive the comment seemed Emmie knew that it was true from the pictures and visions. She just didn't know how much he had planted here for her to validate his story.

Something bugged her with Grace though. He couldn't possibly plant visions and dreams. They were hers alone, which might mean he was telling the truth and that was unthinkable. She wouldn't allow herself down that path.

'Where are they, Scott?'

'Swallow Heath Cemetery. Home. Where you need to be. I can't take any more of this, Emelia, I can't have my kids, but I'm damned if I will lose you as well. I've had a tough couple of years but I'm okay now, we can make this work again.'

And what about me? I'm not okay. I'm not okay with any of this.

And Where the hell are Grace and Charlie? Could he really be so blasé if all this were true? Did a few photo's and visions mean anything or was this just a part of the lure? Maybe it was a coincidence that he had described the things she had seen. A pain was starting to wind it's way through her chest making it hard to breathe.

What am I supposed to believe? What am I supposed to do? Let him take me home? Whatever he's done with them he won't say until I go with him, and if I need to do that to get them back?

I have no choice, do I?

'Emelia?'

She nodded, and he grabbed her arm pulling her to her feet again.

'Well then, let's get going.'

She felt weak and battered as he strode downstairs ahead of her. She grabbed the bannister following him slowly. In the back of her mind, her dads voice was denouncing him with every step.

No sorry, no hugs, no we'll get through this? Just I'm okay, so now we can start again? What about you, Em? Where do you fit into all this? Where's the love and compassion? Do you not deserve that much?

She ignored him. She had no fight left in her. Her mind was whirling, and she was worried to death for Charlie and Grace. Scott wasn't an unknown, she had done it before, and she could do it again. If it meant getting the children back, then it was what she would do. It was all she could think to do.

Chapter 66

Scott smiled as he strode down the stairs. Things were finally going his way, and by tomorrow he would have Emelia right back where he wanted her. It had been easier than he thought, but he should have remembered that she didn't respond to the soft stuff. Once he had checked himself and started to go in hard, she had finally taken him seriously, giving in almost immediately. He could have done without her throwing up, though. It disgusted him to think of it sitting up there on the landing. It took all he had not to give her a cloth and tell her to go and clean it up.

He glanced up at her as he reached the bottom of the stairs. She was holding the bannister as though she were eighty years old, at this rate she may not even be downstairs by tomorrow. Irritation tensed his jaw, but he bit it back.

It was a pathetic little act she was performing, and he would need to get it under control, but he would have plenty of time to knock her into shape back at home.

She owed him. Lots. For the children, the divorce and moving up here.

And he intended to collect. The first thing on his list was to re-marry, the divorce should never have gone ahead in the first place. It was incredible to think that he had gone that far but he had needed to make her see the consequences of her actions.

In the end, though, she knew as much as he did that they were made for each other.

Soul mates.

She could do with some makeup though, he thought. She looked terrible.

Emmie reached the bottom of the stairs, sat down with a thud and put her head in her hands, her shoulders shaking. Scott sighed and rolled his eyes.

'You have five minutes to get yourself together, Emelia,' he said.

She didn't acknowledge him, so he went into the kitchen to see if there was anything they could take to use back in Surrey although after the living room he didn't hold out much hope. There the furniture was worn, and the TV looked as though it belonged in the 1980's. The kitchen wasn't much better. Everything seemed a little worse for wear; even the large table looked second hand. Scott wrinkled his nose in disgust and shuddered.

How many times had he told her that being an artist wasn't a proper job? And fiddling with paint obviously wasn't helping her out here either, at home, he had been subsidising her with a damn good wage. She should have given it up and been satisfied with looking after the children, after all, how many husbands allowed their wives to stay at home and do nothing all day? She was damn lucky. Come to think of it, if she hadn't been at some promotional thing she was all proud of, she would never have been involved in the accident at all, and everything would have been very different now.

His breathing was getting heavier and more ragged as the memories came back and he put a hand on the table for support. Everything would have been very different, indeed.

Anger flared in his gut. She wouldn't be allowed to carry on painting in his house. It had killed his kids. *She* had killed his kids with her stupid fiddling around. He had paid dearly for letting her have her obsession.

He took a moment to calm himself before crossing the almost bare playroom without a second glance, nothing in here, and entering the sunroom.

It was freezing in here. The French doors were still open, the wind and snow howling into the room. Scott pushed at the snow on the floor with his feet and shut the doors with a thump. He looked up, catching his reflection in the glass. He hesitated.

His reflection wasn't the only thing there.

The shadow outside the window was big, menacing and very man-like.

Or was it inside? It seemed to be looming up behind him.

He staggered back heart pounding as he swung around.

What the fuck?

He surveyed the empty space behind him and swung his head back to the glass. No shadow. Only his reflection remained.

Had he imagined it?

He put his face closer to the glass searching as his eyes adjusted to the darkness outside. Nothing. Shit, the shadows played tricks in these open spaces, the sooner they got back to Surrey the better.

He turned away from the doors, goosebumps running down his arms, and stopped when he came across a photo of Grace and Charlie on the little table. He faltered, stunned for a moment, thrown off stride. He stared before picking it up and running his fingers over it.

They seemed older in this picture, which was impossible.

Shuddering he stepped back into the living room, seeking warmth after the cold of the sunroom, still clutching the photograph.

Something about the setting seemed familiar, but it wasn't somewhere he thought he had ever been with them. He looked down at the photo again. Then he noticed the settee they were sitting on and the magnolia wall behind them.

Scott stopped dead and turned, his back to the fire. He looked at the photo, back up into the room, and back to the photograph.

'What the fuck?'

Is this how far she would go in an attempt to keep them alive?

He cursed and screwed the paper into a ball, throwing the photo into the fire in disgust. What did she think she was playing at mucking around with pictures to make them seem current? It was deluded, *she* was deluded, and she would be going straight back to therapy. That would be priority number two when they got home.

Scott shuddered. He had to get out of here. This place was starting to put him on edge. It was like she was getting into his mind and clouding his judgement. And that fucking wind sounded like the hounds of hell were loose outside. There was nothing here of use, all she owned was a pile of second-hand shit.

Time to go.

He went back into the hallway and saw she was sitting in the same place he had left her. A new stab of anger ran through him.

'Ok Emelia, enough is enough, it's time to go. Get yourself together I won't have this snivelling all the way back to Surrey. We have a lot to discuss we can make better use of the time.'

She looked up, white as a sheet, her eyes red. She looked so sorry for herself that Scott almost felt a stab of pity, but he had work to do driving them back home in this storm. He wouldn't let her drag him down.

'Get up, Emelia, it's time to go.'

She struggled to get up and fell sitting back down again with a huff. With a sigh he strode over to her and pulled her up, grabbing her coat, and putting it on for her like she was a small child. God, She was utterly useless when she heard news she didn't like, it had been the same when her father had died. It was only when he had got strict and had forced her to get up and carry on that she had stopped the moping. She would soon be over the children, and she could move forward as he had. She was fragile, she just needed a push to help her along.

He zipped her coat up as she stared into space. At least the tears had stopped, but she looked like hell. He wrinkled his nose in distaste and turned toward the door.

Things definitely needed to change.

Chapter 67

Emmie watched Scott's back as he walked toward the door. The set of his shoulders, the way he carried himself, the gait of his walk. She knew it all. It was so familiar it was like slipping back into a pair of old shoes. The trouble was, these shoes weren't very comfortable, they held a feeling of instability, tension and unpredictability.

Unease swirled in her gut. If she went back to Surrey, she knew all the feelings she would go through living with him again; unease, uncertainty, worry, fear. All the emotions that had ruled her marriage to Scott. At the time she had thought it was okay, it was worth it, she had loved him immeasurably, and he was the children's father. She had felt the good outweighed the bad, and anyway, she hadn't known where she would go or what she would do without him. His intense love and control had been her security.

She hadn't thought she could cope without him.

But she could. She had. She had more than survived here; she had thrived. And all without Scott's help.

Are you ready to throw it all away and go back with him? Back to the crap you used to deal with each day?

Her heart pattered as he threw open the door and looked back at her.

And there it was. That face, that look, that stance.

She faltered, a flutter of both resolve and fear trickling through her. She couldn't risk everything she had here. She had to buy time, to think what to do about the children, but there was no way she could leave with him. She couldn't be with him ever again.

What do I do? I need to get back upstairs I didn't look for the kids in my room, they could be there. Couldn't they?

She felt a little sick at the thought of the Grace and Charlie, and her heart started to thud.

What in the heck is going on? Where are they? And why would he feel the need to tell me they died in the crash? What advantage does that give him?

She couldn't think of one which made her blood run cold.

But they had been here. Emmie already had so many memories of them here, how could all of that be wrong? And yet something nagged.

Scott sighed and stared at her with his hands out, palms up.

'Christ, Emelia! The storm is raging, we have a long journey ahead of us, and you're standing there like a vegetable. Pull yourself together we need to go.'

'Maybe we should stay. The storm is supposed to abate tomorrow we could stay here tonight and leave in the morning when it's light.'

He looked at her incredulous.

'I'm not staying any longer in this cold, shitty, little house. It gives me the creeps out here. I don't know how you sleep. Now let's go.'

He stepped forward to grab her arm, and she inadvertently moved back. A hard look passed over his face, and he was back to working his jaw again.

'What's the matter now?'

'I … don't get angry with me, Scott, please. Not after what you just told me. I couldn't deal with that now too.'

His face softened, and she let out a small relieved breath through her nose. He gave her a quick pat on the shoulder, taking his hand away but staying close, his scent turning her stomach over for the second time.

That smell enveloped an abundance of memories and feelings she would rather forget. It reminded her so much of the life she had left behind. The life she hadn't realised was so rigid until she'd had the freedom of living alone, on her terms.

'I'm not angry, Emelia. I want to get out of here and take you home. Being up here has dragged you down, darling, you need to smile more.' He paused smiling at her, 'Not to worry, I'm planning a little party when we get back, a little pre-wedding affair because I want us to get married again, Emelia. I want to start over.'

How fabulous. Are you going to ask me if I want to marry you? Or do you think I should just fall in line while you start over?

I think that's precisely what you're supposed to do Em. Suck it up, you lucky lady. Your ship has come in Scott style.

Emmie closed her eyes fighting back the tears. Where the hell were Stu and Nat and Mike? She didn't know how much longer she could keep him stalled without angering him, and Scott wasn't good with tears.

One slipped out anyway, running slowly down her cheek. To her surprise, Scott's hand appeared on her cheek to rub it away, and her eyes flew open at his touch. He was smiling, and she forced a small one back. Her head was starting to pound as much as her heart.

'I know, sweet pea, it's too much, isn't it? It's got to be one of my happiest days too. I've missed you so much. And how much have you missed all of your friends? Lots I'll bet, and I'll invite them all. Amy too, I bet you are just dying to see her, am I right?'

Emmie looked at the floor and nodded chewing her lip remembering the conversation at the falls. He gripped her chin forcing her to meet his eyes.

'Well?'

'Yes, Scott.'

A small spark of anger ran through her stomach.

... And I bet you are just dying to see her too you bike riding, whore shagging bastard. How many ways have you taken her in our bed, Scott? And now I'm supposed to move home and play happy families and best friends? Lie where she lay and spread my legs for you? Ha!

The ache in her jaw was becoming unbearable, and she tried to peel his fingers from her chin. A flicker of emotion crossed his face as he let her go and stroked a hand down her cheek instead.

An icy chill crept down her back, enticing a blanket of goosebumps out from under her skin. She barely controlled a shiver as she stood, not breathing, waiting for Scott to finish as he traced his fingers down her neck and around under her hair.

'You're going to be a good girl, Emelia, aren't you?' He whispered, 'I've missed you so much. You'll get over the children, and we will be as happy as we've ever been, you'll see. You can have anything you want, darling.'

She closed her eyes again. Disgusted that he could mention the children so casually. A dull ache filled her heart. She was so confused and so damn worried.

Even with her eyes closed, she was hyper-aware of how close Scott was and the fact that his hand was still in her hair at the back of her neck. His fingers massaged upward winding through her hair which seemed to be standing on end at his touch.

And then Scott pressed his lips to hers, free hand coming up to cup her breast. She cried out, eyes flying open, heart pounding out of her chest. Slapping his hand away, she pushed him back with a grunt, planting both of her hands on his chest. He stumbled back in surprise, swinging her around and dragging her with him by the hair as he clamped his hand shut. Finding his footing, he twisted hard making her yelp as he turned her toward him. He glowered, wrapping tighter, drawing her near. Pain screamed at the back of her neck, and she felt hair tear loose in his grip.

'What the fuck was that?'

Fear and panic gripped her as anger penetrated his dark eyes.

'I ... I ... you scared me, Scott, I'm s ... sorry. I d ... didn't expect it, that's all.'

'Oh, I scare you? Is that right, Emelia. I fucking *scare* you? I knew it was too good to be true. You don't know how to behave, you never did, making my life harder with your smart mouth. Thinking you can go and do whatever you want; whenever you want. I've got news for you. The rules are going to be different this time around.'

He pulled her in close to him still keeping his iron grip on her hair. His lips were drawn back over clenched teeth, spittle landing on her face.

'You'd better start learning fast darling because your life will be a lot easier if you don't pull stunts like that. The crash, losing the kids, it changed me. I can be a sweetheart, of course, but I can also be an unforgiving bastard. You don't want to fuck with the bad side of me now, Emelia. I'm no longer a pussycat when I'm pissed off. Your life will be as good as you make it.'

Emmie swallowed hard whimpering at the level of pain just from a hand in her hair.

The resonance and truth of the statement hung inside her head. Life would be as good as she made it, and it was up to her alone to sort the mess out. She needed to get Scott out of her house, and then she could concentrate on the children. Logically, he hadn't had time to have taken them anywhere. They had been upstairs, so they were either still hiding up there or … well.

She pushed the thought down. She needn't think about that right now. Scott's voice cut through her thoughts as he twisted harder, pulling more hair loose and making her yelp.

'You also need to listen. That was never your strong point either was it? What did I just say, Emelia?'

She scrabbled for her thoughts frantically, what the hell had he just said?

'M … my life will b … b … be as good as I … I make it.'

He let go of her hair, relief flooding through her as the pain relented.

And then his palm connected with her cheek wrenching her head sideways with a sickening crack. Pain exploded through her jaw the impact almost knocking her off her feet. She fell, landing on the cool floor, the wind knocked out of her lungs. Trying to catch her breath, she blinked as he stood towering over her. Slowly she crawled onto all fours pain shooting through her right elbow and hip where she had landed. Scott kicked a boot at her catching her ribs forcing the breath from her lungs again. Rocking her back onto her heels.

'Stay down there. I don't want to look at you. I'm going to tell you what will happen now, Emelia. I've had enough of this shit. We are getting up, and we are going to the car. I don't care whether you like it or not, whether you even think you want to. You will come home, where you are supposed to be, and you will learn not press my buttons like you just did. I love you, Emelia, and I don't want to hurt you. If you just learn to behave we can have a damn good life. We were meant to be together, and I will not let you destroy us like you destroyed our children. Did you hear that? or were you busy staring off into space again?'

Oh, I heard you asshole, and it will happen over my dead body. I'm through letting you push me around.

Squatting back on her heels, it hadn't escaped her attention that she was directly in line with his most delicate area. She gritted her teeth and pushing through the pain in her elbow, she brought her fist back and fired it at him with all the force she had, hitting him squarely on target. Unprepared, he grunted and doubled over.

Emmie got to her feet, ignoring the pain, and dealt him a further swift hard kick to the same region. Her boots had more impact, and he fell to his knees, eyes bulging.

Taking the opportunity, she ran to the living room. She needed a place to hide, and fast, she could hear his grunts in the hallway and knew he would soon be after her.

But there was simply nowhere to hide in here, and she kicked herself for only acquiring basic furniture. Adrenaline surged as she ran into both the sunroom and the playroom, quickly assessing that there was nowhere in those rooms either.

At the door from the playroom to the kitchen, Emmie came to a stop. She swivelled her head between the sunroom door and the kitchen, heart thudding, as she tried not to breathe. Was Scott still in the hallway? If he was, she would come full circle and meet him.

A shuffle emanated from the direction of the sunroom, and the hairs stood up on her neck.

Was that Scott? Or just a house noise? She felt frozen to the spot unable to decide, until she heard him call.

'Emelia? Where are you, sweet pea? Come to daddy, honey. I need to show you how wrong that was, and on how many *fucking* levels.'

His voice started sweetly enough but ended in rage. Emmie began to shake breathing hard, but she was pretty sure his voice had come from the living room. Moving into the kitchen, she quietly pulled the door closed behind her and crept to the fridge wedging herself between it and the kitchen door to conceal herself. Peering around the door, she saw the hall was empty.

Her breathing came fast and raspy, and she felt her head spin as she tried to think.

Come on, Em, concentrate, you can't keep running in circles. Where can you go except outside where you'll freeze to death? We need to play hide and seek, not cat and mouse.

There was a bang from the sunroom, and she realised he was either throwing furniture or at least pushing it around in temper, which was usual in Scott land, but she thought of his earlier words about no longer being a pussycat, and she knew she had to move. There would be no talking to him once he really let the anger go and he was escalating pretty quick, even by Scott standards.

Hide and seek.

Emmie gasped as she remembered Grace's hiding place in her wardrobe. The little cubby hole concealed behind her clothes.

She had no idea whether she would fit, and she would be trapped upstairs if she couldn't, but at this moment there didn't seem to be any other solution, and he was gaining on her fast. She unzipped her coat, dropping it to the floor; there was no way she would get into the small space with extra layers.

From behind her came a low growl, and Emmie almost jumped out of her skin as Scott pushed the door from the playroom into the kitchen so hard it crashed into the back wall.

Fear propelling her blindly toward the stairs, she ran, convinced he would drag her back at any second. Swinging around the bannister, she took the stairs two at a time as she heard his voice carry into the hallway.

'Ah! Unless an elephant is ascending the stairs it appears you'd like to trap yourself up there would you, Emelia? All the better for me, my love.'

Emmie's heart dropped, and she lunged for the top of the stairs before he could get into the hall and see her. On the landing she had trouble getting to her feet, so she crawled on hands and knees to her room, thanking the lord it was the closest to the top of the stairs.

'I'm coming sweet pea, remember you just told me you were scared of me? You'd fucking better be after that little stunt, darling.'

She heard him start up the stairs as she entered her room. Scrabbling to her feet she swung the bedroom door closed cringing at the squeak from the hinges, and moved to the wardrobe as quickly and quietly as she could. She opened the door and swung her clothes aside. Now that she knew the little cubby hole was there it seemed glaringly obvious. She faltered. Was she was digging her own grave?

Scott reached the top of the stairs, and Emmie quickly opened the hatch. It was small - really small - but she had no choice now. Climbing into the wardrobe and shutting the door behind her with a quiet click she turned to fold herself into the gap.

She froze mid climb as she heard the door to her bedroom squeak open.

'Emeeeelia. Where for art thou Emeeeelia?'

His voice was low and sing-song, and her heart pumped so loud she was sure it would give her position away. She stayed as still as she could trying not to breathe while paradoxically needing to gulp air to stop the blackness that was starting to grey the edge of her vision.

He entered the room, His boots thumping as he searched. He rustled the bedclothes, looking in it or under it, maybe both. And then he reached the wardrobe. All went quiet. He was breathing heavy and fast, and was so close Emmie thought she could even smell him through the solid wood.

She closed her eyes knowing that he was right behind the door and if he opened it she would be seen immediately. She didn't dare breathe, her eyes opened, boring into the door waiting for any slither of movement that would cement her found and at his mercy.

And then he moved away, footfalls retreating from the room as she heard him call down the hall. She let out a shaky breath, and trembling from head to toe, pushed aside her hanging clothes as quietly as she could enabling her to fold her shaking, jelly-like body into the small crevice. Sweat ran in rivulets down her face, and her shaking fingers slipped as she tried to hold on to the sides pushing herself inside bottom first, head bent down, tucking her legs in front of her. There was a little more room widthways, so she scooted herself around until she was side on to the small door, head bent down to her knees.

She could hear Scott in the other rooms banging around, overturning God knew what. His voice had got less sing-song and more aggressive as he travelled from room to room and came up with nothing. She heard his thumping steps come back down the hall and knew he had stepped into the bathroom when she heard the shower curtain flick back.

Panic took hold as she realised he was near. He hadn't upended anything in her room yet, he had probably come back to have another check, and that would involve the wardrobe this time, she was sure. In her haste, Emmie pulled the door too hard by its little leather handle and it swung in an arc catching some of the clothes hanging on the rail above. Coat hangers screeched and knocked on the metal rail as clothes fell and others got dragged by the edge of the little door.

She heard the pause in his movements, felt his curiosity and his anger in the silence. Working as quickly as she dared with shaking hands she pushed the clothes caught on the door out of the way and tried to pull it shut, but there was still something stuck. She tugged the strap, frantic, as Scott's grunts reached the wardrobe, but it wouldn't click shut.

'I should have known you would have chosen the most childish place to hide. Really, Emelia.'

She barely contained a small whimper of terror. She pulled hard on the strap, glanced down and realised it was her shoe, her own damn shoe, that was holding the door open, she moved her foot a fraction, and the door clicked flush as the wardrobe door swung open.

Shaking and sweating curled up in the little alcove, Emmie hugged her legs, head on her knees. The only position she was able to be in the confined space. Heart thumping and breath ragged between her knees, she struggled for air in the box. Everything seemed to slip away from her.

Scott had heard the click of the door for sure, and even if he hadn't, it stuck out like a sore thumb in the white wall. Even if he didn't realise what it was, he would only have to lean on it for it to pop open.

Clothes swished on the rail, screeching along the metal as he moved them.

'Got ya.' He shouted, making her flinch in the small space. But the door didn't open. Instead, she heard him tossing around her shoes and pulling everything down from the shelves. Finally, it went quiet, and there was only a grunt. Emmie closed her eyes and tried not to breathe. The seconds ticked by excruciatingly until he banged the wardrobe door shut and stomped out of the room.

'Emelia! Where the fuck are you, you little bitch?'

Emmie broke down in the box, tears coming thick and fast, fear and hopelessness taking over.

Where was everyone? If they were much longer, she thought they might just find her butchered in her own house. Another sacrifice for her bloodthirsty Bruadair. Sobbing, she realised she had no idea how to stop the raging bull that used to be the person she loved more than anyone in the whole world.

She shuddered, scrubbing at her tears, trying to think. This box was torture; she couldn't stay here. It was hot and claustrophobic, and air seemed to be none existent. There was also the small matter of being so crunched up she couldn't move.

What the hell am I going to do? I can't sit here and wait for help. I need to sort this mess out; the state Scott's in I don't know how far he'll go and I don't want Stu, Nat or Mike hurt because of me.

She racked her brains, coming up with nothing at all, until Grace came up with the answer, her voice so clear she could have been holed up with her inside the box.

'Get the dead gun, mommy, the dead gun!'

Chapter 68

Down in the living room, Scott dug the heel of his hand into his breastbone as the pain stabbed in his chest. The rage had descended, his breathing was ragged, red falling over his vision, but he had nothing to direct it at except furniture.

He wanted to direct it at her.

Little bitch, he'd offered to take her away from here, marry her, and give her the life she wanted again. He had offered her a second chance, even after what she had done. He wanted to ask her just how many husbands she thought would be willing to take back a wife who had murdered his fucking children.

He knew the answer was none. Which made him a fucking saint and she'd kicked him in the balls for his effort?

He turned to the chair, one of the only things left upright now, lips curled back in a snarl and grasped the underneath, hurling it into the cupboard, and then he turned and pulled the ugly bulk of the clock away from the wall, giving it a shove as it fell. It managed to flip over, despite its size, landing face up across the doorway, glass shattering loudly. He looked at it, breathing hard.

The infernal ticking had stopped at least.

He put a hand up to his chest, massaging. He couldn't remember if he had hurt himself during the rampage at home, but it felt like something was tightening inside him cutting off his breath, maybe he had pulled a muscle.

Fucking typical, but no big deal. Emelia was his priority at the moment.

He listened to the house, but there was no sound apart from the crackle of the fire.

Where the fuck had she gone? The bitch had literally kicked him in the balls and disappeared off the face of the earth. It was driving him insane, how hard could it be to find someone in such a sparsely furnished house?

He had already destroyed most of the furniture down here, checking every little nook and cranny. His muscles were thrumming with the effort, sweat ran down his face, which felt on fire, and his breath was coming in big, short ragged gulps over the sharp pain.

He pushed it aside, pain or no pain, when he finally caught up with her, he would rip her apart with his bare hands. He had no doubt that he could accomplish it, she was tiny, he would snap her like a twig and go home. It was a shame, and he would miss her. He already missed her, but he couldn't live his life with her being so unruly. She had to go.

Act One over. Slate clean. Start a-fucking-gain. Simple.

He snarled, stalking out of the living room and back to the stairs. He would turn all of the rooms over again one by one, and if he still couldn't find her, he would set the house on fire and smoke her out.

She was up there somewhere; he could almost hear her heartbeat as she waited in terror. Well, he would put her out of her misery.

He took the steps two at a time.

Chapter 69

Emmie listened inside the cubby hole. She needed a sign; something to pinpoint where Scott was so that she could make a move. The gun was her only hope. Her only defence against someone so big and volatile.

She had a feeling Scott was still downstairs, but the sound of destruction had stopped, and she didn't want to open the door until she knew for sure.

Then, another resounding crash from downstairs.

Emmie's heart pumped.

Shit, he's going to wreck my house, there'll be nothing left.

Shaking she clicked the door open and pulled herself out as smoothly and quietly as she could, relishing the cold air that wrapped itself around her. She was soaked in sweat, hair hanging in wet tendrils around her face. Her hip and elbow throbbed from the earlier fall, and being squashed up in the tight space. She pushed her fringe back out of her eyes waiting for another crash from downstairs before opening the wardrobe.

The room was empty.

As she crept onto the landing, she could hear him below, muttering obscenities. She stayed back from the spindled rail. If he were in the hall he would see her, and if possible, she wanted the element of surprise. Instead, she lay down on her belly and shuffled forward, peering down into the hall as much as she dared.

She waited, listening.

He came into view from the living room, and she drew in a sharp breath. He no longer seemed like a man. He appeared bull-like. Head down and hair mussed in a way he would never usually allow he blew heavily, almost grunting, through his nose. He stalked to the stairs, his body rigid under hunched shoulders and clenched hands. His head snaked from left to right like some strange mythical creature. He looked up toward the landing, and the sight of his face almost stopped her heart.

Scott was beet red and flushed, mouth set in a perpetual snarl. His eyes narrowed as he looked up from under his heavy dark eyebrows. Emmie could see that his hazel eyes were bloodshot and as she watched a string of saliva left his mouth and hung before dropping to the floor.

She put her head down to the floor to avoid being seen and then listened in horror as he started to climb the stairs.

Fast.

And now she was in plain view, lying across the landing.

Back Em! Back! Back! Back!

Heart flying up into her mouth she scooted backwards on her belly, hoping his footfalls would mask any noise as she aimed herself at the bathroom behind her. Crossing the threshold, she scurried inside on her knees just as he reached the top. Heart hammering, she pressed herself quietly behind the door, watching through the crack by the hinges.

From here she had a perfect view of the top of the stairs. She watched as Scott paused, holding the bannister panting. He rubbed his chest as he cocked his head stiffly still blowing through his nose like a crazed animal.

'Emelia? Come to daddy Emelia.'

He grinned through the snarl (or was it a grimace?) and stalked down the landing to the children's rooms.

Emmie gasped for air behind the door. She had no idea who or what that was, but it was no longer Scott, and she was no longer scared of him.

She was terrified.

So terrified she wanted to curl up into a ball and cry, only stopping when it was all over, and he had gone.

Move Em. Now! There won't be another opportunity with him as far from you as he is at the moment.

Her dad's voice was both soothing and firm, and she knew he was right, but she physically couldn't move.

I'm scared, dad. I don't know if I can do it.

You have to honey. You have no choice. He's out of control. Move now! Go!

She forced herself out of the bathroom, stepping onto the landing. She didn't need to check where Scott was, she could hear him in Grace's room. He was huffing and grunting as he threw things around. If he continued with that noise, she had the advantage. Her dad was right, it was now or never.

She moved to the edge of the wall, heart pounding in her ears with every frantic beat, legs barely supporting her. She pressed her back to the wall, took a shaky breath, and peered around the corner toward the children's rooms. There was no sign of Scott, but he was still in Grace's bedroom, she could hear his ragged breathing. The heavy throwing had stopped, and she didn't know whether this was a good thing or a bad, but while she couldn't see him, she had to move. Taking a breath, she ran.

At the top of the stairs, she grabbed the bannister and descended as quickly as she dared on rubber legs.

She was at the turn when she heard him.

'Welcome back, bitch. Where do you think you're going?'

His voice boomed, coming in bursts with his heavy breath as he crashed down the landing. She whimpered and looked back catching his gaze full on. He was coming fast, red-faced, hand still on his chest, bloodshot eyes bulging as they bored into hers and for a brief moment she thought he looked unwell. And then she caught herself. He *was* unwell, that was a fact.

Emmie jumped the bottom few steps and ran to the kitchen. She skidded around the door stopping herself with the door handle of the fridge which shook on its base making the contents jangle and crash together. She heard Scott hit the bottom step into the hallway and the thud of his boots coming toward the kitchen as he grunted.

She put her hand up to the top of the fridge fingers fumbling for the Smith and Wesson she had placed there only days before. She nudged it with the tip of her fingers, pushing it away and frantically grabbed for it again, her hand closing around the grip as Scott came in through the kitchen door. She fumbled with the gun trying to get a solid, believable grip as Bill had instructed, while her hands shook so violently she could barely hold it.

Scott had come straight into the kitchen, past the fridge, giving her valuable seconds as she backed up to the wall and got both hands around the gun, one shaking forefinger over the trigger. As he turned, Emmie put her trembling arms straight out, pointing the gun at him.

Scott reeled back. He still had his hand on his chest, his breathing ragged and shallow. The snarl was still on his face, although Emmie wasn't sure that it wasn't a snarl of pain, not anger. She kept the gun trained on him.

'You're going to ... fucking shoot me?' He said, gulping a noisy breath.

Her voice wavered, and she fought to sound confident.

'If I need to. It's you or me, Scott. I can't go on like this, and I'm not going back with you. Being alone has made me realise how tense I was when we lived together. I was constantly on edge, always fearing your moods when you came home. I can't live like that again. We're divorced now, Scott, lets just leave it alone.'

'Leave it alone? Not a chance, sweet pea, I've driven miles up here to get to you -.' He stopped pushing his hand into his chest momentarily before looking back at her. '- And I just re-pulled a muscle playing your stupid games. It fucking hurts, and I'm pissed Emelia. I want to go home.'

He did look hurt. And that was okay. It was to her benefit. Surely Nat, Mike, and Stu couldn't be much longer. She just had to hold him here with the gun for a while, and she would be okay.

'Go home then. I'm not stopping you, but I'm not coming with you. I'm happy here, the happiest I've ever been.'

Scott eyed the gun angrily, and she knew he was deciding if the risk was significant enough. She was feeling more comfortable now. The gun was working on him, and the shakes were slowing. She was starting to gain confidence. She pointed it at him with more intention. He stayed where he was glowering at her.

'Oh you're *happy* here, are you? Happy?' He laughed. Harsh, ragged grunts, before abruptly becoming serious. 'Who the fuck is he? I'll tear him a-fucking-part. I knew there was someone the way you reacted in the hall.'

Emmie huffed a laugh.

'Oh Christ, Scott, it always comes down to that, doesn't it? And you're a hypocrite. I'm aware you've been sleeping with Amy. She let it slip when I spoke to her Saturday.'

He didn't flinch. He merely cocked a lip and rolled his eyes. Emmie steeled the gun at him and almost wished it was live and loaded. She would happily have emptied all six rounds into his chest for that look.

'I was. Not anymore. She was a treat in bed. She could teach you a thing or two, Emelia, but in the end, she was just too fucking whiny. I don't know how you put up with that infernal whining about everything. She actually thought she could take your place which is just a big joke really isn't it? She isn't a patch on you, she just fulfilled a need while you were busy running around up here pretending to live your life.'

Emmie's heart pumped as anger swelled inside her. Fulfilled a need? Amy had been her best friend. Whether she still was was debatable, but Amy should have been off limits no matter how far away she was. Emmie was as disappointed in Amy as she was in Scott.

'Well, that's okay then. I guess we're even. You're right, there is someone, and you know what Scott? *You* aren't a patch on him. If you love me so much, you should go home and let me pick up what's left of my life.'

Scott's face contorted in anger. He took a step nearer, only the table between them, and she watched as he grabbed it and flung it aside, vegetables and paring knife flying across the room. She whimpered, lowering the gun involuntarily, and struggling to raise it up toward him again. He may not look well, but his strength was still there, and she was still terrified of the inhuman look on his face. He hesitated, hand back to his chest, face contorting in pain as he leaned forward gasping air. She noticed his face losing some of its redness, his skin taking on a clammy, pale pallor as he stood back up. She faltered, gun lowering again.

'Are you … are you okay, Scott? You don't look well.'

He snarled again, gasping for air as he spoke.

'I'm just fucking dandy … Sweet pea … don't you worry. You're coming home … to … to finish the life… we started. You belong to me … no one else gets to have you … you dirty whore.'

He lunged forward, and Emmie jumped back reflexively, but her back was already at the wall. Her elbow crashed into it, and she tried to keep the stars out of her eyes at the surge of pain. Scott grabbed at his chest again and staggered to the fridge putting his free hand out to catch his weight and then he made a grab for her.

She yelled, her finger involuntarily squeezing the trigger of the gun. Scott caught himself on the fridge again as there was a small click. The snarl on his face turned to a half contorted grin as he looked at her, and Emmie's heart plummeted as she realised the implications of what she had done.

'Oh … oh dear. No bullets?'

She tried to run, but he staggered forward grabbing her arm, and then she was falling as he let out a blood-curdling moan. She realised he was falling with her, and for a second she thought she would be able to get out of his way, but he struck her with his full force knocking her into the overturned table. Head crashing against the edge she collapsed to the floor, his weight on top of her.

The lights went out. Her world turned black.

Chapter 70

Emmie found herself ankle deep in snow, a blizzard flurrying around her. The snow fell thick, and flakes landed lightly on her nose and cheeks. Charlie and Grace were next to her, both unnaturally quiet. Charlie, in a blue hat and snowsuit, was holding her hand, and Grace, in an identical red set up, was holding onto her leg.

They had no gloves, any of them, and Emmie wondered why in the world she had come out here without them. It was careless. She had no idea where she was, but taking the children out in a storm was stupid. She had to get them back home.

She shivered as she searched for something - anything - an anchor point to work from to figure out where she was, and where she needed to go, but everywhere looked identical. There was nothing but white. No contours, no breaks in the white landscape, and it was cold, so damn cold. She rubbed at grace's back as she stood shivering, fear fluttering through her.

Get out of the blizzard Emmie. There are too many flakes. It will swamp you.

'Dad?' She said, eyes widening. She tried to face where she had thought the voice had come from, grasping for direction in the linear landscape.

They're clouding your vision. You need to get out.

'I don't know how. I'm not sure which way to go.'

You know the way, it's time sweetheart.

'Should I come to you?'

No honey, I'm not an option. Go back.

'Back where? There's nowhere to go.'

Get out of the blizzard. Get to the clearing.

Emmie looked behind her. He wasn't making any sense. The view seemed no different to the one in front, but if he said to go back, then she would go back. Wherever that was. She turned and began to walk, slowly at first, going at Grace's pace as she picked her way through the snow and then faster as the landscape didn't alter and the snow kept falling.

With a grunt of frustration she picked Grace up, holding her in one arm, and jogging as fast as she was able, holding Charlie's hand with the other.

It wasn't long before her lungs burned with the frigid air, and her face and hands felt as if they were made of ice. Placing Grace back on the floor, Emmie raked in breath after breath, each one burning like fire. She straightened, breathing heavily, careful to keep facing the same way. She didn't know why this was important, but she had to stay on track.

'Dad?'

There was no answer, just falling snow. Snow which had already risen to Emmie's calves and was nearly covering Grace's thighs. She frowned.

Was it that deep a few moments ago?

She had to keep going. They couldn't stay here.

Lifting Grace out of the snow, she started to walk again, Concentrating on keeping as straight as she could. At one point she glanced back over her shoulder, but no trace of their footprints remained. It was as if the blizzard was erasing all existence as they went. It was as if they were on a treadmill, getting nowhere.

Stopping again, pain from the cold edging its way into her fingers and toes, Emmie shifted trying to keep warm. The snow was creeping up higher, flake by flake. It would come over the top of her boots soon, it was already over the top of Charlie's, and he was starting to look pale.

Panic curled its way into fear as she realised her dad was right, the snow would literally swamp them if she didn't get out; and quickly.

'Dad?' She shouted. 'Help me please, I don't know what to do. I can't get out, it all looks the same.'

Frantic, Emmie kicked at the snow in frustration as his voice came back.

Running is not the answer. Stand and face it.

Emmie wished he would stop speaking in riddles. If running

wasn't the answer then what? She couldn't get out if she didn't move. She shouted into the storm.

'Face what? I need to get out the snow is rising, it's too fast. The children will be covered, dad! Help me, please.'

Emmie, you need to leave the children, they can't make it, let them rest.

'They don't need to rest,' She shouted.

They can't keep up with you, let them go.

'No! I won't leave them.'

There is no way for them to get out, you know it in your heart, let them go, the snow will claim you if you stay. They will be safe here.

Emmie shook her head, hair sticking to her face in wet strips. Grace clung to her neck as she held her, but she could see the snow climbing up to Charlie's thighs. He would no longer be able to walk soon either, and she hadn't got the strength to carry them both. She pulled him to her side, panic rising to terror.

No!' She shrieked into the snow, 'They'll be killed. What do I do? Tell me what to do, I can make it with us all.'

That's not an option. You need to go forward. The children are safe there is nothing more you can do. Stop carrying them.

'I won't do that. I can't.'

You have to Emmie.

'I don't have the strength to leave them. It will kill me.'

You don't have the strength to take them.

'I'll die trying.'

That's a certainty you can't afford; you have things left to do. You need to get to the clearing.

'Mom, we can stay. The snow won't hurt us, I can get Grace out. I can keep her safe.'

Charlie. Emmie swung her head down to him as Grace tightened her grip screeching into Emmie's ear. She blinked. It was as though the children had been turned back on.

'I'm not tired,' Grace screamed, 'don't leave me, mommy. The man scares me. I don't want to go with him.'

Emmie held her tight.

'I won't let you go. There's no need. Charlie the snow is rising I won't leave you here.'

'We're just holding you back. We're safe, mom, I don't want you to die.'

Emmie felt the bottom drop out of her stomach as the weight of his words hit her. He was getting paler, and the snow was nearly at his groin. She could no longer feel her hands and feet, but as she held his hand, she felt the warmth radiating into hers. She looked at Grace and realised she was now as pale as Charlie although when she felt her hand, she too was warm.

'Why are you warm? How can you be warm? It's not possible.'

Charlie's big eyes were watery, and Grace was crying, making cold, wet patches on Emmie's face.

Let me take them. The longer you stay here, the harder it will be for you to get back. Time is running short.

Dad's voice sounded nearer now, and as she looked up a form was emerging out of the white.

Shadow man. Tall and black, no features, just shape. The same shape she had seen from the house many times.

She took an involuntary step back, snow shifting and compacting around her thighs now. Standing had made her joints and muscles rigid with cold, and pain shot through her feet. Whimpering, unable to run or hide in this cold white desert, she grasped Grace and Charlie tight as she watched him come closer. Terror and panic coiled inside her. Charlie was still and quiet, but Grace was screaming pressing her face into Emmie's neck. Emmie wanted to join her, but her voice didn't seem to want to work any more than her legs. She squeezed her eyes closed, heart thudding behind her ribs, waiting for whatever blow he was going to deliver.

Emmie, let me take them, sweetheart.

She slowly opened her eyes. Her father stood before her as real as he was in life, the only difference was the Stetson hat. The one that he had been wearing in the last photograph she had seen of him. The shape registered instantly.

'Dad? I don't understand. You've been scaring the hell out of me.'

I didn't want to scare you, honey, you wouldn't let me in, and I didn't want to push you. I have a job to do here, as do you.

Tears of relief rolled down her face, freezing on her cheeks as she stepped into his warm embrace. And it was warm, radiating off him like bath water. He hugged her and Grace, who was still in her arms, and she only vaguely let into her mind that this couldn't possibly be real. For now, she was overwhelmingly happy to see him, to feel him, to smell him. She clung to him as she had when she was a child.

The events accumulating are no accident, sweetheart, and you have to face them. Time is ticking. You need to get out of the snow. I will look after the children until you see them again. I promise they will be safe.

Emmie stood back confused, looking up at him, unsure what to do. Grace had stopped crying after being a full-on part of the hug up there in Emmie's arms and was assessing the grandfather she had never known with curiosity.

'Why don't you just tell me how to get them out of here?'

They can't go with you. They're holding you back. Forward is the only way now. You have to let them go.

Grace immediately started crying again, but Charlie let go of Emmie's hand and stepped toward him.

Panic clenched her heart, and she made a clumsy grab at Charlie, missing his clothing as he moved away. Grace screamed as she pitched forward in Emmie's arms.

'No Charlie! Don't. Why can't I take them? I don't understand.'

You do understand. You just need to acknowledge. They don't belong there anymore; you know that. You need to face it and move forward.

Emmie shook her head vehemently. The insinuation of his words frightened her.

'I can't. I don't want to.'

You have to. Life comes and goes, starts and stops, Em, that's the nature of the universe. Accidents happen, and they happen to good people. It's no-ones fault, but Charlie and Grace are needed elsewhere. As you are needed at home. Your life will only start when you face it and let go. They will always be here waiting until you see them again.

'I can see them now, they've been with me. I don't want to lose them, dad. If I lose them I lose everything.'

No Darling, you have lots to live for. Everything happens for a reason, even if it seems to be the most terrible thing on earth, and it hurts us beyond measure. You were in that time and place to stop the cycle. To break free. There is no turning back the clock. The children are safe with me. Let them go and live. Don't let their deaths be in vain.

At the word death, her heart hurt and tears slipped down her cheeks. She held Grace tighter, but she seemed to have less substance. She felt lighter somehow, and the sweet smell of her strawberry shampoo was fading. Emmie looked at her. Grace was no longer pale, she was becoming grey.

'But they're my children. My life. I would rather be stuck in the cycle and have them with me.'

And that is why life deals us these blows. We would never choose the path for ourselves. Sometimes we need a nudge to make a change, to be put in the right direction.

'I didn't change. How could I? I thought they were okay. I really thought they were okay.'

But you did change, even as your mind protected you from the pain you still did it. You started a new life, broke free of the old chains. You did that by yourself.

'But I thought they were with me. It was the divorce that forced me to change. I don't want to lose them, dad.'

And it was the accident that forced the divorce. We're all linked and affected by events. Each event works to put us where we need to be. You lose them only for a short time, and they will always be with you in your thoughts and memories. A piece of music, a painting, a hair clip, a butterfly, the wisp of the wind past your face. You won't forget, and they won't let you forget, but you need to let them rest now. You need to grieve and move on. It's been long enough, sweetheart. You can't keep carrying them around.

Pain filled her in every nook and cranny of her body. Emmie knew he was right, she felt it, and it killed her. Grace was getting lighter, and her snowsuit had disappeared leaving a brand new Peppa pig top in its place. Charlie too had lost his snowsuit and was wearing the same brown jumper he had worn on that day. Emmie's stomach flipped, it terrified her to think that she may have to see them as they had been after the accident.

'No, Not yet, I need more time … I need more time-'

And yet, she knew if she didn't move she would be getting far worse memories of her beautiful children than the photographs could have shown. She had no choice but to be ready. The cold was penetrating her bones. The pain almost unbearable in her fingers and toes.

They would be okay here with her dad, wouldn't they? There was no one better she would have left them with in life, and if he had been taken as part of the cycle to help her now, then it was the best outcome she could have hoped for. If her thoughts hadn't confirmed it, Charlie was already stepping into the man's embrace with all the confidence of any child visiting a relative. He was smiling and calling Grace as the colour returned to his face.

'Come on Grace we get to play with Grandad now. Mommy has to go.'

Grace looked at him and then back at Emmie. The tears were still streaming down her face, and Emmie thought her heart might literally break in two.

'I don't want to leave you, mommy.'

'I don't want to leave you either, sweetie.'

Emmie, you won't make it back. Go.

She held on to now almost feather-light Grace with arms that felt like lead weights not wanting to put her down and break the contact. What if she just stayed? Would it be so bad confronting her own mortality?

'What if I don't want to go back? I can stay. We can all be together. What kind of mother walks away from her children?'

One that has no choice but to go on without them. You're in different worlds now, and you have people who care about you. Keep moving forward it's the only way.

'I don't know how. I don't have the strength.'

One step at a time, everything is achieved one step at a time. One breath, one beat of a heart, leads to the next, and then the next, until it is second nature and we move onto the next step. I have one last bit of advice, honey. When you wake, the pain will hit. Let it out. All of it. Feel everything and ride it through, it doesn't matter how long it takes. You ride it the way you need to until the pain starts to lessen. And it will lessen over time. Understood?

Tears streamed down Emmie's face wetting under her chin and the collar of her coat.

'I really have no choice?'

No, it's not your time.

He pulled something from his pocket and held it out, and she moved awkwardly to him in the deep snow to take it. It was the photograph of Grace and Charlie that she had left on the table in the sunroom. As she focused on it, he took Grace from her arms. Sniffling, Grace put her arms around his neck as Charlie reached up to hold her hand.

Emmie carefully pocketed the photo and looked at Charlie and Grace. They were already looking better, healthier, colour coming back to Grace almost instantly.

They were better here. She realised she was killing them over again keeping them with her. She swallowed hard. The time had come.

'I love you guys so much. You be good now, both of you,' Her voice cracked through the tears. Charlie ran in for one last hug, she held him tightly, breathing him in, and then she stepped up to Grace hugging her too before finishing with her father.

'Take care of them, dad. I love you.'

I will. I love you too sweetheart. Now go Emmie, before it's too late for you. Your body won't recover from this temperature.

She nodded, and a flutter of fear started in her belly, the only part of her that now seemed warm. She looked at the snow, now almost reaching her chest. Her body below it seemed not to exist. She couldn't feel it, and she couldn't see it. She saw now that Charlie had been right. They were safe in the snow; where the three of them stood, the snow had disappeared as if their warmth shunned it away.

The tears fell, blurring her vision, as she took a last look at the children standing hand in hand with her dad. Her heart shattered into a million pieces, and the pain engulfed her, meeting with the pain of the cold.

Shadow man - dad - pointed to the right, and only one step in the direction of his finger took her out of the snow and into a warm and barren landscape. There was a large campfire right in front of her, she felt its heat hit her immediately. Boulders surrounded the edge just like the ones they had made on holiday, and to one side was a little wooden bench. Emmie collapsed onto it, warmth and crackle of the fire familiar and comforting.

She watched the flames for a while, numb, before putting her head in her hands and weeping with abandon. She was supposed to protect her children and instead had placed them in the path of fatal danger.

She cried until there was nothing left, she felt hollow and numb, and then she let the fire dry her tears with its warmth.

Her mind was waking up with piercing clarity, and she got up slowly. Her dad was right she had a job to do, and she knew she had to finish it. Scott had to be stopped, he had to let her go. She took a large shuddering breath and stepped around the fire into darkness. As it encompassed her she heard Charlie and Grace.

'Bye, mommy, we love you!'

And her heart broke all over again.

Emmie opened her eyes one at a time, surprised to find she was back in her kitchen and not lying in a blizzard or by an over-sized campfire. Her heart ached, and her head pounded, she brought a hand up to a patch that throbbed above her right temple. There was a swollen lump there which stung. She quickly took her hand away and saw blood on her fingers.

For a second she wondered what had happened, and then she remembered falling. She remembered Scott falling with her, on top of her.

So where was he now?

Fear gripped her heart. She scrambled up onto her hands and knees scooting toward the back wall. She spun around planting her back to it, and then noticed the gun. It lay at the edge of the overturned table. She reached for it on all fours and scudded back to the wall.

That was when she saw Scott. On the floor by the fridge. He wasn't moving, but she could hear his thin, raspy breathing. She didn't trust that he wasn't playing a game, trying to get her closer, so she sat against the wall, gun trained on him, heart pounding. Knowing he knew the gun didn't work, but not knowing what else to do. When she had sat that way for so long her arms shook with fatigue, and her heart had long since slowed, she let herself admit that he was no longer coming for her.

She tucked her knees into her chest and placed her arms over them letting the gun hang in her right hand. She dropped her chin down onto her arms, watching him.

Her thoughts drifted to Charlie, logical old headed Charlie, and sweet little Grace. They were her family, all she had left, and now the last eight years of her life had been flipped on its head with that metaphorical flick of a coin. The ache that started in her chest seemed to drag downward stretching until it encompassed all of her.

She let out a howl of injustice and despair, and the tears came. Retching sobs that came up right from the soles of her feet and threatened never to stop.

Chapter 71

Someone was calling. Another voice. It took Emmie a moment to realise it wasn't inside her head. It was Stuart.

A tidal wave of relief flowed over her. She wanted to call out, to get up, but her body wouldn't comply. She was shivering hard, the ache heavy in her heart, debilitating exhaustion combining with the numbness.

Stuart strode into the kitchen, frowning as he quickly surveyed the upended table and chairs, and the vegetables scattered across the floor. Then he saw her curled up against the back wall. He paused only for a beat before he was crouched in front of her, hands rubbing soothingly at her arms.

'Christ, Em, I'm so sorry I came as fast as I could, there was a tree down over the lane I had to go back for miles, and the storm made it impossible to move above a crawl.'

The wind battered at the front window, shaking it in its frame in agreement. Emmie looked up with mild surprise, she had completely forgotten about the storm. She hadn't even heard the wind.

'I'm so, so, sorry sweetheart, are you okay?'

She looked into his concerned eyes not trusting herself to speak. She wanted to tell him about Charlie and Grace, but it hurt, and she knew she wouldn't be able to get the words out without another barrage of tears. She already felt emotional from the relief of knowing that she was finally safe, at least from here on in Scott would think twice about what he did to her.

If he ever got up off the floor that was.

A pull of worry circled in her abdomen. Whoever Scott was now; they had brought two children into the world together. He had been through hell after the accident, and most of it was her fault. If he had changed through that one incident, then the blame was solely on her shoulders, and she felt it's weight there as real as the weight in her heart for Charlie and Grace.

She shuddered at the thought of the children. How had they been gone all this time when they had felt so real? Tears threatened to take over again. Emmie sighed heavily, gulping them back down.

Stuart pushed the hair back out of her face gently but caught the egg where she had fallen onto the table. She winced pulling back, and he frowned looking the lump over, before carefully letting her hair fall back over it. With a sigh, his hands went back to her arms, his face etched with concern.

'Em, sweetheart, you're worrying me. What the hell happened and where is Scott?'

'He's over there,' She whispered, looking toward the fridge.

Stuart followed her gaze to where Scott lay, huddled on his side by the fridge. He went to him, looking him over and checking for a pulse, reminding Emmie of Natalie. She fleetingly wondered if Nat and Mike were okay in the storm. If Stuart had trouble getting here from five miles away then Nat and Mike would undoubtedly be struggling.

Emmie watched Stuart check over Scott's large frame. Scott wasn't moving which was disconcerting, but apparently he was still with them because Stuart asked if she had called an ambulance.

She shook her head, feeling numb, and that was when Stuart noticed the gun hanging from her right hand over her knees. A flicker of worry crossed his face. He came back to her without a word, taking the gun from her hand gently. She didn't resist.

'What did you do, Em?' He said slowly, 'And where did you get the gun?'

'Nothing,' She whispered, swallowing hard. Her throat was dry, her voice hoarse, 'I … I didn't do anything. Bill gave me the gun. It doesn't work. Scott fell. Knocked me down with him. I was too scared to check whether he was okay. Is he okay?'

Her voice sounded low and throaty to her ears. Stuart was looking the gun over. He either knew what he was looking for, or noticed the weld up the barrel pretty quickly, because he nodded satisfied and put it in his pocket out of the way.

Or out of *her* way. She wasn't sure which.

'Well, he's alive, but I think he's in a bad way, I'm going to call an ambulance. I'll be right back. There was a blanket over the chair in the living room, right?'

'There was, but I think … I think he destroyed everything down here.'

Stuart nodded putting a hand to her cheek and with a sigh got up and left the kitchen. Emmie's eyes fell back to Scott, unmoving on the floor. She could hear Stuart on the phone, speaking so fast, and slipping into an accent so thick, she almost couldn't decipher what he was saying. She put her head back down onto her arms, chin tucked into her body and closed her eyes. She tried to clear her foggy head but kept seeing her dad with Grace and Charlie as clearly as if it had been real. Which it couldn't. Her dad was dead.

And so were the children.

She let out a low moan and tears dropped onto the floor.

Snapping her eyes open to break the vision she pulled in some deep breaths, trying to keep some control. The depth of the despair that lay ahead of her was terrifying. She gulped air as she fought to hold on to her sanity.

Chapter 72

Emmie didn't hear Scott until his breath rasped in her ear and she felt his hand grasp her hair pulling her head up out of the crook of her arm. She gasped, pain running through her scalp, heart leaping into her ears as her head banged the back wall. She looked up into his face shocked.

'Scott!' She couldn't manage more than a gasp.

He was on all fours, face close to hers, one hand propping him up while pulling her hair with the other. His face, splattered with small, red, popped veins gave him a flushed appearance, and his eyes were bloodshot. Thick dark red patches of congealed blood gathered around his pupils. His nose began to bleed.

Looking like something out of a horror movie, he swayed in front of her, but his grip was firm in her hair.

'You …' He said 'you're mine. No one gets you … but me. You … destroyed my life. Murdered my … kids. You don't get … get to walk away … I will fucking … kill you first, bitch.'

Emmie whimpered turning her head sideways against the wall. Her heart crashing in her chest as terror took hold. She wanted to scream, to alert Stuart, but found she couldn't. Scott came in closer. He was struggling for breath, pale and sweaty. She felt his ragged gasps for air on her face.

'Don't turn away … from me!' He roared

She was hauled upward, the strength in him inhuman. One minute they were on the floor and the next he was on his feet taking her up the wall with him, the relief of his hand leaving her hair replaced with the crushing force of it on her throat. She tried to inhale, but couldn't draw a breath. Emmie looked at him, his dead eyes showing only hatred as they bulged within their sockets, nose steadily dripping.

Then he brought the knife to her cheek.

The same damn knife she had been chopping vegetables with what felt like several eons ago. He traced it from her eye socket to her mouth as he watched her reaction with a grin.

He means to kill me. Oh god, he really means to kill me!

Panic engulfed her every pore. She tried to kick at him but his body pressed against hers, painfully crushing her to the wall as his hand clamped harder on her neck.

'Relax, sweet pea … it's only insurance,' he muttered, 'but looking at you … I won't … won't need it, I may actually finish … you off with my bare hands.'

The room started to spin. Blackness edged her vision and panic escalated to terror as she tried but couldn't draw in any damn air. Her eyes rolled, her lungs ached, and she caught sight of his grin as she felt darkness closing in.

And then he was gone, torn away from her..

Emmie dropped to the floor, sweet air rushing into her lungs, ears ringing with the accumulation of pressure in her head. Shouting accompanied the whine in her ears and she saw Stuart swing Scott around, pushing him hard in the chest, causing him to stagger back. Emmie scooted back to the wall massaging her throat. Her lungs were burning, her eyes pulsed and ached. Knees tucked into her chest, she shook with renewed fear.

She saw Scott regain his balance, clumsily swinging a fist as he came forward. Stuart grabbed his raised arm, forcing it down and twisting it up his back as the knife clattered to the floor. He glanced down at it with surprise before grabbing the neck of Scott's coat with his free hand and forcing him to the wall, right arm hard across his back. Scott's right cheek mashed against the paint. Emmie's heart took up a gallop against her knees as Stuart leaned in toward Scott.

'What the fuck are you playing at?' he growled, 'Was wrecking her house not enough, or do you want to see how far you can push until you kill her?'

Scott was gasping heavily, and Emmie knew he was winding up. Stuart must have thought he was hurt as he let his arm go and eased the pressure against his back. Scott didn't need another opportunity. He flung himself around, bouncing back against the wall as Stuart immediately reapplied pressure, his arm now across Scott's chest. The two men faced each other Scott craning his head as far as he could toward Stuart who didn't move an inch.

'Fuck you. You know ... nothing about her. She killed ... my fucking kids. She needs to come home ... go see a therapist instead of running off ... off up the British Isles pretending ... to be normal. If you've any ... sense you'll step back and let her go. She's crazy, her mind ... is fucked.'

Emmie's heart plunged.

'No, that's not true. It was an accident.' Her voice was a hoarse whisper after the pressure on her throat. Stuart turned to Emmie, keeping his forearm tight over Scott's chest.

'Charlie and Grace?'

Emmie nodded up at him swallowing hard. He frowned, confused.

'Emmie, where are they? Are they safe?'

She looked at him. Safe? They hadn't been safe with her that day in the car. Fighting back tears she shook her head, losing the battle as one slipped over her cheek. She tried to push them down, but god it hurt. Stuart watched her.

'You're going to have to help me out, sweetheart, I'm not on the same page.'

Emmie dipped her head, took in a shaky breath and told him everything. Adding what Scott had said to what she now knew through a barrage of fresh tears. She left nothing out even though it hurt like hell to hear it out loud and she could hear herself sounding as crazy as Scott said she was. It didn't matter; nothing mattered anymore. She felt numb and empty.

Stuart listened quietly, shock registered on his face, and she could see him struggling to take in the enormity of what she was saying. He unconsciously loosened his grip on Scott who stood quietly with a grin on his face, and finally clapped, long and slow, as she finished.

'Now she finally gets it.' He turned to Stuart, 'See? Mad ... as a fucking hatter. Not looking so hot now ... is she?'

Stuart was back on him almost dragging him up the wall as Scott had done to her.

'You want to repeat that?' he hissed through clenched teeth, face inches from Scott's.

Scott only grinned at him even as he struggled for breath. His mouth was pulled back in that horror-mask grimace he had worn before he had collapsed and taken her down with him. His eyes flashed with humour, and beyond the mask, his face lit up. He was enjoying pushing Stuart. Scott wouldn't have missed him calling her sweetheart any more than he would have missed a pot noodle in the kitchen cupboard. His jealousy would be in full swing under that grin.

The air of tension around the two men now would have taken a chainsaw to cut. It didn't matter how gentle Stuart was, or how much Bill had said he wasn't a fighter, Emmie knew that if Scott pushed him further, it would be a foregone conclusion. The anger in his voice, his stance, the tightly clenched fist of his free hand and his face, inches away from Scott's as they eyed each other, told her as much. She was no stranger to anger, and she didn't want it in her kitchen right now.

The room spun as she got to her feet, using the wall for support. She had never seen Stuart angry and, acting on the same instinct she had learned from living with Scott, she intended to put herself in the middle of them. Breaking his focus was the only way with Scott, but Emmie couldn't stop herself from shaking enough to move from the wall.

Scott laughed. Or at least she thought the strangled noise was supposed to be a laugh.

'Cut and run while you still can. She's … fucked up worse than … a brothel full of whores, and a whole … lot worse in bed. But … you probably know that already, eh? … fucking bitch.'

Emmie tried to shout, but her voice was still little more than an urgent whisper as Stuart drew his arm back, fist clenched, ready to go.

'Stu, Don't! He's not worth it.'

Keeping his eyes on Scott, Stuart nodded lowering his hand. Emmie let out a breath that she had been unaware she was holding and closed her eyes with relief. Relief that was more about Stuart being a world away from Scott, who wouldn't have heard her shout, never mind whisper, during his rages. And wouldn't have taken any notice anyway.

She opened her eyes. Stuart was shaking and breathing hard. He leaned towards Scott until they were almost nose to nose.

'If what she's just told me is true, and that's your reaction, then you're the one fucked up. You don't deserve her, and she certainly doesn't need you.'

He gave Scott a final hard shove against the wall before letting him go. Scott rubbed at his nose and pushed down his coat trying to glower but falling short. His hands shook and he grabbed his chest doubling over, his breathing ragged. Stuart picked up a chair and scooted it toward him.

'I think you need to sit down. There's an ambulance on its way, and god knows you look like you need it.'

Scott didn't have the strength to argue. It seemed the battle for breath was bigger than the fight with her for the moment. He took the chair and sat down leaning forward, still clutching his chest and spitting blood between his knees. She looked at him, marvelling how far from her husband this man had become. She also knew with horrifying clarity that if Stuart hadn't arrived when he had, she would have been dead by now.

Gone. Lights out.

Stuart moved over to her, and she took his trembling hands in her own.

'I'm sorry, Em, I'm so, so sorry. I just lost it …'

Emmie looked at him.

'It's okay, don't be sorry.'

Stuart closed his eyes briefly, pain flashing across his face as he took her in his arms, holding her tight. She clung to him just as tightly, wishing he would never let go.

A wooden chair scraped across the floor, and Scott roared.

'Don't EVER think you … can put your hands … on my wife. No one else gets to have … her. I'll fucking kill you both. You don't get to walk away Emelia … especially with him. I told you, bitch.'

Pulling away from Stuart, Emmie saw Scott lift the chair into the air and launch it at them. She stood aghast, not able to move. Stuart's reflexes were quicker. Taking action from the look on her face, he pulled her around the overturned table as the chair hit the wall, smashing the legs and gouging a hole in the old plaster. Scott was starting around the table as they ran into the hall.

Stuart turned to face the kitchen, pushing Emmie behind him, just as there was a thud, and an unearthly groan. After a short silence there was a noise like a straw being blown underwater, which Emmie realised were Scott's attempts to breathe.

Stuart glanced at her and started for the kitchen. Emmie pulled back on Stuart's arm as hard as she could with both hands, terrified it was another of Scott's games.

'Stu, no! Don't go in there. Please. It's a trick. It has to be.' she whimpered.

Stuart turned back to her as there was a clatter and the gargling stopped altogether. Emmie's vision was starting to cloud and her head spun. Her heart drumming a double staccato, she broke out into a cold sweat as her legs shook and buckled.

Stuart grabbed her arms holding her upright.

'Deep breaths Em. Stay with me.'

He kept her focused until the feeling passed.

'Stay here,' He said finally, rubbing her arms, 'I'll check what's happened.'

'No! Please. Don't go in there. I don't want you to leave me. Please, please. I don't want you to get hurt.'

'Scott may be hurt though, Em.'

She was shaking now, tremors running through her and she knew she was losing control, getting hysterical; but she also knew how quiet Scott had been before when he was down, and he had seemed to rise from nowhere in seconds.

'The ambulance is already on its way. Please, Stu, don't go in there.'

Stuart glanced toward the kitchen and then back to her.

'I can't leave him in there hurt. I promise I won't be long, and I will be careful. Stay out here.'

Emmie backed up to the stairs where she slid to the floor sitting with her back propped against the panelling, watching the kitchen door as Stuart disappeared through it. She waited for the roar that said Scott was better and ready to take them down. She waited for the dull thump that meant he had hit Stuart. She waited for sounds of a struggle. Tears of fear and exhaustion slipped down her cheeks as she sat watching the doorway with her heart in her mouth. But nothing happened. And then Stuart was back, face grave.

'What?' She whispered.

'He's not good, but he's still breathing, for now. He really needs that ambulance.'

Emmie nodded.

Stuart sat down next to her taking her shaking hand and leaning his head back against the panels. They sat in silence listening to the roar of the wind outside. It was strong, and the house groaned and whined as it received its own battering. Emmie thought it sounded more blustery now, not so much of a rage.

'I'm so sorry, Stu.'

He turned his head to look at her.

'For what?'

'For getting you involved in his stupid game.'

'There's no need to be sorry.'

'You could have been hurt. You don't deserve this. Me; barrelling into your life from nowhere and putting you in such a position. I wasn't thinking. None of this was your problem.'

'Aye, it was. It became my problem when you walked into the bar and turned my life on its head. I could no more have left you alone to deal with this than I could have sawn off my leg with a bread knife. If I'd have got here just a few minutes later…'

He broke off, swallowing hard, rubbing a hand above his eyes. Emmie closed her eyes. She knew where he was going, Scott wouldn't have let up until she was dead, she knew it in her heart, and it sent ice down her spine. He was in too much of a rage to comprehend what he was doing. It was as if he had transitioned to another level and something else was in control. She eyed the kitchen doorway before turning to Stuart.

'I'm okay. You made sure of that.'

He looked at her, holding her gaze before he spoke.

'Want to hear something crazy?'

She tried to smile although it seemed to take the effort of raising the Titanic.

'As crazy as I am?'

'Maybe more.'

She nodded, the smile slipping away as she struggled to hold it.

'I have a feeling losing you just then may have knocked me down all over again. Which is completely nuts, I know. I'd not even met you before last week. I don't know what's going on with me. Have I only known you a week?'

She leaned her head on his shoulder, and he tilted his head to rest lightly on hers.

'It feels like longer, lots longer.'

'Aye.' He sighed heavily. ' Listen, Em, I don't know what's going to happen after this, but I know that if what Scott says about the children is the truth you won't be capable of anything but grief. I just want you to know that I'm still here for you, anything you need, you know that right?'

She nodded against his shoulder and squeezed his hand as she felt conflicting emotions swamp her. Affection for Stuart, anger at Scott, worry for Nat and Mike, despair for Charlie and Grace, anger and upset at the state of her home and what Scott had just put both herself and Stuart through.

'I don't want to lose you through this,' she whispered, 'I've lost too much tonight. I wish he'd never come here. I just want to rewind to this morning and do everything differently.'

He turned, pressing a long kiss to her head.

'None of this is your fault, sweetheart.'

'Not this, no. The accident was my fault though. G … Grace and Charlie … they were my fault.'

She took a shuddering breath and closed her eyes as the pain ground into her heart as though someone was crushing it with a mortar and pestle.

'No, Em, that was an accident, you didn't put them in that situation on purpose, these things happen. Trust me, I know that better than anyone. Are you absolutely sure Scott was telling the truth? Wouldn't your sister have said something before now?'

Emmie shrugged. She was finding it hard to even think about them, talking seemed impossible but she tried, she owed him that much.

'They're not here Stu. They never were, I know that now. I … I didn't remember … from the accident. I bl … blocked it. I don't know why, maybe I am crazy.'

'You're not crazy. Whatever happened we'll get you through it, however long it takes.'

She knew he meant it and somewhere in her messed up emotional state she loved him for it, but now she was thinking of the children fully, the pain washed over her. The weight of them pulling her back under. The tears came again like a tidal wave. She couldn't have stopped them any more than she could have stopped time. Stuart gathered her in his arms, pulling her to his chest. He rubbed her back gently, murmuring as she sobbed against his coat. Clinging onto him, she felt he was the only thing tying her to this world right now, and that she would float off into oblivion without him.

He tightened his arms around her and sat quietly letting her get all of the emotion out. She thought it would never stop. They would just be sitting here forever. And maybe that was okay. She didn't want to do anything else anyway. What was there to carry on for without Charlie and Grace? Everything of who she had been before tonight had been wiped out like she hadn't existed. She felt like shadow man. Featureless, black, lifeless. As if she were made of the same swirling black smoke. Nothing about her seemed solid or real anymore.

Chapter 73

'Shall we talk about it?' Natalie said gently.

Panic bubbled in Emmie's stomach, and tears welled in her eyes. They were still sat at the base of the stairs where they had been when Natalie and Mike had arrived. After brief introductions and an update on what had happened, mostly from Stuart, Mike was now keeping an eye on Scott, as Natalie stooped in front of her.

Emmie didn't want to talk, it hurt too much, even thinking of them was too painful right now. Stuart took her hand and squeezed it as she shook her head.

'No. I don't want to.' She whispered.

Natalie looked at her carefully.

'Okay. Perhaps not tonight, okay, but I want you to remember that when you're ready, you can ask me anything. Anything at all.'

Natalie seemed upset, but Emmie had no room left to accommodate her. The pain was starting back up in her heart, and her head was thumping. There was a high pitched whine in her ears that wouldn't let up. She looked to Stuart, and he gazed steadily back, his patience calming. He had been through similar and got through it. She looked back down at her hand in his and prayed this wouldn't be the last time he held it like he was.

'I'm not going anywhere,' He said quietly. Emmie blinked back up at him trying not to cry again.

She gazed down at the front of Natalie's boot, trying to compose herself enough to talk. She did want to understand how all this had happened. How this could have happened.

'They were at the hospital,' she whispered shakily, 'That's where I first saw them. After. They … they didn't have a scratch on them. I … I guess that's why I knew Scott was telling the truth. They couldn't have got out without any injuries.'

Natalie took her time answering, and the room started to spin.

'No honey, there was nothing left of the back of the car it was crushed beyond recognition. They said … they said it would have been instant for them … like turning off a light.'

Natalie's voice broke, and tears slipped down her cheeks. She heard Stuart mutter something as he ran his free hand over his face. Emmie's throat constricted, she could hear her breath, scraping along the roof of her mouth with each inhale and exhale, adding to the whine already buzzing in her ears.

Scrape in. Scrape out. Scrape in. Scrape out.

She tried to focus on keeping it steady, not thinking about Charlie and Grace. Her babies. She felt numb as an ache engulfed her, the pressure in her head threatening to explode.

Natalie wiped her tears collecting herself, and Emmie shut her eyes. The image appeared instantly as though it had been fire branded onto her brain.

The car.

The wreckage was total, metal twisted and bent into shapes she hadn't known possible of a vehicle. She wouldn't have known which end was which, it was only from previously being told that she knew the front of the car faced right. A twist went through her gut, and the realisation that what Scott had said was true hit her with the force of a physical blow. She sat back against the panelling breathing hard, pulling her knees to her chest in an unconscious barrier between herself and Natalie whose words she didn't want to hear. Her heart pumped. She knew that she was lucky to be alive.

Lucky.

The word reverberated around her head.

'When was the accident?' Stuart's voice dragged her back into the hall.

'Just over two years ago,' Natalie replied.

Emmie felt him squeeze her hand rubbing his thumb over the back.

Two years.

Had she been seeing the children for two years since they died? How could that happen? Where were the people who helped you with these things? How had she been allowed to pretend they were around? She must have looked crazy.

And yet the pull in her stomach said they had been real. She had taken them to school this morning. They were playing upstairs when Scott had arrived.

She put her head down into her free hand running her fingers roughly through her hair. An angry swirl punctured the pain in her gut.

What is going on with my head? Am I insane?

'Why wasn't I told?' She said, looking up at Natalie.

Natalie looked back at her blinking.

'Why didn't you tell me? Why didn't Scott tell me? I thought he was being pretentious. I had no idea what he was talking about, but everything he said makes sense now. Why didn't someone tell me?'

Natalie looked as though she may cry again and Emmie wanted to slap her. What right did she have to cry? She hadn't lost her children tonight. Her kids were alive to tell her they loved her, to whine about dinner, to moan about wearing hats and scarves.

'We were told not to, Em. I'm sorry, I really am. Initially, the Doctors said the denial could be brain trauma from the skull fracture. They told us not to encourage it, but to let it slide when you said anything about them. As the months went on and you got better physically it became obvious that you weren't letting go, that was when they diagnosed you with PTSD. Post Traumatic Stress Disorder.'

'She fractured her skull?' Stuart said quietly

Natalie broke off and looked at him.

'Her leg too, and she suffered a collapsed lung. To be honest, Doctors were surprised it wasn't a whole lot worse.'

Emmie felt the room spin as the thought of her injuries brought back memories of hospitals, beeping machines, and excruciating pain. With a shudder she changed the subject.

'What happened with Scott, Nat? He lost them too.'

Natalie looked flummoxed, but Emmie needed to know how he coped. She had put him through hell, and maybe that did go quite a way to explaining his behaviour, back then, and tonight. As Scott had said, she had broken the marriage, and she had forced the divorce.

Natalie blew out a breath and rubbed her hands over her face.

'Well. Okay.' She said, 'He dealt with the children alone. He refused any help. He doesn't do emotion well. You know that. He carried on, identifying the bodies, sorting the funeral, burying them and grieving. It killed him, I know it did, and for a while, I had a lot of sympathy for him. He *was* broken by it Em, but that doesn't excuse his behaviour, no matter how many times we told him that you needed help, he just wasn't interested, he was so nasty. In the end, I guess … I suppose he broke and that's when he knocked you across the room and threw you out.'

Emmie felt like she had been slapped hard across the face. All this time she thought that Scott had become a monster, when she had been moulding him into one herself. When he had hit her, she hadn't been entirely sure who he was or why he had done it. Now it was making sense. He had been telling the truth. He hadn't wanted the divorce. He just needed some time out. She blew out a breath, struggling to comprehend how much she had hurt him.

She tried to pull her focus back to Natalie.

'I was glad when you moved in with us, I thought I could try to approach the issue myself, but the doctors said that you should be left speak about it on your terms or we could induce more denial or a complete breakdown. So we did what they said and ignored anything you said about them. When you were starting to get along a little better, I was going to see if we could approach it differently, and then he slapped the divorce on you and knocked you straight back down again, so we left it. The children gave you a reason to get up, to keep going, and at the time you really needed to do that to be able to fight him.'

She took a shuddering breath, tears welling in her eyes.

'And God, he *was* a bastard, Em. Really. I know you're confused because his behaviour adds up to what was going on at the time and I know you're thinking you should be shouldering a lot of the blame but you have to remember, he had a choice. He chose to make damn sure you suffered, and that you came away with so little from the divorce. Each time you were starting to get back on your feet, he turned up to knock them from under you. Every blasted time. He's done the same here tonight. You're up here doing well, and here he is again to knock you straight back down. If he loves you, he has a funny way of showing it. He can't keep treating you like this.'

Emmie looked away. She was still partly to blame. The anger was starting to subside, but she didn't like the horrible numb emptiness that was replacing it.

'I can't remember anything, Nat. I know what I thought was

happening but it obviously wasn't. I feel like I've lost time.'

'You may never remember, honey. It was never going to be a light bulb moment, it might come back slowly… or it may not. That could be to do with the head injury or just the trauma. I don't know. You completely blocked it out.'

Emmie felt a flutter of fear as she thought of all the times she had been out with Charlie and Grace. How many people had seen her talking to herself or sitting at the school gates alone? Little wings took flight in her stomach as she turned to Stuart.

'What happened to the J2o's?'

He shook his head, confusion on his face.

'J2o's?'

'Friday, I ordered the children two J2o's … or did I? … Did I? Or did I imagine it?'

Catching up quickly, Stuart nodded.

'Aye, you did, I remember. I put straws in the bottles because we were so busy the glasses were constantly in use.'

The flutter of fear was growing bigger as the outside repercussions of her behaviour must have shown signs of someone at least a little crazy. She swallowed hard.

'So what happened to them? If the children weren't there to drink them what the hell did I do with them?'

Stuart shook his head thinking before he spoke.

'I don't know, Em. Nothing that stands out, but that night was so busy I didn't stand still. I'm sorry, sweetheart, I really can't remember, but certainly, nothing that made me think you were anything other than a normal mother with two young bairns.'

Emmie nodded, relieved and pleased that he hadn't seen any evidence of craziness in public, but her heart was starting to pound anyway, there must have been many other occasions. What about school? She put her head in her hands and scrubbed at her face before turning to Natalie.

'I must be as messed up as Scott said. I don't … I'm not sure things were ever as bad as I thought. Maybe I just imagined ... I can't work out what was real and what I made up.'

'All of it was real, Em. Scott has always had problems with anger and jealousy, he was malicious and manipulative, and he accused you of ridiculous things. It was madness, but I know you loved him, I couldn't tell you what I saw because you wouldn't listen.'

She gave a sad smile and sighed. Emmie reached for Stuart's hand again feeling a little more at ease. At least her brain seemed to have got part of the scenario right. She heaved a sigh.

'Don't doubt yourself, Em.' Natalie said, 'I know hitting you wasn't the norm, and Scott was under a lot of stress at the time, but you don't deserve the way he's treated you, verbally or otherwise. I know you never let him keep you down, and I admire how you adapted, whether it was right or wrong that you stayed. But I also know the uncertainty of his moods took it out of you, especially trying to shield Charlie and Grace from the anger. I don't know how you coped with that, you're strong Em, really.'

Natalie took her free hand, and Emmie shook her head lightly tears coming back to her eyes.

'Why does everyone keep saying that?' She whispered. 'I didn't have any choice.'

'Aye, but you didn't crumble under pressure either.' Stuart said.

'Well, I'm not sure I can deal with Charlie and Grace without crumbling.'

She took her hand from Natalie's and wiped away a stray tear. Her body felt laden; like she had the world on her shoulders and was forced to hold it upright or risk tipping the lot, spinning it into infinity until she no longer knew where she was. She gripped their hands trying not to let the dam that held her tears break.

'I think you have permission to crumble now, sweetheart. No one should have to deal with the loss of a child and stay upright.'

'I agree,' Natalie said quietly.

Chapter 74

Sat on a chair at the kitchen table, Emmie had drank the tea that Mike had made, her stomach lurching with each sip, as two men bustled around with medical bags, checking Scott over with quick professionalism.

She had tried to stay calm as they took information. What had happened? How long had he been down? The events that had preceded it, his reactions, his mental state, medical conditions, tablets. The list was endless, and by the time they had finished, and pressed Emmie to involve the police, she was starting to shake.

Scott had been given oxygen and injected with something so that he was looking a little less like he wore a horror mask as they stretchered him out. Mike had gone with him at Natalie's insistence.

Now Emmie waited absently on the only upright sofa in the living room as Stuart made sure the fire was out, and that the back doors were still locked tight. Then he had placed what was left of the heavier settee from the playroom across the sunroom doors. Natalie had tidied the kitchen, done the little bit of washing up that was left, and gone upstairs to clean the vomit off the landing.

When the house was as secure and clean as it could be without sorting the furniture Natalie called Mike at the hospital so that he knew where to come when he was able to leave. They had all agreed that the guest house seemed the only solution for a few nights, and Stuart said that they were to treat the place like home, there would be no renting of rooms, they would have free reign of the private quarters.

Emmie thought they would never understand just how grateful she was not to be carted straight back off to Surrey. The thought of life down there and the memories that would flood back scared her to death, and there was no way she could deal with living with Natalie and Mike's children right now. That fight would be one for the future.

Mike relayed that Scott had suffered two heart attacks caused primarily by his high blood pressure not being regulated, and the onset of his sudden and furious anger. The first one had been relatively mild as heart attacks go, but his second outburst of violence had put too much pressure on his heart triggering a continuing pattern of arrhythmia, resulting in Cardiogenic Shock. Mike said Scott was doing okay but was still having chest pain. The next forty-eight hours would be critical, and he would have to stay in hospital where they could stabilise him before they could assess damage and decide how to proceed with treatment. Surgery apparently not being out of the question. Ironically for the moment, it seemed he would be dealing with low blood pressure.

Emmie remained disinterested. Maybe that would teach him to take his medication in future.

Natalie offered to pack some things into a suitcase for her, but Emmie refused. She did want to take a few things, and she needed a moment alone, she ascended the stairs leaving Natalie and Stuart finishing up downstairs.

From the look on Natalie's face she knew she should probably be worried for Scott, but she couldn't summon the feelings. She was devastated about the children. That hurt like hell, but for Scott? Who had made her life hell, stalked and followed her up here, spoken about the children in such a cold way, and then tried to kill her?

It fleetingly crossed her mind that he might not go to prison. What if he was let off? What if he got bailed out? What would he do when he was better and was able to come after her again, would he bother? It scared her that he might want to finish what he had started up the kitchen wall, but in context, she knew he was a broken man. Maybe he would get better and move on. Maybe he would get the help he needed in prison.

She pushed the thoughts away. She would rather go ten rounds with Scott than have to deal with losing Charlie and Grace. But that wasn't an option. She had no choice but to walk through this hell barefoot and see where she ended up.

Emmie gathered some clothes from her wardrobe, retrieving a suitcase from the floor where it lay after Scott had been up here. She threw some clothes inside and was about to zip up when she saw the little white box of photographs, back on top of the dressing table.

She hesitated.

Charlie and Grace were in that box, but was it the good versions or the bad? She couldn't bring herself to look, so she pushed the box down the side of her clothes. Fastening the suitcase, she stood up with a sigh. Her eyes flicked to the wardrobe and the little square of the cubby hole. She wondered how the hell she had managed to squeeze inside; but then she knew from living with Scott that fear was a great motivator for a lot of seemingly impossible feats.

A little of the terror she had felt in that hole as Scott had hunted her down flooded back through her. She shuddered, a blanket of goosebumps spread over her as she picked up the suitcase and walked back to the stairs.

At the top, she paused, listening, wishing irrationally that she would hear the children in their rooms playing, that it had all been a mistake and they had been here all along.

Surprise!

Tears escaped her swimming vision, rolling down her cheeks. She took a breath.

Come on Em, get yourself together.

Natalie and Stuart were waiting at the bottom of the stairs talking quietly. Emmie wiped at her tears shakily as she gravitated down to them.

She put her arms into the coat Stuart had held out ready for her as Natalie took her suitcase.

And then they left, Stuart switching the hall light out and locking the front door behind them.

Outside it was still well below zero, but the storm seemed to be abating. The wind calmed to a moderate breeze. The snow continued to fall, swirling about them in the air, on the ground sat just over a foot, reaching halfway up Emmie's calves. A lump came to her throat as she thought of how she had been so excited to take the children out into a decent snowfall. The flakes flew gently around her face in the breeze caressing and taunting her in equal measure.

They traveled in Stuart's car as Mike had taken their hire to the hospital, Natalie insisted Emmie sat in the back with her. Emmie leaned back into the seat as Stuart started the engine, looking out of the window into the darkness and past the car Scott had arrived in just a few hours ago.

Was it new?

She found she didn't care.

Shivering, she put her hands into her coat pockets searching for warmth. Her left hand hit paper, and she frowned, confused. Tissues and toys were always in her pockets but paper? She grasped it and pulled it out as Stuart started to manovoure the car. Her heart began to thud as she realised she was clutching the photo of Charlie and Grace, the recent one that appeared to have been taken in the living room of Bruadair. Fresh, raw pain washed over her as she ran a thumb over the shapes of their faces in the darkness tears slipping down her cheeks. She put it back in her pocket vowing to add it to the white box.

Letting the tears fall she looked back at the slowly retreating house and thought she saw shadow man in his usual spot by the fence. She blinked tears and scrubbed her sore eyes, wondering if it was her imagination, and then she saw the shadow move and glide toward the house.

For the first time, she felt comforted rather than chilled. She put her fingers up to the window.

Look after them, dad. I love you guys.

And then she broke down, letting the pain and grief wash over her as the dam burst and the tears came.

Epilogue

Two years later

The bench was hard underneath her, cold frost seeping into her sweat soaked leggings. She liked that. It made her feel real, connected to something as she sat, bent forward, elbows on her knees. Her chest burned and her breath came in heavy gulps. Her face felt flushed in the cold air, sweat drying quickly in the early morning sun.

She closed her eyes and listened to the rushing water, falling away to hit the rocks below, the birds with their constant chatter - like Grace - the breeze rustling the leaves above her. She knew the feverish patterns the little birch leaves would be weaving on the stony path as they danced in the sunlight, their frenzied dance on the branches as the breeze tousled and tugged at them. Sometimes one let go, pulled it from its anchor, tossed it up into the air, tugged back and forth in the sky with no control, and no idea where they would land.

For a long time, Emmie had felt like those leaves, disjointed and tossed around. Not knowing where she belonged and why she was still here when her children had gone. She wondered if the arms of grief would ever release her and put her down on solid ground. Sometimes she thought it would never be possible. How could it end when they were gone? How was she supposed to let go? And did she even want to? How would she function and what could be 'normal' after this?

But it turned out that with time normal was, in fact, an achievable state, and the normal of now was as good as the normal of before, better in many respects, save for the Charlie and Grace shaped holes that were left. She still had good days and bad days, as any mother who loses a child will do. She felt she had walked through a hundred mile war, but she could say she was content now, happy, although she was still very much a work in progress.

In the beginning, after the initial flood of tears, Emmie had been numb, long hours spent staring at nothing. She couldn't eat, couldn't move, couldn't cry. She felt hundred ton weights pulling her arms and legs. The effort of merely getting out of bed too much, and food lost all its appeal.

Her heart hurt, not metaphorically, but physically hurt. A dull ache that persisted in her chest with debilitating consistency. Sometimes she sat in a chair in the living area of the guest house and just breathed. It was all she could manage, one breath following another.

In. Out. In. Out.

She understood that people were worried, but she had no room left in her to give them. Grief consumed her every pore with a vengeance, and the days melted into one long painful blur.

Natalie and Michael stayed in the guest house for the first month after the scene at Bruadair, and her mother flew up from the Isle of Wight the next day.

Emmie had been aware of Natalie, in some alternate universe, telling her that Scott had passed away after a massive cardiac arrest in hospital. The only news that allowed a different thought process from the tracks she was hurtling down.

Scott was dead.

She turned it over in her head for a while. Trying the words out, twisting them around, and then she found she couldn't find the energy to process what that meant. Charlie and Grace took the reins again and she sank back into the familiar wave of pain.

Scott's affairs were sorted by his parents, and his funeral was held three weeks after his death, down in Surrey. Michael flew down alone to attend on behalf of Emmie. He said that it was a low key affair, and that he had been buried next to the children. His will had been two lines that declared that everything he owned was now Emmie's. Including the house.

Emmie demanded the house be sold out of her silence one morning, shocking everyone. One by one they told her to hold onto it until she was in a better frame of mind, there was no rush, but she knew she didn't want any ties left down there. It was the only feeling that punctured the tide of grief in those early weeks. The thought of the house stirred up memories she would rather forget. She knew that she would no more go back there than she would get an apartment in hell. Eventually, Michael applied for probate so that he could act on her behalf and sort the sale of the house.

Money made it's way into an account opened up on her behalf, and much later, when she had room in her, she would become angry at the meagre settlement Scott had allowed her from the divorce. While she certainly wouldn't have enough to keep her secure for life, she wouldn't have any money worries for a fair amount of time

After the funeral Michael left to go back home to the children and work, but after Emmie said she couldn't go back to Surrey, and with Stuart's insistence that she was alright to stay, Natalie managed to secure a years sabbatical from work. She flew home one week of every month to spend time with her family, but their mother was there constantly. Between them, they were on at Emmie daily to get up, get dressed, eat, shower, go to bed.

She saw Natalie spend days sitting in the chair beside her, chatting at first, and finally falling silent as the hours had passed. Both of them just breathing.

She saw her mother plumping cushions, straightening pictures, watching the news. Commenting, as she did, about all the worldly goings-on as if they could compare to what was going on right here, right now.

She saw Edith bring things around from the shop to try to entice her to eat and drink. Edith, who spent most of her lunchtimes shutting up the shop and sitting holding Emmie's hand in the living room. She would talk nonsense and Emmie wished she would go away. On the really bad days, Edith had been with her almost constantly, asking one of the other ladies from the village to look after the shop as Len descended further downhill with his chest.

Emmie saw all of it unfolding around her but watched it as though through a dust-filled lens. It was like a movie of her life that she couldn't process. This was the wrong version she wanted to shout; this is not how my life goes. This isn't how it ends, where were the writers of this edit?

Stuart understood that she just needed to be left alone, how he put up with the gaggle of women that now invaded his space with their own ideas was beyond her, but she never heard him moan. He carried on as normal, running to the falls early each morning, running the guest house, looking after Connor, guiding people away when he thought she'd had enough, sitting with her when he could. Sometimes he completed paperwork or read quietly, other times he would chat, but not like Natalie, Edith, or her mother. He didn't expect answer or acknowledgment. He talked about the pub and the customers, regaled things that happened day to day, chuckled as he told her tales that she would previously have found funny. Some of these things filtered through mixing with the grief, distorting it a little, but mostly she focused on his voice, the soothing, familiar accent and deep tones an anchor point in the fog.

Stuart was with her when the first real tears came one evening after the pub closed. He was chatting as he tidied up, but then caught his foot on the rug and tripped. Everything launched into the air as he staggered forward, but it was the cup that had done it, coming back down to hit the back of his head with a hollow clonk. Emmie felt a familiar surge well up inside her. It had been so long that she couldn't place it at first, but then she knew.

Laughter.

She observed the feeling like an outsider looking at it objectively.

Laugh.

Was she really going to laugh when Charlie and Grace had gone? How could she?

And then the feeling spilled up through her chest and out.

It didn't come out as a laugh it came as a howl, all the despair and anguish of the last five months of near silence pouring out. The tears followed, the dam, not burst, but blown to pieces. Stuart held her and told her to let it come even as he rubbed his head, but in truth, she had no choice once they had started. Sobs wracked her body each day after, making her ache. Her throat became hoarse and tears blurred her vision, the only thing that stopped them was exhaustion and fitful sleep, which always involved dreams alternating between Bruadair, Grace, Charlie, and Scott. Each time she awoke was like groundhog day. The pain would hit her all over again, and the tears would start.

By December the tears started to dry up, there was nothing left. It had been eleven long months since Bruadair and losing the children. She was tired mentally, physically, and emotionally. Tired of the fussing around her, people faffing over showering and eating, and tired of letting people sit her in the same damn chair. Tired of allowing grief to swallow her, she had nothing left to give, she was raw and broken, stripped to the very bare bones of her self.

Shafts of sunlight coming through the window caught her attention one afternoon, the simplicity of it, the fall of the light, the dust motes swirling. Snapshots in her head of long ago in the attic, same fall of light, the same swirl of dust.

Stirred, she asked her mother what month it was with a voice that didn't sound quite like her own, and then she watched as the she rushed out of the room to tell everyone that Emmie had just spoken, as if she had emerged from a coma.

A flurry of activity emerged, and suddenly everyone was in the room asking if she okay, did she need anything, was she hungry, was she thirsty? Irritated she blocked them out, focusing instead on the dust motes swirling in the sun. She put her hands over her ears ignoring the whine as people yapped at her and sat that way until Stuart appeared. Being the person she zoned in to for comfort around all these blessed women, the soft lull of his deep voice, and his calmness and level-headedness soothed her. She also knew he would answer her question as her mother hadn't.

'It's December,' He said.

She felt like screaming at them all.

See? That is how you answer a bloody question.

She couldn't be bothered to say it out loud though, not wanting to hurt them however they annoyed her at the moment. Then it hit her.

December?

But she had been sure Scott had been to the house in January, and that hadn't seemed all that long ago.

It was the jolt that pushed her further out of the lull. The children were gone, and it hurt like hell but she was still here, and these people had put their lives on hold for her.

The next day as she watched the dust motes swirl an urge welled up inside. She couldn't sit here on this couch and rot with these women faffing and worrying over her all day. As Natalie cleaned around her, dusting the sills and shelves and chatting about the usual rubbish, Emmie had an intense need to get out and breathe the cold air. She wanted to feel it penetrate her; her throat, her lungs, her stomach, her nose, her head. She needed to push out all of the staleness that was inside her and just breathe.

While Natalie was cleaning the mantle of the fireplace, Emmie stood stiffly without a word, stepping around the chair and out of the door to the right. She wanted to avoid the busy bar, and this door went past the kitchen and to the corridor that lead to the back entrance. She was at the door before she heard Natalie's voice calling, but she slipped through it anyway.

The cold was all consuming and beautiful. Taking her breath away as it cleared her lungs. The smell refreshing and earthy. Noises she hadn't heard in such a long time reached her ears. The birds, singing under the cold sun, leaves rustling softly in the breeze, the rumble of a car heading up the lane, the rush of the swollen river. It seemed to Emmie as if the world had suddenly turned back on, her senses waking from hibernation.

She crossed the car park to the little steps where the river ran, the rush of the water and the roar of the waterfall in the distance pulling her. She went down the steps to the edge of the river where she stood shivering, watching the river rumble past in perpetual motion. Mesmerised by the swirls and bumps on the surface as the water made it's way forever downstream she was thinking of nothing but the motion, lulled by it, entranced, when Stuart had stepped up beside her.

She expected to be taken back inside, and braced herself for the argument, but he simply put a coat around her shoulders and told her there would be a hot drink waiting when she was ready to come back in.

After that, her trips outdoors became a daily thing. Of course, Natalie and her mother worried. Stuart told them that they had to trust her. She needed to get out, and the time alone in the fresh air would do her good.

All she knew was that she enjoyed the chatter of nature and the fresh reviving air far more than the two of them waiting on her all day and sitting in that damn chair.

She started out just watching the water and then she walked; not far at first but further as her strength and appetite improved. By the end of February, she was walking to the top of the falls daily. Sometimes she would sit on Judith's little wooden bench, cold but relaxed, listening to the wildlife and watching the trees move, sometimes she would shout and scream unleashing all of the unfairness, frustration and agony down the falls, letting her voice compete with the roar of tumbling water, Sometimes she would lie on the bench and cry with abandon, sometimes she spoke to Charlie and Grace, told them how she was feeling and that she wished they were around, they didn't talk back anymore, but that was okay. A birds call or a gentle breeze at the right moment was all she needed.

Sometimes she spoke to her dad and sometimes even to Judith, feeling nearer to her as she sat on the little bench. She told her mostly about Stuart and what he was up to, how grateful she was to have him help her through this and how she was sorry she had been such a burden when she knew Judith would want him to be living his life.

In March Natalie and her mother finally went home. At that point, Emmie was chatting and smiling, although laughter still seemed out of place.

On the outside, she presumed it looked like she was doing okay, and she supposed she was to a degree, but inside she still felt hollow and lost. She still dreamed of the children, Scott, and Bruadair, and always woke in cold sweats shaking with emotion.

She supposed this was what her mother had called dressing for the job. Outside she seemed to be doing well, inside she was still breaking, going through the motions. Edith, Bill and a handful of villagers she had gotten to know through their concern over the last year dished out the compliments when they saw her. How well she looked, how she had picked herself up, how strong she was, blah blah blah.

Stuart knew that none of it applied to her, probably because he'd been the same after Judith, and now that he was in sole charge of making sure she was okay he set up a scale so that she could tell him how she was feeling each day. The scale simply went from one to ten; where one was equal to being in the depths of despair, ten was feeling fabulous, and the only rule was that she tell him the truth. She rarely reached one or ten but often fell somewhere between seven and three.

When she was down he made sure he was around if she needed to talk, or a moment alone from visiting company, but he was never overbearing as Natalie and her mother had been. He had no choice, he had a job to do. When she was up higher on the scale, he was upbeat, chatty and attentive.

When she felt strong enough, she went out into the bar in the evenings. At first, people avoided her. They didn't know what to say, but as they got used to her being around, they would stop to chat or give her their good wishes. She always smiled and said she was well, whether she felt it or not, and any unwanted attention Stuart would quickly move on with mind-reading ability.

She rarely drank anything other than water, but she enjoyed watching Stuart work as he pulled pints, poured wine and spirits, and the twinkle in his eyes as he chatted and laughed with friends and customers. She also enjoyed listening to the banter in that Sottish lilt although most of it contained words that would make her mother go running for the soap to wash their mouths out. The bar still had the friendly atmosphere she had remembered from that first Burns night when she had stumbled in terrified, and there was rarely any trouble.

Stuart would often tip her winks and smiles that would make her stomach flutter as he worked, or stand chatting with her when the bar was quieter. After feeling numb for so long, she enjoyed these little moments of raw emotion that were finally making an appearance again.

These days after the pub closed she enjoyed curling up in the crook of his protective arm. Sometimes they watched TV or talked, Sometimes she sat in quiet contemplation as he read. Always it was the only place she felt utterly protected and safe.

'When does it stop?' She asked him one night after he had closed up the pub and they were sitting together sipping hot chocolate before bed.

'It will never stop unless you let it, sweetheart. You have to stop feeling guilty and let life back in.'

'I don't know how. Everything hurts, I think about them all the time.'

'No one says you have to stop thinking about them, there's no doubt you ever will, just let life back in a little at a time, just as you did when your father passed. You've done it before you can do it again.'

'Dad didn't hurt this much.'

'But it hurt all the same.'

'I suppose.' She put her cup down and bit on the nail of her right index finger anxiously.

'And you thought it would never end. But it did, and this will too. Let life back in little by little, and in time you will start feeling better and figure out where this journey will take you next.'

In August she started to join Stuart for his daily morning run. She found the freshness and the quietness of the morning invigorating, even bad mornings had gone up the scale by two or three points afterwards. She told him not to wait, but to carry on at his pace so that she had a benchmark to work to. It helped to have little goals to focus on, and in the beginning, he often left her behind panting and gasping at the bottom of the falls. It would have been embarrassing if she hadn't known him better, but he never said a word. When he came back down, she jogged the rest of the way back with him. He laughed saying anyone watching from the village would have seen her run up and back with him not knowing she had stopped at the gatepost to the climb as he'd gone on to complete the four-mile run. She smiled and told him she intended to get up there one day.

That day had come late September on a day of relentless rain. The day she almost expired, but managed to match him step for step up to the top and back. Her legs screamed as they carried her back toward the bottom, feeling like lead weights. Her chest hurt with exertion and the stitch in her side almost crippled her halfway down, but she didn't give up. She pushed through the pain and matched him all the way onto the car park where they stopped, panting, Emmie's hands on her thighs as she caught her breath. She was soaked to the skin, but the exhilaration was beyond anything she had felt for a long time, and she found herself laughing along with Stuart. It was the first time she had laughed openly and fully since she had learned about the children the previous year and it felt good.

No, it felt *great*.

Grinning, Stuart lifted both of his hands up to her, and she had given him a double high five before he swept her into a hug. She had clung to him, breath slowing, head on his chest, wondering how she had managed to stumble across such an amazing, caring, and giving man. And then he had lifted her chin running a thumb over her cheek, one arm still around her waist and she had felt the familiar magnetic pull as he looked at her. He smiled, and then they were kissing. She had no idea which one of them started it, just that it was full of need, deep and urgent, rain running down both of their faces. If she'd had any fears that his feelings had changed over the last eighteen months, he dispelled them with that kiss and the way he looked at her afterwards as they clung onto each other shaking. It had been her first ten scale day, and after that, there had been more up than down days as she learned to let life back in.

And so it was this morning in March, with frost still on the ground, that Emmie had managed to beat Stuart up to the top, and was sitting, waiting for him to reach her, the frost from the bench seeping through her leggings. It was an unworthy victory; he hadn't been well for a few days which, in itself, was unusual. Today was the first day of the last four that he had joined her. As she sat getting her breath back, he finally appeared and dropped onto the bench next to her, breathing as heavily as she was. She put a hand on his back and rubbed.

'Don't worry Stu I'm sure you'll catch me again one day. You just need the practice. You're getting old, that's all.'

He looked at her, eyebrows raised, and she grinned toward the falls shoulders shaking with suppressed laughter.

'Old? I let you go ahead on purpose, Em, I was enjoying the view until you sprinted off.'

'And I totally believe you. You have to get at least one foot up here before me every single morning, Mr Competitive.'

He laughed, and she giggled leaning in as he put an arm around her shoulders.

'Okay?'

She smiled at him and nodded.

'I'm great. Every day is getting better. If I could scrub away the crap in the middle, and put aside Charlie and Grace for a few minutes, this would be the happiest moment ever, right here with you. Did that even make any sense?'

He held her gaze steadily, eyes full of warmth, and not for the first time she thought he was the most beautiful man on earth, inside and out. Her heart somersaulted as he smiled. She had been living with him for the last two years, but the romance had only rekindled in the previous six months, she still felt giddy when she thought about how things had turned out.

'Aye, I know what you mean.'

'What about you? Are you okay?'

She only meant was he okay running up here after being so ill. His answer took her by surprise as he looked back at her.

'I'm more than okay. I get to spend every day being charmed by you and your 'very average story'.

She wrinkled her nose at him.

'Are you ever going to let me forget that?'

'Probably not. It ended up being the most understated statement I've ever heard. I might get the words framed, hang them on the wall. 'Let me tell you my very average story…'

She rolled her eyes shaking her head, and he grinned and leaned down to kiss her gently, taking his time. Breaking away, he gazed at her, and she was unable to look away. He put a hand up to her cheek, and she closed her eyes heart doing its usual pattering.

'I love you, Em.' He whispered.

Her heart lurched. She opened her eyes and looked straight back into his.

'What?'

'I have for a long time, sweetheart.'

She grinned at him and put a finger to his lips.

'Shhh, you can't say things like that we're on Judith's bench.'

'Sorry Judith, honey,' He said shrugging, 'I'm afraid this one's too special to let go.'

She smiled, turning to cup his face with both of her hands.

'I love you more, Stu Henslow.'

She planted a soft kiss on his lips and turned to sit close beside him as he put an arm back around her shoulders.

'And I think that may have been my happiest moment right there,' He said squeezing her close.

Emmie smiled and leaned back into the crook of his arm, pulling her feet up onto the bench knees to her chest, holding onto the hand of the arm that was around her shoulder with both of hers, enjoying the suns spring warmth on her cooling body as the birds sang and the water roared. This had to be the very definition of bliss she thought.

As they sat in companionable silence, enjoying nature in a rare moment of stillness before they descended the hill back to reality, two red admiral butterflies appeared, dancing and chasing each other in the sunlight before finally flying over the drop to the falls.

Emmie smiled.

Today was turning out to be above and beyond a scale ten already.

THE END

What happened to Bruadair after Emmie left?
Is this unlucky house destined to become a forgotten
ruin once again? And what of the ghosts that roam there?

**Sign up to my mailing list to find out with this
exclusive Ruin content.**

You also get access to exclusive behind the scenes
content and extra's, and you'll be the first to hear about
promotions, discounts, forthcoming titles and competitions!

Signing up is completely free and you will never
receive spam from me.

To sign up visit - www.rebeccaguy.co.uk

You can opt out easily at any time

If you enjoyed this book it would be fantastic if you
could leave a review.

Reviews help to bring my books to the attention of
other readers who may enjoy them too.
Help spread the joy!

To leave a review click the link on Ruin's book page at
www.Amazon.co.uk

Ruin

Thank you!

SHATTERED

Everything you know is a lie… and the truth is worse than you can imagine.

DECEPTION. GREED. VENGEANCE. BETRAYAL

Forced to Northumberland to care for her dying Aunt, Charley Costin is determined to put aside childhood fears, and a twenty year feud, to prove her family wrong. Elizabeth Kane is not a witch, she is just an old lady, and Charley intends to make her estranged Aunt's last days as comfortable as possible.

But doubts creep in when Elizabeth proves more work than Charley ever imagined. Intimidating and demanding, with violent hallucinations, episodes of paranoia, and an agenda of her own, Charley discovers dementia is much more than loss of memory, and her Aunt is as far from 'old lady' as she can get.

Already on edge, Charley discovers Fortwind House hides not only a sinister presence, an unruly bell, and a study door that opens itself, but also a terrible secret. A secret that gardener Axl Maddox would kill to keep buried. A secret that Elizabeth needs to tell. As her Aunt's paranoia grows, an unnerved Charley questions just how long her Aunt has left, and the real reason she may have less time than she thinks.

Disturbed, watched, and afraid, Charley feels out of her depth as over twenty years of deception, betrayal, vengeance, and bad blood rise to the surface with disastrous consequences. What Charley discovers at Fortwind House will blow her world apart and challenge everything she has ever known.

SHATTERED

The next paranormal thriller from Rebecca Guy due for release October 2020

Keep your eyes on your inbox for more information.

RUIN

CPSIA information can be obtained
at www.ICGtesting.com
Printed in the USA
BVHW071027120520
579571BV00001B/18